CURSEBREAKERS

CURSEBREAKERS

a novel

~

Madeleine Nakamura

CANIS MAJOR BOOKS

Book design by Mark E. Cull

Library of Congress Cataloging-in-Publication Data

Names: Nakamura, Madeleine, author.
Title: Cursebreakers: a novel / Madeleine Nakamura.
Description: First edition. | Pasadena, CA: Canis Major Books, [2023]
Identifiers: LCCN 2023016186 (print) | LCCN 2023016187 (ebook) | ISBN
    9781939096128 (paperback) | ISBN 9781939096135 (ebook)
Subjects: LCGFT: Fantasy fiction. | Novels.
Classification: LCC PS3614.A5737 C87 2023 (print) | LCC PS3614.A5737
    (ebook) | DDC 813/.6—dc23/eng/20230414
LC record available at https://lccn.loc.gov/2023016186
LC ebook record available at https://lccn.loc.gov/2023016187

The National Endowment for the Arts, the Los Angeles County Arts Commission, the Ahmanson Foundation, the Dwight Stuart Youth Fund, the Max Factor Family Foundation, the Pasadena Tournament of Roses Foundation, the Pasadena Arts & Culture Commission and the City of Pasadena Cultural Affairs Division, the City of Los Angeles Department of Cultural Affairs, the Audrey & Sydney Irmas Charitable Foundation, the Kinder Morgan Foundation, the Meta & George Rosenberg Foundation, the Albert and Elaine Borchard Foundation, the Adams Family Foundation, the Riordan Foundation, Amazon Literary Partnership, the Sam Francis Foundation, and the Mara W. Breech Foundation partially support Red Hen Press.

First Edition
Published by Canis Major Books
An imprint of Red Hen Press
Pasadena, CA
www.redhen.org

To Jay, my tireless, brilliant creative partner. Her contribution to my work and the value of her friendship can't be overstated.

Preface

In my greater and lesser moments, I fear that I must be fated for sainthood. Martyrdom, then, as they're so often one and the same. The only question in my mind becomes, how will the worthy death come, and what will I be sainted for? I could be the saint of lightning. Laudanum, perhaps. Either could be the killing instrument. They've both sustained me, in different manners of speaking, but we all slip up eventually.

I tell you this because what follows is a historical account, and these facts are integral to your understanding of it. A competent scholar ensures the comprehension of his audience. I've tried my best to construct a coherent narrative of the events of 3016, and I would hate for it to go to waste. My name is Adrien Desfourneaux. Please pay attention.

Chapter 1

The day before extravagant disaster set in, I was walking alongside the Aqua Circadia; the canal was swollen with the ongoing downpour. I barely paid attention to where I was going. The error I'd made revealed itself when I ran right into someone, a black streak in the rain. The streak resolved itself into a Vigil officer; I prepared to be executed on the spot.

I said, reflexively, "Stars and saints."

He said, equally reflexively, something unspeakably impolite.

He was a young man, only a little older than some of my students—in his earliest twenties, I guessed. A lieutenant's star gleamed on his uniform. He pushed an unruly sweep of black hair out of his face and pointed his chin at me, narrow eyes dark with scorn. He was soaked to the skin, but he didn't seem to care.

"Excuse you," the officer said. "Watch it."

True, I'd walked into him, but I bridled nevertheless, biting my tongue to suppress a waspish response.

I stand by my aversion to the Vigil; their uniforms are designed for intimidation, all black and sharp edges, and their rache hounds are bred to terrorize. Strange animals, neither wolves nor lions, ill-tempered to a one. This officer's rache was much smaller than most, not quite coming up to his knees, but the sight of her still drove a shiver through me. The yellow eyes set deep in her black, foxlike face shone with a dreadful intelligence. "I said excuse you," the officer said. "I said watch it." His rache lashed her tail, sending raindrops flying.

"Yes, I heard," I said delicately, taking a measured step back. I regretted my choice within an instant—I should have been practical and apologized. He scowled, one hand drifting to the hilt of his saber. I remembered my earlier thought that he might simply run me through in the middle of the street.

But other people had noticed there was something amiss and were watching. The majority of passersby who had stopped in their tracks were university students and other faculty, most of them soaked just as the soldier was.

People are unused to inclement weather in Astrum, but I'd brought an umbrella. One of the advantages of my affinity for lightning is a sense for storms.

The soldier looked around and noticed his audience; I saw him weigh the situation. He sighed, and his hands went in his pockets instead.

"I could take you in for assaulting an officer," he said.

"It was an accident."

"Whatever."

"It's still the first week of the new semester," I said blankly, not yet processing his threat. "I really shouldn't be late."

He drew closer to me, and I stumbled back—right by the side of the nearby Aqua Circadia. I managed to hold onto my umbrella. "Should I push you in?" he asked. The question sounded almost genuine.

"Well, no," I said.

"Why not?"

I discovered myself at a loss for words, a singularly rare occurrence.

Again, he came closer. I edged farther toward the canal. The small crowd of onlookers muttered amongst themselves, none willing to challenge a Vigil uniform. I imagined the indignity of falling into the Circadia, and then the indignity of being killed, and found neither agreeable.

"You shouldn't push me in because that would be rude, and people are watching," I said. I felt a few sparks of lightning gather around my hands and stifled them, for fear of shocking something in the rain.

He observed the lightning with distaste. "Magician, huh."

"Most Pharmakeia professors are," I said.

"Never liked magicians."

I have never liked Vigil, I thought. "Really, I'm going to be late," I murmured.

He grinned. "I could make you *late* for sure."

The pun on death did not impress me.

Then the officer's rache meowed at him, a bizarre sound from her fanged mouth, and he seemed to miraculously settle himself. He tilted his head at me, inscrutable, and stepped back.

I moved around him to regain some space from the water. "Lucky you," he said. "Now go away."

My gaze flickered to the rache: had she told him to leave me alone? The thought seemed almost impossible. I had never known a rache to express an iota of care for anyone other than its officer.

She looked back at me, and I couldn't tell at all.

"Before I get annoyed," the Vigil officer said.

Incredulous of my good fortune, I fled. My heartbeat didn't settle until I had reached campus. This was an ill omen for the new semester, I thought, and I had never been more correct in my life.

〜

The next day, the rain fell in sheets against the arched glass ceilings of the Academy Pharmakeia's hallways as I made my way to class; the ambric lights strung along paneled wooden walls flickered threateningly from the storm. The smell of petrichor rose into the gray sky, laced with magic. The Pharmakeia crackles with that feeling—it's the only place in the city where magicians outnumber those without the rare talent. From noon to two o'clock, I was scheduled to teach Introductory Magical Theory. The hall of St. Osiander was my regular lecture hall, my favorite; it had the chalkboard space I needed, and the acoustics were passable.

When I got to the hall, the same soldier who had terrorized me just yesterday was standing outside the door. I saw him and dropped my briefcase.

"Excuse me," I said, retrieving it with my eyes on the officer's saber. Owing to our last interaction, I thought he wouldn't instantly murder me, but I had been wrong about things before.

"You. What do you want?" he said.

"It's just that I need to go through the door." I sounded meek; I coughed and tried again. "I teach in this room. May I ask why you're here?"

"Supervision," he said. His rache padded forward toward me, and I jumped. He grinned.

"This is a Pharmakeia building," I said once I'd settled myself again. "There's no reason for the Curia Clementia to be supervising anything here." The Vigil belonged to the military court of the city, and it had no place inside my classroom.

"Want me to get my captain?" the soldier asked. "I bet she'll enjoy telling you to mind your own business." He stepped forward. He was shorter than I, but not by much, and I leaned back.

I adjusted my glasses. "Not particularly." What I wanted was to know why he was there, but I wasn't going to get an answer. "I'd like to go into the room."

He stood aside to let me in. Something in his gaze made me hold my breath as I passed; despite his grin, he had nothing behind his eyes.

His rache meowed roughly at me, and I startled yet again, skipping a step on my way down through the amphitheater. About half of my students were already in their narrow wooden seats, thirty or so faces turned doubtfully toward me. A few of them pointed to the door, pantomiming confusion: *Why is the Vigil here?*

With an apologetic shrug, hoping the officer couldn't see, I went to the lectern. I set out an anamnesic pseudogram before me and shook it; the mekhania gears and cogs inside the small glass cube began to turn. For the benefit of the Pharmakeia's pseudogram library, I liked to record my lectures. The weight of quality glass comforted me; this was a good model, capable of infinite playbacks.

The rest of the students trickled in, each passing by the officer and his rache in acute discomfort, shoulders tense, making wounded eye contact with me as they found their seats.

Magicians are never fond of soldiers. The feeling is mutual. Too many Vigil are eager to see witches wherever they look, even among licensed practitioners.

The clock struck twelve; I heard the bells of the university's tower ringing, a rich, deep sound. "Let's begin where we left off last class," I said, quieting the murmurs filling the room. I could feel the officer's gaze burning through me from where he stood leaning against the door, arms crossed.

I realized that I had no idea where, exactly, we had left off. I was too shaken. "Remind me," I said after a long pause.

"Contemporary magical theory," a girl near the back provided.

That afternoon, it took me a few long minutes to forget our new company and lose myself in the lesson. The recitation of Astrine magical theory is a rote process, with little room for variation. Martyr's Reach is a hive of doctrinaires. Its capital city is no exception.

"The predominant theories of today tend toward the dynamic," I said, and drew a line down the middle of the board, enjoying the chalk's crisp rasp. "In the Reach, at least, magical analysis focuses on potentiality, actuality, and the relationship between them." I labeled the board as neatly as I could, which was never very neatly. *Potency* on one side, *entelechy* on the other.

I caught a glimpse of the Vigil officer as I turned to address the class again, and I stuttered, a long-conquered habit from childhood. He was still watching me. It wasn't the gaze of a listener; it was the gaze of a starving dog. His rache caught me looking at her and licked her lips. I turned away.

"The word 'entelechy' also refers to the physical realization of magical phenomena."

A student in the front row raised his hand. I nodded toward him.

"Is the proper term not 'entelecheia'?"

"It's more classical, certainly. They're interchangeable," I said. "Likewise, 'potency' and 'potentia' denote much the same thing, for our purposes."

I subtitled my labels with his preferred terminology to keep the class moving along.

He raised his hand again; I nodded a second time. "What about systems in other nations?" he asked. "In Torrim, it's completely different. And doesn't Saebar theory divide magic into four main categories?"

"It does," I agreed. "Magic is nothing so much as a metaphor; we're all welcome to our various fancies. Still, today is about Astrine theory." In the end, classification can only take you so far. I wasn't going to pretend otherwise.

"If it's a matter of personal preference," he said, "why teach this class at all?"

I smiled thinly at him. "I often wonder much the same."

He raised his hand.

I recognized the look in his eyes, suddenly, an angry smugness. An *I've got you now*. I felt myself go ashen; my heart twinged. No matter how many times I relived the same interaction, it never lost its edge.

"So what did you classify mind magic as when you were performing it at the Philidor solarium?" he asked.

A murmur went through the room.

"Entelechy," I said flatly, addressing myself to the whole class, feeling their eyes on me, an ecstasy of gazes. Always this question. Always the solarium disaster. "The other researchers and I were practicing entelechy."

The boy was not satisfied. I wouldn't have been, either, in his position. "Why are we learning from a witch, Professor Desfourneaux?" he asked.

It was not a surprise. I flinched anyway.

A few of the other students gasped: witchcraft can be a capital crime. I wondered if I should pause the pseudogram recording, but a pang of masochism told me not to. "I was cleared of all witchcraft charges," I said, and despite my best efforts, my throat closed a little. I looked the student in the eye. The entire lecture hall was frozen in various attitudes of either discomfort or delight. "We were all absolved."

"You shouldn't have been," he said into the deathly silence.

I had no real objections to anything he was saying.

"Professor Gailhardt teaches another section of this class," I said. "I advise anyone who prefers a different instructor to attend her lecture instead. She's an excellent speaker."

He didn't get up.

"I can't tell you to stay for the sole purpose of interrupting me, however," I said. I might not disagree with him, but I had work to do.

That has always been my excuse for not doing something dramatic to myself on account of the Philidor solarium. I have work to do.

The Vigil officer at the back called, "You want me to take this guy away?"

I wheeled on him, feeling lightning spark at my fingertips, and quickly clasped my hands behind my back. Lightning makes people nervous, and I did not want a nervous soldier in my presence. I smelled ozone, sharp and clean. "Absolutely not," I said. I made sure my voice was carefully controlled. The image of that rache biting one of my students presented itself to me, and I shoved it away. "Absolutely not."

He shrugged.

I looked out over the sea of faces. No matter their expressions, no matter if they had known who I was before now, they were all thinking the same thing. Here is Adrien Desfourneaux, a lead researcher of the Philidor solarium disaster, and he is no better than a murderer.

"If you wouldn't mind staying after class," I said to the student. He said nothing.

The ache of an old, abiding guilt shook me for a moment. Wracked me. I turned to the board. "This definition of the dynamic theory is incomplete without a discussion of teleology."

I delivered the rest of the lesson without ever really hearing what I was saying, without looking at anyone. The angry student sat wordless—cowed by the Vigil officer, maybe. At the end of the two hours, I looked up to see the board covered in diagrams I only vaguely remembered drawing.

Slowly, with furious whispers, the students gathered their things and trailed out of the lecture hall. The officer's rache purred at them as they went by, and they shied from the uniformed figure standing at the door. I shook the pseudogram once to stop its recording and put it back in my battered briefcase.

When I saw that my talkative student remained, I remembered with a cold start that I'd asked him to stay behind. He remained seated, tapping a pen against his desk.

I turned to erase the board; my hands shook. They're prone to that.

"I can't recommend Gailhardt highly enough," I said into the slate.

"My mother works at the Chirurgeonate," he said. I closed my eyes. "When she heard I was taking a lecture from you, she told me what you did at the solarium." The disgust in his voice was deeply familiar. I knew it from without, and I knew it from within.

"I left the Chirurgeonate for a reason," I murmured, and turned to face him at last. Losing someone's good regard is a unique feeling, one I was well acquainted with.

"You should be in prison," he said. I realized with muted horror that he had begun to tear up. "What you did to those patients."

"Yes," I said gently.

"Witch."

I straightened my jacket and tie. "What's your name?"

"Rosello," he said, and stood up. "Pietro Rosello. Are you going to have me disciplined?"

"What year are you?"

"Third," he said, crossing his arms guardedly.

He was just about to finish his license, then, nearly a legal magician. Almost done with the trivium.

"You certainly waited for some time to take this mandatory course," I said. "Why not take Magical Theory earlier? Most students make it their first class."

"I put it off because I don't need it. They waived the prerequisite for me at first, but the policy changed this semester."

I sighed, because I knew in exact detail what kind of student he was. I'd been the same way.

"You might leave this section if you don't want me to teach you," I said. "Take up with Professor Gailhardt and ask her to advise you on a quadriviate degree. I think you'd make a good candidate."

I thought the upper division program could use a few more people with a sense of ethical vigilance.

He stood, clearly wanting to argue with me about something else, *anything* else. I bowed goodbye, gathered my things, and started up the steps to leave the amphitheater.

Somehow, I'd almost forgotten the Vigil officer. He was staring unabashedly. "A moment, please," I said to him, and drew him aside so Rosello could slip by on his way out. The boy avoided my eyes as he went.

"So what's the solarium?" the officer asked.

I didn't answer. "Are you satisfied with your supervision?" I said tightly.

He nodded. "Listen," he said. "I don't really care about whatever you people get up to around here, but I was stationed here, so I have to watch."

"I think I have a right to know *why* you were stationed at the Pharmakeia." I was fully aware that I had no rights whatsoever against the Vigil, against the Curia Clementia. No magician does.

He blinked at me, his eyes very black. "Brass just wants us to keep a closer watch on this place. I'll be here for a while with some others."

"You won't find anything amiss," I said.

He exchanged a long-suffering glance with his rache; she turned her sharp nose up. "You're covered in chalk dust," he said with extravagant boredom.

I was, but it was a permanent condition. I shuddered and swept away, back through the Pharmakeia's halls, back under the pouring rain battering the glass ceilings. The ambric lights flickered harder as I passed.

⁓

I knew I was imagining it, but I still felt sure that everyone I passed as I walked must be looking at me. Judging me a witch. I'd been with the Pharmakeia for only a little more than eight years, and I had never stopped feeling as though the buildings themselves must surely want me gone. Every theater, every tower—they must know I didn't belong.

Paranoia may be a symptom of an unwell mind, but a guilty conscience will do it too. My particular unwellness often makes me think people are staring, but then, they often *are*. Making distinctions can be quite a chore.

After my classes were done, I ducked out into the rain, dodging between the Pharmakeia's graceful spires, cold and out of sorts. The other problem I had, coincidentally enough, was that I needed to go to the Chirurgeonate. I dreaded it every single time, for manifold reasons, and that day the dread was thick enough to choke me.

The Chirurgeonate is best described as a medical complex, a village of blue-clad doctors and chirurgeons. It's a dozen hospitals in one, a dozen research facilities, a dozen morgues and lych-houses and ossuaries. Life and death combined, all for the good of the city's health. I hated going there more than almost anything else.

But I went every Trimidy at five o'clock sharp, though I despised myself for it. What I have always wanted is to be useful—and nothing else made me feel more useless.

~

The Chirurgeonate is directly across from the Pharmakeia's own campus; they're both in Deme Palenne, and between the two of them, they take up half of the area. They used to be one and the same, centuries ago.

Like the Pharmakeia, the Chirurgeonate has a preference for glass. The expense of it all is hardly justifiable, but that's neither here nor there. The two haven't been separated for long enough for their architecture to diverge; they're both neatly laid out, gracefully planned, mathematically beautiful. I kept my eyes on the ground. It seemed presumptuous to enjoy the aesthetic.

I went to the private office of Dr. Malise Tyrrhena, as I did every week, and left my umbrella leaning against her doorframe outside after shaking it out in a small shower. As one of the most established doctors, she had her own tiny building. The door was propped open on a paperweight, a stone snake; I knocked anyway. The smell of cinnamon drifted out. "Wipe your shoes before you come in," a soft, steady voice called from within. I did.

Malise tackled the decoration of her office as she tackled everything in life: with ruthless, organizational cheer. Blue fairy lights, neat rows of books alphabetically filed on her blue bookcases, and a blue settee. A tiny potted plant with blue blossoms sat on her desk.

"You're a bit late," she said, her nose wrinkled. The rain had frizzed her tightly curled black hair.

I checked my watch and sat down. "I had to talk to a student," I muttered.

She looked me over carefully. I brushed some of the chalk dust from my shoulders. "Here we are, then. Are you well, my dear?"

She always asked me the exact same thing, in the exact same steady tone. It always took me off guard.

The terminology of insanity is an endlessly difficult subject. What words do we choose to describe the indescribable? *Daimoniac* is impolite, *madman* is outdated, and *crazy* is nonspecific. A fondness for the clinical always seems to be the safest bet. With that preference in mind, the term for what I am is *akratic*. I suffer from dithymic akrasia, and so I am an akratic. *I* call it the daimon, but you may not.

I thought very carefully. Was I well? The daimon tended to wake in the fall. Had I been sleeping and eating? No fits of rage, no days spent in bed? Dithymic akrasia consists of unchecked highs and lows, mania and depression, separated by stretches of tolerability.

I was all right, I decided. For now. I could feel something starting far below the surface, but I hoped Malise would help quiet it. She was a healer and an alienist, uniquely qualified for the job.

She raised her eyebrows at me, patient as ever. A hint of a smile played around her mouth. "So?"

"I'm just a little cold," I said. "Do you mind if I close the door?"

"I like the petrichor."

I left it propped open.

She left her desk and came to sit next to me. "You seem fine to me," she said gently, and I felt myself relax. I could trust her judgment. We were old friends; she'd seen me at my best and worst. She'd seen me after the solarium.

"Kirchoff is at it again," I said, without bothering to ease the conversation through another transition. I have never been a smooth conversationalist, and I wasn't going to start then. One of the gifts I could bring Malise in exchange for her help was gossip about Marsilio Kirchoff, the head of the Thanatology department. Malise thought he was a scoundrel, I thought he was an idiot, and we both liked to tell each other so.

"Go on," she said, and took my head in her hands, blue magic sparking in the air around her.

"He's—ah." I stuttered.

The feeling of her treatment never changed, but I never got used to it. It was cold, smooth, liquid, like the burn of sanative alcohol beneath my skin. The cold was owing to the fact that Malise's talent was with ice as well as healing. I was always afraid that her magic would stop working one day, or ruin me in the same way my solarium patients were ruined. Malise was a prodigy, but even prodigies can slip.

I felt the magic soak down my spine and kept talking.

"He's trying to convince Marta Xu to cut funding from the Music department to give to Thanatology. He says he'll petition to have the entire department moved to the Chirurgeonate again if they don't get their money. Personally, I say good riddance."

"If he comes here, I'll tender my resignation," she said loftily, moving her hands down to my neck. She wasn't applying pressure, but I fought back a cough regardless. "I'll never set foot outside Halicar's." She split her time between the Chirurgeonate and a small church in Deme Cherice, serving as its hedge healer whenever she wasn't in her office.

"It's just posturing," I said. "He'd never do it." Her magic pulsed, and I gasped as something moved in my head. A sharp shift, a sickening pull.

"Tell me about your latest project," she instructed.

Despite myself, I smiled. If I was going to be unwell, at least I had a regular captive audience other than my students. "I have a theory I'd like to disprove," I said.

"What's that?"

I moved my hands while I talked; I couldn't help it, but I kept my gestures soft out of respect for her process. "It's possible to argue that healing magic is a specialized form of time travel," I said. "Maybe we've already found a way to bend time, but we can only apply it to living beings, and only in one direction. The magic itself isn't repairing anything—that's why limbs can never fully be regrown. All we can do is speed up the natural processes."

The eerie light of Malise's magic threw shadows across her skin, blue on soft brown. "Nonsense."

"Well," I said. "Yes. If it were true, healing magic would worsen wasting issues like phthisis. It doesn't. Still, I dug up a few monographs espousing the theory, so I thought I'd try to put the matter to rest."

"Hold still."

I nattered at her for a while in the same vein; she replied with *I see*, and *Is that so?* She didn't pretend to be fascinated, and I had no intention of requiring her to. I had my academic predilections, and she had hers.

I was starting to forget myself, forget the Chirurgeonate, until something hurt deep in my skull. I stopped talking.

"Are you devising an experiment to test the theory?" she asked, looking me in the eye.

I clasped my hands to keep them still. "I was thinking I'd try exposing plants to healing magic and checking their maturity. I don't know. I don't know."

She sat back and brushed my hair out of my eyes. She was done; the sound of the rain seeping through the door filled our familiar silence. We had been friends even before I became her patient, and although that was unusual, I would have died before losing her.

She stood and watched me, squinting, dissatisfied. "You're finally going gray," she said.

I was vain as a young man, and that hadn't quite faded yet at forty-one; I checked my reflection in the nearest window. "Thank you so much," I said. "You look twenty."

"It's good on you," she said decisively. She was particular for women, and I for men. We could say these things to each other without complication.

I rubbed my hands together against the cold, suppressing a shiver, and she relented and stood to close the door before returning to her desk. The noise of rain softened to a dull patter. "How are the students?" she asked.

I remembered Rosello's disgust. *Witch.* "Talkative," I said.

She *tsk*ed, straightening a stack of papers. "You're one to make that judgment."

"I'm going to go mad," I said, a very poor joke. "Teaching the trivium is draining the life from me."

She smiled. "Chin up. They have to start somewhere."

"Are *you* well?" I said. She was a depressive, and she deserved the question just as much as I did—if not significantly more.

Her smile faded. "Personally, yes. I've been feeling all right. Professionally, less so."

Something in her tone set me on edge. I prompted her with a nod.

"We've received a troubling batch of patients."

Precious few illnesses troubled Malise. "How so?"

She took a breath, as if bracing herself for something. "They're presenting with symptoms like the Philidor solarium patients," she said calmly. "They were in pain, and then they fell unconscious."

My heart stopped. An overused phrase, perhaps, but it's overused because that's exactly what it feels like. A brief, businesslike death.

"It's a group of Vigil officers, ten or so of them, and a couple of Pharmakeia students. They're still unresponsive."

The afternoon shattered. I stood quickly to pace, lining up a series of questions. What kind of pain? How unresponsive? Did their pupils still dilate? Were they feverish? But before I could say a word, she caught my eye sternly and shook her head.

"I told you this because you'd find out eventually, and I wanted to give you the news myself—so I could ask you to be sensible about it. Don't make me regret it. As your doctor, I advise you not to go over there."

"As my friend," I replied, "you know I must."

Lightning flashed outside. I felt a spark jump from my hand in sympathy and took my glasses off to clean them, buying myself a second before I replaced them. "If you wouldn't mind telling me the building," I said, in a quiet, pathetic voice. The air felt much colder now.

"The Hessalon building," she said. She knew I would find the patients eventually, with or without her. The only difference was how much time I wasted looking. "In the east wing."

I visited my former patients in the Chirurgeonate every week, after my treatment. The surviving ones lay comatose in the Hessalon building's east wing as well.

"Thank you," I murmured.

"You won't be able to do anything," she said. Her kindness was of the most admirable sort—honest.

"Maybe, but I still want to check." I don't know what I thought I'd find. Likely, I wasn't thinking at all.

"You'll send me gray too after all," Malise said disapprovingly.

I scrubbed my face and laughed. "It'll be all right," I told her. Heaven knows why. I was the last person to be able to give her that guarantee. Still, she nodded at me, and I felt somewhat better for having said it.

I turned toward her office door. I was sorry to leave her so abruptly, but I had found a new way to make myself miserable, and I've never been good at resisting that siren call.

"Adrien."

"Mm."

"Be smart," she told me. "If you send yourself into a fit over this, I'm going to have words for you. Be very smart."

"I always am, my dear," I said, a bracing indulgence in narcissism: I was going to hate myself very shortly, and I thought a quip might at least carry me out the door.

Chapter 2

Now is the time, I suppose, to explain the Philidor solarium. I'll try to keep the pathos to a minimum. Selfishly, I'd prefer to be brief. Explaining it gives me no great pleasure, but the details are necessary.

Here in Astrum, we call our sanitariums *solariums*. The meaning is twofold; they're fitted extensively with glass to allow sunlight in, and the staff hopes to similarly illuminate the afflicted within. For all of Martyr's Reach's faults—and they are innumerable—our attitudes toward the akratic are less barbaric than they could be. Not ideal, mind, but I've spent time inside the solariums myself, on occasion. They suffice.

All this to say that I worked at the Chirurgeonate. I was a doctor, a healer. I was a lead researcher for a program at the Philidor solarium.

There had been developments in mind magic. An influx of research, plenty of foreign monographs and studies. We had access to a pool of willing patients. I helped develop an experimental treatment, and it looked promising in the first human trials.

I vow to you: we believed that it would work.

We implemented the procedure on a group of fifteen desperately ill patients. We waited for windows of lucidity during which to ask permission, and we consulted the families. We prepared our magic as carefully as we could.

Then we ruined their minds from the inside out. To a one, all of them were destroyed. Empty, unthinking shells.

It isn't important what the guilt did to me. Trust me, however, that it was significant. It remains, and shall ever remain, significant.

Forgive me. I said I'd avoid pathos.

The only way a licensed magician may be branded a witch is if they're convicted of the knowing, willing, wanton infliction of harm on another living creature by magic. My peers and I were all tried for witchcraft, and each of us was absolved. We had done our due diligence, the judging committee said. We couldn't have known.

I left my profession and found myself, a few years later, at the Pharmakeia.

Miraculously, I was allowed to work, a privilege I am forever conscious of. Ironic, after everything, that I would still seek treatment at the Chirurgeonate for my own condition.

I turned these facts over and over and over in my mind again and again and again as I made my way to see the new patients.

∽

The Hessalon building's east wing was softly lit, deathly quiet, and sterile enough that I felt like a contamination whenever I visited. I left my umbrella out front.

Everything echoed; footsteps and voices carried very far through the white stone halls. There was no ambric lighting to flicker in the storm—as a ward for the unconscious, the east wing had appropriately sleepy sconces set into its walls, small witchlights illuminating the space.

I found myself instantly at the door to my first solarium patient's room. I'd walked there without realizing it, in an absent daze. It wasn't the door I wanted, of course; I caught a passing doctor's eye. I didn't recognize him, and he didn't recognize me, a small blessing.

"The Vigil officers and the students," I said. "Where are they being kept?"

"Rooms nineteen through twenty-four. Two to a room. Why?"

I'm curious sounded too much like the words of an experimenter. *I want to drown myself in newfound guilt* was inadvisable. "I thought I'd see if I can be of any help," I said.

He looked at my professor's clothing, devoid of blue, but he shrugged. Irresponsible. "Go on, then."

I started with room nineteen. It sat in silence, sparse and peaceful, fitted with clean linens and cream curtains. The officers inside looked peculiarly nonthreatening without their uniforms; they were dressed in soft hospital clothes, and their raches lay next to their beds in tawny, muscled heaps. The animals were comatose as well. A Vigil's rache is bonded to their psyche in the most intimate of ways.

The officer from the hall of St. Osiander was there, sitting in a chair and watching his comrades with his rache on his lap. When compared to her fellows, I realized exactly how undersized the animal was.

"Ah," I said.

"Go away," the officer suggested with great sincerity.

"I used to be a healer," I began, and he stood up, letting his rache jump down to the floor.

"Yeah, I know," he said. "You *used* to, but you messed up. So why are you here?"

That caught me well and truly off guard; I shook my head. "How on earth do you know that?"

He grinned, a singularly unpleasant expression. "I got curious and asked around. *You know that skinny guy, four-eyes, annoying, black hair, skittish? What's his deal?* And one of the other professors told me. She seemed pretty eager, too."

I stared, somewhat wounded. I knew all these things about myself individually, but to hear them laid out in sequence was a little much. "It's nice to meet you too," I said. I didn't bother asking whom he'd talked to. The knowledge would do me no good.

He shrugged. "You're the one who didn't bow when we met," he said.

I realized that he was right. I'd been too preoccupied with his rache's teeth and the shine of his saber to offer any pleasantries.

Mekhanically, I bowed. "Adrien Desfourneaux."

He squinted me down and did not return the gesture. "Gennady Richter." His tone was an exact copy of mine; either he was mocking me, or he was unsure of how to introduce himself politely. More fondly, he nodded to his rache. "This is Lady."

Most Vigil give their raches names like *Ripper* and *Titus*; I willed myself not to smile. I knew enough about the Vigil to address myself directly to the rache. They must be treated as people, or the soldiers get up in arms.

"A pleasure," I said to her. She nodded, her long muzzle waving delicately.

The marginally less hostile moment passed in a blink. "You have some kind of fetish for this stuff?" Gennady asked, gesturing toward the beds. "Is that why you're here? You turn one group of people into vegetables, and now you can't wait to get a look at the next batch?"

"I'm going to leave," I said, and turned to see if the other room was any less inhabited.

He followed me, a guard dog in the extreme. His rache padded along behind him. "So? What's your business?"

"I thought I'd see if I can be of any help," I recited for the second time. "Seeing as I have some experience with these kinds of symptoms."

There were no visitors in room twenty. I stared down at the unresponsive soldiers, feeling a prickling sensation travel up my neck. One unconsciousness looks much like another, but I imagined that I could see the resemblance to the solarium patients.

"Were you there when they fell ill?" I asked Gennady.

"No," he said mulishly, pacing.

"But you know some of them."

"Sure," he said. "Some are from my commissariat. From my unit."

Vigil form strong bonds with one another, maybe to compensate for their categorical lack of bonds with anyone else. Despite his attitude, I could see that he was worried. The empty-eyed hostility I'd seen in him at the Pharmakeia was muted, although not gone; as if to confirm my suspicions, his rache let out a doleful howl.

I had no comfort to offer him. At least they were no longer in pain, as Malise had said.

As if to punish me for the assumption, at that very instant, one of the soldiers began to convulse. Deep, wracking spasms, her newly open eyes unseeing, a guttural rasping forcing its way from her lungs.

Her hands and feet drummed the bed. It was violent. It was terrifying.

This, too, was familiar.

The sight chilled me through. I knew what to do for the patient, what a doctor would have done—and I found that I could not. Instead, I dashed from the room to find someone in a blue coat. I caught a young licentiate passing by and showed him inside with a scattered explanation, and then I fled.

I've never trusted my hands, you see, since the solarium. I used to sketch; I played piano. No longer.

I realized, once I could breathe, that it was unacceptable for me to come to the east wing to examine the patients and then turn away as soon as they showed symptoms worth examining. I leaned against the wall outside, dizzy, until the sounds of convulsion ceased. Then, grimly, I forced myself back into the room.

There was something new to see. The officer lay unconscious again, and from her mouth streamed a beautiful river of magic. I say *beautiful* not as a value judgment. It was horrifying, miserable. Regardless, the motes of raw, colorless plasma filling the air were undeniably lovely. The doctor I'd shown inside stood speechless, his hand over his mouth, shying away.

I felt a twisted gratitude that there was something to distinguish the scene from my solarium patients, and not a moment later, I felt a familiar lance of guilt for my relief.

The magic had no particular specialization—not like my lightning, not like Malise's ice, nothing set in its form. It was pure. I looked at Gennady. "Do you know if she's a magician?" If she was Vigil, the answer would have to be *no*.

He shook his head, not frightened, not unsettled, his shoulders set toward the scene as if it were an enemy he could weather. He was cold, a condition I was beginning to suspect was permanent. "She isn't."

"Then this shouldn't be possible," I said. Normally, I hate that—something happens, something is *clearly* happening, and someone protests that it shouldn't be possible. In this case, however, I couldn't stop myself. If she wasn't a magician, she had no magic, and that was the law of the universe. I recognized this magic's nature, as well; it wasn't an invading force being expelled. It was coming from within.

Logically, then, she had *become* a magician. That should have been impossible as well, but it was the only option.

The young doctor, on cue, said, "She is *now*."

There was a way to tell for sure. I looked at Gennady, looked at the doctor. "If I touch her on the arm, I can tell whether or not she's developed her own magic." Ideally, I would have gotten the soldier's permission herself, but that wasn't going to happen.

The doctor nodded helplessly, and Gennady stared. I returned his gaze, ashen but level.

"I don't know what's going on, but I'll kill you if you mess her up," he said conversationally.

It seemed a fair deal to strike. I turned and laid a hand on the soldier's feverishly warm arm.

Not many magicians can extend their magic outside themselves into another person's soul. It's a rare gift, the product of remarkable talent. I am, I like to imagine, remarkably talented. Magic speaks to me as it does to few others. I closed my eyes and sent my power out, meticulously stripped of lightning, the thinnest thread sinking into her skin.

It hit a second force. She had her own magic. We'd been correct.

"Well," I said, and stepped back, faintly nauseous. "Yes."

The sleeping Vigil officer coughed, and the motes thickened in the air: I fancied that I could see a piece of her soul wisp away. Call it intuition, call it a wild assumption, call it histrionic paranoia—saints know I'm prone to that. Whatever you call it, I knew that her new magic was taking her apart.

"They've all been having seizures," the doctor said quietly, "but I've never seen this."

"I have a feeling that may change," I said, and left the room again. There was nothing more to be done, and I couldn't bear it any longer.

I stood and watched people pass in the hallways, counting methodically to slow my pulse. If any of them took any notice of the anxious, awkward man stuck against the wall, they gave no sign. As soon as I had my wits back, I left Gennady and the young doctor to their hovering and went to room twenty-four to see the two stricken Pharmakeia students. It might have been favoritism, but I cared most for them.

This room was more warmly decorated; more attention had been given to it, perhaps by friends or family. There were potted plants left for the patients, fragrant, almost burying the smell of sanative alcohol that haunted the Chirurgeonate.

The students were quiet, sleeping soundly. No seizures. Not yet. I fretted, wanting to check their pupils, feel their pulse, work some magic to try healing them. None of it was advisable. I wasn't their physician, and I had a cursed touch.

I was beginning to realize that I'd been masochistic to come. Malise was right. I'd done no one any good, and I'd be preoccupied with this for as long as it lasted. She'd *warned* me, and I had insisted anyway, even knowing how often she was correct. I dug my nails into the skin of one arm, testing some pain. Poor judgment. Eternally poor judgment.

The Chirurgeonate holds it to be true that even visiting a patient can have beneficial effects. Even being in the same room as someone can bring some nebulous comfort, awake or not. I pulled up a chair and found a book in my briefcase, absently feeling the creases in the cover.

I was sure Gennady wouldn't care much that I'd gone, as long as I wasn't around any of his comrades. I was wrong. After twenty minutes or so, the door opened, and he was staring at me suspiciously from the threshold.

I closed my book, wondering if he might somehow blame me for the seizures. I could maybe run past him, I thought, if he drew his weapon. "Yes?"

"So can you help them?" he asked, as if we'd ended our conversation only moments ago. Gennady was not one for social cues, I was realizing.

"No," I said shortly, feeling unusually stupid. I spend a great deal of time thinking about my flaws, thinking about myself—you may have noticed—but stupidity isn't often an item of concern.

Gennady sat down in the other chair with a sullen flounce. "I asked to be stationed around here," he said abruptly. "So I can keep an eye on them. Vigil needed volunteers to come watch you people scurry around."

Joy, I thought. "You mentioned I might be seeing more of you, yes."

He leaned forward. I realized, with a lightning strike of intuition, that he wasn't quite sane. I can't say exactly what it was. A light in his eyes, perhaps, or the tilt of his head when he looked at me. A strange hum in his voice. I don't know. "You'll figure out how to fix them, though," he said. "You will."

"Ask one of the doctors around here about that," I said cautiously. "They're the most equipped."

I had to wonder. Why was he the only Vigil quite so dedicated to keeping an eye on the stricken soldiers? Why so guarded, so watchful?

He growled in frustration.

I decided to say something unwise. "Do you know something, lieutenant?"

For a moment, I feared that I had misstepped. He looked at me, silent, utterly blank. A wary predator. I got ready to run.

The moment passed jerkily, floundering away. He stood and slapped me hard on the shoulder. I dropped my book; he smiled beatifically. "No. Just figure out how to fix it. You know about this stuff. You said so yourself."

"Stop making me drop things," I said, more or less involuntarily. I left the book where it was so I wouldn't have to lean down in front of him. "If I think of anything I can do, I'll do it. Otherwise, I don't know what you expect."

His rache reared up to put a paw on my chair, and I scrambled up, beginning to feel well and truly claustrophobic in the small space. I couldn't bear to have the animal in the same room as the comatose students, all of a sudden; I quickly retrieved my book and ducked past Gennady into the hallway, assuming he'd follow me out. He did.

"I'll be around," he said. He didn't seem to have the capacity for any tones besides sullenness, emptiness, and a peculiar kind of sunny menace. "I'll check in."

"Don't," I recommended, and hurried away, breathing a sharp sigh of relief when he let me leave without any further comment.

I wasn't convinced that he truly knew nothing. The worry he'd shown had been urgent, specific.

I could dissect the problem later. I still had to check in on my solarium patients. Even considering the new worries, it was an unbreakable appointment—a weekly penance, a useless ritual. Nothing ever changed, and nothing ever would, but I had to ensure their faces wouldn't fade from my memory.

～

The rain wasn't letting up, and the sun was nearly hidden; no light streamed in through the Chirurgeonate's glass as I walked to pay my visits. As I passed patients and doctors in the halls, the agitation of my conversation with Gennady faded into a familiar malaise, the paranoia of many eyes.

Ten of my patients were still alive. They had spent years trapped in their own shattered minds; it was peculiar to see them age. Part of me always expected them to stay the same, as if their bodies were in stasis as well.

Willette. Carya. Sandro. Rene. Yao. Gedros. Marius. Khada. Jehan. Corinna. Rooms forty-three to fifty-three. They had all been interred in sequence.

I visited each of them for a few minutes. In the beginning, I'd spent hours at the Chirurgeonate, flitting from bed to bed in a silent dream, but I'd learned to cut down on such excesses. If it didn't help them, anything more than the brief, sincere visit I owed them was only a selfish performance. Many of the healers staffing the Hessalon building knew me by now; they let me wander freely.

I prayed a little. I care something for the stars themselves, but less so for the gods they're meant to embody. The constellations have none of my faith. Regardless, I thought I should do everything I could, so I prayed to Anima Iatros. *Please heal them.* I prayed to Anima Kephis, my birth constellation. *Please heal me.* Two sentences, but earnestly meant. That was it. If any divine powers existed, and if they were truly inclined, that would do it. Kephis's domains are sickness and penance, a distasteful bit of trivia.

～

A few days passed. I woke one morning in a strange, distant mood, convinced that some new disaster was waiting to make itself known. I barely managed to get myself standing. The next night, I didn't sleep, working on some project or another until the sun rose, perfectly convinced that everything would be all right.

The daimon was coming, I know now; an episode was on its way—but I hadn't realized it quite yet. No matter how many times the pattern repeats, it can be difficult to catch.

The rain still didn't let up. Other Vigil officers began to appear in the Pharmakeia, accompanying their raches through the halls and standing watch inside other classrooms. Gennady had been telling the truth about the military's plans for increased surveillance.

I lectured on light and optics, philosophy, mekhanical advancements. More often than not, Gennady haunted the hall of St. Osiander, keeping my students on edge, staring at me as I taught. He'd walk back and forth in the amphitheater, sometimes, a black-clad specter of the Clementia. His pacing developed an anxiety to it, a guilty stutter.

Occasionally, I went back to agonize over the new comatose patients at the Chirurgeonate, and sometimes I'd see him there, circling around, keeping watch over his fellows with a suspicious eye. The seizures stopped, eventually. All the new patients were confirmed to have developed their own magic, knowledge that was no help whatsoever as long as they remained unresponsive.

I decided once and for all that Gennady knew something when he waylaid me before a class one evening and asked, "What kind of stuff could give someone magic? Would a magician have to do it, or could a regular person manage?" That question alone might not have tipped the scales, but Gennady was a spectacularly bad liar. He shuffled; he fidgeted. He avoided my eyes one moment and stared me down with comical intensity at the next.

"I don't know, Gennady," I said tiredly. "Maybe you'll help enlighten me one day."

So he drifted away without a word, distrait.

"Figure anything out?" he'd ask me whenever we crossed paths after that, and I would shake my head, perennially unnerved, always failing to work up the courage to interrogate him further.

"Get to it," he'd say, uncomfortable with his secret, jealous knowledge. I began to feel something of a hostage.

There was nothing for it but to continue life as normal, in between visits to the Chirurgeonate. I became accustomed to Gennady's presence at the back of the lecture hall, and my students learned to accept the Clementia's watchdog looking over their shoulders.

That's the key phrase, of course. *Continue life as normal.* I failed to do so.

All the while, the daimon drew closer. More unconscious patients began to appear, Vigil and students both. On Septidy, the witchfinders came.

Chapter 3

The witchfinder corps is a grim organization, another branch of the Curia Clementia, brethren to the Vigil. They're metal-eyed vultures, sniffing out witches to lock up or kill. They come equipped with mekhania lenses set into their heads in place of a left eye; the mekhania grants them small magics, and they use those spells to the disadvantage of their prey.

That's always offended me. The gift of magic isn't something to be stolen and worn like plundered jewelry. Imagine my enthusiasm, then, when pairs of them began to appear throughout the Pharmakeia. They fixed those eyes on the professors and students, studying us, letting us know without question that the only things separating us from the witches were our licenses and the Clementia's hard-won approval.

Two of them cornered me just outside my office. I should have been there earlier; I'd begun to talk too much during lectures, lose track of my thoughts, spend all of class chasing down ramblings. Try as I might, I never ended class on time. I was sorry for my students, but, daimonic or not, talking has always been a vice of mine. I was enjoying myself, in an unsteady sort of way.

Witchfinders always work with a partner. Two women, each dark-haired and broad-shouldered, approached me. "Professor Delacroix," one said.

"Desfourneaux," I said brightly, not expecting them to care. I've never understood the trouble people have with my name: it's three syllables. Still, I was feeling good, for the moment. "May I help you?"

I should have left it at that, but I couldn't stop talking. "I notice you've been enjoying yourselves around here, taking advantage of the academy's hospitality. Has everything been to your liking? We're not exactly accustomed so many visitors from the Clementia. You and your Vigil friends are taking up quite a lot of space here; I hope you're not getting too used to this post. Although—with the rain, I can hardly blame you for needing the shelter. I doubt you spend your usual days inside like this. Chasing witches through dark alleyways has to be a cold business, yes—?"

As I say. I couldn't stop. I was falling.

They looked at each other, a quiet gesture of contempt. "We've been hearing whispers," the second witchfinder said, interrupting me.

I fell prey to pettiness. "I understand witchfinders are given to eavesdropping," I said, far less brightly. "It makes sense that you might."

Her mekhania eye grated and spun in annoyance. I could smell oil and metal on her; I regretted my fundamental waspishness, as I often do.

Her partner put a hand on her shoulder. "Whispers about unrest in the Pharmakeia," she said. "Maybe some of you have been dreaming about a little rebellion. Maybe making some people sick."

My blood stilled. "Sick?"

"You've heard about that poor group of Vigil officers who came down with something awfully strange," she said.

"I have. Some Pharmakeia students are ill as well," I said. "It's spreading." Four more victims had appeared, three Vigil and another student. I'd found them the last time I visited the Chirurgeonate.

"Inside casualties, maybe," the first witchfinder suggested. "Maybe the magicians here have been trying out some new spells on the soldiers, hmm? Maybe a few of those spells backfired."

"I know nothing about that," I said, the remnants of my brightness fading perilously. I felt the seasonal autumn irritation, a monster with bottomless vitality waiting to bite. Ready to turn like the edge of a knife. If I snapped at a witchfinder, I would regret it dearly, and then I would lose my temper, and then God only knew. A witchfinder had never used their eye on me before, cast one of their darling cantrips on me to quiet me down. I had no desire to change that.

"I know nothing," I repeated.

She scratched her nose. "All right," she said. "You let us know if you hear anything." With that, she and her partner walked away, chatting companionably.

I knew without a doubt that they would be watching me. They were watching all of us.

I'm often given to the idea that people are talking about me, waiting for me to slip. It gets worse, at times, with the daimon. Certainly, at that moment, the akrasia didn't *help*, but I told myself that I was far from delusional in my suspicion.

I went inside my office to hide from the metal eyes. Immediately, I felt a measure of comfort; I'd arranged it to fit me perfectly, and it never failed to soothe. It was on the second floor of the same building as the hall of St. Osiander, tucked into a cramped nook somewhere out of the way. It felt smaller than it was, owing to the bookshelves filling it, but that was no flaw. I enjoyed the closeness of the walls. The smaller the space, the easier to control.

One day, I intended to straighten the room up, but I didn't suspect that day would be soon. The scattered pieces of tiny mekhanical projects lying around had made their own homes in the space, and until I finished those projects, I hated to disturb them.

It'll be all right, I told myself, and began the task of sorting the monument of papers on my desk.

～

It was not, as it happens, all right.

The witchfinders' supervision continued. My resentment toward them bled into my resentment for the Vigil officers—they were all Clementia, all military, all menaces. The Pharmakeia began to feel unsafe. My colleagues were watching me, my students whispering about me, and now that wasn't all. Raches prowled. Mekhania eyes flashed. I began to lose my patience.

I've never had much patience to lose, even on the best of days. With the mounting akrasia on one side and the Clementia on the other, I never had a chance.

Gennady was the first to catch my ire, undoubtedly because familiarity breeds contempt. I'm not proud of that, but it's what happened. I'm bound to tell you. Specificity in all things.

The incident opened with a lecture on ethics. It began well enough. As Gennady oversaw the class, I thought I saw him—bizarrely, miraculously—beginning to *listen*. It was a shame; Ethics was my least favorite class, below even the trivium subjects. I felt myself fundamentally unqualified to speak on the subject.

"Alexarchus of Elora believes that character is a matter of habit," I said to the class, speaking a little too quickly despite my best efforts. I had practice with mitigating pressured speech, but practice can only do so much. "In his dialogue with Siphos, he argues that goodness is a discipline, a skill that can be honed. Our natures aren't static; we can improve ourselves through careful, consistent work."

I've always been fond of Alexarchus, long-dead though he is. By all accounts, he was an excellent magician and a passable scholar, if famously irritating. I think we would have been friends.

In the corner of my eye, I saw Gennady stop pacing. He stood there, still and silent, for the rest of the lesson. After class was out, he strode toward me, brows furrowed; I retreated to the chalkboard. Frankly, I hated the sight of him.

"You really believe that shit?" he demanded, stopping a few feet away from me.

"We covered several subjects today," I said testily. "Which do you mean?"

"That guy who says people can make themselves better."

"Alexarchus of Elora." I started to clean the board, taking my time. Long, slow motions with the brush, giving myself an excuse to avoid eye contact. "I believe him."

He waited, strangely keen, for me to go on. I shrugged. "Why? Are you looking to improve yourself?"

It was something of a cruel joke, but he startled and pinned me with an alien stare. "No," he said at length.

"You're a strange person," I said. He had little tact, and I felt free to meet him where he was. We owed each other nothing.

He grinned emptily, nothing more than an imitation of grins he'd seen before. "I know that."

With that, as suddenly as he'd spoken to me, he went back to the door of the amphitheater and stood there to loom over my students as they left. They were preparing for an exam, already frayed and unhappy. As they walked past him on their way out, I saw him touch the hilt of his saber once, making them jump and scurry away.

A fire bloomed; it had been waiting for a signal, lurking for the past few days. I snapped.

"Gennady," I said, very quietly, from where I stood at the lectern. The hall's acoustics carried my voice to him as well as if I had shouted. The ambric lights dimmed and surged.

He turned. "Yeah?"

"Get back here."

If I'd been completely well, I would never have dared. I wasn't. Akratic elevation and irritation banded together to give me the strength to be careless.

He ambled over, his hands in his pockets, Lady panting happily at his side.

"Speaking of self-improvement," I said, "stop frightening my students. I've had enough of it."

He heard the challenge in my voice. "Or what?"

I considered. I couldn't appeal to his superiors. I couldn't appeal to his better nature; I wasn't entirely convinced that he had one. He'd just told me so.

Alexarchus could endure a little disappointment. I heard myself say, cheerfully, "Or I'll fry you into smoke."

Akrasia is, in the original, nonmedical terms, the abandonment of good judgment because of a lack of willpower. I can think of no better example. I realized, finally, that the daimon was here. It had turned. I'd been right: something was coming. It was all, as ever, a matter of time.

The students who were still in the process of leaving stopped walking and started staring. They were frightened—I'd frightened them. I couldn't quite care. Not with Gennady in front of me, the symbol of all my recent terrors and travails.

He had the legal right to drag me to prison on the spot, and he knew that.

"Professor," a few young voices said.

"Go on," I said to the lingering crowd. "Remember, an exam is coming up."

Lady barked at me, her strange, rough voice grating on my ears. I flinched, but I didn't move back. The students regained their wits and hurried out. I could only hope none of them would report me for what I'd said.

Gennady stood very close to me. "You'll fry me?"

I spoke on sheer, warped, venomous instinct. "If you insist on scaring people like a wild animal, yes. I'll do it in an instant, and you'll have no way of stopping me."

I have no idea why I said it. I could never kill. I could never hurt anyone— not willingly, that is. I could never use my magic in the service of violence. Never, never. So I told myself. I said it anyway.

As soon as the words were out, a full crush of misery descended upon me, bone-deep. Malise's protections were breaking, and the pattern was recognizable. It wasn't solely the gray of a downswing, and it wasn't the untethered mania on the other edge of the knife. This fit would be both of them, mixing, alternating, bringing me to my knees.

In my opinion, a better term for mania would be *teratothymia*. The spirit of a monster. I thought I would die.

Gennady shrugged. "Okay," he said.

My breath left me, a sharp gasp of horror. "I'm sorry. I didn't—"

He and Lady exchanged quizzical looks, and he eased back a step. "Like I care that much. It was fun, but if you're going to be dramatic about it, I'll quit it. Just to shut you up."

"I didn't mean it," I said, scattered, and gathered up my things in a blind panic. I left the rest of the chalkboard uncleaned. Gennady's predator's gaze never wavered.

"See you tomorrow," he said unreadably, absently. He was looking past me at the board—at a quote from Alexarchus.

Heedless of my next class, willing to desert it, I hurried to the Chirurgeonate to see Malise. The witchfinders and Vigil infesting the Pharmakeia's halls all watched me as I left.

∼

At the very least, it wasn't raining when I left campus, and I barely felt the cold. I stopped outside Malise's closed door, hovering and staring at the solid oak, realizing that we had no appointment. She might not be in. I counted to three, took a shuddering breath, and knocked.

No answer. I had no idea where to find her, and even if I did, I had no right to interrupt her day any more than I already planned to.

So I waited for about an hour in the gathering gloom of the approaching evening. I stood under her awning, watching the Chirurgeonate faculty come and go throughout the grounds, watching the patients taking their air. The glass and brick glowed comfortingly in the lowering light; I felt ungrateful for not appreciating it.

When she finally arrived, she lifted a hand in uncertain greeting, coming to join me at her door. She had shadows under her eyes. I felt the overwhelming urge to tell her that I had only come to check in on her, to see if she was all right. To portray myself as something other than a selfish akratic, here to demand her help.

But she saw my face. Like Gennady, I am a poor liar. "You're getting sick," she said immediately.

"Mixed," I mumbled, alive with humiliation. I had gotten used to reciting the nature of my fits to Malise, but I never managed to look her in the eye when I did.

She unlocked her door and pulled me inside by the hand.

I stood frozen in the middle of the room, unwilling to use the settee, unwilling to take up any more space than I already was. She shrugged her coat off and left it hanging on her chair before coming to stand in front of me, gently pressing me down by the shoulders. "Go on."

She was much shorter than I, but it never felt that way. I sat.

With a sigh, she went to her desk to find a pad of paper and a dip pen. "I should have known," she said, finding her ink. Blue, of course. "We haven't eaten together since last week. I haven't talked to you—I should have known something was happening."

I shook my head silently, wanting to lift the blame off her shoulders. I had been avoiding our regular meals together between appointments; it was my fault.

"Tell me about it," she said.

"There's not much to tell. I've been—"

My voice failed. Fear. There's a special kind of dread that comes with the start of an episode. I'm facing down the daimon, and I can do nothing to stop it.

"How long has it been?" she asked.

"A few days. I can't tell exactly. The anger," I said, and fell silent again.

She wrote everything down. I had no idea why. She'd seen it all before.

Apologetically, she said, "Have you done anything unfortunate yet?"

She had to ask. I understood that. It burned me nevertheless. "I told a Vigil officer that I was going to kill him," I said.

She winced sharply and wrote for a while longer as I willed myself to dissolve.

"What did he do? Did he report you? Is everything all right?"

"He didn't do anything," I said.

She shook her head and moved on, still unnerved. "Hallucinations?" she asked. "Paranoias?"

"None of the former, as far as I can tell, and a few of the latter."

"You caught it early," she said with soft approval. "Very early."

Don't take that tone with me, I wanted to say, feeling patronized, enduring a shiver of outrage. Instead, I nodded. I always saved all my self-control for her.

She came to sit next to me, her magic already humming; the air chilled in response.

"I'm so tired of it," I said, sounding like an indignant child. "Malise, my God, I'm so tired. I can't take it again."

"You can," she told me simply, and pressed her hands to my temples.

The regular burn went deeper this time. It hurt more; it was much colder. I gritted my teeth and held still. She stayed at it for a long, long time, purging me, slowing the daimon to a glacier.

Of course, a glacier always gets its way.

The anger smoldered to a halt and lay purring below the surface, and I felt some of my nervous, thoughtless energy wind down. At the same time, a deep grayness wrested away the upper hand.

There was a choice to be made: Malise could only ever help me with one thing at a time. In a mixed state, she had to decide between the high and the low. With experience, I knew that the high would be far more dangerous. It might bring joy, for a time, but that was nothing more than a sweet poison.

When she took her hands away, I buckled forward and covered my face, taking my glasses off for a moment. "Thank you," I breathed.

She embraced me. "It won't last," she said. "It never does."

I leaned on her, too grateful to be standoffish. "But it always comes back around."

She had no answer to that. There *was* no answer. She let go after another long moment, moving back, and I replaced my glasses so I could see how, exactly, she was looking at me. It was with distress, I discovered. "Have you been straining yourself lately?"

I thought of my now-habitual agonizing over the growing numbers of comatose patients at the Chirurgeonate and looked away.

"Adrien."

"More Vigil and students are falling ill—I know you know that, I'm sorry— and the witchfinders said they think the Pharmakeia is at fault."

"They can think what they want. You're going to obsess over it," she said, bitterly resigned.

"I can't help it."

"You *can*," she said. "You could take some time off, rest, forget about the things you can't change, and be safe while you get better." She spoke fiercely, as though she could change me into the type of person who would take advantage of such practical things.

My dithymic akrasia is survivable; my fits rarely last beyond a few months, and I never descend into violence. If I was lucky, it would be over soon enough that taking some time off might genuinely help. I should have felt grateful for that knowledge, but I'm often an ungrateful person.

I knew without a doubt that next, I would be visiting to check on the new patients and make myself miserable over them. I knew that I should not, but I was going to. Poor judgment. Weak will.

"I'm sorry," I murmured. "You deserve a better patient."

"Don't self-flagellate," she said sharply. "I want you to take care of yourself. That's all."

"May I come to see you more often, then?" I smiled weakly: a compromise, since I couldn't promise I'd behave with any real sense.

Why couldn't I promise that? Why, precisely, was I so determined to do what I could only assume would harm me? Because comatose cases are often time-sensitive, and so is akrasia. There was a slim chance I could figure something out before either I or the patients went too far, and it was worth the risk. Even if I knew more or less nothing, the *chance* was still there.

In hindsight, yes, it's very silly. I know that.

Malise took my hand and squeezed. "Of course you can come more often. But you should tell Casmir."

I took my hand back, gently, and stood. "No." My voice almost broke; I coughed, as if I had any hope of covering it.

Casmir was my keeper.

"Better safe than sorry," she said.

"I don't need him."

"If you're going to be working yourself up over the Chirurgeonate—"

"Don't tell him," I said, and I was begging. "Don't tell him."

"*You* should," she said, lifting her chin. "It's what's smart. It's what's safe." Her tone was meticulously controlled. "You don't have to live with him. You just have to let him know."

A keeper's duties vary from patient to patient. Casmir lived with me when I needed him, kept track of my finances and took what he was owed, kept me from my manic excesses, kept me—excuse the indelicacy—from suicide. He tried, at least. The times I needed him were hell on earth for both of us.

In short, I did not want to tell Casmir Leynault that I was, once again, going definitively crazy. We saw each other often, between fits, but it was as comfortable friends and coworkers. Not as a keeper and his charge. I wanted it to stay that way.

"What did you feel?" I asked Malise. "When you were treating me just now. What did you feel, that you think I need him this time?"

She didn't answer me.

I paced, a spooked cat. "Is it going to be *that* bad?"

"You know I can't predict it with much accuracy."

"But you felt *something*." Her blue ambric fairy lights were flickering; I forced myself to calm down, and they quieted.

She inclined her head a bare inch. "I think we should tell him, Adrien. I can treat you, but you're not going to be happy."

Startled, lost, I turned away. I was realizing that I was going to submit to her better judgment, and I was going to hate every second of it. "All right," I said indistinctly.

"Every day," she told me. "Come to me every day at five."

"I told him I'd use my lightning," I said, instead of agreeing with her as I should have. I meant to obey, but I couldn't make myself say so. "The Vigil officer. When I said I'd kill him, I said I'd do it with lightning."

She looked away from me.

I found myself with my nails in one arm, digging crescents in my skin. The pain was a pleasant, bracing sting. "Please keep me down."

"Don't scratch." She tugged my sleeve to stop me.

I hated myself dearly.

It began to rain again, as if we needed any clearer indication of drama. "Go find Casmir," Malise said, giving me a light push toward the door.

"Thank you," I murmured. "I will."

Then I started off toward the Chirurgeonate's library instead, because I am nothing if not predictable.

Chapter 4

The Chirurgeonate's library is not quite as extensive as the Pharmakeia's, being far more specialized, but it still holds a place in my heart. All the city's libraries do. The Chirurgeonate's is well organized, and I'm shallow: I think the hardwood floors and soaring, vaulted ceiling lend it a distinguished air.

The library is always crowded with hollow-eyed students trying to pass their licensing examinations. However, one of the best features of libraries is that they guarantee you'll be alone, no matter how many other visitors there are. I slipped into a private world and made my way to the third floor.

The Philidor solarium disaster garnered its fair share of fame within the Astrine medical community. In the years following, treatises were written about it, many of them by the original researchers. I never published my own. I did, however, spend the occasional day sequestered in the library poring over our dedicated shelf in history, hoping against hope that one day I would find something I'd missed.

There were volumes upon volumes to choose from, with titles of varying sensationalism: *Clinical Details of the Philidor Solarium* by Ranbir Aelius to *Horror Under Glass: A Dark Tale of Malpractice* by Iva Zerkov. I'd read each of them dozens of times—I could have done something of actual use with the days I spent on those books.

Maybe this time would be *the* time, I told myself, when some vital detail would catch my eye, and I'd learn how to put it all right. If I could solve one set of patients, why not the newer set as well? I pulled up a chair and immersed myself, feeling the last few traces of Malise's magic trickle through my veins and disperse. Sound faded; dust settled. The cramped shelves formed a separate plane of existence.

Familiar records, familiar interviews, familiar illustrations, and familiar turns of phrase on each page—it was an intimately familiar activity, and one that always had the exact same effect. I detached from myself and sorted the information like an automaton. It was a relief; I settled in for several hours. My heart rate finally slowed as the smell of paper soothed me.

Any relief vanished when Casmir Leynault came up from behind me and took the book I was reading out of my hands. *Cacochymionic Phthisis in the Philidor Solarium Patients* by Chih-Hung Li went back on the shelf.

I turned. "You're not supposed to reshelve them," I said blankly.

"You stupid bastard," he hissed.

Casmir was unusually pale for an Astrine, a little too gawky, and his brown hair was just slightly too long to suit his face, but he had a wonderful voice. Strong and clear, with the faintest hint of a baseborn accent. I was in love with him. I suppose that's salient.

We'd met when I'd first come to the Pharmakeia, still raw and hollow from the solarium disaster, and he'd treated me well. He treated me like a person rather than a menace; he showed me how to survive the academy's intricacies. I fell in love, and he did not—although he never took his leave of me. Eventually, I asked him to be my keeper, and he obliged.

I regretted my request on occasion. That day, I certainly did.

Casmir took me by the wrist and pulled me out of the library. I declined to resist; I'd made enough scenes for the day.

We hid from the rain under the overhang outside the front doors. The plants framing the door tickled our shadows. I had no idea where I'd left my umbrella. "Malise told you after all," I said, trying and failing to be indignant.

He nodded. "We knew you'd be at the library," he said. "You really never learn."

I hugged him before I knew what I was doing.

Grimly, he pried me away. "She thinks it's going to be bad this time," he said, as if I hadn't touched him.

I stood adrift, forcing down a fledgling desperation. I hadn't wanted to see him, and now he was all I wanted in the world. He *was* the world. "I know."

He crossed his arms, staring me down, and a dreadful pang of déjà vu shook me. I remembered this. I remembered how it was to have him look into my soul in the midst of a fit. "Then why are you here making yourself worse?" he said.

"There are these new cases at the Chirurgeonate," I began, and he shook his head.

"I swear, Adrien—"

"I just want to help," I said, much too loudly, drawing the eye of a doctor passing by us into the library.

"You should want to get better."

The daimon's anger, buried so skillfully by Malise, clawed its way to the surface again. "Of course I want to get better," I snarled. "Just because I'm trying to make some use of myself doesn't mean I don't want that."

"Saints," he said, with what I thought must be disgust. "Is this why you've been avoiding me? To stop me from seeing that you're getting sick again?"

I hadn't talked with him often lately. That much was true. We normally had lunch with each other whenever Malise wasn't free; we saw a play together now and again—he was a professor with the Light Studies department, and we saw enough of each other at work. With recent events, though, I'd been taking all my meals alone.

"It's not intentional," I said weakly.

"You never learn," he said again.

I could have had a different keeper than Casmir. I could have found someone kinder, someone softer. I didn't, and not only because I loved him. A keeper must be *effective* above all else, and he was effective. He kept me in check.

I couldn't meet his gaze. "The witchfinders think the Pharmakeia is behind the illnesses. The Vigil is breathing down our necks. They're watching us. Maybe if I can find something out . . ."

"You're a narcissist," he said, hard and sharp. His magical talent was with rock and earth, and it often showed in his bearing.

He was right about me. I just wasn't sure what he was referring to, specifically. "How so this time?"

He began to pace. "You think you're so special. If someone is going to find the answer, it's going to be *you*." He paused near me and leaned in. I felt a flush threaten. "You think you're the only one who can possibly figure any of this out, even though the entire Chirurgeonate is examining those same patients—even though you're not a doctor anymore."

"If I could *help*—"

"You can't."

I had the good sense, at least, to remain quiet.

"Should I move in again?" he asked, clipped. He'd shifted from friend to keeper effortlessly. I wasn't quite as ready.

I bit my tongue to keep myself from being unkind. "Not now. Not yet."

"She said you're not hallucinating."

I hissed and looked around for anyone who might be listening, finally flushing despite my best efforts. "I don't—for God's sake, Casmir. Must we do this *here?*"

He relented, stepping back. "At your house, then."

I lived in Deme Palenne, only a mile or so from the Pharmakeia. I knew that he wanted to go there because the state of my house would tell him how deep I'd gone. Luckily, between manic cleaning and depressive inattention, things were more or less normal. "All right," I said.

He'd neglected to bring an umbrella, and I had no will left to go searching around for mine. Accordingly, we walked silently in the downpour for twenty minutes, out of the Chirurgeonate's grounds, past the Pharmakeia's own spires, through the many charming little streets filled with charming little houses that were drowning under the rain.

I'd never experienced a more vivid discomfort. The Aqua Circadia ran through Palenne; as we came to my house, I found myself eying the canal wistfully. Drowning might be better than facing Casmir.

Regretfully, I resisted the urge and went up the whitewashed front steps. The edges of the Circadia were nearly overflowing. Living beside a canal can be scenic, but there are certain generous drawbacks. "If I'm flooded, I'll burn whatever's left to the ground once it's dry," I muttered viciously, fumbling with my keys.

"Dramatic as ever," Casmir said, sounding more tired than disapproving. As we went inside, he tracked mud onto my floor. I couldn't care. The realization that he was *here* in my home struck me like a lightning bolt, and I wavered.

Even soaked to the bone, he looked lovely. The daimon sank its claws in very deep. I could stand it all, I thought, if he kissed me.

He didn't. "It's not as much of a mess as I thought it would be," he said.

"I told you I don't need you here," I said, and winced at how cold I sounded. "Please. You know what I mean."

"I know." He ran his hands through his hair, wringing some water out, and shook himself like a wet dog. A quick shower spattered the hardwood floor. I watched closely; he'd always had a casual, unselfconscious grace that shone through in every action, no matter how uncouth.

"You're standing near a bookcase," I said with soft dismay, drying my glasses on my shirt.

"It's your place," he told me, brows drawn severely. "I always am."

He was right. Like my office at the Pharmakeia, my house was small, filled with books and mekhanical parts, and deeply untidy. Not *messy*, exactly, just organizationally illegible. The one extravagance was a piano in the living room's corner, gathering dust.

"Stay out of the atelier," I said. Not even Casmir was permitted in my workshop. With that, I went into my bedroom to change my clothes and recover myself. He was welcome to stay and drip in the living room for as long as he pleased. If he was going to insist on coming to my door to interrogate me, he could wait.

My house had a wound in it, an empty room I kept for Casmir. A space for my illness to live. I didn't look at it as I passed.

I took my time. Once I was dry, and I thought I could talk to him without losing my temper, I went back out to find him sitting at the coffee table. He'd slung his soaked coat over the back of his chair.

"So," I said, and took the chair facing him. It was satisfying to be able to sit across from him, perfectly warm, and watch him puddle on the floor. I had so few upper hands; I couldn't resist acknowledging one of them.

"Are you sober?" he asked.

My threadbare satisfaction dissolved. "Casmir—"

"Are you sober?"

Akrasia often comes with a set of specific habits.

"Yes," I said stiffly, and stabbed a hand out toward the other rooms of the house. "Do you see any needles?"

"Addicts are often good at hiding them," he said with a brittle smile. "So that doesn't mean much to me."

A flash of nausea climbed up my throat; I huddled into myself. I had gotten sober before I'd ever met Casmir, but even he saw me as an addict.

After a long, chilly silence, he sighed. "I'm sorry. You know I have to ask."

I did know. I said nothing. We were both looking toward his empty room, I realized, both wondering if it was going to stay empty.

"Malise is keeping me down," I said, nearly whispering. "She'll keep it steady. I don't need you. I promise."

Finally, he looked at me with something other than irritation or inscrutability—a quiet regret. "You said that last time," he said, with enough tenderness to cut me to the bone.

Last time. The words made me sick. There had been a last time, and there would be a next time. For as long as I lived, that would always be the case.

One of the greater ravages of my daimon is that I can never trust myself.

My judgment is worthless. My instincts are perennially suspect. Every emotion is a potential mirage; my basic self is pathologized. I was *sure* I didn't need Casmir, and that meant nothing. I had been sure many times before.

I sat with my mouth open.

"Either forget about those patients and leave the Chirurgeonate alone, or let me move in," he said.

I thought about living with Casmir sleeping near me at night, out of reach, and broke. "I'll forget about them. I'll check in with you every day," I promised. "You don't have to stay here. I'll talk with you every single day."

He nodded, relaxing minutely.

Just before silence could fall, I jumped to intercept it. "The witchfinders," I said without thinking, my mind leaping to the next available subject of contention. A desperate defense—I couldn't stand Casmir's pity, so why not say something I thought might start a fight? "Do you think they're right?"

Long-suffering, he sighed. "Right about what? That the Pharmakeia is behind the comatose curse?"

I hadn't considered labeling it that way. Not a new plague, but a curse. It was more apt; a curse is *inflicted*. I remembered the river of plasma motes streaming from the Vigil officer's mouth and gave Casmir a half-nod.

"Saints," he said. "Of course not, and if *you* do, you're more paranoid than you think."

That stung.

"You're not interested in what's going on?" I asked him. "What's causing it? Why they're getting sick, why it looks just like—just like the solarium?"

For a moment, he softened. He got up and came to stand in front of me; it took all my willpower not to let myself melt into his presence. Instead, I sat rigidly, looking away.

He put a hand on my shoulder. "Of course I am. I'm just not obsessed. I'm willing to leave it to the people who are trained and paid to deal with it."

"You were always incurious," I said bitterly, to drive him away so I wouldn't have to feel his warmth next to me any longer.

It worked. He stepped back again, indignant. "You mean I've always been more sensible than you."

"They're not mutually exclusive," I said, a poor excuse for an apology.

"I'm here because I wanted to make sure you were all right," he said. "The least you can do is be decent about it." Decent, not good. All he wanted was *decent*, and I couldn't oblige.

I lifted a hand in protest. "The first thing you said to me was *you stupid bastard.*"

"Well, I stand by that," he said, reignited. His blood had always run hot. "You've got to leave the whole issue alone. Ignore the witchfinders. Ignore the Vigil. Ignore the patients."

A thought struck me. Casmir might be so insistent about me leaving the matter alone because he was involved in it himself. Maybe he was behind the curse, somehow. Maybe he didn't want me thinking about the witchfinders because he *knew* that they were onto something. Maybe, maybe.

I took a fistful of my hair and pulled. He was right; the paranoia was worse than I'd imagined. "I'll try."

"Adrien," he said, watching me closely. He took my right hand and slid my sleeve up to check my arm. I realized with chagrin that the crescents I'd left in my skin with my nails before were still visible. Careless—I'd been careless.

I've always kept my nails short, but they're never quite short enough. I pulled my hair harder. "Would you please," I said, "let me go."

He shook me. I savored it. "Stop."

I stopped. He let my arm go; I laughed, a thin, irritating sound. "I'll be good," I said, and for the most part, I meant it. "Please leave my house. I'll find you in your office tomorrow and check in then."

He stared at me, mad with worry, chewing his lip—I could tell that he wanted to argue with me. He wanted to insist on taking up that empty room after all. All for a few marks on my arm.

"I put you through hell, don't I?" I asked neutrally.

Wordless, he nodded.

Some last piece of resolve inside me crumbled and fell away, softened by the downpour.

"Would you kiss me?" I said. I couldn't hear myself. I was speaking through a mile of ice. "If I asked you to, if I begged, would you kiss me?"

He retrieved his coat from the back of his chair and let himself out.

I'd asked him once before, during my worst fit. Thankfully, he'd declined then as well. A responsible keeper to the end.

I sat there for a long time, staring at the mud he'd left on my floor, aching with the urge to do myself harm. To resist, I forced myself into my atelier; I sat at the table covered in mekhania pieces and diagrams, lenses and screws—useless things. I had no spark for any of my projects, I realized. I picked up a few half-assembled devices I'd been tinkering with, and they sat dead in my hands. I could barely feel my lightning.

Malise's treatment was working perfectly well.

It was perhaps six o'clock at the very latest. I closed my blinds and went to bed. The Aqua Circadia rose steadily in the back of my mind while the sun set.

Chapter 5

The next day, I dragged myself to work only with difficulty. Obediently, I went to Casmir's office first thing in the morning. He had no classes until eleven, but I knew he'd be around.

"Come in," he called from within when I knocked.

I opened the door, jaw set, thinking of yesterday—*Would you kiss me?*

He didn't meet my gaze; he stared down at his work, pen still in hand. I expected it, but it stung nevertheless. "So?" he asked. His office was far neater than mine, sparse, with everything in its place. A small collection of rocks scattered across his desk added a spray of color.

"I'm still all right," I said. "No change." There was no use addressing what I had said before. He'd written it off, no doubt, as the ramblings of a daimoniac on his way down. Nothing to devote any further thought to.

He glanced up, cataloging me. I knew I looked tired; I knew my clothes were unironed. I could keep myself neat, but I couldn't quite manage any flourishes. Whatever he saw, it satisfied him, and he nodded.

He opened his mouth to say something, and I turned to leave, abruptly embarrassed beyond measure. He didn't call after me, which meant it wasn't important.

Undignified, I hurried to the hall of St. Osiander, refusing to meet the metal eyes of the witchfinders I saw still drifting from floor to floor. For the first time, I hoped to see Gennady at the classroom. More than anything, what had gotten me out of bed was the need to tell him I was sorry. I'd threatened to kill him. Apologies had to be made; I wasn't Clementia, so I had no ready excuse.

Against all odds, then, I felt a measure of relief when I saw him lurking outside the door as usual. Lady lounged next to him, her head resting on her scythe-clawed paws. She yawned cavernously as I approached.

"Morning. You look awful," Gennady told me, as if he were delivering vital information. He leaned forward to inspect me; I leaned back.

"Thank you," I said, and planted myself resolutely before him.

"No, really," he said, with the black, alien glee I was starting to become familiar with. "You look like—"

I interrupted. "I'm sorry."

He frowned, purely quizzical. Lady stretched and showed a spotted tongue. "What?"

I paused, struck by the idea that he might actually have forgotten. I had no clue what the average attention span of a Vigil officer was. It might very well be shorter than a day.

No matter. I was obligated to apologize. "I'm sorry for saying I would—*fry you into smoke*, I think the phrasing was." I coughed. "I truly didn't mean it."

He reached out to clap me on the back, but I was ready for it this time. I skipped out of range, feeling accomplished. "I thought it was funny," he said, with an air of faint disappointment.

"It wasn't," I said fervently.

"Just don't try it again," he said. I fancied that his teeth looked too sharp when he showed them in another one of his unconvincing smiles.

Just as I was about to take my grateful leave, I saw him remember something. He put out a hand again, this time as if to stop me from going anywhere. "Another couple of guys I know got sick," he said. The topic flipped with disconcerting, disconnected ease. I was prone to the same leaps, at moments; I let him go.

"I really can't help," I said, with more finality than ever before. "I need you to understand that I have no way of doing anything about it."

Just like that, the majority of his facade fell away. To see his fake smile drop was something of a relief, but the sullen agitation underneath wasn't much better. He pulled his hair lightly, and at his side, Lady chewed a paw. "I thought you were trying."

I winced, struck by reluctant sympathy. "Stop that," I said, hearing Malise and Casmir's voices under my own.

He let go and bit his thumb instead, too hard to be a mere nervous gesture. "I thought you were trying," he repeated.

We don't know each other. Don't make me your only hope. "You still won't come clean with what it is you know, I see," I said, somewhat unkindly.

He made a fabulously rude gesture.

"I'm sorry," I said, once again, and slipped past him into the classroom. Lady whined at me as I went by.

The lecture I delivered on Saebar mekhanical advancements after the Yang

Reconstruction wasn't good, but it was completed, and I finished on time. I did my job. I may not have remembered a solitary thing I said afterward, but I was making it through my day. That was a positive sign, and I was going to have to content myself with it.

If Gennady seemed to watch the lesson more unhappily than before, that was unfortunate, but I could do nothing about it.

Good enough is an insidious enemy. Countless great endeavors are ruined by *good enough*. For an akratic, however, the sacrifice is necessary. I swallowed my pride and continued on through the motions.

～

Every morning, I went to present myself to Casmir and hope that I met his expectations. I did, if not by much. At five o'clock I went to see Malise, and she kept me firmly pinned under the ice. She held me down as she had promised, and if the daimon resented her for her efforts in slowing my mind, I did not.

You see how I split myself, how I pretend that my lesser nature is another being. Allow me that, so I may live with myself.

I saw my keeper, I went to work. I stumbled through lectures, I saw my doctor. I went home and lay in bed to stare at the cracks on the ceiling. Nothing more. Paperwork piled up, unattended. I stayed away from the Chirurgeonate, away from the library, although they beckoned. All the while, the witchfinders and the Vigil crowded the academy. Gennady stalked outside the hall of St. Osiander with wounded confusion, hassling me in increasing desperation every time I passed by.

All this to say that I managed to keep my promises to Malise and Casmir for a full week. Ten whole days.

On the tenth day, after my last class, Gennady and Lady followed me to my office. I refused to look at them as we walked—I had barely gotten myself to the Pharmakeia that morning. There was no energy left for strange, awkward Vigil boys.

"I need to tell you something," he said.

"No."

"I have to tell you what I know. I know something. Okay? You were right. I know something." His tone was sharp, miserable, a furtive hiss.

A dull throb of curiosity made it through my haze. "No," I said, with less conviction, and opened my office door. I was aware, suddenly, of the state of it: enough papers had piled up that I had trouble making my way through.

I tried to shut the door behind me in Gennady's face, but he stuck his battered black boot out to stop me with a thud as the door bounced off it. "Please?"

To hear a Vigil officer say *please* is a remarkably rare thing. I stopped. Alexarchus would approve of his effort; I had a teacherly obligation to reward it.

"I don't know who else to tell," he said.

"What?"

"You're the only one I can tell."

He had imprinted on me, I realized with despair: I'd showed him some modicum of attention, and I was now his favorite magician. He was bizarre and unlikable—

But he'd listened to my lectures, so he was half a student, and he pulled his hair like me.

"Goddammit," I said. "What?"

He blew a sharp exhale of relief. Lady sauntered into the office with me, and he stepped inside after her and slammed the door shut with a resounding crack, shaking the frame. I covered my ears a second too late.

The room began to feel much, much smaller. I sat down at my desk and peered up at Gennady over the stacks of papers.

"This place is a mess," he said. "Even for a wizard."

"Magician," I said, fighting a yawn. "I'm a magician. *Wizard* is an old-fashioned term—a relic of mysticisms past. I'm a magician, just as a mekhanic is a technician." I heard my voice slipping into a lecturer's tone, unbidden. Habit always takes over when there's nothing else left.

"Do you hear yourself when you talk?" he asked me.

"Often," I said, and gestured toward a collection of pseudograms stacked perilously on top of each other nearby. Their glass would shatter if the tower fell, but I couldn't summon any concern. "I'm immune to it."

"Whatever. It's a mess."

"I've been disinclined to—" I said, and stopped. *To organize*, I meant to say, but there was no real use in specifying. He wouldn't care. "I've been disinclined."

He leaned up against a wall, refusing to look at me, the brass buttons on his uniform glaring under the single ambric light. "Whatever," he said again.

"Why don't you take your own turn talking?" I suggested.

"I think I know why those people have been getting sick." He spoke as if he were trying to whisper, but didn't know how.

"Clearly." I knew that if he told me, I'd be helpless against the temptation to do something about it. I'd disobey Malise and Casmir; I'd make myself sicker along the way if what I learned distressed me. I realized that, but curiosity is yet another vice I'm traditionally helpless against.

He wavered.

"Is it the Pharmakeia?" I asked. Best to be blunt. "Is someone here experimenting on people?"

With no real upset, I realized that I would be the first suspect if that became common knowledge. I would be up for investigation, and there was no guarantee I'd pass, no matter my actual guilt. I didn't have the luck to survive *two* witchcraft trials. I should have felt afraid, but I was altogether too tired to muster the appropriate response.

Gennady shrugged. "I think it's the Vigil," he said, his hand checking the hilt of his saber—a self-reassurance, not a threat.

I sat mystified. "The Vigil? How? Why? Why do you think so?" I had my fair share of suspicion for the Vigil, but it didn't go quite that far. They might inflict harm on the Pharmakeia students—that much I could imagine. But on their own soldiers?

Gennady looked at Lady. She gave a small, encouraging yelp.

"A bunch of the sick Vigil are from my unit," he said haltingly. "My first unit, not the one I have now. A *bunch* of them. People I knew when we were kids."

Vigil begin training at ten years old, for the most part. Stragglers might join as late as thirteen. I looked away from him, reminded of that fact and struck by reluctant sympathy. "And?"

"So we still talk a lot. We're friends." He spoke defensively, as if jealous of the fact that he had friends at all. "Some of them told me some things before they got sick. Weird things."

I could make no sense of *weird things*. I scrubbed my face. "I can only offer you so much patience, Gennady," I said. "This may be difficult for you to spit out, but I'd rather you do it sooner than later."

Although he snarled, it was biteless. "Blanche and Cinna told me they were going to go see our old captain. They told me that, and then they got sick. And then Li and Mikhail mentioned the same thing to me. And now they're sick."

The dull throb of curiosity sharpened to a painful point. I looked up quickly. "You think your old captain is somehow rendering your former unit comatose?"

After a long moment, he nodded. "I talked to some of my other unitmates. They think I'm crazy. Say I'm paranoid. Say it's nothing."

He broke off, waving his hands awkwardly, unable to express himself. Child soldiers aren't taught to articulate.

"But you have a feeling," I provided.

"I guess."

I recognized his expression, that specific type of frustration. *No one believes me.* "It's probably not *nothing*," I said gently.

He chewed a fingernail. Slowly, he said, "Blanche woke up today. She's the one you saw having that fit. She can't talk yet, but . . ."

With that, I was lost. I stood, picked up my briefcase again, and began to head for the Chirurgeonate with Gennady at my side.

I passed Casmir's office on my way out and willed myself not to so much as look at his door. I thought he'd sense me being unwise through the wood barrier and come rushing out to scold me. He didn't; we left campus without any trouble, although a few of my colleagues did give me furtive, sympathetic looks when they noticed I was being accompanied by a Vigil officer.

Lady purred enthusiastically as we walked. "So?" Gennady said. "You're going to help?"

"I'm certainly going to *see*," I said. "Anything more than that, I can't promise."

I had no upcoming class to abandon, but I would have, if required. I'd cared for nothing at all in the past week, not really. To have an outlet for a genuine interest was too much to resist. It was, without exaggeration, a reason to live.

My heartbeat began to pick up as we got closer and closer to the Chirurgeonate; the short walk was almost too much to bear. If one of the patients was alive and awake, that meant there was hope. It could be that simple—maybe, finally, one of them would be able to explain what was going on for themselves.

Gennady pulled me to the room as if I wouldn't have remembered on my own. "Blanche is in here," he said, also unnecessary, but I couldn't blame him for trying to fill the silence.

She was sitting up, there was no river of beautiful motes flowing from her mouth, and she wasn't seizing. That didn't mean she looked *healthy*. Her ashen skin was papery; her reddened eyes were glassy. The room smelled sweetly of sickness. There's a certain look the ill sometimes acquire toward the end, an emptiness unlike anything else. It didn't matter if I hadn't been a physician in some time. That look is unforgettable. She had it, badly enough that I was surprised when she spoke.

"Genya," she said. I was startled to hear the diminutive; Gennady hardly struck me as the kind of person to earn a pet name, even from a comrade. "Back again?"

Gennady went to sit near her while Lady curled up with the other rache on the bed; the animal raised his huge, tawny head with difficulty to lick her face.

"Back again," Gennady said.

"Some of the others have been around too," Blanche said. Her voice was vague, directionless.

I'd never seen anything nearing tenderness from Gennady, but for this woman, he seemed to be trying his best. "About time you learned how to talk again," he said. "Why'd it take you so long?" Belying his words, he brushed her hair from her face. It was a false gesture, unnatural—as ever, he seemed to be imitating motions he'd seen before. An unskilled mimic.

"I was sleepy. Who's this guy?" Blanche asked, nodding toward me.

I braced for Gennady to say something scathing.

"Just some Pharmakeia professor," he said. Before I could relax, he added, "He wants to experiment on you. Help make you better."

"I do *not* want to *experiment*," I hissed. "I absolutely do not. I'm here to talk to you, and nothing else. Gennady, if you'd refrain from putting words in my mouth—"

"High-strung," Blanche said weakly. I stopped talking.

"I've got a question for you," Gennady said to her with a reasonable facsimile of apology, ignoring my frustration.

"Mm," she said. She seemed to know what was coming.

He took a deep breath, and I found myself fascinated by the nature of their interaction. They had locked the rest of the world out; there was only them and their raches. Comrades of the most exclusive sort. "Did Captain have something to do with this?" he asked.

She turned away.

Gennady moved in front of her again, eyes emptier than usual. "You can tell me," he said. "Captain Corvier, is he . . . ?"

"I won't talk about this," she said. Loyal to her old captain even on what I suspected was her deathbed. She was awake, but she wasn't getting better. It was her body's last effort before the end.

"You went to see him before you got sick," Gennady said.

Many Vigil have no homes but their commissariats, no family but their comrades. I could imagine that an officer's first captain would be something like a parent. I looked away.

"Leave it alone, Gennady."

Gennady began to pull his hair. The stillness in the air stretched taut and broke. "He's doing something. He did something to you."

"He wouldn't hurt us," she whispered, as if vehemence were beyond her. "I volunteered. You have to leave it alone."

I spoke without thinking, interrupting their private world. "Volunteered for what?"

Blanche made her best attempt at an exhausted scowl. "None of your business."

Vigil. I half-raised my hands, exasperated beyond words and unable to express it to a dying woman.

"You go away now," she told me. "Or I'll call the doctors and tell them you're bothering me."

Her rache switched his gaze on me. I looked to Gennady.

"Go on," he mumbled. His usual menace had been thoroughly extinguished.

I took half a step backward, and then a full step forward. "No." She was bluffing, and I was prepared to call it. "I'm sorry, but Gennady requested my presence very insistently, and I'm going to oblige him to the fullest."

"I hate the way you talk," Blanche told me.

"You're welcome to," I said, without resentment. Many people did.

I could have left Blanche to spend a little more of her remaining time in the singular presence of a comrade. I could have, but I wanted more information.

"Blanche," Gennady said. "Seriously."

His tone was unreadable to me, but she heard something in it that moved her. "He just wants to make us stronger," she said. Her rache dropped his head heavily onto the covers, panting. "It isn't his fault."

I opened my mouth, but she shook her head. "I'm tired now."

Gennady brought his gaze up to meet mine, and I saw that he would kill me if I disturbed her any further.

I bowed to her. A first and last goodbye bow, most likely. "Thank you," I said firmly. "I truly hope that you feel better soon."

She closed her eyes. I think she knew that she wouldn't.

"We can talk about this later," I told Gennady in an undertone.

Before my composure could break, I left the room, and I didn't wait for Gennady before I began the trip back to the Pharmakeia.

As I walked, what concerned me most was: *What does this mean for me?*

Not very noble. I know. But I never have been, and at that moment, I had no idea what I could possibly do for Blanche, or Gennady, or the rest of them. I retreated to my office, dug up a pad of paper and a pencil, and sat down to draw out the situation:

1. *A Vigil captain is involved in causing the curse.*
2. *The victims are both Vigil and Pharmakeia.*
3. *So is someone at the Pharmakeia involved as well? The witchfinders think so.*
4. *What am I supposed to do?*

I stared at that fourth item for a considerable time. The daimon was settling back in. I could feel it looming over my shoulder; its breath was cold against my neck. I was tired—too tired to think of anything I could do. I could barely think at all. The momentary spike of interest had carried me to the Chirurgeonate and back, but alone in my office, I began to falter.

5. *Unacceptable*, I wrote, and waited for five o'clock. I'd go to see Malise. I'd beg her to pick me up, and then maybe I'd be able to look the problem in the eye.

The hour dragged closer at a glacial pace. In the normal way of things, wasted time is anathema to me. I can't sit and do nothing. I have to use my hands and mind, or the time poisons me. I wanted to do something, anything—organize my desk, grade papers, tinker with a project—but in the end, I stared at the office door with its cluttered corkboard and did nothing at all.

My eagerness to end the time overcame my aversion to the Chirurgeonate, at least; I left at ten minutes till without a second thought. The rain had gone for good now.

Malise was going to argue with me, I knew. Even if I didn't tell her why, she'd struggle against using her magic to nudge the akrasia toward mania. I didn't care.

Chapter 6

"Absolutely not," said Malise.

"I can't do anything with myself," I said. "I need you to lift it just a *little*."

We had been at the argument for some time. She was sitting in her chair, and I was standing, and although it felt miserable to tower over her, I couldn't keep myself still. It was either pace or tremble.

She shook her head. "Do you remember—?"

I swept my hand to the side, cutting her off. "I remember," I said shortly. "Whatever you're about to ask, I remember. I remember the money I've spent. I remember every fight and every tryst. Everything I've broken—yes, Malise, I remember."

She folded her hands tightly, eyes narrowed.

"Accordingly, this isn't a casual request," I said, lowering my voice, already ashamed of my ire. A spark of lightning played at my fingertips, and I put my hands in my jacket pockets. She would know it wasn't a threat—could never have been a threat—but the display was unwelcome.

"Please," I added. I was thinking of Blanche, all of a sudden, thinking of Gennady's captain. There would be no greater frustration than to have a mystery at hand and none of my faculties available to solve it.

Methodically, clinically, Malise recited, "It could prolong the episode. If I misstep even in the slightest, you could come undone."

I shrugged: I was treading in very deep water. A reprieve could come at any cost, and it would still be welcome.

"You've never once misstepped," I said. "You're the consummate healer. We both know that."

Thin-lipped, she shook her head once again.

It's a pointless endeavor to describe the hollower side of the daimon's embrace. Dark, yes, painful, yes, a languorous strangulation, yes. None of that suffices. It isn't a poetic subject. I thought of all my wasted time and forced myself to sit on the settee, holding her gaze.

"I need a little color," I said roughly. "I need some *light*, or by all the saints, I'm going to walk into the Aqua Circadia. Please fix it."

We sat in a ringing silence as I realized exactly what I'd said.

"Do you mean that?" she asked.

I decided that I did and nodded.

She was ashen. I wished, not for the first or last time, that I could learn to shut up.

Moving as if it pained her, she rose to come join me on the settee, leaning herself up against the wall behind it. "I know you went to check on the patient who woke up," she said. "I know you haven't been leaving it alone. You've been pushing yourself, and *now* look."

I spoke before I could think, eager to defend myself. "That's because there's something going on," I said, distracted, picturing Gennady pulling his hair. "Someone is doing it to them on purpose. They're not victims of some unknown phenomenon—it's some sort of experiment that's going wrong."

"A conspiracy," she said unreadably, after a thick pause.

I hummed in agreement, relieved that she was following without complaint. "One of the Vigil captains is involved, somehow."

She looked at me as though I had broken her heart.

"Oh," I said, and set aside the urge to burst into tears.

"You're delusional." I'd never heard anyone speak with such gentleness.

"No."

"I'm going to pick you up a little, as you ask," she told me, "and then you're going to go find Casmir, and he's going to stay with you until this is over. Do you understand?"

It was a predictable outcome. All the more embarrassing, then, that I hadn't predicted it in the slightest. "Malise," I said.

"Do you understand, my dear?"

I'd trapped myself. "I understand," I whispered. The threat of my old stutter kept my response to a few syllables.

With my surrender, she gave me what I needed. Blue light began to fill the air, and she pressed her palms to my temples.

She loosened the daimon's chain a bare inch—it rose, and I rose with it. It didn't feel like a glacier melting. It felt like a hot needle. I must have made a sound; she shushed me softly: *It will be over soon.*

It was, and it was wonderful, a rush of chemicals better than any drug, and the relief was enough to send me into her arms.

I could breathe again. She'd shifted the balance enough to open a window somewhere. There would be consequences later, other deficits to deal with, but the world was no longer monochrome.

"Thank you," I said. "Thank you."

She hugged me back and then held me at a distance to look at me. The desire to insist that I wasn't delusional came and went; I didn't think either of us could stand it. I couldn't blame her for her conclusion, but it ached too much to speak of.

"You're going to be all right," she said with determination. "You'll be careful, and you'll be all right."

I smiled, enjoying the novelty of it, and sent a gentle surge through her blue fairy lights, brightening them for a moment just because. Not even the knowledge that I would be seeing Casmir soon could erase the simple pleasure of feeling *alive* again. I'd have the energy to think now. I'd be sharp enough to turn my attention toward Gennady's information without the haze of ice getting in my way.

Malise didn't seem to share my relief.

"I think you're a miracle-worker," I said shyly—a tone rarer than all others.

She crossed her arms, looking much older. "Would you say that if I hadn't given you what you wanted?"

I'm a difficult friend. Capricious, irritable, quick to judge, quick to bruise, worrisome. I've always known so. I held that knowledge close to me before I spoke. "I would say it even if you stopped seeing me," I said, looking her in the eyes. "I would say it at the end of the world, my dear."

She relaxed by the slightest measure, not reassured, but reaffirmed. "Let's hope it doesn't come to that," she said gently, pointing me out the door. "Find Casmir."

"One day I'll make it up to you," I said, and went to deliver myself to my keeper before she could respond.

I savored the walk to the Pharmakeia and Casmir's office as much as I could; it was the last time I'd be my own person for an unknown while. I ran through what I'd say to him in my head as I dodged through the crowds of students and faculty, avoiding eye contact with everyone as studiously as possible. *Hello, Casmir, Malise thinks I'm experiencing paranoid delusions. Hello, Casmir, it's time for you to upend your life again for me. Casmir, the spare room is ready for you, because I always keep it ready, and I need you now, because I always need you.*

My knock at his door was very soft. "Come in," he called. I steeled myself to face him and went inside.

He looked tired, eyes ringed with gray, and I felt a pang of guilt. I was going to make his life harder, once again, a pattern as certain as the daimon's cycles. "You're looking better," he said after a thoughtful pause.

"Momentarily," I said, walking in to stand in front of his desk. "Malise picked me up a little."

"Risky," he said disapprovingly.

I spoke with rote concentration, my lecturer's tone. It insulated me, detached me enough to allow me to get the words out. "She thinks I'm delusional. She treated me again on the condition that I ask you to move in."

He leaned back in his chair. "Delusional."

I smiled, not entirely pleasantly. "If I told you I know for certain that the curse is being deliberately inflicted on the patients, most likely by one of the Vigil captains, would you look at me with pity and quiet horror?"

He looked at me with pity and quiet horror.

"It's true," I said, for no reason other than to hear myself talk. "I could prove it, if you'd let me."

"That doesn't seem wise," he said.

"You and Malise can concede the point later," I said, feeling my voice waver in my throat. "In the meantime, I have no choice if I want to abide by her wishes. Please move in for a while."

I was struck by how natural it felt to fall over this edge again, once I'd been given the initial push. I could complain as bitterly as I liked, but at the end of the day, part of me was always ready to be kept. To mute my potential hysterics to a minimum, I bit my tongue; the pain and pressure steadied me.

"I'll come around tomorrow," he said stiffly. Sad for me, afraid for me. Delusions were rare—very rare. He was probably considering the possibility that I might be slipping further and further, someday to be out of reach.

I held my hands behind my back to keep myself from worrying my arm with my nails. I would need to find a less showy habit. "Thank you," I said. Despite everything, I meant it. That he was willing to uproot himself to watch me was a strange thing, inexplicable, deeply precious.

"I'll send word to the bank to give you a hold over my money," I added. Financial independence isn't always a permanent option for an akratic. If he was coming to live with me, he'd need access.

He dipped his head. "All right."

"I won't be taking time off work, though." I taught in a few different disciplines, but the chair most responsible for dealing with me was Cosima Rabena of the Mekhanical Studies department, and I'd taken too much advantage of her good nature during past episodes. I could hold my own this time, especially if I had Malise's tiny hint of color to get me up in the mornings.

Casmir shrugged, reluctantly conceding. "Maybe it'll be good for you to have something to do."

It hurt, all of a sudden, to speak with him at such a distance. I missed the normal way of things; I missed eating with him for no other reason than the pleasure of his company. I missed being able to make him laugh, and I missed looking at him without the daimon telling me that if I begged enough, he would love me.

"I'm aware of the things you sacrifice for me," I said, without bothering to ease toward the subject. "As my friend. As my keeper."

I felt a thousand more words priming themselves, the newly whetted edge of the akratic knife already beginning to turn, and forced myself into silence. *Parasite*, the daimon said.

"You are who you are," he said. It was more damning than a condemnation could ever have been.

Through his window, I saw the rays of the sun beginning to scatter and die; they bathed him from behind. "You look like a saint," I said involuntarily, and covered my eyes at once. "I'm sorry."

When I forced myself to look back up, he was staring at me. "Go home," he said, offering me a weak smile.

I was growing tired of being told where to go. "I only meant—the sunlight—"

"Try to sleep," he said, with uncharacteristic patience. It didn't suit his voice. "I'll be there tomorrow."

I left him to his work.

$\sim$

As I walked along the edge of the Aqua Circadia on my way home, watching its waters glimmer, I wrapped myself painstakingly around the thread of light Malise had given me, trying to keep it shining. It could hurt me if it grew, but I could risk holding it close. I *had* to risk that, to keep Casmir's unconvincing smile from withering me.

It worked, to a degree. Although I was stinging, the Circadia looked much different than it had during the rain. It was swollen still, but I no longer imagined that I could see the water beckoning. My hands were steady when I stood at my doorstep and readied my key for the lock.

Except the door was already unlocked.

I can be absentminded at the best of times, and it was not the best of times. The door was unlocked simply because I'd forgotten to lock it, I decided, scolding myself.

But sitting on the floor in front of me when I stepped inside was a single paper crane.

I've never bothered to learn zhe zhi; the art never appealed. I couldn't make a paper crane.

The air was very, very cold. I entertained the possibility that Malise had, in fact, misstepped, and I was, in fact, hallucinating. "Hello," I said to nothing at all, and left the door open as I ventured farther in. An unwise thing to do, I realize in retrospect, but wisdom was in short supply.

The house echoed unhelpfully back at me, so I called a thin bolt of lightning to my hand and crept past the first set of bookshelves. The bolt threw twisting shadows against the walls; I moved forward through my living room, my heart whispering feverishly inside me.

Another paper crane flattened under my shoe with a delicate crunch, and I jumped back.

There was a neat row of them. One after another, lined up, trailing in a lovely parade from the atelier to the living room. They were folded from good paper, thin and even—*my* paper.

When I realized that someone was in my atelier, my reaction was, principally, indignation. The fear came as a close second, and together, they sent the lightning in my hand into a guttering surge.

No one's there, I told myself. *You're going to go inside, and it'll be empty, and you'll turn around, and the cranes will be gone, and then you'll have to tell Malise you're seeing things after all.* I wasn't sure which I preferred—to be going psychotic, or to be alone in my own house with someone I hadn't invited.

A shadow that wasn't mine graced the atelier's doorway. It didn't move like a person.

I stood frozen. "Hello," I said again, a bare whisper, with the evening breeze rolling into my house from the open doorway behind me.

I heard a noise from within, a soft, animal snuffle, and readied my grip on the lightning in my hand. Stars know why—I could never have fought with it.

Someone tapped me on the back, and I shrieked, and all the ambrics in my house shattered at once.

In the flash before the filaments died, I saw a rache barreling toward me from the atelier, her eyes lit by the lightning in my hand. I resigned myself to death.

"Goddamn," said Gennady, while Lady put her paws up on my waist. "You are so dramatic."

The lightning flickered and faded. I didn't quite go to my knees in relief, but it was close. I staggered away from Lady to stare at them both.

Gennady made a small, contemptuous noise. "Dramatic," he repeated.

I dragged some of the lightning back to brighten my path and went to retrieve a lantern from on top of the hearth. The neat line of paper cranes gave way before me. "You're in my house," I said, incapable of relevance, and lit the lamp with a spark.

His grin was wide in the dying sunlight. "Welcome home, professor."

I made my way to the couch. "*Why*," I said. "Why have you done this? Are you going to kill me? How did you get inside? You broke in—did you pick the lock? Why are you here? Why were you waiting? Why did you sneak up on me? What are the cranes for? Why? How do you know where I live? *Why?*"

I ran out of breath. Lady whined inquisitively. "You want me to answer all of those at once?" Gennady asked.

"Get to it," I said, as fiercely as I could manage.

He went sullen. "I was kidding," he said, fixing his gaze somewhere far over my shoulder. "I can't actually remember anything you said. Ask them one at a time."

I paused to give him time to focus, and to give myself time to lower my voice. "Gennady, why are you here?"

"Wanted to talk to you alone," he said, growing uncomfortable. "Where no one else could hear."

Of course. I folded my hands to steady them. "Did you ever consider letting me know of this plan ahead of time?"

"Clearly not," he said.

"You *should* have," I said, with more despair than judgment.

He sniffed. "Too late now."

I leaned over to pick up a surviving paper crane and examined it—it was folded well, if not expertly. I hadn't taken him for any kind of artist, but it was time to give up on trying to predict anything of his character. "Explain these," I said.

He blinked his odd black eyes at me. "I got bored. I thought I'd make something while I waited. You were way later than I expected."

I shook my head sharply, unsatisfied. "Why leave them lined up like that? It's something a serial murderer would do."

Unashamed, he shrugged. "I thought they would look nice that way."

For lack of anything else, I said, "That was my good paper."

"Shut up," he said cheerfully. "Let's talk strategy."

A moment of perfect fear gripped me, just as my heartbeat had started to settle: surely no real person in the world would behave themselves like this. Maybe Malise and Casmir's suspicions didn't cover all of my potential delusions. Did I have any true proof that Gennady was real? Apart from my own judgment, flawed as ever, what was my guarantee that Gennady Richter existed?

He saw me wavering and frowned. "What's wrong?"

My students had flinched from Gennady; they'd seen me talking to him and hadn't seemed surprised. I'd met him before my episode had started. He was real. "A *lot* is wrong," I said.

He rolled his eyes.

If I was going to survive Gennady, I had to accept that he existed outside the realm of normal human politesse. "Strategy," I murmured. "You mentioned strategy."

He threw himself onto the couch next to me; I got up and took a chair instead. Lady followed him and stretched out, her ears flicking lazily.

"My sister Mariya is a mekhanic for the witchfinders," Gennady said. "Fixes their eyes and all that. She's pretty good at it."

"And," I prompted.

"And she says she keeps hearing stuff about how they think the Pharmakeia's involved."

"They haven't been keeping it much of a secret," I said. "What good does that do?"

"It means she'll tell me if she hears anything *else*. Inside information."

I forced myself to nod, as if impressed.

"Anyway, Blanche died," he said blithely, not allowing so much as a pause between thoughts.

I froze.

"Yeah," he said, for all the world as though he were speaking of a stranger. "Apparently, she kicked it a couple hours after you ran away. I wasn't there."

Before I could wonder if he was a sociopath after all, Lady betrayed him with a mournful howl, ear-splitting.

"I'm sorry," I said.

He gave me a halfhearted scowl.

I hadn't thought she'd be gone within the week. Soon, yes, but not *that* soon. Certainly not in a single day. It didn't sit right with me. "How did she die?" I asked carefully. "She just fell asleep and didn't wake up?"

He toyed with his saber. "Don't know. What's it to you?"

It was a certainty that Gennady and I would be far from the only people to take an interest in Blanche's brief awakening. "Someone might have hurried her along," I said. My words were slow; I knew that it was a supremely dangerous suggestion.

"Well," he said, smiling brightly, "the last person who was with her after me was our friend Alim, so—no, no one hurried her."

I stayed silent. My suspicion wasn't solid enough to argue.

"You understand?" he said, leaning forward, his head cocked at an angle— another predator's stance.

"For God's sake, yes, fine. Don't do that," I snapped. Malise's bright thread flared inside me, more fire than sunlight this time. I fought to stay even and neatened my clothes; I couldn't afford to show Gennady any more of the daimon.

To my relief, he relented and settled back. "I'm going to figure out who's doing this," he said, and put his boots up on the coffee table. A mug there rattled, a jarring sound. "So."

I stared at him, but he failed to present anything else. "What exactly do you need me for?" I was already resigned to help, but I needed to know with *what*.

There was a long, dull pause. He'd broken into my house to ask me for help, ostensibly, and now he was having trouble admitting it. "Can you ask around the Pharmakeia about this?" he said eventually.

I gave him a bare nod. "I've already posed the issue to a few people," I said, somewhat resentfully. "They didn't know anything."

"You'll keep trying, though?" He kept his voice flinty, trying to disguise the flash of gratitude I saw on his face.

"If you answer me one question."

He narrowed his eyes suspiciously, arms crossed, expecting the worst of me.

"Why me?"

I saw him laboring through a thousand rude things he wanted to say, one by one. "Coincidence," he said. "Because you were there at the Chirurgeonate that day."

"That can't be it," I said.

"Alexarchus says that making friends is good," he said mulishly.

I fought the urge to tell him that Alexarchus had been a great deal more specific and eloquent in his points, and I fought the urge to tell him that we were not friends. I couldn't punish him for trying.

"It's never too late to learn," I said instead, an acceptable compromise, and left it at that. He'd explain himself more fully when he wanted to.

Ludicrously, I thought I saw a spark of relief light his eyes for a moment. "Whatever," he said, the same relief brightening his voice. "It's hard not to listen to *something* you say. There's so *much* of it."

"Thank you," I said. "Another question."

"I only agreed to one."

"Did you break anything in the atelier while you were amusing yourself?"

He grinned; I rubbed my eyes until I saw stars, reminding myself that patience is a virtue.

"Not really," he said. Lady meowed guiltily.

"You have to leave now," I said into my hands. It was too far. The brief fear of death I could withstand, but an incursion into my workspace was too much. "Leave, and never do this again. Come here with advance warning and an invitation, or not at all."

I should have known better than to expect him to take instructions. "Or what?" he asked. "You going to threaten to kill me again?"

"Or nothing," I snapped. "I know very well that I can do nothing to keep you from breaking and entering. It's a polite request. People make those sometimes. There's a lesson for you."

He made a great show of considering it.

I decided to be a good example. "Please," I added.

"Ehh," he said, as close to an acquiescence as I was likely to get. Lady jumped up from the couch to pad toward the door, still open, and he joined her after another moment spent staring at me. I wondered if he was going to make any sort of goodbye.

He didn't. With that, he strolled out into the evening.

I got up to light a few more lanterns and went to the atelier to itemize the damage.

Chapter 7

It was gratifying, in a twisted way, to know that there truly was some manner of conspiracy underway. Whatever the rest of the facts were, whether or not Blanche had been murdered or someone at the Pharmakeia was involved, someone was inflicting comas on a definable set of victims. I wasn't losing my mind.

The satisfaction was limited, of course: I still went to bed that night vexed and terrified. When I went to see Casmir for my routine obeisance in the morning, I was relying on very little sleep and some amount of caffeine. Usually, I avoid coffee—but I was getting into the habit of making exceptions.

When I knocked on his door, he looked me over far more thoughtfully than I was accustomed to, and I found myself shying from his gaze. "Still all right," I said.

"You didn't sleep."

"A Vigil soldier broke into my home to ask me for help in fighting the conspiracy," I said indifferently. "The curse. You recall. I was up worrying about it." I knew he wouldn't believe me; I didn't bother to make my tone convincing.

He recoiled with a deep wince, dropping his head into his hands. "Saints," he said between his fingers.

"Good thing you're moving in," I said, keeping my bitterness down to a trace. I couldn't quite expunge it.

He looked up at me, unsure what to make of any of it. "I should have come last night. I shouldn't have waited."

"Trust me," I said, "that would have been no good at all." The longer I could ensure that Gennady and Casmir never met, the better. It might be briefly satisfying to be believed, but I didn't want Casmir involved.

"Adrien," Casmir said, adrift.

In the normal way of things, I loved to hear him say my name, loved to hear his steady voice wrap around it. Not so, then. "I'm all right. Really. Thank you, Casmir." Then I left him again, as abruptly as ever. I didn't look back to see whether it affronted him. Guiltily, I hoped it did.

My walk to the hall of St. Osiander was a labored one. I found myself stopping at every corner to watch the witchfinders, wondering just how much they knew. One of them pinned my eye with his mekhania and smiled; startled to be caught staring, I hurried off to my first class without any more stops.

Gennady was guarding the door as usual. He brightened when he saw me.

"Have you talked to anyone yet—"

"It is eight in the morning," I said. "I have not."

That brightness faded, and I regretted my sharpness. "Fine," he said.

"I'll tell you when I do," I said. "I'll find you here, and we'll talk in my office. All right? Not at my house. I'm going to have company there for a while."

"And you don't want me to meet your company?" he said, playing at tender feelings.

"No."

He considered. "Who is it?"

"None of your business. He's a magician with a temper, though, so I'd be careful about breaking in again." I was overstating Casmir's temper somewhat, but I thought Gennady could use the deterrence.

"Boyfriend?" he said.

"No."

He grinned evilly.

"I can tell you're about to say something absolutely dreadful," I said, "and if you do, I cannot be held responsible for how I react."

He shut his mouth.

"Goodbye, Gennady," I said, and went into the lecture hall. I was teaching Mekhania Studies, and I thanked Malise's thread of light yet again; I held class without hating every single word.

∼

I spent my free time that day asking the other faculty about the comatose curse with increasing awkwardness. There was no natural way to introduce the topic, and I had no plausible reason to be asking. All I could do was try to keep the oddity of my inquiries from provoking outright suspicion.

Marta Xu knew nothing. Pyrrhus Pavarotti knew nothing. Septima Theverard thought at first that she might know something, but on reflection, she decided that she did not. Janin Gailhardt knew nothing, although we had a pleasant tea. All the while, I grew more and more tired of asking, and more and more certain that all I was achieving was making myself look either paranoid or guilty. Interacting with most other people has always been a strange, taxing chore—it involves exhausting calculations. When to laugh. When to smile. When to say, *Oh, naturally,* or *Oh, of course not.* The more I forced myself to do it, the less skilled I felt. Still, I continued on.

By the time I got to Marsilio Kirchoff, I was sure no one had anything to offer. Inevitably, he proved me wrong. He was fond of doing so whenever he got the chance.

Kirchoff was the chair of Thanatology—a department-wide freak show. You'll recall that I disliked him. The study of death and its magical implications could have been a standard, respectable field, an asset to the Pharmakeia, but the department had attracted a certain unpleasant element. The effects had grown from there, until Thanatology was a collection of the least pleasant people the academic community had to offer.

I may be biased. Regardless, Kirchoff was unkind, and impolite, and lacked the talent to justify his arrogance. I swallowed my dislike and visited him around lunch. Despicable or not, he was a department chair.

His office felt like the mouth of a great cave, and it was full of skeletons. Reptile skeletons, a few apes, countless small rodents, and a single human looming from a corner—he refused to allow any visitors to forget his discipline, even for a second. Murky shadows bobbed in the tanks of water lining his walls. I couldn't be sure whether the faint, musty smell was coming from them or not. Kirchoff had covered most of the surfaces in black velvet: an aesthetic disaster.

I stayed standing, unwilling to make myself any more vulnerable next to his lifeless menagerie.

"So nice of you to visit me, Desfourneaux," he said, seated at his polished oak desk. He had a sharp face, good for sneering, and fine brown hair hanging over his eyes. "What brings you here?"

Let's keep this as brief as possible, I thought. "I was wondering if you knew anything about the comatose patients at the Chirurgeonate," I said, reciting the now-familiar query. "There are more and more of them as time goes on. It seems to be getting more urgent."

"What's your interest in the matter?" he asked, looking me over with curiosity. "The Pharmakeia has no claim over that. Lingering affection for your former home, maybe?"

My erstwhile affiliation with the Chirurgeonate was, of course, common knowledge.

Kirchoff wasn't incorrect. I shrugged. "We all have our pet projects." It unsettled me to put it in such terms, but I knew ambition would appeal to him more than altruism.

He toyed with a paperweight on his desk, a frog's skeleton encased in resin. The dim light glinted off its surface. "These are fascinating times, aren't they?" he said. "I've taken the liberty of examining a few of those patients myself. You've heard they seem to have developed their own magic?"

The way he was watching me set my teeth on edge. Keen, quiet. I give him a bare nod, with Blanche's face in mind. "It's killing them."

Slowly, he turned the paperweight until the frog's skull was pointed toward me, its empty eyes staring. "The Clementia has been visiting our halls for the past few weeks because they think we're to blame," he said in a voice of silk.

"So I've noticed," I said. "Do you think their suspicions have any merit?"

He sat still for an extended moment, until I began to worry that I'd misstepped. He seemed to be making some sort of unknowable calculation, and I had a feeling it was an unpleasant one.

"Suppose they did," he said. "Suppose they weren't far off the mark at all."

I wanted to tell him that I could think of nothing more unfortunate, but I knew him. He might very well be the type to shrug at shattering a human consciousness forever. "That wouldn't make it any less fascinating," I murmured.

"You're likely the professor here who has the most experience with such things," he said. "The Philidor solarium disaster's effects were quite similar, yes?"

"Of course," I said. I kept my voice even, although my chest ached. If I could affect boredom, I thought, all the better.

He stood up to pace; it was false, theatrical. Some people pace to clear their heads, others to keep their thoughts rolling, and others because they simply can't stay still. Kirchoff was pacing as a performance. I wasn't entertained.

"You must feel jealous of whoever has been using your style," he suggested, layered in the most amicable sort of poison.

I had a choice to make. If he was involved, faking a lack of contrition for my past sins was by far the safer option. If he *wasn't* involved, I could damn myself very effectively by doing so. My good standing with the Pharmakeia wasn't guaranteed. If Kirchoff gave word that I was somehow suspect—

"Your trademark, so to speak," he added, with what passed for a flash of genuine respect. I could see his soul, in that moment. He'd always thought I was more like him than I wanted to admit. There were always those who imagined that the Philidor solarium researchers had enjoyed our results, that we had set out to ruin our patients. For the most part, those who believed so wanted nothing to do with us. To those like Kirchoff, it made us kindred souls.

I shrugged, doing my best to make it nonchalant. "I'd like to compare notes," I said. "Give my own insights." Maybe just this once, I could make myself a better liar.

A slow smile warped his face. Something about his complete pallor reminded me of a dead fish in the eerie light of his office. "I've never liked you, Desfourneaux."

"And you know I've never liked you," I said impatiently, an easier emotion to fake than affinity. "So what?"

"I've never liked you," he said, "*but* I've always suspected that you have more ambition in you than you choose to admit to the meek and mild-mannered around here."

You were never a healer, he meant. I nodded and waited for him to get to the point.

"I'm not sure about you, but I've grown tired of the witchfinders' metal gazes," he said. "I'm through with shying from Vigil swords."

"Of course I agree," I said.

He stared me down for a time, dragging me through the pause on his tether. He was satisfied, apparently; he wrote something on a piece of stationery and slid it across his desk toward me. I stepped forward to take it, the skin on the back of my neck prickling.

1370 Via Charenton in Deme Aufford, 8:00 p.m., Oktidy, the note read.

I didn't recognize the address, but I knew Deme Aufford. I'd been raised in the neighborhood, and I knew that it was crawling with Vigil. A military deme.

"You'll have two days to decide whether to drop by," he said.

With his flair for the overstated, I was surprised he hadn't already printed custom cards to hand out. I folded the paper and put it in my pocket.

"Why exactly—"

He didn't let me get any further.

"Magic is a blessing," he said. "A magician is the grand beneficiary of a gift from the stars."

I thought the same thing: magic is the saving grace of an otherwise disastrous cosmos, the purest example of nature's art. Still, I fought the urge to roll my eyes. "A little flowery," I said. Only Kirchoff could make something I agreed with sound so unappealing.

He gave me a thin smile. "Perhaps. The point is that the Clementia forces us to blaspheme our own power."

He sounded like an apocalyptic preacher. "Of course they influence our lives unduly," I said. There wasn't an Astrine magician alive who didn't chafe under the Clementia's yoke.

"If there were a way to undo the bonds of the licensing process," he said. "If there were a way to restore us to our untrained vitality, would that not be worth pursuing?"

"You'll need to tell me more," I said.

A window closed behind his eyes. "Join us," he said, "and perhaps you'll see."

I opened my mouth to ask him what would happen if I refused. He was ahead of me. "I trust you'll do the right thing with the information," he added.

It was a threat. I realized that I had no idea what Kirchoff was capable of, but if our conversation was to give me any clues, the answer was one that should put me on my guard. His magical talent specialized in water; I had to wonder if he would drown me.

Newly trapped, I nodded and turned away toward the door.

"Be well, Desfourneaux," he said. "I trust in your ambition."

I said nothing at all and left him alone with his skeletons.

The Pharmakeia may as well have been empty; I barely noticed the other people going about their business. It was a mistake. When a witchfinder caught my arm, I startled hard.

"Jumpy," he remarked, and his partner blinked at me. His eye whirred red, and hers silver.

"Most people are startled by rudeness," I said, on pure instinct. He'd stopped me within a stone's throw of Kirchoff's office.

He gave me a withering smile. "You seem quite eager to take your leave of Marsilio's company," he said, nodding toward where I'd come from.

"You're on first-name terms?"

"Well," his partner said. "We're all friends."

I was more tired of witchfinders than I had ever thought possible. "I'm not your friend," I murmured stupidly.

They exchanged looks. I saw them make a judgment: I was odd and difficult, but no real bother.

"Friends or not," the first witchfinder said, "is there anything you want to tell us about old Marsilio?"

I could see that they were only fishing. They didn't have any concrete reason to suspect him—not unless I gave them one.

And I *could* give them one. I could reach into my pocket and hand them his note. I could pass responsibility of the situation over to the witchfinders, and they'd take care of it all, and I'd be free to go on my way. No more dealing with comatose patients and strange Vigil boys and my least favorite colleagues.

Except that if the witchfinders caught on to Kirchoff, he would know how. I trusted him on his threat. I trusted him implicitly, and I didn't have the strength of will to test him. At the same time as I'd found my answer, I'd lost the ability to do anything constructive with it.

That didn't mean I had to defend Kirchoff's good name.

"He's unkind," I said, "and impolite, and he lacks the talent to justify his arrogance, and the entire Thanatology department is a freak show." I took a breath, as if I might continue for some time, and the witchfinders both shook their heads. They were unwilling to subject themselves to the minutiae of an academic's grudges.

"All right," the second witchfinder said, wrinkling her nose. "We get it." They turned to hurry away.

I dashed off before anyone else could waylay me. In record time, I'd gotten my answer. It was the bitterest sort of irony; my questioning of Kirchoff went so very smoothly because I had already proven myself to be reprehensible. If I had been a better man, a better physician, he would never have told me a thing.

⁓

I had no time to sit and contemplate my discovery, or its implications, or my thoughts on the matter, or Kirchoff's threat. I'd told Gennady I'd let him know as soon as I learned anything, and it was time to go find him.

The hall of St. Osiander was in use by another professor; I found Gennady standing outside it as usual. Once he spotted me, he trotted forward to meet me like nothing so much as an oversize dog, his rache at his heels.

He peered closely at me, worrying the hilt of his saber. "So?" I'd thought he might be reluctant to leave his post. Per usual, my expectations were worth nothing with him. "You hear anything?"

I nodded and shepherded him to my office. In a small blessing, he was silent all the way there, and I shut the door behind us as emphatically as I dared.

"The Pharmakeia is involved," I said quietly, dropping into my chair. "Some of us, at least. One of the department chairs—Marsilio Kirchoff, he certainly is—and there must be others. I was asked to lend myself to the effort, whatever the effort may be."

He pulled his hair briefly, then spun to face me. "You still don't know?" he asked, fierce with annoyance. "How'd you get through a whole conversation about it without asking *what* they're doing?"

"He was cagey," I said, stung. "He invited me to come see and wouldn't say anything else. It isn't my fault he wasn't willing to give it all away during a first conversation."

He caught a word out of the air. "Invited. He invited you somewhere to see it actually happen?"

I wrapped my arms around myself, feeling a shiver threaten. "I believe so. I think he means to show me the procedure."

Gennady grinned, and it was one of the least pleasant expressions I'd ever seen, sharp enough to cut. Beside him, Lady stretched luxuriously. "Did he give you a time?"

I handed him Kirchoff's note over the desk.

He looked at it, crumpling the paper. "I'll go with you," he announced proudly. "Perfect. We'll see what's going on, and then—"

"And then *what*?" I asked, far more sharply than I intended. "No matter what we see, what can we do with it? A Vigil captain and a Pharmakeia department chair are involved, at the *least*—who's to say it doesn't go much farther up?"

"So what if it does?" he asked. He squinted, wounded with confusion, knocked off balance.

"*So* we'll be limited in how we can respond," I said. "Say I go to the Archmagister, or you go to one of your Prefects. If they're involved, they'll just kill us and continue on their way. We'll go to the demi-lune and lose our heads, and they'll march on."

Hysterical, paranoid words, but far from baseless. I didn't truly think the Pharmakeia's Archmagister was implicated in a conspiracy, no more than I believed either of the Curia Clementia's two Prefects was—but it was a *possibility*, and a uniquely threatening one.

"We'll have to figure it out afterward," he said, as if that settled the matter. For all the world, he sounded as if he'd discovered an airtight solution. "After we go and see what's going on. It can wait until later."

I put my head in my hands, down on the desk. "Gennady," I said. "That's not a plan."

He flared. "Why not?" he demanded. "What's wrong with it? How *else* are we supposed to figure out what to do, until we actually go and *see*?"

"Rushing in won't help anything. There has to be some sort of happy medium," I said, hoping desperately that I was correct, trying my best to think.

"I'll just go alone," he said after a disgruntled pause, arms crossed as if to shield himself. "I don't need you to hover over my shoulder. I'll go alone. I'll figure it out. I'll deal with it myself."

As far as my own welfare was concerned, it was the perfect solution. If he was correct, all the better. If something went wrong for him, it wouldn't come back to me.

"Don't," I said. "Going alone isn't smart. If you find yourself in trouble—"

"You'll be no help for trouble," he said cruelly, and put Kirchoff's note into his jacket pocket. "No professor is going to help me out of any binds I get into. It doesn't make a difference if you stay."

That wasn't entirely unfair. I still couldn't encourage him, in good conscience, and I had so very little good conscience to spare. "Tell me how to dissuade you," I said.

From the floor, Lady yipped warningly. "Made up my mind," Gennady said. "You stay away safe and cozy, and I'll go to Via Charenton."

I had to laugh in disbelief. "That won't *work*. You weren't invited. You'll be unexpected—they'll know something's wrong right away."

"Says you," he said.

Stubbornness had officially passed into stupidity. "You're being an idiot," I said, before I could stop myself.

He started forward at me, and I jumped back in my chair. A spark of lightning leapt from one hand and almost hit a stack of papers. "Don't," I said, preemptively.

"I'm not an idiot," he snarled. "I'm just not a coward." Whatever limited rapport we'd developed was crumbling—all because I wouldn't endorse a useless suicide mission. "You're not going to tell me my business. You're not going to stop me from doing what I want."

I'd forgotten how young he was.

"Quite possibly," I said, "you'll die for nothing."

He rolled his eyes, and I realized something: he was always ready to die for nothing.

"Just think about it," I said, nearly begging. I had no idea what to do, but *this* wasn't it. "Allow yourself some time to think about it."

He turned and jerked the door open, as if it were an effort not to simply pull it off its hinges. Lady stalked out in front of him. He turned to give me one last glare.

"No one else wants to do anything about it," he said. "No one wants to fix it. Maybe I'll go to Via Charenton right *now*. What about that?"

With that, he was off, striding away—against all logic, going to storm a location that would be empty at best, and deadly at worst.

I stood to follow after him. If I needed to make a scene in the Pharmakeia's halls, so be it.

He stopped short in front of me, only a few steps out the door.

"Prefect," he said.

Over his shoulder, I saw Tessaly Velleia, the first Prefect of the Curia Clementia, with her executioner's sword on her back and her monstrous white rache at her side. She was at the Pharmakeia. She was here.

Chapter 8

"Soldier," Prefect Velleia said.

Her voice was low, a dark-steeled knife. She let her black hair fall freely to her waist. Her cold, clear gaze spoke to her ruthlessness more than the golden honors pinned to her uniform ever could. I fought the instinct to close my door behind Gennady and hide from her.

The six Prefects of Astrum, two per Curia, are the most powerful people any average citizen is ever likely to see up close. The Prefects of the Clementia in particular are rumored to be quick with their tempers—the Divae are holy; the Eulexica are prudent. The Clementia are killers. They're only ever Vigil, never witchfinders, which I've always thought must chafe the witchfinder corps.

Gennady snapped to attention, and the pose looked dreadfully unnatural—I didn't think he would have struck it for anyone short of the Prefect. Now that he had the opportunity, he did a poor job. Like me, he kept silent.

People were staring, students and staff frozen midstep to watch the Prefect interact with the lower orders. The fever-dream thought that she might somehow be here specifically for Gennady or me gripped me, and it refused to let go until she turned away.

"At ease," she said. She dismissed Gennady with a perfunctory nod; it was nothing but a coincidence that he had happened to open the door directly in front of her. There was no danger, except the inherent danger of her very presence at the Pharmakeia.

As she turned, her ceremonial executioner's sword gleamed, and I allowed myself a deep breath of relief.

Gennady was eager for ruination. "Prefect," he said. "Can I talk to you?"

My blood turned to dust. She faced him again, slowly, and I registered with faint surprise that she was even taller than I. Her massive rache snorted. Tessaly Velleia was feared for her ruthlessness, renowned for her impatience. I wondered if she would simply cut off his head where he stood.

"What's your rank, soldier?" she asked. It wasn't a sincere question; if

I could tell from his uniform that he was a lieutenant, she would have no doubts whatsoever. She was telling him that he was nowhere near important enough to be speaking to her.

I could only be glad they were both ignoring me.

"Lieutenant," Gennady said, unaware. "I just need to tell you something. It's about the sick people. Do you know about that? Me and this professor figured something out."

He laid it all out very exactly, sacrificing us both without a thought. I put every ounce of effort I could into preventing any stray sparks of lightning from making their appearance.

Gennady grabbed my arm and dragged me out in front of the Prefect. I stood straight, with effort—hating him, to a degree.

She examined both of us in turn, inscrutable, judging each detail, dissecting us like cadavers on a slab. The white rache—I knew his name was Amphion; everyone in the city knew it—stalked forward to stare at us.

Eventually, she said to Gennady, "Report to Deme Eudora after seven o'clock tonight. Bring him."

Only that.

Without another thought, she dismissed us again, a soldier and a magician both far below her notice, and started on her way through the Pharmakeia's halls once more. Amphion kept up at her side. The animal's movements were beautiful, in their own way. He moved like a powerful piece of mekhania, heavy and carefully controlled.

We stood frozen until she rounded a corner out of sight. At length, the other people staring dispersed as well.

"Gennady," I said softly, "why would you do that?"

No one could refuse a summons from Tessaly Velleia. We were going to have to go meet her, and if she was involved with the curse, she was going to kill us. I wondered if she'd use her executioner's sword to do it, or if she'd merely send us to the demi-lune to lose our heads.

"I couldn't help it," he said. He sounded dazed, faraway, as though he could barely believe himself either. "I wanted to do it, so I did. I can't stop myself sometimes. Maybe it wasn't a good idea."

"It wasn't." I left it at that. There was little point in scolding him further. He'd already explained himself as well as he could: he did what he wanted.

I retreated back into the office and lowered myself gingerly into my chair again. He stayed where he was, as close to abashed as I thought he could manage. "What's in Deme Eudora?" I said. "Where are we supposed to meet her?" The city's largest prison, the Penumbra, was in Deme Eudora. I had to hope she didn't mean to summon us *there*.

"The Clementia keeps an administrative office in Eudora," he muttered. "Sometimes the Prefects hold audiences. She means that."

"Wonderful," I said, deep under my breath.

Lady whined softly. "I did a bad thing," Gennady said, and pulled idly at his hair. "Oh, I think I did it wrong. That was the wrong choice."

I recognized something in his voice. The perennial *why did I do that?* The quintessential *I couldn't help it.* He might quite possibly have set my course for something awful, but I still couldn't bring myself to harangue him. Not with the way he stood in my doorway with his back to the outside world.

"We'll deal with it later tonight," I said. "At least that's something to do besides go to Via Charenton alone, with no plan."

He dipped his head slightly, the barest concession toward a nod.

"You might want to let me do the talking," I added grimly. It was a terrible suggestion to make, but it had to be made. Between the two of us, daimon or no—and I could hear it speaking inside me—I was the best candidate.

"I just wanted to do something to make it better faster," he said, speaking with difficulty. He sounded as though he were trying to walk himself through the fields of his own mind. "That's all."

I couldn't yell at him, but I couldn't deal with his presence any longer, either. "What's the address for the administrative office? Write it down," I said, tearing a corner off a nearby piece of paper at random and handing it to him along with a pencil.

He scribbled for a moment and tossed the scrap toward me; it fluttered in the air and fell slowly to the floor.

"Thank you," I said, and left it there. "I suppose I'll see you after seven tonight. Please leave now." I needed him gone before I could decide for myself exactly how bad things had gotten.

He looked like he wanted to say something very cutting indeed, but before he could, he made a sharp turn and let himself out; I heard a faint noise of protest from a student he pushed out of his way as he strode through the hallway.

I could feel the daimon slipping through. Malise's bright thread was beginning to split and broaden, sending forks of light throughout me fit to crack. Stress and fear—two of the most reliable ways to send me reeling.

Before I could do anything else, I was going to have to see Malise and ask her to right me again. Velleia's summons was for seven o'clock; I had time.

Whether I would be around to help Casmir move in was a different matter. I'd explain to him when I got home, I decided, even knowing that he wouldn't believe me.

∼

Five o'clock came, as it did every day, by some miracle beyond my comprehension.

The first thing Malise said to me when I swept into her office like a frazzled hurricane was, "My goodness."

Her hair was standing on end; the fairy lights flickered. I'd brought static into the air with me. Shadows danced on the surroundings.

"Excuse me," I said, and built a wall around my mind until the charge calmed.

"That's better." She sat me down.

I folded my hands tightly. With a soft sigh, she joined me on the settee as usual. "Are you well?" she asked, a weighted question this time.

I felt a now-familiar pang: *She doesn't believe me.* "Tessaly Velleia summoned me for an audience with her at seven o'clock tonight," I said, understanding that she would take it as the ravings of a sick friend. "I'm frightened. I don't want to go, but I have to. She's observing the Pharmakeia; anyone there can confirm it."

She closed her eyes for a moment. "I do know she's been spending time there," she said, with utmost softness. "I understand why she might be influencing your . . ."

"Delusions," I provided.

"Your state of mind, I was going to say."

"I wish you believed me," I said, keeping my voice level. "It's more frustrating than I can say. Something awful is happening, and no one believes me."

I don't need to be liked, really. I prefer to be, but I can get along without it. What I need most is *respect*. To be thought despicable is one thing. To be thought incompetent by a dear companion is quite another.

She took my hand. "I think it's time I sedate you again," she said. The thread of light inside me protested.

As always, there was a choice to be made. The daimon's flaming claws, or its frozen breath. One edge of the knife or the other.

"Can't I just be well again?" I said. It was less rhetorical than I would have liked.

"Not yet, but we can manage it," she said quietly.

I thought of facing Velleia without all my wits intact. With Gennady along, we would already have one person present who couldn't control himself. I couldn't reasonably introduce another.

"As you like."

She winced. "I don't *like*. None of this brings me any pleasure," she said.

I felt the urge to be unkind to her, and I knew that she was right. "Keep me down," I said.

So she put her hands to my temples and took away that thread of light. She closed up the lovely wound. I felt it die, felt its heat wither. I was in the dark again.

As ever, beyond the small horror of the experience, I was taken with her skill. "You're a wonder," I said, with my head on her shoulder. "I hope you know that."

"You're very kind," she said. Then she smiled. "But yes, my dear, I know." We stayed there for a while as I settled into my new melancholy.

I sat up, embarrassed, and neatened myself—as if dusting my clothes off would help.

Graciously, she let me stay silent for a time. I watched the Chirurgeonate through her windows, feeling the cloudy pull of nostalgia. Never did I miss medicine quite so keenly as when I was sitting for Malise's treatment. "Do you remember medical school?" I said. We'd attended the Pharmakeia together, and the Chirurgeonate as well.

She shrugged, an open, vulnerable gesture. "I try not to," she said. "I was unhappy then. Unwell, you know."

Sickened physicians, the both of us.

"I'm sorry."

"It made me a better healer," she said, her eyes clearing. I was grateful. "*You* were unbearable. Especially in the beginning. You thought you were the only genius in the world."

"Am I better now?" I asked, not quite meeting her tone. She was teasing; I was not. "Am I *any* better?"

She smiled. "Usually. I know you try."

A sigh of relief took me. "I try."

With a nod, she stood and returned to her desk. "I know. What about me?" she said, raising her eyebrows. "Have I held up over the years?"

"I thought you'd be Prevot of the Chirurgeonate by now," I said, "but I should have known you were too sensible to actually go for the position. You've held up."

Malise was unsusceptible to insincere flattery. Fortunate, then, that I was being entirely honest. She smiled. "Thank you."

But the moment couldn't last. "Casmir's moving in tonight, yes?" she asked, more businesslike.

"Yes," I said. I couldn't suppress a thin laugh. "But I won't be able to help him. I'll be seeing Prefect Velleia."

I wondered where she thought I'd *really* be. Wandering the city aimlessly? Talking to walls and shadows?

"I see," she said, looking haunted once more.

"Wait awhile before you ask him if I need a solarium," I said. "I'd appreciate that favor."

"I'll wait."

I thought of Casmir's hands and his lovely voice. "It's going to be a misery, having him near," I said.

She put her chin on her hand and watched me. "You're still . . ."

"Yes. As I ever will be," I said, a reasonable prediction to make.

"You could find another keeper."

I shook my head.

She didn't argue, although it seemed an effort.

"I can't imagine why he doesn't want me," I said with a brittle smile, unable to leave it at that. "I'm brilliant. I'm good-looking. I'd give him everything he wanted."

She nodded gravely; we were both keenly aware which faults of mine might serve to put Casmir off. "I don't know, Adrien," she said, indulging me in our playacting. "It's a mystery."

The plainest way to put it is that to me, every manic tryst had Casmir's face.

The subject turned to poison in my mouth. I looked away, checking my watch. "I think I have to go," I said, and stood.

"Be well," she said, as if it were an incantation.

I cracked the door open. The cold air hit me, and all of a sudden, the memory of Kirchoff's paperweight and its staring eyes touched upon my mind. "One thing."

"Hmm?"

"Stay away from Marsilio Kirchoff," I said, making sure to hold her questioning gaze. "I know I don't need to tell you that, but . . ."

She seemed relieved to finally have a piece of my paranoia she could safely assuage. "I won't let him near me," she said firmly.

"Then be well," I echoed, and set off to spend the remaining hour or so until my meeting with Prefect Velleia as usefully as I could.

∾

I failed in my bid for usefulness, as it turned out. I didn't go back to the Pharmakeia to catch up on paperwork; I didn't go home to neaten the space for Casmir or tinker with anything in the atelier. I walked through the Chirurgeonate, hating the sight of it as usual, and I fought the unbearable itch to go see my solarium patients or the victims of the curse—just to reassure myself that they were there, that I hadn't hallucinated *them* from whole cloth.

By the time I needed to catch a caleche to Deme Eudora, I had accomplished nothing more than making myself anxious. The caleche horse looked at me skeptically as I got inside; whatever it saw, it didn't like.

The building in question looked much as I expected. The Clementia has a particular aesthetic sensibility that's impossible to mistake; they keep everything under their control grim and understated, blocky and gray. This administrative center was no exception. The knot of Vigil officers guarding the front doors scowled my way, not reassured by my professor's clothing and obvious nerves.

"Business?" one of them asked. Her rache showed its teeth.

"Prefect Velleia called me," I murmured.

Maybe they assumed that no one would dare lie about such a thing. Whatever the reason, they didn't need any more convincing. With a single glance amongst themselves, they all moved aside to let me in. I ascended the austere stone steps as though walking up the scaffold of the demi-lune.

The interior of the building was as cold and unwelcoming as the exterior. It wasn't quite an ancient castle, nothing so antique, but the spirit was clearly there. A small labyrinth of hallways spidered from the main entrance, and I realized I had no idea what room I was looking for. The place smelled of raches.

As if on cue, Gennady and Lady rounded a corner. "You showed up," Gennady said, with enough surprise to offend.

"I had no real choice. I was ordered to come, and I told you I would. No one said *please*." The only issue left was how dearly it would cost both of us.

He blinked at me for a moment. "Please," he ventured.

A personal improvement. I was taken aback enough that I had no answer besides a brief nod, and he moved on without any further pause. "You look kind of beat," he said. Malise's influence was visible, evidently.

"It's nothing."

He shrugged, supremely unconcerned, and beckoned me. It was almost seven o'clock. "It's this way."

I expected any room in which a Prefect would receive visitors to be lavish—a Prefect of the Curia Divae would have the place dripping in holy relics, and a Prefect of the Curia Eulexica would be displaying the city's wealth as prominently as possible. Not so for Velleia's office. The wood and stone were of quality, yes, but the effect was one of sincere, deadly competence. There was no ostentation in sight.

She was seated in a simple chair behind a desk, mostly bare except for several small stacks of paper and a pen. There were two chairs already waiting for us, and Amphion was lazing in front of them.

She inclined her head to us. Her executioner's sword stood leaning against her chair. "Sit."

Gennady sat promptly; I edged my way past Amphion to my own place, and when he raised his head to look at me, I swallowed a noise of dismay. The hollow echo of our footsteps made his ears swivel.

"Prefect," Gennady said, speaking without being prompted. I winced.

Velleia allowed it, though she raised an eyebrow.

"Sorry," he said, and neglected to elaborate. Immediately, he looked proud of himself, as though he had achieved some great feat. In a way, I supposed that he had.

She chose not to address the mysterious apology. Instead, she steepled her hands and settled herself, gracing us both with a fathomless gaze.

"You were very insistent on telling me that you know something of the comatose curse," she said. It seemed that terminology was catching on. "I've been conferring with the Vigil and witchfinders posted at the academy to learn what progress has been made in determining the Pharmakeia's role."

Gennady straightened up eagerly. "It's not just them, see," he said, comfortable again. "Someone in the Vigil is doing it too. I know it for sure."

I couldn't tell for certain, but I thought I saw a flash of confirmation on her face. She wasn't surprised to hear it.

Still, she let him talk himself out. I dug my nails into my arm without meaning to.

"I think it's my old captain," he said. "I think he's one of them. My first captain. Hiram Corvier, in Deme Fienne? I think he's recruiting the people from my first unit to get experimented on, or something, and they're getting sick. Apparently one of the Pharmakeia people—at *least* one—is helping to do it too, so that means they're working together, I think. One of my friends pretty much told me so, and then she died."

I looked for a place to interject, but he took a breath and continued.

"So I really think that's important, and I think you ought to know, and maybe you can help stop it, because it's making a lot of us sick. And the professor is—"

He looked at me, as if suddenly unsure what I had to do with anything.

"I helped advance the theory," I said, stiffly enough that I barely recognized my own voice. The old childhood stutter threatened to rear its head, but I fought it away. "I helped confirm some symptoms of the curse. I discovered the involvement of the one of the Pharmakeia department chairs." *Primarily, I was dragged here as a security blanket for Lieutenant Richter*, I thought.

Velleia tapped her fingernails on her desk, repeating a steady pattern. Taking her time. "I know something of this," she said at length. "It's an issue I intend to take care of."

A great weight lifted. Barring dishonesty from her, she wasn't behind the curse. Even if she *was* being dishonest, at the very least she wouldn't strike us dead where we stood.

"Shit," Gennady said, and brought a great deal of that weight back down. "Now that's a relief. See, we weren't sure."

I had never seen someone who could blink dangerously before. Velleia managed it with aplomb. "You thought I might be behind the sickening of my own soldiers," she said silkily. "Me, Prefect Tessaly Velleia. You imagined I might be guilty of such a crime, and yet you still chose to offer me your information. Disrespect and foolishness all in one."

Amphion was watching us hungrily.

Gennady sat with his mouth open. "Well," he said eventually, while I put my head in my hands. "I guess when you put it that way."

A Clementia Prefect must be accustomed to ill-mannered subjects. Witchfinders are traditionally hard to deal with, but the Vigil in particular are famously trained from childhood to be difficult. That may have saved Gennady.

"Watch yourself," Velleia said, but the moment of danger had passed. She crossed her arms.

I needed to get us back on track. "Why wouldn't the Vigil just begin to recruit magicians?" I asked. "Why not just train their own?"

"Vigil training takes a lifetime," Velleia said shortly. "It takes everything you have. It couldn't be completed concurrently with a Pharmakeia education. We need to choose one or the other."

A magician's training is indispensable; it's not an afterthought. Without craft and form, power is worth nothing. I kept that opinion to myself.

"Forgive me," I said, after I'd gathered the nerve. The short distance between us was not quite enough for my liking. "What would you have us do now?"

Her nose wrinkled a little as she took me in further. The customary Vigil distaste for magicians was present in full force with her, it seemed. "I've been looking for a way to understand exactly what process they've come up with to achieve their results," she said. "I'm interested to know what they're *intending* to achieve, if not a coma. An inside look would be welcomed."

I thought, *Oh, no.*

She smiled grimly. "Since you've offered this information, perhaps you'd offer something further."

"Sure," Gennady said, all openness.

She pointed to me. "You'll volunteer your services as a magician to implement the procedure." And she pointed to Gennady. "You'll volunteer to undergo the experiment at a later date. You'll both observe what happens without actually taking part, and then you'll leave. You'll report back later."

"There's a meeting on Oktidy," Gennady said proudly. He'd found a way to serve his Prefect, and he was going to stretch it as far as he possibly could. "That's perfect."

"Except there's no guarantee that they'll let us leave," I said, wondering why that wasn't obvious to either of them. "It's quite possible that they'll kill us if they suspect we aren't sincere. If we fail to lie gracefully enough to excuse ourselves . . ."

"Aw," Gennady said, realizing.

Velleia, on the other hand, didn't move. I could see that she understood it might be a suicide mission, and she was content with that choice. She wouldn't have much trouble finding other candidates, when all was said and done. She had nothing to lose if we failed. We were less than pawns; we were barely part of the game.

My opinion of the Clementia was stronger in that moment than ever before.

"I have faith in you," Velleia said. With that, Gennady was lost, and I had no way of protesting.

Amphion rose and padded to her side; they looked at each other for a few moments, communicating in a way the outside world would never be able to access. His white ears twitched. She smiled fondly. "Are we clear?" she asked. "Do you understand what I want?"

"Yeah. Yes, Prefect," Gennady said.

I nodded, silent.

She switched her eyes on me. "I said, *do you understand?*"

Hastily, I repented. "Yes, Prefect."

"Excellent." She paused for a while, contemplating if she had said everything she needed to say, perhaps trying to calculate our odds of success. When she was finished, she rose. I felt the dismissal like a slap.

"Thanks," Gennady said blithely.

"You're excused," Velleia said, she nodded toward the door.

I fled. Gennady ambled after me.

The hallways seemed to echo even louder as we found our way back through the labyrinth. Once we were safely out of earshot, near the entrance again, he turned to me. "That wasn't so bad," he said, grinning.

My whole body was leaden. "It was *so* bad."

"You're just skittish," he said reprovingly. "You magicians. Jumpy."

I remembered that I had said I'd do the talking and wondered how I'd ever been so stupid.

"Oktidy," I said, and my voice trembled. The walls were closing in. I had no choice; I'd had no choice ever since the day I'd laid eyes upon the first comatose patient. My own stubbornness had ensured that. "We have to. We have to go on Oktidy."

He slapped me on the back, ludicrously hard as always. I stumbled forward. "It'll be fine," he said. "Then we'll finally know what's going on. This is great."

I turned on my heel and hurried out of the building, with the guards' curious gazes dogging me as I went.

Gennady didn't follow me. I hailed the caleche home in a daze, berating myself the entire journey there. Casmir doubted me; even *Malise* doubted me—it would have been best to leave the curse alone from the start. But I had Gennady's corroboration to tell me I was right, and I had the Philidor solarium's specter hanging over my shoulder, forbidding me to turn away. It was too late now.

The walk up my front steps went painfully. When I reached the door, it was unlocked. Casmir was there—Casmir was home. I prepared myself to meet his ire and explain why I hadn't been there to greet him, and I went inside.

Chapter 9

Casmir was sitting on the couch, reading something he'd taken off one of my shelves. I didn't let people touch those books, ordinarily, but now it was his house too.

He stood to greet me as I crept inside, ashamed. "There you are," he said. "Finally."

The house was lit by lanterns instead of ambrics. Demonstratively, he flipped a switch on and off. "Your lights are out," he said.

I winced. "I was upset about something," I said, as vague an answer as I dared. "They're broken."

He fixed me with a disapproving eye. "This isn't the first time that's happened. Why do you insist on using ambrics?" He raised his hands and waved his fingers—imitating my lightning, possibly. "Most of the city gets along fine without them."

I couldn't tell him that I rather enjoyed watching the bulbs flicker and glow along with my mood. Having the lighting in my home obey my psyche was a bit of aesthetic flair I wasn't willing to give up. "I like to be modern," I said delicately.

"What were you upset about?"

"A . . . difficult project."

He came a little closer to me, almost warily. "Oh? Is that what kept you out tonight?"

"I was busy," I said. "It couldn't wait. I'm sorry."

With a half-shrug, he dismissed my apology and dropped my gaze. "What were you doing? What project?"

I bit my lip hard, realizing that no answer I could provide would satisfy him. The daimon drew me close. I might as well be honest if there was no right choice. "I was talking to Prefect Tessaly Velleia," I said, in the same hopeless tone I had used with Malise. "She has an assignment for me."

That made him look up.

"I can prove it if you want," I said, and went to hang up my coat. "I can prove all of it if you'll let me."

He shook his head. "Come here."

I did. He tilted my chin up to get a good look at my eyes. Checking my pupils.

"I'm not," I said. "Stop."

He saw that I was telling the truth and let me go. "Where were you, really? Can you remember?" He was being gentle, patient. I was sober. To him, whatever delusions I was having weren't my fault.

I stayed close even after he'd stopped touching me, imagining that I might hug him when I found the courage. "With Velleia," I said, nauseous with resignation.

His unhappy look withered me. "I made you tea," he said, and sat back down. "It's cold now."

"I'm sorry," I said again.

He took a deep breath and held it, clearly trying to decide whether I was worth arguing with. When he spoke again, it was with a trace of hurt. "I know you don't want me here," he said, "but I thought you could at least be bothered to help me get settled."

I willed myself not to go to his room and see just how comfortable he'd made himself. Had he unpacked? How long was he expecting to stay? "It's not that I don't want you here," I said. I *didn't*, fully, but that wasn't the reason I hadn't been around.

After a tense silence, finally, he relented. "Come eat something," he said. "I've missed eating with you lately."

The relief was depthless.

"Lunch at work is boring since you've started shutting yourself away," he continued, and turned to go into the kitchen. I was lost, of course. I followed him without a second thought.

There's something intimate about having someone rifle through your kitchen. I poured the waiting mug of cold tea regretfully down the sink and watched him try, in vain, to find the ingredients for a decent meal.

"You have almost no groceries," he said with weary outrage, his head still stuck in a cabinet. "What have you been eating?"

I considered. "Takeout." Usually, I loved to cook. Usually, usually, usually—all my excuses these days consisted of *usually*s.

He made a disapproving sound and emerged, finally, with bread, jam, and a bottle of wine. The jam went on the bread; the wine went down the sink.

"Expensive," I noted. "Expensive and unopened, thank you." Alcohol was never my vice.

"I'm not an idiot," he said, and went to find plates for our dinner, such as it was. I got us water.

We ate at the kitchen counter, standing. Despite everything, it was the most pleasant meal I'd had since the beginning of the curse. I found myself desperately trying to think of an amusing story to tell him, something a coworker had said, something a student had done, but I had nothing. All my stories were things he did not want to hear. I didn't even have the presence of mind to invent something.

I had to ask him to provide instead. "Tell me what you've been up to," I said meekly, to show that it wasn't a demand.

He lit up. I wasn't the only one who took pleasure in work; Casmir might be more grounded than most of the other academic magicians, but he still had that fundamental spark of curiosity. "I've been experimenting to see if one artificial construct can power another construct," he said. "If I imbue one statue with life, is there any way to enable it to pass my power onto a *second* construct by proxy? If it works, it'll open up whole new avenues for automation."

I made a sound: *Go on.*

"If I can find some way to get the constructs to generate their *own* power, they could feed each other forever. It would be a paradigm-shattering discovery."

I thought he was chasing shadows. Only true life force can innervate a construct, and beyond that, it sounded like a perpetual motion machine in disguise—an unattainable phantom. Still, I nodded. I liked to see him excited, and I'd seen for myself that the laws of magic weren't as immutable as I'd imagined.

"Send me an advance copy of your treatise," I said.

"Even if it doesn't work," he said with a nod toward my atelier, "it's something to tinker with. You understand."

I did, intimately. "Of course."

It was worth more to me than I can say to have a conversation that wasn't about any sort of impending doom, whether actual or akratic. We were speaking as friends, colleagues—warmly, and with purpose.

Casmir seemed to feel it too; he gifted me with a smile and took my plate to put it in the sink. "I think you'll be better soon," he said after he was done clearing the dishes. He didn't seem happy, not exactly, but his bearing had relaxed. He was remembering why we were friends.

I thought of Oktidy. If I died then, it was probable that I would never be found. Casmir and Malise would both assume I'd done something to myself. I couldn't even try to make oblique goodbyes, just in case. All it would do was send them into a worried frenzy.

"I think so too," I said.

There were questions I had for him, questions I would never be brave enough to ask under normal circumstances. *If you don't want me, why do you tolerate me still? Do I ever disgust you?*

He left the kitchen. I followed, and as I watched him in the dim lantern light, I realized that I was going to have to remove myself before I decided to ask him anyway. "I'm going to get ready for bed," I said. The humiliation that had been circling for some time hit me hard; I turned away.

Graciously, he let me go.

Sleep came in fits and starts. I jerked awake several times with lightning at my fingertips; I dreamed of swords and raches—one moment Gennady was my killer, and Prefect Velleia the next. When I woke in the morning, Casmir was gone for work.

~

The remaining days until Oktidy passed in an unremarkable, depressive haze. Casmir was a courteous houseguest, and I did my best to be a good host. I wasn't in any state to make him happy, but I could at least give him the benefit of my relative absence.

My routine continued. During the usual times, I saw Gennady at the lecture hall, and he seemed no more anxious than he had before. I was the only person, apparently, who had any misgivings about what needed to be done.

When I went to 1370 Via Charenton in Deme Aufford on Oktidy, I brought a notebook, a good pencil, a blank anamnesic pseudogram to record the proceedings, and a kitchen knife. I put everything in a messenger bag, with the knife in an outside pocket, and hoped to God that no one would search me.

Gennady and I met at the Pharmakeia after dark to walk to the location together. I spent my fair share of time at work after hours, but the darkened spires still looked threatening that night, as if a spiny beast had come to haunt the skyline of Deme Palenne. Even my second home held no comfort in the face of our night to come.

We arrived at Via Charenton on time. It was an abandoned warehouse; the conspirators hadn't missed their chance to be cliché.

"Figures," Gennady said, and Lady huffed in agreement. I reached into my bag to give the blank anamnesic pseudogram a shake to start its recording—with annoyance, I realized that the pseudogram was a cheap version, lightweight and capable of only a single playback. Velleia would have to be satisfied with one listen, if we managed to get the evidence back to her at all.

The lights were on inside the warehouse as we approached. Outside the door stood two Vigil officers, a small woman with a massive brown rache and a blond man with a midsized, dagger-clawed specimen.

"Genya," the man said with great surprise. "No way you're here to get fixed up?"

I prepared to see just how badly Gennady would lie.

To my surprise, he held it together well enough. "Marcel. What do you mean *no way*?" he said. "Didn't think I'd want in?"

The man tilted his head with a lazy sort of curiosity. "I just didn't think Captain had told you yet. He hasn't asked everyone from the old unit." There was a significant pause. "Not everyone's suited, he says."

I could hear the hurt in Gennady's voice when he spoke again. No matter that his captain had betrayed him and all the other soldiers—he was still upset not to have been included. "He didn't, but someone else did," he muttered. "So now I'm here."

Unconcerned, the officer shrugged, looking me over briefly. "Well. Good for you. I heard the magicians saying they think they've got it right this time."

"I sure fucking hope so," Gennady said flatly, and the woman standing beside his friend snorted.

"My turn is next week," Marcel said. "It'd be nice if they figure it out before then."

I had to interject. "You're going to submit to the process even if you aren't sure it won't send you comatose?"

He raised his eyebrows at the sheer disbelief in my voice. "That's orders," he said. "I can't say I look forward to it, but it's for the cause."

The extent of the brainwashing some Vigil are subjected to never ceases to amaze.

Unimpressed and unsettled, I nudged Gennady forward, and we stepped into the warehouse to finally find our answers.

Somewhat childishly, I had expected glowing equipment or tables strewn with sinister instruments, but there was only a lonely circle of chairs. A small, uncomfortable group of fifteen or so people milled in the center of the space, casting long shadows across the stone floor; only a few were seated. The low, flat ceiling seemed ready to crush us.

"My old captain's not here," Gennady said, aggrieved. For the most part, the guests were young Vigil, but I saw two Pharmakeia students standing side by side off in a corner, ashen. Two Vigil in captains' uniforms and two Pharmakeia professors rounded out the gathering. The professors were Kirchoff and an older woman I didn't know well, Winifred Tenniel. Her talent was with wind magic, if I remembered correctly.

"Desfourneaux," Kirchoff said once he saw me. He gave me a delighted smile. "You made it. Who do you have here?"

I'd thought of my excuse for bringing Gennady already. "He's the son of an old friend," I said stiffly. "I was raised here in Aufford, actually."

To my relief, Gennady had enough sense not to object. Kirchoff barely looked at him, beyond a cursory glance. "Did you? My condolences," he said, loudly enough for the other Vigil around him to hear. "Military demes are so unpleasant. No place for raising a child."

Silently, I had to agree. In all probability, I'd escaped being tithed to the Vigil only by virtue of my magic. Watching the majority of my playmates sacrificed one by one to the Clementia's machine never did much to improve my opinion of the Curia.

Around us, the Vigil scowled. "In any case," I said hastily, "his mother was happy to volunteer him. Since you invited me, I thought I might as well bring my own prospective subject. You will need subjects, I assume?"

If I trembled with disgust as I selected that phrasing, I hoped that Kirchoff would chalk it up to the chill of the warehouse.

He smiled at me, as if a long-held suspicion of his were being confirmed. That smile meant, *I was right about you.* "I've brought a couple of my quadriviates," he said, nodding toward the two Pharmakeia students in the corner.

Advising a quadriviate is an investment in someone's future. I kept myself utterly still. "Ah," I said. "Well."

Gennady cleared his throat, tired of being ignored. "I'm Gennady," he announced, with his usual volume and lack of grace. I nodded at him, disproportionately relieved to be interrupted.

"Quite," Kirchoff said, his smile dropping another few degrees toward a sneer.

Winifred Tenniel drifted closer to us, setting me in her sights, red-haired and toothy. "Hello, Desfourneaux." She put a hand to her mouth, as if amused beyond laughter. A few tiny dust devils swirled on the floor; her magic was picking up on her glee. "I didn't think you'd be interested in our little project."

Kirchoff's involvement didn't surprise me in the slightest. He was just the type. Tenniel, on the other hand—I wouldn't have guessed. The deep sting of indignation gave me an ounce more courage. "I'm afraid I figured you out easily," I said with utmost pleasantness. Just a joke between two likeminded colleagues. "You should have taken more care in covering your tracks. Once I brought my suspicions to dear Marsilio, he couldn't wait to invite me."

"The more the merrier," she said. She was with the Celestial Studies department, I remembered. Did she think the stars would bless her for her efforts?

I turned my attention back to Kirchoff, keenly aware of the recording pseudogram sitting at the bottom of my bag. "*Now* will you tell me exactly what you're after?"

"Impatient," he chided, but he nodded. "During the process of earning a license, a magician is constrained in certain ways." He had adopted an instructive tone, as though I were a student. I sighed and waited. "The training we receive shapes us, forces our magic into narrow channels. We learn discipline and restraint, and by the same token, we lose a great deal of our flexibility and power."

Not the worst tradeoff in the world. Even a Pharmakeia-licensed magician can wreak havoc, and an unformed, untrained *witch* can bring down hell. Discipline is worth something. Of course, for Kirchoff and Tenniel, I hummed in agreement. Unsubtly, Gennady snorted with disapproval.

"The licensing process creates a callus around our magic," Kirchoff continued. "A scar. If there were a way to rip it away . . ."

"The magicians of Martyr's Reach deserve to own their gift fully," Tenniel said, cutting him off. "Look at Torrim. They have no Clementia to keep them leashed, and their advancements in magic are some of the most impressive in the world."

Kirchoff looked at me speculatively. "You have a Torrine name, Desfourneaux, although you don't look it; does your family have any ties with their grand seigneurs?"

"Torrine mother," I muttered. "The name is from her. My father is Saebar. But no, there aren't any ties."

I've never quite approved of the Torrine magocracy. Those who suggest that Martyr's Reach emulate it are usually fanatics of some order or another. When only magicians may rule, the talentless suffer.

"In any case," Kirchoff said, "what we're doing here has the potential to produce Astrine magicians of unrivalled talent."

"So you're breaking through the scar to strengthen them," I said, willing myself not to look at Kirchoff's frightened quadriviates. "Except it's shattering their minds instead."

"We'll perfect it soon," he said with a wave of his hand. "A little more time, and then we'll administer the procedure more widely."

"In service of what?" I asked. "A rebellion? If so, why work with the Vigil?"

Gennady started forward, violently eager. I'd almost forgotten him. "Yeah. What do Vigil have to do with it?" He hooked a thumb toward one of the Vigil captains. "None of us give a damn about any of that."

The disdainful look Kirchoff gave him was potent enough that I felt its sting as well. "*Unfortunately*, there's safety in numbers. It was advantageous to partner with a few of your people who had interest in the same procedure." He rolled his eyes at me, as if to suggest that Gennady was stupid. I'd had the same thought several times in the past, but now I had to suppress a glare.

"We're not magicians," Gennady said. "I don't see what we get out of this."

"You're not *yet*," Kirchoff corrected. He spread his arms grandly. "What is magic, if not life force given purpose? The only thing separating a magician from the average person is a barrier between the power and the will."

"Stars and saints," I murmured. The motes of light that had poured from Blanche's mouth filled my head for a moment.

"Our process could make a god of a magician and a magician of a talentless soldier," he said.

"We don't need any Vigil magicians," Gennady said impatiently. "We have the Stardust Artillery."

The Clementia keeps a division of drugged witches under its control. Witches dangerous enough to warrant death, but useful enough to warrant detainment. In lieu of execution, the witches serve.

Kirchoff's points about the tyranny of the Clementia took on a little more shine at Gennady's comment. What better example than the Stardust Artillery?

Tenniel broke in, speaking to Gennady with a sickly sweet bite. "Apparently, your people think it would be nice to have some magic at their disposal that doesn't come with the cost of pounds and pounds of stardust. We all know how difficult those poor witches are to control."

I worried my wrist with my nails for a moment, feeling the walls threaten to close in, imagining what the Clementia would be capable of if the average soldier could wield magic. Their grip on the city would be absolute; no foreign war would be beyond them. "This alliance can't last," I said.

Kirchoff shrugged. "It's distasteful, but we can deal with our grievances after we both have what we want." Theatrically, he leaned in to whisper to me. "And we both know who's going to come out on top."

Gennady's hand hovered near the hilt of his saber. I felt our futures balancing on its point.

He recovered himself. "Sounds fun," he said, devoid of tone. I smiled at him, trying to reassure him somehow—as if I were in any frame of mind to help.

"A temporary alliance with Prefect Mulcaster and his people is the best way to ensure we can complete the project without Clementia interference," Kirchoff said, beginning to grow bored. "That's all."

Prefect Everett Mulcaster. The second Prefect of the Curia Clementia. Tessaly Velleia's equal. With a surprise beyond horror, I decided I couldn't handle meeting both Prefects in one week.

The warehouse door opened; two men and their raches walked in.

Gennady said, "Captain."

I said, "Goddammit."

I'd seen Prefect Mulcaster at Hallow festivals, when the government gathered the citizens to tell them how the city was faring. I knew his face from a great distance. Up close, I'd underestimated just how large his rache was, just how harsh his features were. A broad scar interrupted his short fuzz of brown hair, sweeping across one side of his face. Like Velleia, he bore an executioner's sword.

The thin, graying man next to him would be Gennady's first captain, then. I risked a glance at Gennady—he was stone-faced, vibrating subtly with rage.

I was afraid. The more superstitious citizens of Astrum tell each other that the Prefects have divine powers, that the stars whisper secrets in their ears, that they can read a person's mind on sight. I thought I could safely discard that idea, but there, in that moment, I doubted. Surely Mulcaster would look at Gennady and me, and he'd *know*.

He didn't. His gaze swept over us without interruption; he barely saw us. Instead, he went straight to the Vigil captains who were already present. The other raches shied from his own, Leo, a mottled black-and-white creature with only half a tail. Amphion had taken the other half, if rumor was to be believed.

Gennady took a half-step toward the other man. On cue, he was noticed; his old captain came to greet him. The man was in his sixties, I guessed, and had liver spots dotting much of his dark skin.

"Gennady," he said. "I'm surprised to see you here. I didn't think you'd be interested."

"You never asked, Captain," Gennady said. I barely breathed. He was going to break at any moment. I was sure of it.

The man raised his eyebrows and turned his attention to me. "I had my reasons. Introduce us."

Gennady stared at me, at a loss. He'd forgotten my name.

"Desfourneaux," I provided.

Gennady pointed at his captain, a weak motion. "Captain Corvier. Hiram Corvier. From Deme Fienne."

We bowed to each other; his sable rache lowered its head. "So you're going to be the one to try the process out on Gennady," Corvier said to me, with speculative amusement. "Take care. I knew him as a cadet. He was one of my own."

Gennady made a very small sound.

I had to play my part. I *had* to. "I wouldn't usually waste my time on one of the Clementia," I said, "but I used to know Gennady's mother. She owes me a favor. I thought I'd test the procedure before choosing my own student."

Corvier snorted and took a step back. "You professors all sound the same."

"Blanche said I should give it a try," Gennady said. Lady chewed a paw. "She really seemed to think this was a great idea."

"Poor Blanche," Corvier said. "She was one of the best of you." He sighed. "It's too bad, but it had to be done." There was genuine regret in his voice, and somehow, that made it worse.

Gennady nodded jerkily as Lady turned in circles, maddened, her nails clicking quietly on the floor. I could only hope that Corvier would excuse

Gennady's grief without suspecting him of uncooperativeness. "Yeah. She was the best of us."

"I would have gotten around to asking you eventually," Corvier said. "You understand that I couldn't tell everyone at once."

Another nod.

Casually, Corvier tousled Gennady's hair, a fatherly touch. "I hope this time it works," he said, and turned to attend to the other Vigil captains. Gennady was dismissed.

There was nothing kind I could safely say to Gennady to keep him even. Practicality was the closest I was going to get. "Remember why we're here," I told him, hoping that would do it.

He opened his mouth, flaring, but before he could get anything out, Prefect Mulcaster cleared his throat.

Everyone shifted and realigned to face him, and the low buzz of scattered conversations died down. Gravity bent toward him. He spoke. "Shall we get started?"

Chapter 10

Mulcaster's raw impatience laced his voice with spikes—immediately, everyone scrambled to do his bidding. Unfortunately, Gennady and I had no idea how or where to scramble. I pulled him off to the side, up against a far wall, and we stood to watch. Whatever he had meant to say before, it was gone now. He was just as clueless as I was.

"The first two," Mulcaster said.

Tenniel sat one of the Vigil officers, broad-shouldered and wide-eyed, down in an empty chair. Kirchoff did the same with one of his quadriviates, a delicate-looking young man who fidgeted constantly as he looked up at his mentor.

The two professors stood before the specimens and looked at each other. "Gentle, now," Tenniel told Kirchoff, with no real sincerity.

Kirchoff smiled. They put their hands to their victims' temples and began to cast.

Performing mind magic is one of the most delicate processes in the world. No responsibility is greater—not even a chirurgeon's hand must be as steady. Kirchoff went at it like a maniac with an ax. Tenniel's style was subtler, but she was just as eager.

In a bright, unsteady flash, I realized my mistake. I'd been thinking of the meeting in terms of selfish hypotheticals. What would people think about me? What would they expect me to do? Would I die? I'd never stopped to think about the realities of what would happen to the people who were being experimented on. The *whys* and *hows* were trivial. What mattered was the curse.

To stand by and watch while it happened made me complicit. I might die if I protested, but if I did nothing, I would forever know that I'd allowed two minds to be destroyed.

I'd expected it to be Gennady who would do something that would bring us unwanted attention. I'd been wrong. "Wait a moment," I heard myself say. My voice bounced harshly off the stone walls.

The magicians stopped. Kirchoff turned, glaring at me. "What? What is it?"

I hadn't quite thought of what I was going to say. "Explain to me what you're doing as you go," I stammered. "You haven't told me how to do this."

He stepped toward me, narrow-eyed, and I held up a hand. "If you want me to have any hope of assisting, you'll need to explain the process," I said.

Tenniel gave a good-natured sigh. "Come stand next to me, and I'll talk you through it," she said.

I forced myself to walk to her, desperately avoiding the eyes of the Vigil soldier she was working on. The young woman's head was lolling; she slumped in her chair. She was still conscious, but I wasn't sure that would be the case after Tenniel was through with her.

"So," Tenniel said, replacing her hands on the soldier's head. "Establish the primary energic flow. A one-way connection, mind. That's very important."

Kirchoff returned to his place as well, although he watched me closely. I couldn't think of another way to stall.

Fortunately, Gennady had a solution for me. *Un*fortunately, it involved drawing his saber. I heard the deadly rasp before I turned to see him holding its point to Kirchoff's throat. His hand was shaking; the blade's tip wavered in the air.

I saw in his eyes that he hadn't meant to do it. He'd only lost control, just for the briefest of moments, and now he was regretting it—but there was nothing either of us could do. "Huh," he said.

"Gennady," said Captain Corvier with soft disappointment.

Tenniel laughed. "Oh, my."

Kirchoff had gone a dangerous shade of white. For the briefest of moments, I closed my eyes, wishing that I were the type of person who might pray in crisis.

I walked forward and jerked Gennady's arm back, away from Kirchoff. "Idiot," I spat. "Put that down."

Numb and bewildered, he lowered his saber.

Before us, Kirchoff's dazed quadriviate made a small, unhappy noise, his head hanging forward. I looked out at the small crowd, meeting each hostile gaze in turn. "My enchantment on him isn't perfect yet," I said impatiently. "It seems there are still a few details to work out. He loses track of himself sometimes—it makes him violent at the most inconvenient moments."

"I beg your pardon," Kirchoff said, incredulity writ large, one hand to his throat.

"You can't think you're the only one with a pet project," I said. As though truly surprised, I turned a quizzical glance toward Tenniel. "It's a wonderful idea you have, using the Vigil as test subjects. I've been trying out my own experiment on Lieutenant Richter."

The enchantment of another human being is perhaps the most heinous use of witchcraft. To bend someone's mind to your will, to make them yours—no magical heresy compares to that. I smiled sweetly and continued. "He's been very obedient so far, on the whole, but when the enchantment slips, the disorientation makes him . . . disagreeable."

"Um," Gennady said.

"Be quiet," I said, as if I expected to be obeyed.

I was. He stood soundless and emotionless. He had realized my goal.

Captain Corvier shook his head. "Magicians," he said.

I raised my eyebrows at him. "You object? You weren't going to make use of him anyway."

He looked Gennady over with only the faintest regret, chalking him up for lost. *Giving* him to me. "It's not what I wanted for him, but I suppose those are the costs of dealing with you people," he said. "I'm only surprised you managed to enchant him at all. He was always hard to control."

You must have made a wonderful father to him, I thought, worrying in earnest that I might be sick.

I turned away and tugged Gennady back, away from the professors. "Stay."

He stayed.

Mulcaster had been silent, and I hadn't dared to look at him. When he spoke, it was all I could do not to flinch.

"You," he said. "What's your name?"

"Desfourneaux," I said, as if I were proud of it.

"Richter is the only soldier you'll be enchanting," he said flatly. "In the interest of our partnership, you may have him, but be warned."

People often speak of the Vigil's unconquerable loyalties, their fanatical devotion to each other. It seemed that I was in a room with the most grievous exceptions to that rule. I saw Gennady panting with rage and nodded quickly. "I won't need another."

"Your enchantment may interfere with the process," Kirchoff hissed. "It might not work on him now. Didn't you think of that?"

"It isn't as though you've gotten it to work on anyone else," I said delicately. "What exactly would be the difference?" *That*, at least, was sincere. "But we'll leave him for another day, if you insist."

"Stop bickering," Mulcaster ordered. "Cast."

Sighing with irritation, Tenniel and Kirchoff set upon their victims again. The quadriviate and the soldier sagged in their chairs.

That was it. There was nothing else I could plausibly do without getting us killed. We'd reached the end of our stalls. I was going to have to watch two young minds shatter in front of me, and I was going to have to pretend to enjoy it.

I kept a tight grip on Gennady's wrist. He stared straight ahead into the opposite wall while Lady watched me. "I owe you a favor," Gennady whispered. I couldn't read his tone.

After another two minutes or so, Tenniel and Kirchoff stepped back. Kirchoff dusted his hands off. "That should do it," he said.

His quadriviate stood, took a single step toward him, and collapsed.

"Ah," Tenniel said, as the soldier in front of her slowly listed to one side and fell to the floor as well, one leg still draped over her chair. A few motes of plasma slipped from her mouth and thinned in the air until they were gone. On the floor, her rache toppled over into a graceless pile with a soft thump.

Even my daimon was silent with horror. I needed no artificial despair.

"Wonderful," Mulcaster said acidly. "Another wasted procedure."

"Maybe not," Tenniel objected. "Put them in the Chirurgeonate. Watch them. They could recover."

Mulcaster looked at one of the other Vigil captains. "Arrange for them to be hospitalized." The captain nodded, thin-lipped.

"Shall we try again?" Kirchoff asked, very eager, and turned toward his second quadriviate, hovering nearby. The girl quailed, and I tasted blood. I'd bitten my tongue too hard.

"If you want to waste another one of your people," Mulcaster said, "do feel free."

I let go of Gennady with some difficulty and stepped forward again. "I'll try."

I could harmlessly put her to sleep. *Easily*, if I could only cast: it was a procedure taught to healers in the pursuit of a Chirurgeonate license, and I wasn't sure I could bring myself to use it. It didn't matter. I needed to.

Kirchoff tilted his head at me, curious.

"Practice makes perfect," I said, and checked my watch as if bored. "No?"

"Fine," he said.

A remaining Vigil officer dragged Kirchoff's first quadriviate away and laid him on his back, away from the chair. The boy left a cleaned patch in the dust on the warehouse floor.

"Take a seat," I told the second quadriviate, and she did.

"Please," she said. I'd never been looked at like that before—with total surrender. My stomach turned. "I want to help, but please be careful—"

I put my hands to her temples. "What's your name?"

"Rosabelle," she said, the word cracking.

"You'll be all right," I said, in my best healer's tone, a long-retired voice.

"Establish the connection," Tenniel said helpfully. I nodded, as if I had any intention of doing what she said.

"Reach the barrier—you'll feel it with your magic. It'll feel like a hard wall. Now tear it. Focus on one place and make a long incision."

Some magical specializations are conducive to putting someone to sleep. Water will do it nicely, and stone presents no real challenges. To soothe with lightning is far more difficult. It requires more talent. I took her out like a snuffed candle, quietly and gently.

She fell forward; I righted her, motioning for the same Vigil officer to lay her on the floor as well. She would wake up later at the Chirurgeonate. She wouldn't be the goddess of magic Kirchoff hoped for, but she'd live.

I straightened up and gave Kirchoff a shrug as Gennady stared at me like a dire wolf. "Well. It was worth a try."

"I'm running out of quadriviates," he said with disgust, and turned away.

With that, the clandestine meeting seemed to be over. The procedure had failed, and none of remaining Vigil officers were eager to be the next casualty. Those in charge of the affair had seen enough. The air of hopefulness dissolved into a sullen disappointment; I saw the professors and the captains eying each other mistrustfully, resenting their alliance.

Tenniel approached me. "Don't you think that was a little wasteful?" she asked me.

It was too much to wish that she might understand the irony in that. "Kirchoff was going to try the procedure on her anyway. I might as well get a feel for it," I said.

She crossed her arms, inspecting me. "You look a little wan, Desfourneaux."

"I've been ill," I said distantly.

Slowly, a smile spread across her face. Fake sympathy, genuine interest. "Oh. Having an episode?"

I'd failed to conceal my akrasia with complete success over the years. My colleagues knew. Some of the more perceptive among them could detect it at times, and it seemed that Tenniel had a sharp eye. We'd barely ever spoken, but she could tell. It was hard to take.

"Mm," I said, and turned away to talk to Gennady. She let me, going off to speak with Captain Corvier.

"What's that about?" he asked. "What's she mean?"

I considered. "I'm prone to fits of pique and bad judgment," I said, obliquely enough to frustrate. "Ignore her. Are you all right?"

"The student you messed up," he said. There was a quiet danger in his voice.

I couldn't risk reassuring him in company. "We should go." I didn't think anyone would care if we neglected to make our goodbyes before leaving.

He pulled his hair. "I need to talk to Captain first."

"You really don't," I said, as deliberately as I could. "Nothing he has to say will help you, Gennady, and we can't be here any longer."

Lady nudged his leg with her head after a few ugly seconds. He relented. Just like that, he was striding away, pushing aside the small crowd to burst through the warehouse door into the night. I followed at my own pace, never looking at the motionless victims laid out on the floor.

ᴖ

We walked silently until we were far out of earshot. I took out the anamnesic pseudogram that had been recording and shook it to stop it. Hopefully, it would be sufficient for Velleia. If it wasn't, I wasn't sure I could stand another meeting.

Once we had rounded enough corners, Gennady stopped, turned, and snatched my glasses off my face without a word.

I reached to take them back, but he pushed me away lightly. Lady sat to the side, her ears pinned back, making an awful chattering sound.

"So they don't break," he murmured. "Hold still."

"Excuse me," I said.

He punched me in the face.

The pain bloomed like a nova. I'd been hit before, but never by a soldier; I stumbled hard against the wall of a nearby building, backing up against the brick. For a split second, I wondered if I should go for the knife in my bag, but I knew there was no chance I could use it against him. He was Vigil. If he was planning to kill me, only my magic might save me—and I wasn't sure I could use it to hurt someone.

While I was dazed, he pulled me up by the collar and put my glasses back on me. "There," he said, with warped satisfaction. "There's the favor I owe you."

I pressed a hand to my mouth and held it up in the starlight; it came away with dark smudges. Gennady lunged at me again; I flinched back, putting my arms up.

"You humiliated me," he snarled, and I realized what it must be like to be his enemy. I'd forgotten what he was. I'd forgotten that he was Clementia, just like the rest of them. His rache was a monster like any other, no matter her size.

I felt a stab of anger somewhere far away, but I couldn't reach it. There was only a deep ache. "You humiliated yourself," I said softly. "You almost got us killed because you couldn't behave."

He shook me by the shoulders; I held up my hand, showing him a spark of lightning. "Let go of me."

It was a bluff, but he didn't call it. He stepped away.

"I *saved* us," I said with deadly exhaustion.

With that, he sank to his knees, his shoulders shaking.

At least if anyone from the warehouse came upon us, I could tell them I was only terrorizing him, I thought bleakly. Carefully, I knelt as well to look at him. I felt the same thing I did whenever I saw one of my students cry: a pinched, peculiar distress.

"He betrayed us," he said. "Captain. He betrayed the Vigil. He betrayed me."

I said nothing, and he sniffled. "We were like his kids," he said. "When we first joined. I thought so, anyway. We were the cadets no one else wanted. He gave us a place, he gave us—"

He broke off.

I'd been right that a Vigil officer's first captain would be something like a parent. I could only trust my suspicion that Gennady had no other parents to pick up Corvier's slack.

I wanted to sympathize, but I could taste copper.

"Why'd you do the same thing to that girl?" he asked, and in an instant, his hand was around my throat. He wasn't squeezing yet. It wasn't even a threat. He was simply readying himself for my answer.

I swallowed. "I only put her to sleep," I said. "She'll wake up in good health.

They'll be sending her to the Chirurgeonate, and I'll check up on her there. I'll make sure she doesn't . . ."

He squeezed lightly. "Doesn't what?"

"Doesn't end up like Blanche," I said, high and thin, wondering how long it would take him to asphyxiate me.

Gennady had no more protests; he didn't try to tell me that Blanche hadn't been murdered. His father had told him otherwise. He let go of me, and I touched my throat reflexively, gasping.

"You're being really dramatic again," he said, watery but contemptuous.

Then all of a sudden, *there* was the anger. I stood, my vision darkening even further—I was tired, so tired, of being threatened. I was the only reason we weren't both lying dead on the warehouse floor, and he'd hit me for it.

Lightning haloed me; shadows strobed across the cobblestones around us. "You *stupid* animal," I hissed. "Can't you try to control yourself for just one *instant*? Just a solitary instant? Is it *so very* much to ask—"

My breath caught. I broke off, horrified, my hand over my mouth again, feeling the wetness of blood. I recognized my tone. It was the same way I'd been spoken to, over and over, in all my lesser and greater moments. I was talking to him like a fed-up keeper.

He stayed kneeling, staring at me, not hurt, not angry—only curious. He'd stopped crying, at least.

"Gennady," I said, "I'm sorry."

He got to his feet. His hand went to his saber, and I feared that I had committed suicide by soldier. "You can't talk to me like that," he said remotely. Lady hissed at me.

I couldn't blame it on the daimon. That had all been me. "I'm sorry—"

I thought he'd snap, but he only pushed his way past me. I let him go; I stood and watched him leave until he was gone. Somehow, I didn't think he would be accompanying me to report back to Tessaly Velleia any time soon.

It took me a while to cut away every trace of lightning, to calm myself and my magic. Once I'd done so, I missed it badly.

When I realized that I still had to go home to Casmir, I started to laugh. By the time I'd gotten ahold of myself, the night had chilled me through, and I walked back to Deme Palenne stiff and numb.

Chapter 11

When I let myself into the house, it was dark inside. Casmir was in bed, of course. I could leave him alone, I thought; I could deal with the results of the night alone like an adult. I didn't have to bother him. I didn't have to inflict myself on him.

Despite it all, I stood in the living room for some time, aching, wanting nothing more than to wake him up. Would it be so wrong to seek the help of my keeper?

It would. The atelier would help me instead. Quietly, as quietly as I could, I set my bag aside in my bedroom and went to find a lantern to bring to the workshop. I had a few half-finished projects lying around I could sink my mind into. Sleep wasn't much of an option, but the pleasant trance of a momentary fixation would be *something*.

The lantern cast a welcoming light over the piles of mekhania in the atelier and the tables covered in incomplete components. I sat down and chose a half-assembled ether meter; I'd been tinkering with it, trying to see if I could improve its sensitivity. If I could modify it to filter out ambient magic from its readings and only measure one specific strain . . .

I lost myself in work for perhaps three hours. Every time I thought about Kirchoff's second quadriviate—Rosabelle—and how I could have hurt her if I'd been just a little less delicate, I disassembled my progress and tried again.

Eventually, a shadow moved from behind me. I hadn't been quiet enough, after all. "What the hell are you doing?" Casmir said. My reverie broke. I jumped and dropped the ether meter; it fell apart on the ground with a tinny clatter, all the different components scattering.

"Oh," I said, staring at the pieces.

"Shit. Sorry."

I'd pick up the mess in a second, I told myself. Just a second.

"You're not manic," he said, quizzical, and bent to do it for me. "Why are you staying up like this?"

Of all things, the broken ether meter was what undid me. The daimon clamored. I pulled my hair; I tried to turn away.

But when Casmir rose to replace the pieces of the meter on the table, he saw my face clearly. The bruising must have been setting in. "Saints," he hissed. "What happened?"

"Nothing," I said faintly, trying to retreat. Before I could go far, he grabbed me by the wrist and dragged me closer.

"What *happened*?"

I shook myself free. "You won't believe me, Casmir. Why should I tell you?"

He'd gone pale. No matter how difficult I get, I've never been prone to fights. He knew that, and it frightened him. "Who did that to you?"

"It doesn't matter," I said, and went to sit at the table and start repairing the meter once again. If I didn't look at him, maybe he'd leave.

He stood in front of me, putting his hands on the table, demanding that I respond. "I want to know."

I weakened. Maybe just a little truth wouldn't doom us. I wanted his sympathy; I wanted what I always wanted—his attention. "A Vigil officer punched me," I said haltingly.

He swore and came around the table, turning my head so he could see the damage. I dropped the mekhania piece I was holding. Again. Every time he touched my face, whether it was to check my eyes or to examine a bruise, there was a moment when I imagined that he was finally going to kiss me. Just then, that pang was nearly more than I could take.

"Why?" he asked.

"I was rude to him," I said.

He sighed and took his hand away. "You had to know that wasn't going to end well."

I scrubbed my eyes furiously and stared harder at the half-assembled ether meter, feeling like a scolded child. "It wasn't my fault. You weren't there."

"What were you doing near a Vigil officer at night?"

There it was; we'd come to the part of the conversation where he couldn't follow me any further. Anything else I said would be taken as a delusion.

"Well?" he prodded, more anxious by the second. "What were you doing?"

Lying to Casmir had always been a unique challenge, but I gave it my best effort. "Working late. He was guarding the Pharmakeia. He hassled me, so I said something."

"For God's sake," he said. "You know the Clementia. You know the Vigil. You're lucky he didn't do worse. Why did you—?"

I cut him off with a sharp motion, looking up at him. "I don't have to listen to you lecture me," I said, my voice wavering. "I didn't ask for your advice. Go back to bed, Casmir."

He glared at me, frustrated—frustrated with my weakness, my waspishness, my poor judgment, all of it, all of me, as he always had been, as he always would be.

I lost my mind.

It was quiet, at least: the hysterics were controlled. I covered my face and thanked the stars my ambrics were still broken; otherwise, they would have shattered all over again. The hatching wound of the night tore open, finally, and I was crying. Fragments of lightning dripped from my lashes no matter how I tried to brush them aside.

"You weren't working late," Casmir said. He took my hands away from my eyes; his frustration melted beneath a wave of pure concern. I hated myself. Using tears to get my way—a perfect strategy for a selfish akratic. "Tell me."

"You don't believe me."

"I believe you got that bruise from *somewhere*," he said, as much of a declaration of faith as I was ever likely to get.

"I went to Deme Aufford tonight because Tessaly Velleia told me to," I said, swallowing a minuscule sob. "Winifred Tenniel and Marsilio Kirchoff are helping Prefect Mulcaster create powerful magicians. They're giving Vigil soldiers their own magic. It's the curse. I saw them destroy two people. I'm a spy for her—and I had to go there with a different soldier. Gennady. His name is Gennady. He hit me."

Casmir shook his head.

I could play the anamnesic pseudogram's recording for him, I realized; he could hear the meeting for himself, and there would be no way to doubt—

But the cube I'd grabbed without thinking was disposable, single-use, and pseudograms are design to prevent replication. I couldn't use a second cube to rerecord. I had to save its one playback for Velleia; if I returned to her empty-handed, I had no idea what her reaction would be. I couldn't risk it. I had nothing, no proof for Casmir.

"Believe me," I said, the last iota of my willpower dissolving. "You have to believe me. Please."

When Casmir spoke again, after a long silence, it was with guarded caution. "All right. I'll ask Tenniel and Kirchoff about this in the morning," he said. "We'll get to the bottom of it. For now, I want you to go to sleep."

I stood with a gasp. Of course. Of course I hadn't realized that if I *told* him, he was bound to investigate. "Oh, you can't. You can't. Casmir, you can't. It'll kill me. They'll kill me."

He shook his head, caught off guard. "Don't you want me to check?"

I took him by the shoulders. "If you mention this to them, I'll die—I'm sorry," I said. "I'm sorry. I take it back—I was lying."

He only stared.

I offered him a sickly smile, my head pounding. I could hear an odd rushing sound, like an underground river. "Just a lie. Just a joke. Don't ask them."

Neither of us breathed for a moment. When the tension broke, he grabbed my arm.

"I won't ignore this any longer," he said. "Come on. We're going to see Malise."

"It's the middle of the night," I said. "We can't go to her house."

"We can, and we will." Carefully, he guided me out of the atelier and to my bedroom to get my coat and a scarf. I'd forgotten the cold outside, but he hadn't.

"No," I said. "No. Let go of me."

"I'm your keeper," he told me. His tone brooked no argument. I'd forgotten the fundamental privilege a keeper holds over their charge: they don't have to listen. If I didn't come with him, he would drag me.

"Casmir," I said, bewildered, as he dressed me for the cold and snuffed the lanterns. "It isn't my fault."

I would have done anything, in that moment, to kill the daimon, to wipe its shadow from my name. But it lived with me all the same, coiled in my skull, threaded between my ribs. I was reduced to the perfect akratic, and it was laughing.

~

Malise lived in Deme Palenne like me, near the Chirurgeonate. It was too late to hail a caleche for a ride to her house. Casmir and I walked the whole way there, nearly thirty minutes. I protested for the first ten minutes or so—*it's too long a walk, I was only joking, I don't want to wake her up, I don't need her.* He barely answered me at all, except to tell me that I was making a scene.

That quieted me. It didn't matter that there was no one around; I was tired of being a scene.

I covered my face while he rang the doorbell. Awkwardly, he squeezed my shoulder. Comfort had never been his forte.

Malise answered eventually, her hair in wild disarray, squinting into the night with immediate alarm. "What? What is it?" There was fear in her voice. I flinched.

Casmir pushed me forward, and I nearly snapped at him, exhausted with being manhandled.

"He needs a solarium," Casmir said tightly. "He hasn't stopped hallucinating. He's delusional—and he was out all night, and he came back bruised. Someone hit him. I don't know what he's been doing, but—"

"I can still *talk*," I hissed. "Let me speak for myself."

With her hands in her hair, Malise led us into her house. It was small and cozy, naturally decorated with blue. Like her office, it smelled of cinnamon. Along with her books, she filled her shelves with medical oddities in jars and anatomical models, surely a ghastly sight to any stranger.

She had ambric lights as well, and they flickered furiously as I stepped inside. I suffocated my magic until the flickering stopped. If I shattered her lights too, I'd die of shame.

Casmir sat me down in her living room, and Malise came to settle next to me while he paced back and forth.

"May I touch you?" she said, suppressing a tremor in her voice.

To be *asked* was a relief beyond words. I nodded gratefully.

She checked Gennady's damage with far more gentleness than Casmir. "Who gave this to you?"

"I can't explain it again," I said.

She bit her lip. "May I heal it?"

Another nod.

Her magic, cool and liquid, spread across my skin for a moment and sank in. I felt some of the splitting inside my mouth close; the ache eased. I'd still have a bruise, but it was far shallower.

"Thank you," I said quietly.

"Tell her what you told me," Casmir demanded. The daimon whispered to me: if I could only convince them that I was all right, they'd let me slip away from them for a moment, and I could find a way to finally get some rest.

"I'd rather not," I said.

"Then I will," he said, and drew a breath to continue.

It was too much. "Casmir!" I cried. "Shut up!"

"You are *so* stubborn," he said, furious and distraught all at the same time. "I'm trying to help you."

"Casmir," Malise said.

He looked at her, one hand raised in disbelief. "What?"

"Why don't you go sit in the kitchen for a minute?" she said.

"No," he said, lifting his chin.

"You're in my house," she said heavily, smoothing her hair down. "Go."

He mouthed a swear and stalked off.

They'd never really liked each other. They got along well enough, and they both had the sense to respect the other, but they'd never enjoyed each other's company. Their main connection—me—was fraying, and I could see the results.

I was shaking, I realized. Nerves and pure frustration. I pressed my hands together to try to stop it. "I'm sorry," I said. "It's late. I didn't want to come. I told him we shouldn't."

She smiled painfully. "No. I'm glad you're here."

"It's not as bad as he's making it out to be," I said.

She didn't answer that. "May I hug you?"

You're an adult, I told myself with grim disapproval. *Act like it.* Then I clung to her.

Patiently, without judgment, she said, "Tell me about it, my dear."

Once I could bring myself to let go, I sat back and kept myself absolutely still. "I'm not psychotic," I said. Every word took more effort than I thought I had in me. "I'm having an episode. But I'm not delusional. I'm not hallucinating." I held her doubtful gaze. "How many more times do I have to say it?"

She moved as if to reach for my hand, but stopped herself. "Who hit you?"

I told her exactly what I'd told Casmir, word for word, albeit much more slowly. I needed to sound deliberate.

The room had grown terribly cold; frost crept on Malise's windows. Her magic was responding to her distress. "Kirchoff and Tenniel?" she asked.

My old stutter weighed on my tongue, threatening me. "Yes," I said carefully, "but if you ask them, they'll know I was spying, and Kirchoff will drown me, or Tenniel will suffocate me."

"The Clementia Prefects," she said.

"Yes."

She didn't believe me. I could see it. "All right," she said.

"Please," I whispered. "Please, please, would you please—?"

Wonderfully, gloriously, I saw a spark. I had a chance of convincing her; she'd opened up for a moment. "The soldier," she said. "What's his name? Can I talk to him?"

Gennady could easily confirm what I was saying. He could prove I was—

Not sane. I'd never be able to lay claim to that. Functional, then.

"Gennady Richter," I said immediately. "He guards the hall of St. Osiander every day. I can introduce you in the morning, if you're willing. If you meet me there at eight thirty tomorrow."

"I'm willing." She sighed, still skeptical, but I could work with that. She was finally considering that I might have proof, and it was enough for me.

"Saints," I said, in sheer relief. Then, more fiercely, "Thank you."

"I still have to treat you," she said. "Even if you may be lucid, you still need a little help."

"Help?"

As ever, she wasn't willing to mince words to spare my ego. She would be kind, but always honest. "You're losing control," she said, nodding at my shaking hands. "If I sedate you at least until the morning, you should be able to get some rest."

I felt a last flutter of willpower protest and then leave me. I'd be able to calm down by myself, given some time and space. I didn't need her to numb me. I didn't need it, but I *wanted* it. I wanted the easy way out. "All right," I said.

She brushed my hair back before putting her hands on my head. I managed to hold back a flinch, remembering Kirchoff and Tenniel's eagerness, remembering the way the Vigil soldier and Kirchoff's quadriviate had slumped off their chairs.

Her magic poured in, chilling me, numbing me.

I sighed in relief—and then she stopped. It was barely anything, only the slightest film around my mind. The thinnest protection. "Wait," I said, more plaintively than I intended. "That isn't enough."

She fixed me with a stern look. "It is," she said. "I know my work. That should hold you over until the morning."

I didn't want to sleep. I wanted oblivion. When I met her gaze, though, I knew without a doubt that she wouldn't be so reckless.

"Thank you," I said.

She squeezed my hand in response. I could breathe, at least; the thought of facing Casmir again didn't send me spiraling any further.

You may be frustrated, at this juncture, with my fragility. Believe me, you aren't as frustrated as I was. Keep that in mind.

The tiny seed of cold Malise had planted spread gradually as I surrendered to it, trying to calm down. Trying to forget the warehouse, forget the daimon, forget Casmir's glare. In time, I was breathing evenly, the pounding in my head reduced to a low thrum.

You're the only thing that keeps me grounded, I wanted to tell her. *You're my daimon's greatest fear.* But I bit back the words. Placing that kind of responsibility on her shoulders seemed like poor thanks for the gifts she gave me. Instead, I said, "I love you."

She straightened my glasses for me tenderly, her unspoken reply. "Should we call Casmir in again?" she asked.

"Are you going to tell him you'll take me to a solarium?"

"No," she said. It was not without some regret. "Not until I see whatever you show me tomorrow morning. He's going to need to watch you closely, but as long as you avoid getting into any other fights, I won't advise it."

The sooner we convinced him that I was fit to go home, the sooner I could leave Malise to her well-deserved rest. "All right," I said.

She looked toward the kitchen, where Casmir was pacing and muttering under his breath, gesturing into the air. "Shall I, or will you?"

If I was going to demand not to be spoken for, I might as well be consistent. "I will," I said, and got up to slink into the kitchen.

Casmir was waiting by the sink with his arms crossed, watching me like a hawk. "What did she say?"

"No solarium," I murmured.

I expected him to argue, to be angry. Instead, he slumped with relief. He and Malise may not have liked each other much, but he respected her professional opinion. I thought about telling him that she was willing to believe me, that I was going to prove it to her, but I didn't have the energy to reenter that debate.

"She treated you?" he said.

I gave him a bare nod.

Now that our initial anger and distress had faded, we were left with a quiet, burning embarrassment. He coughed and stepped toward me. "And how are you feeling?"

The dread of what on earth I was going to say to Tessaly Velleia reared its head. How *exactly* was I going to get out of attending another meeting in that warehouse? "Well enough," I said.

He sighed. "You know I brought you here because I care about you."

"Yes, keeper," I said, knowing that he was telling the truth and not caring.

"I'm not your *master*," he said, indignant. "And I don't act like it."

Casmir's command had been the only thing standing between me and permanent ruination more than a few times. I swallowed my pride and looked away. "I'm sorry. I'd like to go home. We should let Malise sleep."

He went back into the living room and turned to Malise. I tensed, waiting to interrupt if he said anything biting, but he only bowed slightly. "Thanks for your help."

She smiled, and if it was somewhat thin, it was still genuine. "You made the right decision."

Casmir left to wait for me by the door.

"Will I see you in the morning?" I asked her.

"Outside the hall of St. Osiander," she said. Indulging me, always indulging me.

"I'll bring you something to eat," I promised. "And some coffee." I would have preferred to cook or bake for her, but for now that would need to suffice.

"Black," she said firmly.

Finally, I smiled back. Loath to keep her any longer, I bowed goodbye and hurried out.

Without the urgency, the walk back home was grueling; exhaustion dragged at every step. Casmir stayed close to my side, and I let him, feeling our familiar pattern beginning to settle back in. No matter what happened, after it blew over, we would always find ourselves in the same place—friends, but painfully, and no more.

I started to get ready for bed as soon as we stepped through the front door. That, at least, I didn't have to ask Casmir's permission for. I wasn't going to be getting much sleep, but I could pretend. At a loss, he watched me drift through the house. I left the lanterns on; I wasn't going to leave him in the dark if he wanted to stay up.

"Adrien," he said, before I could go into my room.

My heart betrayed me, and I hoped he might ask me to stay with him. I knew he wouldn't, but I hoped.

"Wake me up if you get worse," he said.

That was close enough.

"Thank you," I said, and retreated. In my room, I found the bag sitting on my bed; I took out the anamnesic pseudogram and the kitchen knife and turned them over and over. They were cold, certain, ruthless in my hands. The pseudogram and its single playback couldn't leave my sight until I delivered it to Prefect Velleia.

For a moment, the shadow of a thought occurred: I could turn the knife on myself. Not fatally, just enough to relieve some pressure. I let the urge pass me by and float away unanswered. The relief would be sweet, but I could go without it for now.

The knife and the cube went back in the bag, with Kirchoff and Velleia in mind respectively.

It was only thanks to Malise that I was able to fall asleep at all. I woke often, as I was accustomed to, but any measure of rest was better than nothing. A little time in the dark was worth something.

I dragged myself up early to run and get Malise her breakfast; I hurried to the Pharmakeia nursing a desperate hope. I'd introduce her to Gennady, and no matter if he was still angry with me, he wouldn't deny everything I said. I'd finally be believed.

Imagine, then, my chagrin when I discovered him missing.

Chapter 12

I met Malise in front of the lecture hall at eight thirty, as agreed. She was the only one. When I noticed that Gennady wasn't there, the ground began to crumble beneath me. Of *course*.

Malise received me with raised eyebrows; wordlessly, I gave her the coffee and pastry I'd brought and opened the door to the hall, looking into the room to see if Gennady had gone inside for some reason. He hadn't. My first class didn't start for half an hour; there were no students inside, either.

"So," Malise said.

"He guards this room every single day," I said blankly. "All day. This is the first time he's been gone."

I could see her making her decision. "Is there anyone else I can ask about this, Adrien?" she said, but it was nothing more than a formality.

Anyone else I could direct her to would put her in danger. To involve her any further than I already had would have been unforgivable.

"No," I said.

It might even be preferable for her to believe I was only losing my mind, I realized. In the daylight, I was beginning to suspect that I'd already been too selfish in telling her the truth. I should want her and Casmir as far away from the conspiracy as possible. I was going to have to accept her final decision that I was delusional, and there was nothing I could reasonably do about it—not unless Gennady made his appearance. He'd been angry enough that I might never see him at the Pharmakeia again.

"I'm so sorry," she said quietly, touching my arm. "If you happen to find him later, tell me."

"You don't have to pretend that you think I will," I said with a small laugh.

She sighed. "I don't, really. But just in case."

No use throwing a fit. I'd kept her up last night. I didn't have to ruin her whole morning. A deep breath steadied me; I lifted my chin. "No matter. I feel better today."

She shook her head, but she smiled. "I hoped you might."

It was best to be blunt. "So, am I going to a solarium?" Legally, I didn't need to submit to institutionalization against my will. I could refuse—and I would *have* to refuse, to fulfill my obligations to Prefect Velleia. Despite that, I wasn't accustomed to prolonged disagreements with Malise, and the thought of starting now was profoundly unattractive.

"Promise me you won't be getting any more bruises," she said.

"I promise."

"Then not yet," she said, but she looked much, much older. "Please don't make me regret it."

There was a very long pause while I thanked every single star I knew.

"Thank you. Enjoy your drink," I said. "It's fancy. It cost six dyads."

"You shouldn't have," she said primly, taking a sip, and checked her watch.

"I'm sorry for the scare," I said, aware that it wasn't only my own morning that had been wasted. "I know you have to get to work."

She sniffed. "I'm your doctor. I'm your friend."

I wasn't sure that entitled me to quite so much of her time, but I nodded. "I'll see you at five," I said, resigned, and went into the classroom to set up my lesson early.

If any of my students had questions about the faint, lingering bruise I still had, they didn't ask. I tried not to make myself look overly approachable. Usually, my effort was in the opposite direction, but I was tired of lying. The lesson went in near silence, except for my unenthusiastic lecture.

～

After class, I looked for Gennady. He wasn't outside the hall. He wasn't in any of the other halls; he wasn't near my office. He wasn't in the Pharmakeia's library, although I have no idea why I checked there. He wasn't anywhere in the whole academy—I even asked the other Vigil officers whether they'd seen him. They hadn't. They weren't from his commissariat; they barely knew who he was. I saw Kirchoff in the halls as I searched, and I refused to look at him. If anything, it would have been *more* suspicious if I suddenly pretended to have any interest in him.

I told myself that Gennady missing a single day of work was no cause for alarm. If he wanted to take a break after the night we'd had, who could blame him? Intuition told me I was wrong, but I'd never been in the habit of trusting my own instincts. He *could* be lying dead somewhere in Deme Aufford, but it wasn't likely.

Surely.

The day passed at an excruciating pace, until the light had begun to turn golden. Before I visited Malise, I went to the Chirurgeonate early to check up on the newest victims of the curse—and Rosabelle.

The Chirurgeonate's halls seemed to shrink around me as I found which rooms the new patients had been taken to and made my rounds. The Vigil soldier and Kirchoff's first quadriviate were already in the advanced stages of the curse: seizing, vomiting plasma. They weren't awake as Blanche had been, toward the end. She'd been an anomaly. Either way, it seemed Kirchoff and Tenniel were refining their technique after all. They were streamlining the process.

I braced myself to see Rosabelle. There was a Vigil guard posted outside her door; I sent him away with an impatient bark: "Go be useful somewhere! I need an hour with my subject." My feigned authority worked, to my surprise—or possibly this soldier was overdue for a lunch break.

Once the guard and his rache were gone, I paused to think of what I was going to say to Rosabelle and kept the script fixed in my mind. She would view me as the person who'd nearly destroyed her, and I needed to make my visit accordingly quick.

When I knocked, her reply was tremulous. "Come in?"

I walked in, already tense with inexpressible apology. She drew the covers up to her chest and looked away from me.

"I don't think it worked," she whispered. "I don't feel any different." She covered her eyes for a moment. "I'm sorry if I interfered with the process somehow."

Of course Kirchoff had picked *this* girl to ruin. "No other ill effects?" I asked.

She shook her head. "The others," she said. "They weren't as lucky. Professor Kirchoff told me. I'm not to talk about anything to any of the healers. But I have to stay here for observation."

"He's been to see you?" I said.

"He and one of those Vigil captains."

I took a deep breath. "I think you should go somewhere Kirchoff can't find you," I said. "I think you should leave here—you're not sick; I just put you to sleep—and hide away from him. Away from anyone else who was in that warehouse."

She shook her head, mouth half-open, ashen.

I took a moment to gauge just how loyal she might be to Kirchoff. He was famous for making his quadriviates into nervous wrecks, but she'd been willing to follow where he led. "He doesn't have your best interests in mind," I said cautiously.

She said nothing, but I understood her look: *I know.*

"May I ask what he did to convince you to submit to the process?" I couldn't imagine why a person like her would take that risk, no matter how dedicated they might be to their mentor.

She only shook her head again.

"Threats? Promises?"

No response. Both, I had to assume.

So I said, "I can only save you from them once."

Her knuckles were white, her grip on the sheets as tight as she could make it.

"You'll end up dead if you don't leave," I said, suddenly breathless; her terror was infectious. "Get yourself somewhere he can't find you. Do you have a way to do that?"

"I have family in the provinces. Close by."

"Be quick," I said.

She mouthed, *I will.*

With that, I left. I wanted to give her more, try something else to assure her safety, but any further association with me might be dangerous for both of us. If she left the city swiftly enough, she'd be all right, and the question of her disappearance could be dealt with in good time. There'd be no way to definitively prove I'd had anything to do with it.

I could tell Malise and Casmir to ask Rosabelle about everything before she was gone, I realized. That would work perfectly well as proof. Then I imagined Kirchoff and Tenniel learning that Rosabelle had disappeared shortly after speaking with them, and the option vanished.

～

I waited for another two days to see if Gennady would show up, wondering when Prefect Velleia was going to summon us again. Casmir watched me closely, meanwhile, worried and overbearing. Eventually, it was time to acknowledge the real possibility that Gennady wasn't just sulking. If he was, I'd leave him to it, but I was going to have to *check*.

After asking each and every one of the Vigil soldiers I saw at the Pharmakeia if they knew which commissariat Gennady served out of, one was able to tell me that he was with the Deme Nymphes commissariat. With reluctance, I made a trip there.

For an outsider to go to a Vigil commissariat is rare. There's really no reason to; the Vigil exists to keep the populace in its place, never to lift it up. No one pretends otherwise. Appropriately, my visit was an uncomfortable one.

I was stopped at the front doors, to my great relief. I had no desire to be let inside; being in a confined space with so many raches sounded like a nightmare.

"What do you want?" one of the guards asked.

I'd recited my question a dozen times. I had it ready. "Has Gennady Richter been to work within the last three days?"

The two guards looked at each other, and then back at me. "No," the first said. "Why? Do you know where he is?"

I wouldn't be asking if I knew, I thought, and fought desperately not to say it. If I angered them, they might decide to interrogate me, and I really couldn't have that. "I don't. I've been looking for him."

"What do you want with him?"

"I have a message for him from Prefect Velleia," I said, not *too* far from the truth. I needed to know where he was before we could report back to Velleia.

The effect was immediate; I found myself marveling at the power of a name. No one was willing to obstruct the Prefects. No one was willing to even question me. "Fine, then," the guard said. "Who should we leave a message with if he shows up?"

"Desfourneaux at the Pharmakeia," I said, and hurried away.

So Gennady was missing. I reflected on that, queasy and guilty, as I began the walk back to Deme Palenne. He hadn't struck me as the sort of person to have much to his life apart from work—I could recognize the type very well.

Except—

Was that true? *Did* he really have nothing else in his life? I remembered what he'd told me on the day he'd broken into my house. *My sister Mariya is a mekhanic for the witchfinders.*

I swore viciously as I turned and set my course for Deme Alidor instead, where the witchfinder Watchtower loomed. I'd need to take a caleche—I was going to have to ask Casmir to give me access to more money for the fares that were beginning to add up.

～

The trip took a long time, but not nearly long enough. My feelings on the witchfinders have been made abundantly clear; I'll restrain myself from repeating them. All I'll say is that I was tense and miserable as the caleche finally approached the complex's massive gates and I let myself out.

The Watchtower is the seat of all important witchfinder business, home to their various offices and management. The architecture is jagged and unwelcoming, flat stone broken up by tall, thin spires. It's a sprawling campus—and in the past year, it had been subject to a terrible attack. A group of witches, tired of being hunted, had caused an explosion. The casualties had not been inconsequential, and the reconstruction around the huge crater wasn't quite complete.

Other evidence of the attack was less physical, but just as clear. The witchfinders were vigilant about who walked through the complex's gates. They'd slipped once, and after what it had cost, they were determined never to slip again. As I walked up, two witchfinders fell upon me immediately. Partners, obviously, a tall man with a sharp nose and a nervous-looking brunette woman.

"Identification," the man barked.

It's said that some witchfinders can sense magic—whether through their mekhania eyes or through some warped sixth sense, no one besides them is really sure. They keep their trade secrets away from the public. Whatever it was, these two could clearly sense the talent in me. I was a magician, and I was subject to the appropriate treatment.

When I hesitated, they both drew close, their mekhania eyes whirling.

"Adrien Desfourneaux. I'm a professor with the Pharmakeia," I said tightly.

Anyone who looked at me would come to that conclusion. From my clothes, I could have been an attorney or a clerk—but as a magician, there was one main possibility. They accepted my answer.

"Business?"

I took a deep breath. "Is Mariya Richter here?"

There was a brief pause. They looked at each other, exchanging one of the witchfinders' patented glances, unreadable to any outsider. "The mekhanic?"

"The mekhanic," I agreed.

"Why the hell would anyone want anything to do with *her*?" the taller witchfinder asked, his nose wrinkled. Evidently, Mariya had something in common with her brother: a gift for frustration and the will to use it.

"I need to talk to her about her brother," I said. "I didn't know where else to ask after her."

"If you'll accept supervision, you can come in and ask her yourself," the woman said, begrudgingly. As an affiliate of the Pharmakeia, I posed no threat by witchcraft, but that didn't mean they had to approve of my presence.

I nodded my acceptance, and they shepherded me inside, muttering sourly to each other all the way.

The inside of the Watchtower wasn't quite as I'd imagined it. My whole life, without ever having set foot near it, I'd pictured it as a place of horrors, full of captured witches and sinister hunters with their cruel metal eyes, watching over the city like beasts of prey. What I got, instead, was a place of business.

Aside from the damage from the explosion, the offices were laid out neatly across the complex. Witchfinders streamed in and out of buildings at a methodical pace, moving from one assignment to the next, going about their hunts with casual efficiency. They were killers, but there was paperwork to be done. There were reports to file. I found myself almost more uneasy with the reality than with what I'd been imagining.

My guards took me on a circuitous route around the mostly filled crater to a larger office with more traffic than most. "Mekhania office," the woman said briefly, and waited for me to go inside, watching me with undisguised vigilance. I couldn't quite blame her; the witchfinders depend on their mekhania to a great degree. If something were to happen to their production center or their mekhanics, the Watchtower would suffer.

The office was clean and sparse; there were three rooms, from what I could see—one with a front desk, a storeroom full of mekhania parts, and a workshop. The witchfinders took me past the woman at the front desk and into the workshop, a claustrophobic space full of tables piled with mekhania parts that smelled of oil and metal. I felt, paradoxically, somewhat at home.

A teenage girl turned to greet us. Immediately, I could see Gennady's features in her—sharp cheekbones, bronze skin, and narrow, deeply hostile eyes. She had no mekhania; she was a technician, not a witchfinder.

"What the hell do you want?" she asked, just in case I'd been nursing any lingering doubts about their family relation.

"I think your brother is missing," I said, keenly aware of the witchfinders at my back. There was no use wasting time on polite introductions. "Gennady. He hasn't been seen for three days."

That got her to blink. She came close, staring at me, inspecting me. "And who are you?" Her inflection was close enough to Gennady's that I was a little perturbed; it was as if she was copying him.

"I'm a professor with the Pharmakeia," I said, tired of introducing myself. "Adrien Desfourneaux. I know him because he's been guarding the Pharmakeia, and—"

"Oh, the curse thing," she said blithely. "He's been telling me all about it."

I looked back to the witchfinders behind me in time to see them raise their eyebrows at each other.

"Get out of here," Mariya told them, as if she had full authority to do so. "Go on. Get."

"Little miss," the woman began, and Mariya hissed at her like an angry cat, breaking into a sudden fury.

"Leave us alone, or I'll put spikes in your next lens," she said.

The woman's partner tried again. "Any information about the comatose curse—"

"You won't find out anything you don't already know," Mariya said scornfully, jabbing a finger toward the door. "*Get.*"

The witchfinders got. For the very first time, I felt something approaching sympathy for them, especially when Mariya wheeled on me instead.

"So," she said, and sat down at a table with a box full of cracked mekhania eyes to sift through them, looking for one to fix. "Gennady's missing. You figure he got himself killed?"

The words were empty. She didn't sound as though she cared.

"I hope not," I said, at a loss. "I thought you might know where he is."

"What," she said, "just because I'm his sister?"

I took a good, long time to choose my words. "You were the only person I knew of, apart from other Vigil officers, who might have any idea. He mentioned you once. That's all. If you don't know where he is—"

"If you find him, tell him to stay gone," she said.

I knew I shouldn't ask, that it would only embroil me further in whatever trouble was between them—and I could tell that wasn't a place I wanted to be. Unfortunately, curiosity has always been a vice of mine. "What exactly is your problem with him?" I asked.

She bared her teeth at me. "Murderer," she said. "He's a murderer. Ask him about it."

I couldn't bother to feign surprise. Many Vigil officers are, and Gennady didn't seem likely to be an exception. What did interest me was that a witchfinder mekhanic might have such a strong distaste for killing. What did she think her lenses were being used for? "I can't ask him about it," I said patiently. "He's *missing.*"

She dug a screwdriver into a mekhania eye with gusto, cracking it apart, and began to dig around inside with a horrible grinding sound. "You check his commissariat?"

Quickly, I drew a breath to assure her that I *had*, in fact, because I wasn't stupid. Just as quickly, she waved a hand to cut me off. "Check the Penumbra," she said. "He likes to haunt that place whenever he's upset. Reminds him of when we were kids."

"The prison," I said cautiously. The Penumbra in Deme Eudora is the city's largest prison, a huge, sprawling mass of misery, complete with its own demi-lune. I wasn't sure what reason two children would have to become so familiar with it, but none of the possibilities were good.

"Yeah," she said. "There. He loves it. Freak." She clenched the screwdriver between her teeth as she held the lens up before her eyes, speaking around it in a low growl. "I bet he's *not* missing. I bet he's just sulking there, and he hasn't bothered to tell anyone where he's spending his time. He's just skipping out on work."

She shook a few loose gears out of the eye and looked back up at me, removing the screwdriver. "Bet you a corune."

I tried not to hope too strongly. "Maybe. If he is, do you want me to—?"

"Tell me?" she interjected. "No. He can come see me himself if he thinks I'll care."

I began to miss Gennady in earnest. "Thank you," I said.

She bent over the eye and fished a small, round piece of glass out of a box on the table, a pair of tweezers in her other hand. "Is that it?"

"That's it." I turned to make my retreat before she could demand it.

"Don't come back here asking about Gennady again," she called after me. "I don't care!"

My witchfinder guards were still there, waiting sullenly outside the room; I saw a flash of reluctant sympathy in their faces. Quickly, I closed the door. "She's a handful," the man said, as discreetly as he could.

"About the curse," his partner said, less willing to indulge in smalltalk. "What was she talking about?"

"You already know someone from the Pharmakeia is involved," I said, wishing either Richter was capable of even a modicum of subtlety. "That's all she meant. I have to assume she learned it from the gossip *here*. Her brother was investigating the same issue."

"Witchfinders do gossip," the man agreed, somewhat ruefully, trying to decide if I was worth questioning any further.

I tried my best to look useless. It came easily.

"Time for you to go," he said. Without any more delay, he and his partner escorted me out of the Watchtower, and I could breathe again. I ran the last few steps out the gates.

I wanted to go *home*; the city felt unfriendly. I was exhausted—with the day, with all of it. The only thing that held any real interest for me was going home and sleeping.

Except I knew I needed to visit the Penumbra for the sake of my sanity. I owed it to Gennady to look for him in earnest. I hailed yet another caleche and tried not to drift off inside while it took me to Deme Eudora.

Chapter 13

Not unlike the Watchtower, the Penumbra is a dreadful place. Unlike the Watchtower, it feels old, a stone palace rotted by time and terror. It used to be a basilike, home to the Basilissae—but the empresses and their twin thrones abandoned it long ago. Now it's a gargantuan tumor on the city; it lies at the center of Deme Eudora, gray and uncompromisingly functional. I'd never had a reason to visit it, and I was far from happy to change that.

I wandered through a gathering of the stray cats that make the Penumbra their home as they sunned themselves and put a hand out to one, seeing if it would let me near. It got up to amble a few steps away and settled down again.

It was difficult not to think of the poor souls trapped inside the prison. I had to wonder how many of them were slated for capital punishment—what must the promise of the demi-lune or the gallows be like? But I set my mind to the goal at hand and kept an eye out for any undersized raches like Lady.

The large dirt yard was populated mostly by Vigil, with the occasional nervous citizen interacting with them, asking after incarcerated family or friends. The entire place had a claustrophobic, anxious energy, as if something horrible was waiting to happen.

Mariya was right. I found Gennady safe and sound, surrounded by old unitmates, outside the northernmost set of gates. It wasn't difficult to spot him—I looked around, and there he was, sulking against a wall. Beside him, Lady played in the dirt with another rache. All my worry melted away until I was merely very irritated.

Then I remembered what I'd said to him after we'd escaped the warehouse, and I covered my face. If nothing else, I was going to need to make sure he was willing to testify in front of Velleia with me, and I was going to need to apologize.

Before I could question if it was a good idea to approach, given that he was surrounded by other soldiers, I was walking up to him. When he saw me, he pushed aside the two men he was talking to and strode toward me, face already twisted in distaste.

"Not you again," he snarled. "What the hell are you doing here?"

I put my hands up. "I thought you might have been missing," I said, feeling more stupid for it by the second. "I thought maybe you'd been caught and killed. So I—"

"Stalked me here," he said. Lady gave an accusatory yelp.

He wasn't *wrong*, I realized with deep distress. I'd gone so far as to ask his sister. All because he hadn't come to work for a few days.

I took a breath, held it, and released it slowly. "I'm sorry for what I said," I recited. "It was unacceptable." Again. I'd already had this conversation with him. We barely knew each other, and I'd already been cruel to him more than once.

He froze; he had no idea how to react. I let him take his time processing what I'd said. Eventually, he rolled his eyes. "Whatever," he said. "So you found someone to heal up your face?"

I didn't answer the question. If that was as much of a reaction as he could muster, I wasn't going to push it.

"Additionally, since you aren't dead," I said, as his friends snickered around us, "I thought I'd ask you if you're ready to go to Velleia about what we found." I had to assume there was no use being furtive with the other soldiers around. Gennady had almost certainly told them by now, given the way they were looking at me.

He glanced away, wincing. Apparently, even he had some concept of responsibility—or at the very least, he feared the displeasure of his Prefect. "I don't know."

"I don't think we should wait until she calls us," I said tentatively. "That might incur some anger. It's been a while already."

Above all else, I did not want to her to send someone to come *get* us. Being dragged before her would be hard to stomach, and possibly hard to survive.

Lady lay down in the Penumbra's dirt and whined. Gennady looked around at his small group of peers.

"I don't know, Genya," a woman said. "If you want to get Captain, you ought to go to the Prefect sooner than later."

So Gennady wasn't the only soldier from his old unit who wanted Corvier to answer for what he'd done. I wondered just how many of them felt *otherwise*. How many old friends was Gennady going to have to face down eventually?

He sighed heavily, concealing genuine nerves, and deigned to nod. "Tomorrow, I guess. Does seven in the evening work?"

"Seven works," I said, hasty with relief.

"Now go away," he said, ever so slightly cheered by the opportunity for further rudeness. Then I saw a spark—he was recalling something, remembering some kind of abstract lesson. Alexarchus, maybe. "Please," he added.

I felt the slightest hint of an educator's pride. He was learning, no matter how reluctantly. No matter how sporadically or unreliably, no matter if it was in *spite* of my influence.

"I'm glad you're all right," I said, and turned to leave the Penumbra as quickly as possible, kicking up cloud of dirt. I caught the briefest glimpse of his expression as I fled: total perplexity.

～

So I prepared to meet Velleia again, a process that consisted mostly of creating and repeating various soothing mantras to myself. Keeping my secrets from Casmir in the meantime had become more and more difficult. I hated to lie to him—I'd never been any good at it. He was my keeper, and he could see right through me. He knew that *something* was wrong, that I was keeping something from him, but he couldn't figure out what. It was driving him crazy.

He'd been badgering me night and day—I was worried that he might resort to following me, and I'd already made the hard decision to let him maintain his ignorance. "What are you hiding?" he would say, and I would insist that it was nothing, and he'd stare at me with his wounded hawk's gaze, and all the while, the guilt grew stronger. Inviting him along to see Velleia would be satisfying for an instant, but disaster would surely follow. When I set out for Deme Aufford to meet with the Prefect, I did my utmost to make sure he wasn't going to know where I was.

～

The Vigil administrative office was, if anything, even more austere and threatening than it had been the first time. The dark wood seemed ready to open and swallow me whole. Gennady was punctual, at least; he met me outside right on time. We walked inside together in a strained, uncomfortable silence. I felt the anamnesic pseudogram burning a hole through my bag, and I felt the kitchen knife waiting.

This time, we didn't have a scheduled audience. We had no guarantee that she would be ready to receive visitors—in fact, there was no guarantee she'd be around at all. Unfortunately, there were no other sure ways of determining a Prefect's whereabouts. An educated guess was the best we could hope for.

Luck was on our side, at least in the minute details. She was in, a passing soldier told us, and she was free. "If you think you're important enough, go on in," he said, with the obvious implication that we would regret it dearly if we misjudged our worth.

"We'll be all right," I told Gennady. I couldn't know what spectacular failure of self-control might await us, but I could try to head it off. "All we have to do is be calm, and we'll be fine."

"I know," he snapped, and that was that. We made our way into the audience chamber, already poised for contrition.

She was, unreassuringly enough, polishing her executioner's sword when we walked inside. Amphion hulked near her feet. She took her time before looking up at us; when her gaze landed, it was cool and thoughtful.

"Finally," she said. "I'd almost decided to summon you myself."

"Our apologies for taking so long," I said softly.

She cupped her ear impatiently. "What was that?"

I repeated myself, and she sat back, satisfied. The point of her sword dipped toward the ground.

"We did what you wanted," Gennady said.

"That remains to be seen," she said. "Tell me what you found."

I retrieved the anamnesic pseudogram from my bag and realized that I was going to need to approach her to give it up. It was much easier thought than done. "I recorded the meeting," I said, to buy myself some time.

It wasn't *much* time. Immediately, she beckoned me forward. "Good. Bring it here."

I took a deep breath and forced myself to walk to her desk, past Amphion. He raised his massive white head as I went by, and I bit my tongue hard before dropping the pseudogram into Velleia's palm.

"It's a long recording," I said weakly. "It covers the entire process. The Pharmakeia professors intend to create a new breed of more powerful magicians, and the Vigil conspirators want to give their soldiers magic." She stared at me, waiting. I continued. "They're working together for the sake of convenience. They intend the alliance to end as soon as they both achieve their goals."

She was silent with fury for some time, her jaw tight. When she finally spoke again, it was with measured contempt. I didn't envy Mulcaster and his supporters. "A risky play."

Gennady coughed. "So, do we have to do anything else?"

Her head snapped up; she looked at him in disbelief. "What was that, soldier?"

He crossed his arms and looked away. Beside him, Lady lay down on the floor. "I just wanted to know if we should do anything else," he mumbled. Hurriedly, I made my way back to his side.

"You should be happy for the chance to do anything to rectify this situation," Velleia said. "This is no small matter. This concerns the Vigil's very soul. You should be *eager* to do more."

He was silent.

She smiled. "Or don't you want your captain dead?"

He nodded at her, but there was a hesitation. He might want Corvier to fall, but it didn't make him happy. That was going to come back to haunt him later, I had to assume. "Yes, Prefect," he said. "The others want Captain dead too."

"The others," she repeated thoughtfully.

"From my old unit," Gennady said. "The ones who aren't going along with him." The pain in his voice was unmistakable. Vigil value solidarity above all else. To have his first unit—his family?—split must burn him.

I saw that Velleia was about to ask him to bring them into her service. Just before she could speak, he said, "I'll bring them. They'll help."

Slowly, sharply, she smiled. "They'll be willing to take the same risks as you?"

He didn't hesitate for an instant—not a moment's thought for the possibility that his friends might not appreciate being offered for sacrifice. "I know they will."

"No need to bring them directly to me," she said. "Just use them in your endeavors as you see fit. Make it clear to them that they're on orders from me, now."

He nodded.

In turn, Velleia looked at me. I wondered if she could see what I was thinking and hoped, for the sake of my survival, that she couldn't. "Do you have any similar offerings?" she asked. "It will be good for you if you do."

It will be good for you. Was that a euphemism? A threat? I wondered if she'd kill me if I didn't volunteer anyone. In the end, it didn't make much of a difference to me. My decision was the same. "No," I said, as calmly as I could manage.

She shook her head with exaggerated disappointment. "Maybe later."

"Maybe," I lied.

"In answer to your question," she said to Gennady, "yes, there's more for you to do. You'll attend another meeting and report again on your findings."

What else could she possibly want to know? "I'm not sure we'll find much else," I said, between gritted teeth. "In fact, we run a greater risk of being exposed as your plants."

Amphion rumbled, and she murmured something calming to him, inaudible. "I want him dead to rights," she said to me. "Mulcaster. I want a mountain of proof, undeniable—I want evidence gathered over time. An ironclad case. I'll see him ousted, and I don't want anyone harboring any doubts about whether it was the right thing to do."

Politics. I'd seen institutional politics at the Pharmakeia, but even the bizarre grudges of academia couldn't hold a candle to the rivalries of Prefects. Even in the extremity of Mulcaster's transgression, there might still be Clementia other than his current faction who would take his side against Velleia. If he was going down, she needed to ensure that his coffin was air-proof. She needed to be the Clementia's righteous savior, not a scheming tyrant. The two Prefects of a Curia are meant to be as twins—twin swords, for the Clementia. Velleia and Mulcaster had, apparently, never taken note of that.

Neither Gennady nor I was going to get in the way. If she wanted us to go to another meeting, we were going. "I understand," I said.

Gennady nodded. "Okay."

"Make it quick," Velleia advised.

At my side, I made a fist, digging my nails into my palm. "May we go?"

"Dismissed," she said.

I made sure Gennady was following me before I left. His eyes were glazed over; he'd done his best, but it had taken its toll. Once we'd fled the building, I turned to him. "That wasn't so bad," I said firmly, with a confidence I didn't feel. "We know what we need to do, at least."

"I don't think she likes us very much," he said with vague disappointment. Lady whined in agreement. I wondered exactly how dwarfed she felt by Amphion.

"Probably not."

He looked so dejected that I had to say something else. "At least with your friends helping us, it should be easier."

He perked up. "They'll be glad to have something to do. They've been raring for it."

"If I may ask," I said.

"*Ugh*," he said, and readied a glare.

He hadn't delivered any threats, which I took as encouragement. "There are people from your old unit—your friends—who are going along with Mulcaster. What are you going to do about them?"

"They'll come around," he said, with more hope than conviction. "I know they will. Once Velleia takes down Mulcaster, they won't stick around. They'll see."

There was no value in telling him that I wasn't as optimistic. "I hope you're right," I said.

He turned to start walking, and I took it upon myself to go with him. He looked completely lost. I thought I'd try to at least make sure he knew where he was going.

"I probably have to go back to work, huh?" he said after a decent pause. He wasn't looking at me.

"Probably," I said. "Unless you want your superiors to take further notice."

He sucked a breath in through his teeth, unfathomably irritated. "That's where you'll find me, then. Whenever you figure out when the next meeting is."

I nodded, relieved. A while ago, I would have done anything to get him to stop showing up. Now, he seemed as much of a part of my lectures as any of the students. In a way, he *was* one of the students. It would explain the uncomfortable sense of obligation I felt toward him.

I've never had any real parental instincts; I've never wanted children. However, teaching at the Pharmakeia instills some measure of protectiveness in any lecturer with a heart. The youngest students are sixteen, some of them very far from home, and all of them newly frightened by their own power. They're all desperate to earn their license, to escape the threat of witchhood.

It would take a barren soul indeed to oversee the training of young magicians and feel nothing for them. Gennady was no teenage student, but he had the same air to him, the same fundamental lack of direction. He had the same fledgling hurt in his eyes. I couldn't help it. Now that I'd seen it, I was bound to take *some* interest in his future.

"You're acting weird," he said.

"Not unusual," I said, and resigned myself to reigniting his rage. "You should tell your sister that you're not missing, after all."

He stopped walking. "You talked to her? You talked to Masha?"

Mariya was *Masha* to him, and he was not *Genya* to her. I thought of her obvious disdain for him and winced. "I did, yes."

Lady circled him a few times until he resumed walking. There was no sudden explosion of frustration, no descent into name-calling. "She hates me," he said.

As ever, curiosity got the better of me. "She called you a murderer," I said, although I understood that I'd regret it.

"You don't want to know," he said.

It's difficult to overstate the degree to which I've never been able to leave well enough alone. "I've dedicated the majority of my career to the pursuit of knowing things," I said reasonably. "I think I do."

He didn't stop walking again, but he did look at me. It was a foreign look, an alien look, the gaze of a deep sea creature. A shiver wrenched my spine. "I had a brother once," he said. "Ivan. *Vanya*. There were three of us." His inflection had changed; his tone was something I'd never heard before. The usual acid had evaporated. There was only an expansive flatness.

I nodded.

"He was Mariya's favorite," he said. "Now there are two of us." That was it.

He let me consider that for a few moments, emotionless, watching me with his starving-dog eyes—then he smiled, and it all washed away. He was putting a mask back on, reassembling a great charade. "I'm going back to my commissariat now to report for duty again," he said. "You should go back to the Pharmakeia, or back to that pretty little house of yours, or wherever it is people like you go in your free time. I'll see you tomorrow."

A restless instinct seized me: the instinct to abandon him as a lost cause. A Vigil fratricide was not an ethically promising pupil.

I had my pride, however. It would have been bad pedagogy. "I'll see you tomorrow," I agreed, and we went our separate ways.

Chapter 14

When I went to Kirchoff's office the next day to find out when the next meeting might be, I made sure to remember the kitchen knife in my bag. If he was going to murder me, he probably wouldn't do it in the middle of the Pharmakeia, but I'd seen stranger decisions made in the past few days.

The musty smell in the room had not improved, and the one human skeleton standing in the corner had taken on an accusatory stare. As I spoke with Kirchoff, I entertained various fancies about how he might have gotten it. Taken from the Chirurgeonate? Stolen from one of the graves in the great Vesperide Gardens? An unlucky student, maybe?

We sat opposite each other over the worst-tasting cup of tea I'd ever had, something black and smoky and tepid. "I'm so glad you're keen," he said, examining me without any effort to conceal his evaluation. He was suspicious, but no more than was warranted of any new accomplice. I'd been convincing enough to escape immediate detection, even with Gennady's outburst. Perhaps, I reflected, *because* of Gennady's outburst.

"It's a fascinating undertaking," I said, trying to borrow a hint of Tenniel's lazy amusement. "Of course I'm interested in seeing the outcomes."

"I must commend you," he said. "You managed to leave poor Rosabelle intact, although the procedure failed. That's no small achievement."

He was testing me.

"I went to check up on her, actually," I said, in case he already knew that somehow. "She's quite timid, isn't she?"

"I poached her from Gailhardt," he said with a sniff. "Unfortunately, she seems to have taken after her mentor. I got to her too late. She's unsuited to thanatology, to tell you the truth."

"Well," I said. I could see Rosabelle's face clearly—her hurt, her fear. "It was only a first try."

He smiled. "Such is the march of progress."

"I'm eager to go again," I said, a fabulously impossible lie. "I have some ideas on how to improve."

He raised his eyebrows. "We'll be meeting again this Primidy," he said, watching the shapes bobbing in the tanks on the far wall. "In the same location, at the same hour. I'm hoping to have the Vigil comprise all of the test subjects this time."

"Why?"

His shrug was impatient. "As I said, I'm running out of quadriviates."

I've always wished I could advise more quadriviates; it's one of the more rewarding facets of academia at the Pharmakeia. Given my frequent indisposition, however, I rarely take one on. Kirchoff was doing his active best to ruin the minds of a new generation. I gave him a gleamingly sharp smile, imagining all the things that might happen to him once Prefect Velleia had her victory. "I'll bring Lieutenant Richter," I said.

"Richter," he said thoughtfully. "Your pet. Even for a member of the Clementia, he seems impulsive. Unreliable."

"My enchantment will fix that soon," I said, thinking, *pet*? He couldn't have said anything fouler if he'd tried.

"If you're bringing him on Primidy, ensure he behaves himself," he said.

"I'll do my best," I said, as if it were a joke, and stood up to leave with my skin crawling. "Until then." Primidy was only in two days. It was a shame—I could have used more time away from Kirchoff.

"Until then, Desfourneaux," he said. I thought he'd leave it at that, but he gave me an oily smile. "By the way, feel better soon."

"Excuse me," I said.

He was playing with his frog's skull paperweight again, enjoying himself. He might not have pinned me as an enemy, but he was viperous by nature. He couldn't resist a little needling. "Tenniel tells me you're having one of your fits," he said. "I was surprised—I hadn't noticed. Is it bad? It won't interfere with your attendance or your discretion, will it?"

He'd reminded me of the ache of the daimon. I resented him madly for it. If I'd been well, maybe I would have thought of something clever to say, something witty and quick and cutting. As it was, I was tired. "It's very mild," I said, a comparative truth. "Thank you for your concern."

That was as much of Kirchoff as I could stand. I left with haste and didn't look back.

～

I couldn't stay late after work; I didn't want Casmir bothering me about where I'd been. He was finally starting to settle, finally accepting that there was no longer any crisis to worry himself over, and I needed to avoid setting him off again. I went to see Malise, and I soothed her too. Yes, I told her, I was stable. No, there was no need for any stronger treatment. Neither of them was fully convinced; I had little energy left with which to convince them. Still, it was something. The momentary hysteria had passed.

Gennady and I met at the Pharmakeia to go to Deme Aufford again, and we walked in silence. He kept his distance from me. Neither of us had forgotten what had happened before. Neither of us, I had to assume, were eager for what we'd find this time.

"Please try to go along with the act," I said, once we were almost there. "It'll be difficult to smooth over any outbursts this time. Please," I repeated, as a good example.

I could see that he wanted to object to the instruction, but he knew it was warranted. He gritted his teeth and nodded. "Sure."

"I may need to put you to sleep," I said cautiously. "If they demand I try it on you, I'll pretend as though I am, and I'll send you to sleep without harming you."

"No," he said, before I was finished speaking.

I was prepared for that. "It'll be the only way to avoid death."

He wrestled with himself for a few more paces. "Promise," he said, once he had prevailed. "You have to promise you'll do it good."

"I swear to you," I said.

With that, we made our entrance once again. The scene was much the same, except there were no Pharmakeia students this time, and Mulcaster and Corvier were already there. Corvier gave Gennady only the briefest of looks before dropping him from his attention. Mulcaster didn't even turn his head. Several of Gennady's friends were there, as promised; he greeted them with quick nods. At least if there was a fight in store, we'd have a few more blades by our side.

I hated Tessaly Velleia more than I had ever hated anyone, in that moment. We were going to watch another set of victims be ruined, and we could do nothing. She was making us complicit. She was poisoning us.

Kirchoff and Tenniel came to greet me. "Just on time," Tenniel said, as Gennady hovered uncertainly at my shoulder. He knew he had to stay close, although I'd seen him eying some of the other Vigil officers wistfully, longing for their company instead.

"I wouldn't miss this," I said to Tenniel, concealing a private exhaustion. *I couldn't miss this.*

She nodded at Gennady. "I hope you've decided to try the procedure on him after all."

"If I do, he'll be fine," I said, trying to communicate to Gennady that I meant it.

"Of course, of course," Tenniel cooed.

Kirchoff shrugged. "At least you seem to have a lighter touch than Tenniel and myself."

I wondered if Rosabelle had managed to flee yet.

Before I could think of anything else ghastly to say to my colleagues, Mulcaster cleared his throat. The ritual had begun.

The proceedings seemed rushed this time; it was all far less ceremonial. Corvier and one of the other Vigil captains chose two soldiers and sat them down in the chairs in the middle of the warehouse at top efficiency. Neither of them was Gennady's friend, as far as I could tell. There was no dialogue about who would volunteer, and no self-congratulatory rambling from the professors about whether or not they'd improved the process. It was mekhanical this time, a sinister clockwork, and that was so much worse.

Gennady trembled at my side as his fellows were destroyed. Two bodies hit the floor; two raches lay in heaps. *You're chasing after phantoms,* I wanted to tell Kirchoff and Tenniel. *It won't ever work. This is all for nothing.* But I was quiet, and Gennady was too.

"Two more," Mulcaster said, morose, as the unconscious soldiers and their raches were dragged to the side. "Try harder. We need this soon." In the depths of my horror, I felt a flash of irritation. Beyond the obvious evil, there was a certain *stupidity* in trying the same thing over and over again and expecting the results to change.

Corvier pulled another soldier forward. He was young, Gennady's age. His jaw was set; he was ready. I recognized him, abruptly, once he moved forward into the light. Marcel, the door guard from the first meeting. Gennady murmured his name, half a whisper.

Kirchoff stood before him and looked at us. "You may as well try yours now," he said.

I waited for Gennady to draw his saber again. He didn't. He just stared at me, fathomless, and tilted his head. It may have been a threat, an *or else*, or it may have been an acquiescence. I had no idea. There was nothing else for it; I guided him gently by the arm to a chair in the center and waited for him to sit.

To my relief, he did, without a word. My mind went cold. If I faltered, somehow, if I hurt him when I tried to put him to sleep—

Tenniel coughed, ready to assist. "Establish the primary energic connection."

"I recall," I interrupted. Anything to avoid hearing her voice. I placed my hands on Gennady's temples, as light a touch as I could manage.

"Professor," he said. He was perfectly toneless. His facade had been stripped away; he was incapable of carrying on the charade now. Lady had put a paw over her eyes, on the floor. Around us, his friends stood holding their breath, inches from giving us all away.

"I won't hurt you," I said. The audience would think it a cruel lie. They were welcome to. I didn't say it for them.

"Cast," Mulcaster said. There was a thick pause. Beside us, under Kirchoff's care, Marcel dropped to the floor.

Like Rosabelle, I tried to snuff Gennady like a candle. Unlike Rosabelle, he fought. I could feel his mind struggling; I could feel his surprise, his disorientation, his panic.

It was necessary that I put him to sleep anyway.

I didn't, because I couldn't. No other factors mattered, in the end. He was trying his best. He'd trusted me. I was not going to use a healer's spell to strangle him into darkness. I stopped for a few long moments, letting him recover, planning. A more extravagant lie was necessary, and I'd take the risks gladly.

I conjured thin wisps of lightning into the air around him, drawing them out as if they'd been born from him. They were only the barest sparks, nothing that could do more than sting. I wouldn't let them touch him, but if they did, they wouldn't bite. I haloed him in blue; lightning streamed lazily from his hands, from his mouth, from his eyes.

The finesse required was remarkable. Allow me to brag. Even in the moment, surrounded by the familiar smell of ozone, I felt a hopeless sort of pride.

The room gasped. Gennady sat statue-still, wide-eyed. I stepped back and watched him thoughtfully, faking at being surprised by the results. On the floor, Lady sat up, rigid and watchful, growling deep in her throat. I drew a wisp of lightning from her jaws as well, for good measure.

"That's not mine," I said. "It's coming from him. It seems I broke the barrier."

Kirchoff and Tenniel both advanced to take a closer look. "It isn't anything like the plasma we've seen from the others," Kirchoff said. "It has a fixed techne. Your lightning has contaminated him."

"It looks different because it worked," I said impatiently, as if my professional pride were on the line. "Of course the direct enchanter's techne would be imparted to the subject. Really, why has it taken the both of you so long to figure it out? It was easy, after the first try."

Tenniel grabbed a part of Gennady's arm that was unguarded by lightning and bent it toward her, examining the sparks more closely. I closed my eyes. If she had the same ability that I had, the capacity to extend her magic into another human and feel their own power, she'd know that I was lying. It would be over.

But, as I've said, that level of skill is rare. She hummed in fascination and stepped back, satisfied. "Do something with it," she told Gennady. "Use it somehow."

Around us, the Vigil whispered furiously; Corvier and Mulcaster were engaged in fervent conversation.

Gennady mumbled something too quiet to hear, looking down at the floor. I hadn't seen him frightened before. Not until now.

"Don't be hasty," I said. "Of course he'll need time to adjust. If he tries too hard now, he'll surely break something."

Evidently, that sounded reasonable. Both Tenniel and Kirchoff shrugged.

"Control it," I told Gennady, and let the lightning die away. "Good."

He took a breath to say something, and I shook my head, offering him a hand to help him stand. Whatever he was thinking, he swallowed it and got up, nodding slightly to those of his friends who were watching.

I'd been hoping we could retreat to a corner once the demonstration was over, but I should have known better. Of course the Vigil would want to examine the proof. Mulcaster pushed his way over to us, and without a moment's hesitation, took Gennady's chin in his hand to stare into his eyes. I twitched—I'd had that done to me enough times that I could *feel* exactly how irritated he must be with it. Thankfully, blessedly, he said not a word against his Prefect.

"Say what you're feeling, soldier," Mulcaster said.

Gennady shivered with the urge to wrench away from him, but he stayed still. "It feels like magic," he said, somewhat uninspired. Of course he had no idea what the right answer was. "I don't know. It feels weird."

Mulcaster scowled, his brows lowering dangerously. "Elaborate," he said.

"I can't," Gennady murmured. "That's it. It just feels like weird magic."

"This is for the cause," Mulcaster said. "You're the first successful subject. Explain what you're feeling for the professors."

Lady yelped sharply, unable to contain her agitation. Gennady stood silently.

With a sigh of frustration, Mulcaster moved back. "He was one of yours?" he asked Corvier in an aside.

Corvier nodded.

"It must have been frustrating," Mulcaster said.

Gennady looked like a scolded dog. Lady curled herself around his legs, whining softly. I wondered if all of Gennady's life had been this way—a series of failed trainings and the scorn that came after them.

"We'll keep him overnight for observation," Tenniel said. "Naturally. Well done, Desfourneaux."

"Yes," Kirchoff said, with extreme reluctance. "Well done, I suppose. Let's see if he survives the night—we'll find out how useful he is."

The lie would be almost impossible to sustain. I'd deal with that problem later. For the moment, what mattered was that we were both alive and conscious. "You won't keep him overnight," I said, and watched Gennady relax by a single iota. "He's my subject. I'll observe him, and if I need to take him to the Chirurgeonate, I'll notify you in the morning."

"You seem awfully touchy about this," Kirchoff said, exchanging a look with Tenniel.

"Is something wrong?" Mulcaster asked. He was clearly very tired of the minor quibblings of academic magicians.

I took a deep breath and turned to him. "My colleagues overstep their bounds," I said, and hoped that I'd judged his character correctly. He might not care about Gennady—might not care about any of his soldiers, really—but I was willing to bet he had some sense of possessiveness over them. "They're trying to take custody of Lieutenant Richter for themselves instead of letting him go free."

A storm passed across Kirchoff and Tenniel's faces. They didn't appreciate my play in the slightest. That was all right; it had worked. "Let him go," Mulcaster said.

"Oh," Kirchoff said with a delighted smile, faking a realization. I'd angered him, and now he was going to make sure he had the last word. "Adrien. You show such . . . protectiveness."

"Say whatever you're going to say," I told him.

He leaned forward. "You don't have some manner of improper fascination with the boy, do you?"

I shuddered; I couldn't speak for a moment. I've never been given to *fascinations* with my pupils. Gennady Richter was not going to be the exception. "No," I said exactingly, once my stomach had settled. "But a continuity of care is important." A teaching of the Chirurgeonate.

The professors rolled their eyes while the other Vigil wrinkled their noses. Still, Kirchoff had gotten his comment in. He wasn't willing to go against Mulcaster, not directly. He wouldn't insist on taking Gennady in for observation.

It was too much to hope that we might be allowed to make a timely, graceful exit. We found ourselves obliged to wait nearly another thirty minutes, attending to questions from all the Vigil, hearing the young soldiers' admiration and praise for Gennady. All of them demanded to see the lightning again. I fended them off for him; his friends helped subtly draw the crowd away. I was, not for the first time, glad of their presence despite myself.

Kirchoff and Tenniel took me aside after the Vigils' questions had been answered. "Mulcaster is going to want to see proof. I'm eager to hear your results," Kirchoff said. I looked into his eyes—they were shuttered, guarded. He was still suspicious. "They had better be good, if you're insisting on taking such an . . . exclusive view."

"They will be," I said.

"Good."

My heart dropped. I saw something in him. He was beginning to suspect in earnest that I wasn't to be trusted. Slowly, by increments, we had overplayed our hand. "Do any of your friends know about this, Desfourneaux? Have you extended invitations to any of them?"

"No," I said with perfect indifference. I had to tune my voice exactly.

"Leynault doesn't know? What about that little doctor? Tyrrhena? We've been looking into spreading the word further. Maybe they'll be the next to hear."

He could not speak to Malise or Casmir.

"They don't know a thing," I said, affecting the mildest irritation. "They wouldn't be suited."

He leaned in by a fraction of an inch, as if trying to see into my mind. "I wonder if it will remain that way."

Please, I thought.

"I think it will," he said, "as long as you stay in line."

With that, he swept away. He was never one to waste a dramatic exit.

I had no choice but to continue mingling, with my pulse hammering in my ears. When Gennady and I could finally escape, we made up for lost time, leaving as quickly as possible. I hoped the other professors would simply assume I was eager to begin testing on him. The farther we walked from the warehouse, the more my nerves began to unravel; by the time we were far away enough that we weren't likely to come upon any of the other participants, the edges of my vision were dark.

I'd introduced a lie that was going to be very, very difficult to uphold. In trying to avoid cruelty toward Gennady, I might have consigned us both to destruction. No—*Velleia* had consigned us to destruction. I'd only helped her along a little.

I stopped to try to calm myself down, and Gennady stood watching me, blankly puzzled. "Why didn't you put me to sleep?"

"You were fighting it," I said. "I would have had to force you under. I couldn't do that."

"I bet you could have," he said, still inscrutable.

I straightened up, shaking my head. "I really couldn't."

Lady stepped toward me, and I wondered what I'd said wrong. But she didn't bite—she pushed her head against my leg like an appreciative cat, purring, before returning to Gennady's side. He rolled his eyes. "Coward."

I had to laugh, albeit weakly. He could growl as much as he liked, but his rache would always give him away. They were one and the same.

"Don't fucking laugh," he said.

"I'm sorry."

He pulled his hair, but without any true strength. "We got out alive."

"I have no idea how I'm going to convince them that you have magic now," I said, wishing I'd thought of a better solution. "I won't be able to hover at your side day and night, just in case someone wants a demonstration. They'll suspect us eventually."

"Marcel's sick too now," he said with a glance back toward the warehouse.

His primary concern was with his comrades. "More and more of them. One by one."

"I'm sorry," I said, once again.

He shifted uneasily on his feet, crossing and uncrossing his arms. "I want Captain to pay."

"He will," I said, "once Prefect Velleia has what she needs to deal with Mulcaster." I had no clue what the *dealing with* might entail. Would she kill him? Send him to the Penumbra? Would it be public, or would he disappear without fanfare? Come to think of it, if she wanted to, how would she *deal* with us?

"That thing you did with the lightning," he said.

"It's not dangerous," I said quickly. "Not with a competent caster. I may need to do it again, if we're required to attend another one of these meetings."

He squared his jaw. "I hate it."

I'd recovered my nerves enough to give him a stern look. "If you can figure out a way to genuinely give yourself magic, you're welcome to do it yourself."

"But you won't use it on me if I don't want you to?" he asked. He was testing me, testing my loyalty to my earlier words.

"No," I said, simply, and started walking again.

The reticence disappeared. "Fine, then. You can if you need to." He was silent for a while as we walked farther, until he added, "If you do me a favor."

I prepared for the worst. "What favor?"

"Help me talk to Mariya," he said. "I never know what to say to her. I always mess it up." He pointed at me. "So you'll come along to help me, since you're better at talking. We need to see her again, anyway—check if she's heard anything else."

I'd extended him a little compassion, and I was now in charge of his family life. We'd only just stepped out of the mouth of the beast, but already, he'd moved onto the management of his social affairs. "Gennady," I said cautiously. "I don't think she likes me either."

He shook his head. "She doesn't like anyone. That's not the point. I just need someone to tell me what to say, and you're good at that."

I winced. "That's a damning way to phrase it."

"Am I *wrong*?"

"Not exactly, but—"

He held up a hand to quiet me. "Do me this one favor, and I'll play along with whatever dumb plan you come up with to keep those other professors off your back. If not . . ."

It was becoming hard to muster any surprise or indignation at Gennady's various outrages. "If not, you'll walk us both into the fire, I suppose?" I said, infinitely tired.

He gave me a ragged grin. "You know me. I'm just a crazy animal, right? Who knows what I'll do?"

There was the heart of the matter. "I don't think you are," I said. "You're rude and violent, yes. You're unusual. That doesn't make you less of a person." I paused. "It also doesn't mean you couldn't get better."

"Wow," he said. "Really nice. Thanks."

"You're welcome," I said dryly. "I'll help you with Mariya."

"I'm going over to the Watchtower tomorrow at six in the evening," he said. "Can you make that?"

I could, barely. Malise's more intense treatments usually took about an hour. "If you wait for me outside the Chirurgeonate, yes."

He melted into a puppyish smile. I thought of Corvier's dead disinterest in him and looked away. I was not ready to replace his captain, but it was feeling less and less like I had a choice. "Now go home," I said.

He didn't say goodbye; he nodded, and then he was marching off to wherever he spent his nights, perfectly unbothered. He'd already packed away all his fear and humiliation, hidden it somewhere inside. I couldn't quite envy him the skill. It would have to come up again sometime.

Once again, I was alone with my thoughts of the warehouse, of what Kirchoff had said to me—*Leynault? Tyrrhena?*

Life had become a house of cards, and now it was falling. I hurried home, composing speeches to Malise and Casmir, imagining that I might tell them more about it before Kirchoff could—but the reasons why I couldn't remained the same as always. He was only going to tell them if I stepped out of line, in any case, and I hadn't. Not yet.

I hurried home so I wouldn't keep Casmir waiting any longer, wondering what lie I'd tell him this time, and whether he'd even let me tell it.

Chapter 15

The next day, after Malise was done treating me, Gennady was dithering out-side the Chirurgeonate just as he said he would be. He wasted no time in saying something blunt.

"I thought you quit being a doctor. What are you doing here, anyway, if you aren't working?"

I'd been lying about so many things for so long that I didn't want to add another to the pile, even if it might make our conversation easier. "I see my own doctor here," I said.

He frowned. "You're sick?"

I adjusted my glasses, just to have something to do with my hands for a moment. "Intermittently."

"With what?"

"None of your business," I said. I didn't want to lie. That didn't mean I had to be forthcoming.

"I bet it's consumption," he said cheerfully. "You've got that look to you."

"I don't even have a cough," I said, disappointed in him on an educational level.

He shook his head and started toward the nearest thoroughfare so we could catch a caleche to Deme Alidor and the Watchtower. "Don't tell me. Fine."

"You're in a good mood," I said as we walked, hoping the observation wouldn't compromise that.

Lady barked happily, a short, enthusiastic sound. "Sure," Gennady said. "I'm finally going to be able to talk to Masha and do it right. I'll finally figure out what to say to her, and she'll calm down."

It won't bring your brother back, I thought. Nothing in the world could have induced me to say it.

Instead, I asked, "How long have you been fighting?"

He squinted, trying hard to remember and coming up against some kind of trouble. Some people have difficulty with time, with dates—they drift through their lives without taking note of any milestones, like sand in a tide. I was willing to bet that he did the same. "I don't know. Since we were kids."

He'd killed his brother as a child. I was quiet until we found ourselves in front of the Watchtower.

Once we were standing in front of the complex's gates, I had the momentary, insane urge to throw myself on the mercy of the witchfinders. I'd tell them about the conspiracy, about Kirchoff and Tenniel's ambitions—I'd confirm everything they knew already, and far more. They'd disapprove, of course; they'd send personnel to help quell the threat. The culprits would be charged with witchcraft, as they should be. Maybe I'd be tried as a witch as well, just for good measure, but I'd survived it the first time, hadn't I? Maybe, for once, the witchfinders could do the Pharmakeia some good—

Then I came to my senses. Gennady and I located a pair of witchfinders to escort us inside to the mekhania office, and I said nothing to them. With another member of the Clementia at my side, the witchfinders were less suspicious, but they still followed procedure. They were willing to leave us alone with Mariya, at least; they waited outside the building for us to be done.

Gennady stood outside the front door of the workshop, frozen. "She's going to be mean," he said, as though cautioning me.

"I know," I said.

"What do I say?"

I considered. I have no siblings; I was guessing. "Tell her you care for her," I said. "Tell her you want the best for her. Say you're sorry."

He swore under his breath and opened the door.

Mariya was seated at a bench, holding a mekhania eye close to her face, inspecting it with a look of absolute concentration. Her head snapped up when she heard the door open; she saw Gennady at once, and her face twisted.

"Masha," Gennady said.

"You piece of trash," she spat in guttural Aicorine. With the names they had, it wasn't a shock that they might use the language with each other. I'm fluent in it, for convenience—Aicor produces useful treatises on mekhania and etheric spectrometry. "Get out of my face," she said, and then switched to Astrine when she turned her gaze on me. "You. Get him out."

I'd wondered if I was going to see Gennady timid, for once, if he'd be cowed by his sister and the obvious disdain she had for him. He wasn't, not exactly, but there was a deference in his bearing I'd never seen before. Not even for his captain or his Prefect. "I'm not missing," he said.

She threw her hands up in frustration. "I know that, idiot. I never thought you were—not that I'd care."

"I want to be your brother," he said, blankly, not bothering to veil the non sequitur. At times like that, I could see him slipping. Everything he used to construct his facade began to blur, and he was left without expressions, without any tone in his voice, without all the affectations and performances he usually put into being a person. He was only Gennady, and Gennady was an otherworldly creature.

Mariya snarled. "You *are* my brother," she said. "We share the same blood. What about it?"

"You hate me," he said.

She dropped the eye she was holding and stood up to advance on him. I moved forward, almost apologetically; I couldn't be sure if she was going to attack him.

"You *spilled* the blood we share," she hissed. "Vanya was my brother too. You took him."

He fell silent; he looked at me, supplicant, begging for advice.

"Remember what I said?" I asked gently.

His expression clearing, he turned to her. "I'm sorry," he said. "I care about you."

She said nothing.

An eerie, febrile light sparked in his eyes. "I did it for you," he said. "I always say it. It's true. I did it for you. I killed him for you."

Her strange, exacting similarity to Gennady died down. Her inflections were no longer his. Her expression was blank as well. They were empty canvasses, the two of them. I felt my skin crawl. "You're not getting away with it," she said. "I'm not going to forgive you. Not ever. You can say whatever pretty words you want."

He began to pull his hair. Lady crawled toward Mariya; she gave her a glare, and the rache flinched back. "Will you talk to me about *anything*?" Gennady asked. "Can we just talk?"

Slowly, she sat back down on the bench again. "It won't mean anything."

"Maybe," he said. "But I still want to."

"What about?"

He looked at me again, at a loss. I felt fundamentally unqualified to help— why I'd ever agreed to the outing was a total mystery now. Of course I couldn't help with this. No one could. The Richters existed outside human guidelines, in their own foreign plane. Still, I had to try; I owed Gennady that.

Besides, Mariya might have useful information.

"The witchfinders," I said quietly, fully aware of my selfishness in choosing the topic. "Maybe you can discuss what the witchfinders think is going on at the Pharmakeia. The comatose curse."

She narrowed her eyes. "Oh, you think you're so subtle."

"I really don't," I said. "If you know anything, I'd appreciate it."

She looked at Gennady.

"Please?" he said, desperately uncomfortable. "We sort of need anything we can get."

Her acquiescence seemed to come more from boredom and spite than from any desire to help Gennady or me. She didn't seem to have many other opportunities to discuss things in her life. "The witchfinders say you Pharmakeia magicians aren't even trying to hide it anymore," she said to me. "Everyone knows you have something to do with those people at the Chirurgeonate."

"How many of us are involved?" I said. I'd only seen Kirchoff and Tenniel so far, but they couldn't be the only two conspirators at the entire Academy Pharmakeia.

She spread her arms, as though indicating a vast quantity. "Lots, they say. More and more every day."

That was some kind of news. I'd need to ask around again. I tried hard not to ask myself if the Archmagister herself was on Mulcaster's side. If she was, there was no hope at all.

"Then why aren't they making arrests?" I asked. "The entire enterprise constitutes witchcraft."

"It's not like hunting down regular witches," she said. "You all have licenses. They need real proof to call you witches, and they can't find it. There's lots of talk, but they haven't *seen* it yet."

I could provide the witchfinders with that proof, if I decided to, but I didn't think Velleia would want that. She wanted to be the one to bring down the ax. "They think they'll have it soon?"

Mariya grinned unpleasantly. "Soon. And then you'll all be in for it."

"Most of us don't have anything to do with the curse," I said, perturbed—if some of the academic magicians were found guilty, would the witchfinders prosecute us all?

"Better safe than sorry," she said. "That's the witchfinder motto. I bet they'll have you all burned, just like in the old days."

"Surely some of them must be on Mulcaster's side," I said, ignoring the delight in her voice. "The witchfinder corps is Clementia too, yes?"

Both Mariya and Gennady shook their heads. "They think they're separate from the Vigil," Mariya said. "Mulcaster and Velleia might be the Prefects, but witchfinders answer to the Witchfinder General."

At least we didn't have to worry about Mulcaster having any witchfinder allies, then.

"So," Mariya said. "Was that helpful?" She sounded as though she hoped the answer was *no*.

She was in luck. "Not really," I said. "Thank you."

But Gennady nodded. "A little," he said with brave determination. "I think it was, a little."

"Suck-up," she hissed, baring her teeth.

He recoiled, stung. "Hey."

"Don't *hey* me," she said. "I told you that you weren't getting anything from me."

"I don't know what to do," Gennady said.

I had some manner of answer for him, although I doubted it was one he wanted to hear. "You may want to reconcile with the possibility that she doesn't want to be your sister," I said to him, quietly, as though Mariya wasn't there. "Either way, it's certainly going to take much longer than a single day."

He tore his gaze away, his jaw working, and turned to Mariya. "One day I'll fix it," he said with terrible earnestness. Lady howled plaintively. "Just you wait. I'll figure it out."

For a moment, I thought she'd spit on the ground. She contented herself with a broad sneer instead. "Get out, Gennady."

He fidgeted with a terrible, primal nervousness. "He needed to die," he said, digging himself deeper with each syllable.

I pulled him from the room before Mariya could attack; he slammed the door with vigor, shaking it in its frame.

"Thanks a lot," he spat, with his back against the door as though he were trying to keep her inside the room. "You were so much help."

"In all fairness," I said, "you couldn't possibly have made a stranger choice of person to help you. Anyone else on earth would have been better qualified."

He put his head in his hands for a moment. "I don't know. Maybe. You were just . . . around."

A ringing endorsement.

Mariya's voice sounded from within, muffled but strident. "Get away from my workshop!"

We fled the building and left our witchfinder accompaniment behind. Gennady would have been content to stand around inside the Watchtower, but I was perfectly aware of the looks we were receiving from the witchfinders passing by. I left through the front gates, and Gennady followed. Once we were outside, he started to settle, ritualistically replacing his usual apathetic mask, sliding his bad attitude further back into place.

"Gennady," I said. "What did your brother do?"

His head snapped up. "Why won't you give this up?" he asked.

"You brought me directly into the middle of it," I said. "I'm curious."

For all his recalcitrance, once the dam broke, the flood came quickly. He needed to talk about it. "He was bad," he said. "He was like me. Like I am now, but worse."

I knew better than to offer anything yet.

He pulled his hair. Hard, this time. "And Mariya was sort of like him. You know. Had problems. Our parents didn't want us."

Whatever was wrong with the Richters, then, it was congenital.

"He was funny," he said. "Funny. People liked him. But he was mean. Masha loved him." He paused, fidgeting; Lady paced. "He told me she was my responsibility. Once I was old enough to feed her. Once our parents gave us up."

"I'm sorry," I said.

"I realized she was going to grow up like him," he muttered. "Unless I got rid of him. She was five. I was nine. Then I joined the Vigil."

I didn't ask how he'd done it. Poison? Could a child of nine wield a knife? I didn't want to know.

"I try to talk like him," he said, depthlessly frustrated. "I try to move like him. For Masha. But it doesn't work. I never get it right."

With a tight pinch of horrified empathy, I remembered what he'd said about his time under Corvier. *We were the cadets no one else wanted.* Gennady had come to him a broken child, one of many, and been treated like an untrainable dog. For a fraction of an instant, I saw someone else before me—a different young man, someone awkward but hopeful, if only the Vigil hadn't gotten to him first.

He seemed to know what I was thinking, a rare occasion. "I was glad to join," he said, and nodded down at his rache. "I got Lady."

I wasn't entitled to an opinion on any of it, at the end of the day. I wasn't Vigil. I had never lived that child's life. I was only something like a teacher to him, and my best move was to act like it. "Give it time," I said. "Give it all time." That, at least, was safe advice.

He was finished sharing. Already, the ill-fitting signs of embarrassment were showing on him. "We should bring that second report to Prefect Velleia soon," he said with terrible remoteness. "Tell me whenever you want to go."

With that, he was marching away, moving as though his body were a puppet he was forcing himself to operate.

I went home to my domestic hell with Casmir without any more delays. At dinner, he was quiet and distant, as if nursing a secret of his own. I could barely find it in myself to care. The dread was there; I was afraid of what it meant, but it was all buried very far down, beneath the weight of whatever catastrophe was headed for Gennady and me next.

It's a strange thing, to live in fear. I was getting used to it far more quickly than I could have ever imagined.

～

The world settled into a tense, uneasy limbo—we made our second report to Velleia without incident, and she told us to await further instructions; at least there wasn't a third meeting planned. Not yet. Neither Kirchoff nor Tenniel approached me in the meantime. Not yet. No one demanded proof of Gennady's success. Not yet. We stood at the edge of a precipice, but we could only wait to fall.

When the stasis was broken, it broke in high fashion. It broke with the murders.

Mariya and her witchfinders had been right; the conspirators were no longer being quite so careful. When the news came that dozens of comatose patients at the Chirurgeonate had died at once, all those who had been admitted before a week or so ago, it was obvious within an instant that the deaths had been arranged. A more recent batch had survived, but the conspirators had cleared the board of their earlier failures.

Malise was bound to know something; she was bound to have opinions. The day the news spread throughout the Chirurgeonate and the Pharmakeia,

I went to my regular meeting with her ready to ask questions—and I brought her another coffee. She was going to need it.

When I stepped inside the office, she looked awful—haggard, miserable. She looked up at me from her desk and gave me a watery smile; I set her coffee down next to her and motioned her up.

"Come here," I said.

She dragged herself up and shuffled into my arms. "You heard?"

I made a soft sound of agreement and rocked her a little. I remembered what it was like to lose patients, and I knew that I had nowhere near as much empathy as she. Whatever she was feeling, I could only imagine it. "I'm sorry."

"They all just died," she whispered. "All at once. Overnight. They were stable, but they died."

"It isn't your fault," I said.

"I examined a few of them myself," she said fiercely, beginning to cry in earnest. "They were my responsibility."

"No," I said with determination. Mulcaster's faction had murdered the patients, and they'd left the doctors with that scar. I felt my lightning writhing inside me. "Listen to me. It isn't your fault, my dear."

She sniffled; I tightened my embrace. "They were all at different stages," she said. "It doesn't make sense that they'd all die at once."

"What did the autopsies show?" I said.

"No physical damage." She swiped a hand across her eyes, as if punishing herself for her tears. "It's like someone just . . . turned out the lights."

Only a healer could do something like that. They had people inside the Chirurgeonate working for them now; there was no guarantee the Chirurgeonate was uncorrupted enough to investigate.

Malise knew it too. "Someone here killed them," she gasped. "It was someone here." Before I could respond, she took me by the shoulders and set me back to look at me, her eyes burning. "I've been hearing the strangest things from the Pharmakeia."

Mariya had said the magicians weren't trying to hide it anymore. Word was traveling around the academies. The incubation was complete; now it was coming time to choose sides. It was less a conspiracy than a coup, and I couldn't save anyone from involvement anymore.

Malise shook me slightly. "The things you were saying," she said. "About the patients, about the Prefects and Kirchoff and Tenniel."

There was nothing I could say that wouldn't sound like an *I told you so*. I only nodded.

Her face crumpled, and she brought me close again. "I didn't believe you," she said, "and now look. I should have just believed you—"

If she had been any other human on earth, I would have salted the wound—*You should have*, I would have said. Instead, I brought her to sit down on the settee and kept an arm around her. "You couldn't have stopped them," I told her.

"I feel like such an idiot," she said, leaning on me. "All this time. I've been treating you like an incompetent, and under my nose . . ."

At least Kirchoff hadn't been the one to let her know.

"Prefect Velleia will be able to do something," I said, although I had no idea what. "She's thinking of a way to stop this."

She shook her head. "You're in danger," she said urgently. "It's true—that means you're in danger. You said she has you spying."

I thought of my perilous lie. Gennady and I could only maintain it for so long. "If anyone happens to mention me to you," I said, "it's best to feign ignorance."

"You've been dealing with it alone."

"Not exactly," I said. "There's the Vigil officer I mentioned. Gennady. I found him again."

"I want to meet him," she said.

I winced hard, wishing I had any hope of denying the demand.

"I have to be a part of this now," she said.

Without any real hope of convincing her, I said, "It'll be dangerous if you get involved."

"They killed my patients," she said, like a judgment from the stars. Cold and measured. "They've been hurting you. I want to know everything I can."

"I can introduce you tomorrow." I had no right to coddle her anymore; she wasn't a child.

"We should tell Casmir too," she said.

I closed my eyes for a moment. "If he doesn't already know." I'd have to go home and ask. The murders at the Chirurgeonate would have reached him too; he might have already drawn his own conclusions as well.

"We'll help you," she said, her expression set. The tears had dried.

I should have felt relieved. I should have felt grateful. I felt, for the most part, very tired. Malise was now in danger. Nothing was worth that. "You have to be careful," I murmured. "Kirchoff and Tenniel and whomever else they have. They're dangerous."

Her fear was eating at her, I could see, but her spine was straight. She'd always been one of the only people who could match me for stubbornness. "You have my word," she said. "I'll be careful."

We sat there awhile, each of us in mourning and in fear. She clung to me tightly, fighting off more tears for her patients. I hadn't seen her cry in a long, long time. In between quiet reassurances, I daydreamed about showing Kirchoff a little lightning.

"Your treatment," she said eventually, turning to face me. I jumped guiltily, reluctant to ask anything more of her.

But I couldn't tell her that it could wait. I couldn't skip treatments. Ideally, I needed them at the same time of day; I couldn't even offer to come back later. "If you would," I said softly, instead.

She rested her head on my shoulder for a moment, collecting herself. When she looked up again, her gaze was steady. "At least there's someone I can help," she said, and put her hands on my head. The air was washed with blue.

"You do help," I said. No matter her state, her work was as steady as usual. "You help everyone around you."

Now that she wasn't trying to treat me for a psychosis I didn't have, her magic was gentler, lighter. I let myself enjoy the relief of it for a moment, as I hadn't since before the curse had started. It hit me then—that I was being believed, finally, that no matter what other perils had arrived, my best friend no longer thought I was losing my mind.

When she was done treating me, I took her hand in mine for a moment, squeezed it, and then let her go. "Thank you," I said.

"I'm sorry," she began yet again, but I shook my head.

"I understand that I'm an akratic," I said stiffly. "I understand what that entails. You made the same judgment any other doctor would have. Please don't apologize for it anymore."

She opened her mouth, then closed it and nodded.

I realized that I hadn't taken dinner with a friend in some time. "Come eat with me," I said. "It'll do you good to get away from the Chirurgeonate for a while."

"I need to work," she said. "I need to think of something to do."

I laughed, somewhat strained. "You would never accept the same answer from me."

With red-eyed exasperation, she gave in. "A quick meal."

I have a nice smile, I've been told, when I have occasion to use it. Accordingly, I try not to wear it out. I hit her with its full force, to show her things would be all right. I had little faith that I was correct, but we could pretend for a moment in the eye of the storm. "You choose the food," I said.

We went to a teahouse that smelled of bread and sandalwood. Every time she flagged, thinking of her dead patients, I bought her something else for her sweet tooth, and we made it through dinner with no more scars than we'd started with. I could feel another depressive wave threatening, but that was nothing new. The wall of stress was building; I was unraveling—so what? I'd known that from the start. It was reaching its peak soon, but for a night, it didn't matter. I shut my daimon away.

Chapter 16

"You want me to meet your friends," Gennady said, doubt writ large. I'd just finished my last class of the day. "You want me to come to your house?"

"You were perfectly fine with inviting yourself over before," I said, not without some irritation. "What's the hesitation now? It's the safest place to meet."

He made a face.

"You don't have to," I said. "I'd appreciate it, but I can't make you."

That seemed to convince him. "*Fine*," he said. "If you think we can trust them."

I thought Malise and Casmir could be trusted more than any of the people from his old unit he'd already told. "I do," I said.

He rolled his eyes. By then, I'd learned to ignore the plentiful gestures of derision. He sulked like other people breathed. "If you're wrong, I'll just kill you."

I fixed him with a disapproving look, one I knew from experience to be especially piercing. "Don't say that if you don't mean it. Do you mean it?"

I could see him battling not to say *yes* without actually considering the question. Alexarchus of Elora won out. "No. Not really."

"Better."

"But I *am* bringing my saber with me," he cautioned.

I shrugged. I'd just assumed he brought it with him no matter where he was, without exception. "Be there at six tonight," I said. "If you please."

He tilted his head at me. "I wonder what kind of friends a freak like you has."

So the progress was limited. "Why am I a freak?" I asked.

"All magicians are freaks," he said reasonably. "*And* you're crazy."

I straightened up, wondering, how, how, how—how was it that people always seemed to know? "I'm not crazy," I said, and immediately realized that I'd be proven a liar tonight. He was going to meet my keeper.

"It's fine," he said with an eerie smile. "We can both be freaks. People can tell that I'm crazy too."

Every time I thought I was through with being unsettled by him, he proved me definitively wrong. I turned, fed up and a little hurt, and went to go to the Chirurgeonate to be treated by Malise. We'd walk back to my house and meet Gennady there at six, once we were finished.

I'd told Casmir to expect company, that Malise and a different acquaintance would be coming over to discuss something. I hadn't elaborated—selfishly, somewhat cruelly, I wanted him to be surprised. Malise might have been safe from my *I told you so*, but Casmir hadn't quite earned that benefit. I hadn't forgotten my realization that if I'd refused to come with him to Malise's house that miserable night, he would have dragged me.

Gennady was outside the house when Malise and I approached, kicking pebbles around. Lady snapped to attention, examining Malise with keen eyes and quirked ears. She didn't growl or hiss, a welcome sign.

"This is Gennady," I said to Malise. Nothing more. I'd already told her his role. "Gennady, this is Malise. She's a healer with the Chirurgeonate."

He'd opened his mouth to say something—probably something rude, judging by his expression—but once I'd introduced Malise, he reconsidered. "A healer," he said instead, with something like respect. It was a bizarre tone on him; I turned and stared. He bowed in greeting. "Hey."

"A pleasure," Malise said icily, and returned a shallow bow. She hadn't forgotten that he'd hit me.

Gennady smiled a nervous, rictus smile. I remembered the superstitions some people have about healers. A skilled healer can inflict as much damage as a trained soldier, given sufficient cause. A scalpel cuts both ways. The murder victims at the Chirurgeonate were proof of that; maybe Gennady was thinking of them.

I'd been prepared to tell Gennady that I wouldn't tolerate any rudeness toward Malise, but it seemed that wouldn't be needed. I unlocked the door and let us in, abruptly queasy with the trepidation of what exactly I was going to tell Casmir.

He was in the living room, watching the door as we came inside. As soon as he saw Gennady, he was on his feet. "Vigil," he said.

"Vigil," Gennady said happily.

"Casmir," I said. I could understand his unease about Gennady; I'd felt the same, until recently. Still, he wasn't making anything any easier. "This is Gennady Richter. Gennady, this is Casmir."

Gennady walked forward to inspect Casmir sharkishly. He didn't bow.

Lady opened her mouth wide, tasting the air. I didn't envy Casmir at all; I stood ready to interfere. Gennady looked at me. "This is the boyfriend?"

"He is not," I snapped, ignoring Casmir's look of total bewilderment.

"Who, then? Why's he living with you?"

I was going to need to tell him sooner or later. I wished it was later rather than sooner, but none of us had the luxury of time anymore. "He's my keeper," I said very stiffly. "I am an akratic. I occasionally require keeping."

I saw a small light go on inside his head. Some puzzle pieces had finally slid into place. He sucked a breath in through his teeth, as if impressed. "So you *are* crazy."

"Not *crazy*. Dithymic akrasia," I said, enunciating every syllable. Malise fidgeted next to me, maybe feeling my resentment.

"Whatever," Gennady said pleasantly. "Doesn't matter to me."

I couldn't decide if that was infuriating or comforting. Either way, I had no time to process it.

Casmir cleared his throat. "I know what this is about," he said with the slightest embarrassment. He was looking at the wall behind me, avoiding my gaze. "This whole meeting. You were right about those things you were saying." So he wasn't surprised at all. "You don't have to rub it in, by the way."

My eyes prickled. His words weren't the relief I'd imagined. "You believe me?"

He sighed. "It's hard not to, now."

I do like to be right, and I like to be told so. I tried, miserably, to scrape together some satisfaction. Categorically, catastrophically, I failed. I'd begged him to believe me. I'd begged him in tears. Now, all he had to say was *don't rub it in.*

"Wow," Gennady said, leaning forward. "So he actually tried to tell you, and you didn't listen?"

Casmir stared, caught off guard. "Excuse me?"

I could have stopped Gennady from continuing. I chose not to. "That was pretty dumb," he said to Casmir. Somewhere under the vicious glee, I could see a strange kind of anger—on *my* behalf. "Don't you think that was dumb of you?"

Malise put her head in her hands.

"We're all on the same page *now*," Casmir said grimly, hiding his indignation with effort. Anyone else would have caught the wrong side of his temper, but like any magician, he was shy of Vigil. "That's what matters." He looked to me for support.

Reluctantly, I gave it to him. "That's what matters." I looked out at all of them, feeling the walls of my house begin to close in. "If you want to sit in the kitchen," I said, "I'll make tea."

I shepherded them all to the table. Malise and Casmir sat; Gennady and Lady paced the length of the room, ignoring their stares. Gennady's boots thudded on the floor. I put the kettle on and dug out some green tea. All was silent until everyone had their cups; Malise watched me, Casmir watched Gennady, and Gennady stared into the middle distance.

"So," I said, sitting down next to Malise. "May I assume that everyone remembers what I was saying before, and I don't have to introduce it all again?"

Malise and Casmir nodded. "Word is going around the Pharmakeia now," Casmir said tiredly. He pointed at me. "You're part of that word, by the way. People think you're really with Mulcaster."

I'd been prepared for that since the beginning, but it still hurt, and more than a little. Although I'd never had much of a reputation to lose, I had to wonder how difficult it would be to clear my name if I survived until Velleia could put Mulcaster down. Would my students still trust me?

Casmir must have seen my regret; he softened for a moment. "Don't worry," he said. "You can set it straight later."

"I'll *help* you set it straight," Malise said.

"Thank you," I said gently. "But it's possible that anything I say will only be seen as the excuses of a guilty man."

Casmir didn't try to tell me that people would believe me. How could he? "For now," he said, "let's focus on keeping you alive." He paused. "Both of you," he added begrudgingly, with a look for Gennady.

"He's not going to die," Gennady said, with an impatient wave of his hand. "I'll be around. So he won't die."

His confidence was touching, if misplaced. If Kirchoff decided to drown me, or if Mulcaster's executioner's sword needed blood, one lieutenant was not going to help. "Hopefully," I said. "We should still keep a wary eye out."

Gennady turned to the other two; Lady reared her paws up on the table to look at them. "Well?" Gennady said. "Do you fancy magicians have any better ideas?"

"I only wanted to meet you and assess the situation," Malise said, perfectly level. She *had* assessed the situation, and she'd found it all lacking.

"I wasn't asked about this meeting," Casmir said. He crossed his arms. "Forgive me for not having an agenda."

Gennady heaved a great sigh, exaggerating it as much as he possibly could. "Then I guess we're all fucked."

Casmir gave me an arctic look. "So this is who you've made your alliance with."

He *blamed* me. He thought it was my fault. The room went still. I cupped my hands around my tea, hoping it would warm me. "I didn't have a choice." Because I was not Hiram Corvier, I added, "And he's made a better ally than you think." Then, because I was not a sensible person either, I said. "He's been a better ally than *you*, these past few days."

"You're digging yourself into a hole," he said softly. "All this, because you got curious in the beginning."

I had to wonder if he was right. He was my keeper. He knew me; he knew my downfalls. Was it my fault after all? Had I brought it all upon myself through stubbornness, through my perennially bad judgment?

"Be fair to Adrien," Malise said, but I barely heard her. I wanted, all of a sudden, to throw myself into Casmir's arms and beg forgiveness for every petty slight.

Gennady snarled as Lady hissed. "I got him involved," he said—protecting me. Defending me, after all the small cruelties I'd shown him. I hadn't really had the time to hate myself in the past few days; it now returned in full force.

"I blame you too," Casmir retorted. "That doesn't mean I'm going to pretend he had nothing to do with it."

They were talking about me like I wasn't there. I made eye contact with Malise, and she smiled painfully at me. There was nothing I could say. There was no real excuse I could make. If Casmir thought I'd dug myself this grave, there was nothing on earth to soothe that wound. Especially if he wasn't wrong, as I was beginning to suspect. He'd always been able to do that. He'd always been able to change how I thought of myself, to shine a light on the ugliness I refused to see. It was a necessary trait for a keeper, and it hurt every time.

"Then I think we've already discussed everything we can," I said faintly. Everyone's cups of tea sat untouched. Now all I needed was for them to get out. The vague hope I'd had, that together we might come up with something constructive to do, was dashed. All that had changed was that the stakes were now much higher. I'd chained Malise and Casmir down with me.

"You want to be alone," Malise said. I nodded.

Casmir coughed. "Since you're not psychotic," he said, "should I move out?" Not cruelly. Matter-of-fact.

I flinched. From the corner of my eye, I saw Gennady's head swing dangerously toward him. Malise sighed.

I can think of no other reason besides masochism that explains why I said no. For my health, for my sanity, I needed him gone; I needed my space back. But I was afraid to be without him. I was afraid to be without the pain he brought. A ludicrous fear was rearing its head—if he left, would I do something drastic? "Stay," I said.

I might have imagined the flash of resentment I saw flit across his face. I don't know. It was gone in a moment, though; he simply looked tired. "All right."

Immediately, I regretted it, but I couldn't force myself to say so. I was determined to cling to his presence, no matter the cost.

"I should be getting back home," Malise said with an abiding sadness. She knew what my dilemma was, and she knew she couldn't help me with it.

"Thank you for coming," I said.

"Useless," Gennady said, and turned to leave without a goodbye. The door slammed. For a moment, I was panicked—if both Malise and Gennady left, I'd be alone to spend my time with Casmir, just as I'd asked for. But there was no earthly reason I could give for asking them to stay any longer. I saw them away in a subtle daze, and as soon as they were out of sight, the fear began to come again.

Tessaly Velleia had set our course for destruction. That house of cards was due to fall at any moment. In the middle of it, still, as before and always, all I could do was wait.

I've never been good at waiting. I sat in the living room after Gennady and Malise were gone and focused on trying to breathe. Casmir sat with me at the other end of the couch, staring.

"I didn't mean to be harsh," he said. "I'm just a little frustrated."

"I know that."

"You know I care for you."

Childishly, I was silent.

"Adrien."

"Yes," I said. "I know you care." But we hadn't felt like friends lately. It had been a long time since he'd looked at me with a smile, since we'd talked to each other without a weight hanging over us.

He sighed. "You're nervous."

"I don't want to die," I murmured. I'd flirted with death before; there were times I'd meant to let it have me, times I thought it must be beautiful. Now, I could still see its appeal from afar; the daimon still told me that there was one sure way to get some rest—but I had work to do first. There was a conspiracy to foil, and I wanted to stay until it was done.

"You won't die," he said, pale and wan. "You'll be fine. Just keep your head down and wait for Velleia to do something. It's bound to be over soon."

"They're going to figure us out," I said. "I had to pretend to do the procedure on Gennady. They'll know I didn't."

He took in a deep breath and let it out gradually. "It'll be all right." He was trying to convince himself more than me, I could tell. From the way he leaned against the arm of the couch, it seemed that he was failing.

No matter our differences, I hated to see him afraid as well. For him, I straightened my posture and tried a smile. "Maybe you're right. No need to panic yet."

He stood and ran his hands through his hair, ruffling it—very attractively, I thought, with marked despair. "Whatever happens, I'll be around for it," he said. It didn't matter that he blamed me. He was still willing to stand by my side.

With that, I was lost. My signature penchant for self-destruction, so admirably controlled until then, got its way. "I have a question," I said.

He looked at me.

The words were out before I had much time to think about them. "Why haven't you ever wanted me?"

I'd imagined that when I finally asked him, it would be in some great despair, in the depths of some fit or another. Not just because I was cold and lonely.

"You don't want to ask me that," he said patiently.

"I need to know," I said. I wore my threadbare insistence as proudly as I could.

"You don't."

"You know I'm in love with you," I said. My hands shook; I was getting used to that. I ignored it. "I always have been. But you stay. You don't tell me to leave you alone." I was thinking of every failed relationship before meeting him, and every one since—every time I tried to love another, I'd come disastrously short. I'd always prove too difficult to want.

He closed his eyes for a moment, as if asking the stars for patience. "You're my friend. I don't feel the same, but you're my friend."

I am prone to bad judgment. Bad judgment. Bad judgment.

"I can't help it," I whispered, watching the daimon puppet my body.

"Imagine you and I become a couple," he said with deliberate calm. "Then one day you go manic." He stood over me, grim and intent. "You get how you get sometimes—you know what I mean."

Promiscuous. Desperate. I burned in shame.

"And you try to control yourself. But you can't pull it off." With no evidence of ire, he drove onward. "Maybe you go to a temple, or maybe you just throw yourself at the first man who will have you, no matter who it is. Then you come home to me and you say *Casmir, I couldn't help it*."

I could barely breathe. He gave me a thin smile. "Don't you care what it would do to me?"

"I wouldn't do that," I said, knowing unmistakably that I had no way of making such a guarantee.

"Maybe not *that*," he said. "But one day you'd get angrier than you could control, or you'd dose yourself too far, or you'd do something else." His gaze was steady. "You'd be bad for me," he said.

Of course. Of course he was right.

"*That's* why I've never wanted you," he said.

"Casmir," I said.

"You wanted the truth." He shook his head. "You're not easy to keep, Adrien. You would not be easy to love."

For the first time in a while, the daimon was silent. There was only me, and what I had earned.

"Go to sleep now," he said, a keeper's words. He hadn't forgotten his job. I'd asked him to stay, after all.

Silently, I got up and went to brush my teeth. I was numb and eager to please, especially now that there was no chance of it mattering.

Sleep came like a shot in the dark; my mind gave up on the waking world. I dreamed any number of miserable things. In most of the dreams, the Pharmakeia was flooding, and Kirchoff's magic drowned us all while Tenniel smiled. No matter what I tried, there was nothing to be done. Sometimes Casmir was there, and he never looked at me once.

Chapter 17

I was right that worse things were on the horizon. I managed to wake up, at least, and get myself out the door. My conversation with Casmir tucked itself away in my mind for later, waiting to strike—but not yet. For now, I was still walking.

No sooner had I set foot inside the Pharmakeia than Kirchoff and Tenniel invited me to conference with them—without Gennady, they specified. I resigned myself to whatever else was coming and went to face them with the kitchen knife still tucked in my bag.

I'd only been in Kirchoff's office a few times, but I was already sick of it. The skeletons had gone from unsettling to merely tasteless. Kirchoff and Tenniel were already both seated when I entered the room; they turned to look at me, and I suppressed the urge to run.

"Desfourneaux," Tenniel said, pointing toward the free chair they'd set out. "Please."

I forced myself to sit politely.

"You look tired," she said.

That didn't merit a response; I ignored it.

"Tell us how your test subject is progressing," Kirchoff said. I couldn't read him. I heard none of his usual oily self-satisfaction, at least.

There was no other real option but to lie, of course. "Well enough," I said. "He still hasn't learned to use the magic." I shook my head, as if mortally disappointed. "I'm afraid he never will—he's difficult to teach, you see."

"That's so interesting," Tenniel said brightly.

It was worth a try, I thought, and closed my eyes.

"It looks totally different in our own successful subject," Kirchoff said. "How strange."

That was it. There was no use pretending anymore. Beneath the fear, I felt a wave of relief. At least the charade was over. I could stop pretending that I had anything in common with the two of them.

They watched me, sharp and eager. "So," I said, refreshed, and looked up with a smile. True terror was now somewhat beyond me. "Are you going to kill me now?"

"That remains to be seen," Kirchoff said, folding his hands.

I banished the last hint of tightness in my chest, reminding myself that it was too late to be worried anymore. "Does Mulcaster know we were lying? Has he drawn his own conclusions?"

He shook his head sourly. "The Vigil are clueless about magic. They think the difference between Richter and our new success is merely aesthetic."

That was something.

"Speaking of Mulcaster, you've put us in a real bind," Tenniel said. I knew she was irritated about being left out of the conversation. "Very inconsiderate of you."

I took a moment to calculate. "Let me guess," I said. "If I am revealed to Mulcaster and his people, suspicion automatically falls on all of the other magicians as well. A professor is a professor to them. They won't know who to trust; they may even doubt *you*. It'll undermine your position with them, and that's a dangerous game. You don't want to risk it. You'd rather deal with me quietly."

They both blinked at me.

It feels *good* to steal someone's conclusion out from under them. It's a shame that manners usually prevent it.

"Well?" I said.

Kirchoff bared his yellowed teeth. "We could tell Mulcaster that you let Rosabelle loose," he said. "Would you like that?" I felt a second wash of relief at the threat, more than anything—so she'd escaped after all.

"Same problem. Besides, she was *your* quadriviate," I said. "You're the most likely candidate for having helped her. Bringing that up only makes you look worse, especially if I get the chance to talk to Mulcaster before I die."

They glared at each other, and then at me.

"You won't say a thing to the Vigil," I concluded. "This is an internal affair."

Tenniel gave me a shiny, empty smile. "You seem to have the gist of our dilemma."

I moved methodically down the list of concerns. "If not the Vigil, then do your other magicians know?"

"Many of them," Kirchoff said. "More than you could imagine."

The Pharmakeia was broken down the middle, finally. I felt an undefinable pang of loss. "If any of them move on Gennady or me," I said, "I'll have Tessaly Velleia take all your heads."

I didn't think for an instant that Velleia would interfere on our behalf if it wasn't strategically sound. Kirchoff didn't know that; he hadn't met her. All he knew was that she was eager with her sword.

I let a little lightning play across my hands. I have no capacity as a combat magician, but again, Kirchoff had no idea. What mattered was that I'd always been acknowledged as a very, very good caster. "So will you kill me here yourself?" I paused. "Or will you try?"

Bluffing becomes easier when there's no other choice.

"What's gotten into you?" Kirchoff asked, not without some begrudging respect. "I didn't think you'd put up so much of a fight."

"Has anyone ever told you that you speak like a villain from a pennyblood?" I said. Now that I had no obligation to pretend politeness toward him, either professional or conspiratorial, I couldn't contain myself. "You dress like one, too. You *decorate* like one. You're a disaster, Kirchoff."

Tenniel laughed, startled but genuine.

"Hard words from the academy's resident daimoniac," Kirchoff said stonily, his feathers ruffling.

I wasn't twenty-three and freshly diagnosed. The word didn't hurt. I shrugged at him. "You can try to kill me now, but I'll bring the Pharmakeia down around us, and the stars won't help you if you're caught in the rubble."

He looked fascinated. It seemed my sudden flair for resistance was surprising enough to give him pause.

I stood up. "Or you can try to kill me later, but I've planned for that—if I'm gone, I have more than one person waiting to tell Mulcaster you were my dearest allies."

I made a note to myself to actually do that.

He opened his mouth; I swept a hand in a cutting motion. "Do you think the Vigil will grant you the benefit of the doubt? They hate *all* of us. It'll be safer to replace you, and they won't let you live once replaced."

"Maybe you're secure for now," Tenniel said indulgently, after a pregnant pause. "But not forever. We'll get you eventually. I suggest you stop showing up to those meetings, Adrien."

"Desfourneaux," I corrected, more fed up with her smug cheer than with Kirchoff's menace. "We're not friends, witch."

Finally, I'd gotten a glare from her. A few tiny dust devils danced on the floor; her power was stirring.

I knew she wouldn't do anything to risk Mulcaster's displeasure. A side effect of the Clementia's constant eye on the academic magicians is that it turns many of us into cowards. Her resentment wouldn't change that.

"Out of curiosity," I said, "why warn me? Why not just kill me when I wasn't expecting it?"

"We wanted to confirm you had no other excuse," Tenniel said, her arms crossed. "We were giving you the benefit of the doubt."

Kirchoff was silent, watching me with slitted eyes. The shadows in his tank bobbed. I realized his game. "It was for dramatic effect," I said, and nearly laughed. "You wanted to see me frightened—it was for sport. I didn't realize you hated me *that* much."

"Consider it a compliment," he hissed.

It was nice to know that I wasn't the only person who had problems with bad judgment from time to time.

"I hope that stings," I said. "Goodbye, *Marsilio*. Goodbye, *Winifred*. Watch your backs." And I left in good style, without glancing back.

～

Unavoidably, the instant I was out the door, the crushing weight of the situation set in. I couldn't hope to maintain my convenient composure for *too* long. Still, that couldn't completely wipe away the pleasure of having finally told them what I thought. The house of cards might have fallen, but at least I'd said something about it.

The Pharmakeia's halls passed in a blur as I walked; I crept around the gaze of every magician I saw. *Is he involved? Is she involved? How many are there?*

The matter of how far the Pharmakeia had fallen was no longer ignorable. Students and staff were going missing; the faculty had stopped conversing with each other. Everyone had stopped interacting without layers upon layers of suspicion and hostility smothering them. Departments were splintered; an atmosphere of deep paranoia lay over the entire academy. As I fled from Kirchoff's office, I realized that the Pharmakeia no longer felt like a home.

Gennady needed to know the situation. Malise and Casmir would need to be told as well, but he was the one who might die alongside me. I stopped by the hall of St. Osiander to get him. "Bad news," I said, and pulled him to my office.

He kept quiet until we were inside, and then he burst into questions. Lady paced the floor. "What?" he snapped, eyes wide. "What's wrong? What happened?"

"The other magicians know," I said, and sat down at my desk to panic properly. "All the rest of Mulcaster's allies at the Pharmakeia—they know I'm against them. They know we were lying. They're afraid to tell Mulcaster, but they *know*."

"Shit," he said blankly. "How'd they figure it out?"

"They finally had a success with the procedure," I said with a shudder. Whatever the consequences of that turned out to be, they wouldn't be good. "They did it. I don't know who on, or what it looks like, but it doesn't look like you."

Lady whined. "Then we have to go to Prefect Velleia," Gennady said, pulling his hair hard. "She'll know what to do."

I couldn't follow his blind faith on that, but I had to agree that talking to Velleia seemed like the next best step. *No use*, the daimon said. *You're dead anyway, thank God.* I fought the desire to surrender to it, to acknowledge that it was probably right. I was tired of it slowing me down; I was tired of it dragging at my sleeves. I needed it gone—and that was not going to happen.

"Soon," I said weakly. "We can do that soon."

"This is bad," he said.

I was too tired to snap that yes, it was, thank you. "It was coming sooner or later," I said. "We're lucky we made it this long."

"I didn't think they'd actually get it to work," he said, marveling. "I wonder if it's pretty."

A horrible, humorless laugh forced its way from me, more of a gasp. "I wholeheartedly doubt it's *pretty*. Violations of the laws of the universe rarely are."

He shrugged awkwardly; I sighed. "I'm sorry," I added under my breath. There was no use being sharp with him now.

"Whatever."

"Be careful," I said, taking off my glasses for a moment to rub my eyes. "You must be very careful. I don't know how likely it is that any of your fellows will know soon."

"They wouldn't do anything to me," he said, but I could hear that he wasn't convinced. "Not the ones I used to know, anyway."

"I think they would," I said. I tried not to sound unkind. "I think it's better to be cautious than otherwise."

Lady lay down and curled into herself. "They were my friends," Gennady said. "They were my . . ."

"Your family," I provided. A better family than his own blood, without a doubt.

He nodded jerkily.

I took a deep breath. If I was going to see myself as responsible in any way for his future, for his wellbeing, it was time to act like it. "Sit," I said, and nodded toward the one empty chair near the desk.

He sat. "What?"

"I'm sorry," I said.

He tilted his head in an inquisitive animal gesture. "You didn't do anything."

"It's a general apology," I said, stiff with discomfort. "I'm sorry about your family; I'm sorry you may not be able to trust them. I'm sorry about the ones who are sick—who were murdered."

For an instant, I thought he'd be angry. I could see a habitual resistance to kindness rising in his eyes. But his shoulders slumped, and he looked away. "I don't get it," he said. "I don't get why so many of them are being stupid. We don't need magic. We don't need anything but the Vigil, and they're killing—"

His voice broke. When he spoke again, it was tonelessly; he was slipping again. "Stupid," he said. "It's just stupid. And Captain's the worst of them."

"I think it'll be fine," I said, a flagrant lie. "It may not be good right now, but we'll figure out a way to get through it. And I think your captain is going to get what's coming to him."

"Death," Gennady said absently. "I don't know if I want him to die."

"Prison, then," I said. "Would you want that?"

An odd, dreamy smile crossed his face. "Yeah. He could go to the Penumbra. I could still visit him a lot, but he'd be away from everyone else."

I found myself unfazed, for once. He was losing the ability to unnerve me, slowly but surely. I wondered if I'd ever unnerved him in the same way. I wondered if he trusted me.

Then I realized that I could just *ask*. "Do you trust me?" I said.

He took a good, long pause to eye me suspiciously. "You're weird," he said. "You're annoying. You're mean sometimes." I waited for him to get it out of his system. "You're dramatic. You talk too much. You're crazy."

"My goodness," I said. "Is that all?"

He and Lady looked at each other; he shrugged. "You're a coward, you're a magician, you think you're smarter than everyone else. You complain a lot."

"I *am* smarter than everyone else," I said delicately. "So, do you trust me?"

He checked the hilt of his saber; the nervous tic was becoming familiar. "You're good at it," he said.

I blinked. "At what, exactly?"

He leaned in eagerly, his hands on his knees. "Pretending. Pretending you're like other people. You have to pretend a lot of the same stuff as me, except you're good at it. You're teaching me some of it."

I felt an instinctive rush of indignation—I wasn't, was I? I wasn't like him. Nothing like him. But I couldn't deny that interacting with most people was a performance of the most tiring kind, for me. In the end, I was acting too. "I'm trying my best," I said. *Alexarchus, help me.*

"It would be nice to trust you," he said. "That's what I mean."

I neatened a stack of papers on my desk, taking comfort in the dry rustle. "But you don't?"

He fidgeted, gawky and awkward in the space. Lady watched me with wondering eyes. "I've got to work on it. I never trusted anyone except the other Vigil, and look where that got me."

That was perfectly fair.

"I don't quite trust you either," I admitted. "I've always been wary of the military. That habit of thought is going to be hard to break."

He crossed his arms mulishly. "What's your problem with us, anyway?"

A complicated question. I gave it the time it deserved. "I saw many childhood friends fed to your machine," I said, keeping my voice neutral when I'd composed my answer. "I saw what it did to them—and I see it now." I nodded to him. "I see it in you. I've watched many of my charges shy from the teeth of your raches."

He was silent.

"And I've seen many dissidents put to the sword. Over the years, the Clementia has done terrible things to this city."

"What's your point?" he said. "That doesn't really have anything to do with me."

Deliberately, I said, "As soon as you get the lieutenant's star on your uniform, you all think you know what you are for the rest of your lives. My *point* is that you could be wrong. What was done to you by the Vigil as a child doesn't need to warp who you are forever."

In an instant, he was snarling. "What was done to me? Nothing was *done* to me."

"You were born different," I said.

He nodded.

"They exploited that. They let you languish in the cold." Dramatic phrasing, yes, but he'd already addressed that predilection of mine. "That's what comes of letting children play with swords," I said. "They grow up much as you'd expect."

He was barely breathing, gaze burning. "I'm Vigil forever," he said. "Until Lady and I die."

I shrugged. "You can choose to be a good soldier," I said, "or you can choose to be a good person." I had no idea how far he would allow me to go, how much I could say without truly provoking him, but the hour was too late for me to be cautious.

"I'll never be good," he said. He didn't think about it for a solitary second; he stood up. "I can never be good."

I sat back. "Says Captain Corvier?"

I'd struck a nerve. "Says everyone."

"So prove them wrong," I said. "Do better to spite them."

I had a feeling that motivation might appeal to him better than the argument of goodness for its own sake. I was right; his eyes lit. "To show them?"

"For now," I said.

The academy clock tower struck twelve, almost time for my next class. Gennady flinched and came back to earth—the stalemate of our discussion shattered. "Listen," he said. "No, I don't trust you. But I'll try. Also, you don't know anything about me."

"Maybe not," I said. He looked younger than he ever had. "Do keep what I said in mind, though."

He hovered for an interminable moment. "Okay," he muttered.

I knew better than to push my luck; I nodded toward the door. "Be well, Gennady."

He said nothing, but Lady purred as she followed him out.

I put my head down on my desk and finally breathed easy. He hadn't threatened my life even once. I was still almost certainly going to die, and Gennady along with me, but at least we'd reached some sort of understanding before the end. The panic threatened again, that crushing pressure, but I pushed it aside, telling myself that there were classes to teach. There were students to warn.

If things had progressed as far as Kirchoff and Tenniel seemed to think they had, if the conspiracy was now a proper coup and secrecy was no longer on the table, it was time I told the young magicians to use their heads. Enough of them had gone missing, fed to Mulcaster's mission, that the remainder deserved to be warned bluntly. I couldn't advise them to leave the Pharmakeia outright before earning their licenses, or they'd be declared witches, but I could say *something*.

～

I went to the hall of St. Osiander without my lecture notes. They hadn't been good, in any case: the loss was remarkably small. For once, the minutiae of life at the Pharmakeia seemed very remote. As the students for Advanced Mekhanical Studies filtered in, I wondered how many of them I would never see again, how many faces were already gone forever.

Soon enough, they noticed that I was leaving the chalkboard empty; a few quizzical murmurs drifted around the room. I saw several brief panics as a handful of students asked their peers if there was an exam they'd forgotten about. Once the room was mostly full, I cleared my throat—feeling, for the first time in many years, a fear of public speaking.

"There's no easy introduction to this," I muttered, and repeated myself more loudly when the back rows cocked their heads. "I imagine most of you are aware of the current schism at the Pharmakeia."

The atmosphere plummeted. Instantly, the tension in the air lay like a heavy weight; students glared suspiciously at each other, different factions seething with hatred for each other but unwilling to say it out loud. I was seeing the schism's wounds open fresh right in front of my eyes. How much of the Pharmakeia's slow collapse had I missed while I was preoccupied with myself?

No one nodded. No one spoke. I found myself fighting back my childhood stutter. "There are many Pharmakeia magicians who are conducting experiments," I said. "Harmful experiments in the name of power. That's relatively common knowledge now, and I feel that I should address it."

Maybe some of my students would try to reveal me as a traitor to Mulcaster's Vigil. Maybe not. It didn't matter; the ethics were clear. If anything, I should have acted sooner. If my warning could deter even one student, it was worth it. "I advise you all to stay away from the matter," I said. "Death is too high a price to pay for their ideology."

A rustle of confusion swept through the crowd; I had to assume they were recalling earlier presumptions that I was on the other side. The prevailing attitude seemed to be relief, but I saw a few disappointed glares, thinly veiled.

"If anyone has questions," I said, "please feel free to stay behind. For everyone else, this comprises all of today's lesson." I nodded toward the door.

After a stunned, uneven silence, everyone began to gather their things to leave; the sheer number of whispers was enough to deafen. A few people hovered for a minute or so, debating whether or not to stay, and then decided against it. Some swept out of the lecture hall immediately, either fleeing or desperate to attend to their next order of business. In the end, they all left.

All of them except one. Pietro Rosello, the daring student from the beginning of the semester. He made his way down an aisle to the front of the classroom.

"Professor," he said, looking fragile and pale.

I made an unenthusiastic noise. For once in my life, talking felt somewhat beyond me. Instinctively, I turned to clean the chalkboard before realizing that I hadn't written anything down. With a hiss of exasperation, I turned back.

"It's been frightening," he said.

I gave him more of my attention.

"Watching everything fall apart. Watching people disappear. It's been frightening."

"I know," I said quietly. "I'm sorry. The Pharmakeia is meant to protect young magicians, and we've failed."

He looked away. "When people were saying that you were in on the experiments—"

"You were unsurprised," I said with a thin laugh. I knew what people thought of me. I knew that it would never change, no matter if I died for Velleia or not. "Yes, yes. Thank you."

I was wrong. Defiantly, Rosello lifted his chin. "I hoped you weren't, and I'm glad now."

I went still.

"So," he said. "I just wanted to say that. I know a lot of the others feel the same way."

A dull pang of something like gratitude forced its way into me; I faked a smile with relative success.

"I would prefer to see you all alive by the end of the year," I said. It was the only thing that felt safe to say. "Very much. Please assist with that."

"I'll do my best," he said.

I needed to go home. I needed to hide in my atelier. I needed to beg some comfort from Casmir and hope it would last me long enough to talk to Prefect Velleia again without losing my mind.

He must have seen something on my face; he bowed a quick goodbye. "Sorry to bother you," he said.

"Not at all," I said.

With that, he turned to leave.

"Be careful," I called after him. I was getting tired of telling people to be careful. "Be smart." And he was gone.

Chapter 18

After I finished repeating my warning to every class I had left, each time to the same effect, I hid in my office until the sun began to set. Finally, I left to buy dinner from a street market and slunk home to bring some to Casmir.

He was sitting in the living room surrounded by books, some from the Pharmakeia's library, some from my own shelves. From the few titles I could see—although the light was low—it seemed they were all about the enchantment of humans.

He didn't say hello as I went past him to put the food aside in the kitchen. At least he glanced up briefly—I smiled, and he nodded once before dropping my gaze.

He was distracted, I told myself, and tried not to let it sting. When I came back into the room and stood uncertainly to the side, he looked up again, without malice. A rush of disproportionate relief made me waver. He didn't hate me yet.

"Sit down," he said, and tossed me a book. "I'm just researching."

I caught it and sat across from him. "About the enchantment process?"

He shrugged. "About *reversing* the process. It would be nice if the cure for the remaining comatose patients is in here somewhere. There might be something about how to dispel it."

I'd read everything on unnatural unconsciousness in the city, over the years. Casmir probably wouldn't find anything I hadn't—then again, the curse was not entirely like the Philidor solarium. I couldn't discourage him. "Maybe," I said.

"If they don't kill this second batch before anyone can cure them," he muttered.

"Hopefully the doctors at the Chirurgeonate will keep a closer eye on them this time," I said, knowing that it wouldn't matter if Mulcaster had some of the doctors under his sway already. There were plenty of magicians within the Chirurgeonate; they might not be with the Pharmakeia, but some of them might be eager to receive the augment as well.

I flipped the book Casmir had thrown me open to a random page. It was a historical account of a group witchcraft victims in the Heretical Era; their minds had been broken in a similar way. I read for a paragraph or so, shuddered, and set the book carefully back on one of Casmir's piles.

"You look tired," he said.

Of course I'm tired, I thought. Why did everyone insist on telling me so? "Do I?"

"Don't tell me it's a surprise," he said.

I looked away. "No. I spent all day warning my students."

He snapped the book he was reading shut, abruptly alarmed. "Warning?"

"Yes," I said cautiously. "I thought it was time to say something. They all already know what's going on at the Pharmakeia. It's worth the risk of speaking out, if I can get any of them to keep further away from—"

"Stupid," he said.

Oh, it ached.

He saw it and winced. "I mean—that's too big of a risk. It isn't wise. You shouldn't have."

At least I was feeling well enough to be quarrelsome. "More interesting is that so few of the other professors are doing the same," I said. "Don't you care what happens to your students?"

"Of *course* I care," he hissed.

"Then show it."

"We can't save anyone if we bring death on ourselves first," he said, standing up to pace. I could hear a peculiar kind of hurt in his voice; he was aware that he was being something of a coward, and he knew I was watching.

"Compared to everything else," I said, "it isn't exactly the largest risk to take. The cards have already been dealt."

"Damn it," he said aimlessly.

I tried to sound gentle. "I can't force you to do the same. It's my choice to make, however, for myself."

He squeezed his hands into fists and then let the tension go. "I worry," he said. "That's all. I worry about you."

While I was deciding whether to feel patronized or not, I remembered that I'd meant to come home to him for comfort. "Thank you," I said, and started to tidy his stacks of books. I had to pretend to be doing something before I added, "Casmir?"

He paused in his pacing. "What?"

Debasing yourself for the care of your keeper is a skill that comes only with time. Nearly two decades of time wasn't enough, apparently, because I still felt myself burning. "Would you be kind to me for a while?" I said. "And I'll be kind to you. If we could have a nice night reading together—"

My voice broke then. I wasn't tearing up; it was only a momentary failure. He lifted his hands in perplexity. "What?"

"I want to have a nice night with my friend in case I die soon," I said. "If we could eat together and sit and talk about something normal and read for a while, I think I'd like that."

"Oh," he said. "Come here."

I stood stiffly to go over to him, not daring to hope.

He gave me a brief, bracing hug. I didn't pine for him as a lover, then; all that mattered was that he cared for me, and I for him, and neither of us was dead yet. It didn't hurt when he stepped back. I was only grateful for the gift. "Let's go to the kitchen," he said firmly. "We'll eat."

I gave him the smile I usually reserved for Malise and went to find some forks.

Then, as I was looking, as he was sitting at my table, in my house, he said, "Do you ever think that it might be safer to join them?"

The daimon opened its mouth and bit me in half.

I couldn't stand it anymore; whatever defenses I had left against my inconvenient little disease were swept neatly away. I recoiled from Casmir as if struck, my breath vanishing. When he saw my horror, he cursed viciously and rushed to me, reaching out to touch my shoulder. I threw him off.

"I don't mean *help* them," he said. "I don't know what I mean. I'm not saying anything. I just mean that your best chance—our best chance—"

I wanted him out. I needed him gone. I took his former seat at the table and put my head in my hands. "I'll never forget what you said just now," I said, muffled. "Every time I look at you, I will think of that."

He was ashen, his jaw clenched, fists held safely away. "It was just a hypothetical. Just a tiny suggestion. It was just a *question*, Adrien. Get ahold of yourself."

But I'd heard his tone. I knew that if I had answered with a *yes*, he would have taken it to its logical conclusion. He might not have volunteered to ruin his students by his own hand, but he would have obediently stepped aside.

"As long as you don't act on that, we will never speak of it again," I said. "Never. We can be done with it forever, as long as you promise me . . ."

Fear does the strangest things to you. It hunts and haunts every person differently, just like guilt. *His* fear had him reeling, wide-eyed, and he was having exactly the same thought as I was. "We're not soldiers," he said. "We're regular citizens. We aren't bound to die for anyone."

"I can't do anything," I breathed. "There's nothing I can do to stop you. But— please. Please don't try to convince me to join you, if you choose to . . . stand aside." I paused to struggle for my next words. "And please leave the house."

"Self-righteous," he said. It was the fear speaking; I understood that. It didn't stop my flinch. "You think you're some kind of martyr. You think anyone's going to saint you for this, if you get yourself killed? They won't." He took a wrenching breath. "You'll just be dead, and you'll be stupid in the grave." I recognized the slow, rolling horror in his voice; I'd experienced it countless times. *Why am I saying this? Do I really mean it? Why can't I stop talking?*

I waited a moment longer to make sure he was finished. "I'm going to go out," I said. "I'm going to talk to Malise. Eat without me. After that, I'd appreciate it if you got your things together and left." Casmir had always been able to convince me of nearly anything, and I couldn't risk that now.

I could see that he was stunned, but there was no alternative. I left him alone in the kitchen and went out into the night.

I was going to the Chirurgeonate, yes. True. It was not to talk to Malise. It wasn't even to grieve over the remaining comatose victims or my solarium patients. I wanted nepenthe, and there was no better place to get it.

Any mixture of stardust and an opioid may be called "nepenthe." However, there are different grades of each substance. Nepenthe made of cut stardust and laudanum is one thing, and the combination of pure stardust and morphine is another. I'll let you guess which one I preferred during days past. It was, after all, easily available to anyone at either of the academies.

It had been a little less than ten years since I'd had any. As I walked to the Chirurgeonate, I reflected with distant regret that I wished I could have made it to a full decade.

Ideally, the drug is delivered by injection; I'd always taken very good care of my syringes. I still had a fresh set back at the house, shoved somewhere in the far back of my atelier in case of emergencies. All I needed was to get some nepenthe and sterilize them, and I would have everything I needed.

Nothing else has ever soothed me enough to finally still the frantic, teeming storm of my own thoughts. Nothing else makes the world seem more beautiful. Nothing else makes it easier to sleep or to get up in the morning. A question for you: what's nicer than medical-grade nepenthe?

Nothing. Nothing's nicer than that.

∼

The Chirurgeonate is always open, night or day. I walked through the front gates and under the glaring ambrics inside, and they didn't flicker in the slightest. I wasn't upset. I was determined.

I knew the location of the closest dispensary office by heart, from old habits, and I headed there without so much as a glance for the other people passing in the halls. None of the doctors spared me a look; I was walking like I belonged there, and no one questioned it. With each new face I saw, I wondered if they were one of the people who had murdered the first wave of comatose patients, if they were one of the witches Mulcaster had made. How many were in the same situation I was—aware of the slow collapse of everything around them, afraid of their peers, desperate to save *someone*?

An urge came and passed, the urge to visit my solarium patients after all and make my apologies for being so weak. Then I realized that even if they were conscious, they wouldn't give a damn about whatever I wanted to do with myself. That wasn't a concern for their hollow bodies. It had been a selfish thought.

The dispensary was close; I didn't have any more time to wallow. I walked into the office and began to rifle through the shelves without any introduction to the medical student watching over the room, a curly-haired young woman with terrible shadows under her eyes. "Excuse me," she said, standing. A textbook fell off her lap. The dull thud barely registered to me.

I turned. "Yes?"

"What are you doing?"

"The Hessalon building needs more nepenthe," I said indifferently.

"Oh," she said, uncertain. "You're a doctor?" She was looking at my clothes. No blue.

I turned to give her a severe look. "It's late. I usually use Hessalon's dispensary. Can you just direct me to the right shelf?"

"Top," she said, coloring with embarrassment. "To the left. But you need to put in an order first—"

"We'll file for the larger amount tomorrow," I said. "For now, we only need a couple of bottles to last the night."

She retrieved her textbook from the floor and sat back down. "Well. All right." I've always thought that the practice of using midlicense students to staff the dispensaries is an ill-advised one. At the moment, I was grateful; one of the regular doctors might have recognized me. She'd been young and easy to trick.

I know I've said before that I'm a poor liar. There are exceptions. Addicts lie. Daimoniacs lie. I was both, in that moment, and not much else.

I took two small bottles of nepenthe, but I paused before I left. "You don't happen to keep any sanative alcohol here?"

Wordlessly, she directed me to a box off to the side. I took a small quantity of that as well and left without hurry. The bottles in my pocket had a pleasant, solid, grounding weight.

If I was caught later, I thought, so what? So what?

Yet no one stopped me. I passed Malise's office on my way out of the Chirurgeonate and slowed. In a last gasp of willpower, I imagined that I might stop and see if she was still in, after all, just as I'd told Casmir. She was as prone to late days as I usually was. Maybe I'd ask her to help me, to take the bottles and help me through the night.

The moment lasted all of three seconds. I left without another look back.

I wandered Deme Palenne for another hour, just to be sure I was gone for long enough to convince Casmir for the night. He'd find out soon enough, but it didn't have to be before I got the chance to use what I'd taken. When the night's chill began to bite in earnest, I started the walk home, hoping against hope that he would somehow have managed to move out at lightning speed.

He hadn't, of course. He was still collecting his things when I opened the door again, making a pile in the living room. I passed him to go into the atelier alone, without comment.

He put out a hand to stop me. "What did you say to her?" he said. "Malise? When you talked to her?"

"I didn't tell her what you said about joining them," I said. "Everything else is between us."

With a sigh, he turned back to his pile. "As long as you're happy," he said, an obvious barb. "You're not even going to give me a day to get my things together?"

He might not have *many* things to collect, but I wasn't being reasonable, I realized. More than a single night was warranted.

That didn't mean I had to interact with him in the meantime. Once he was away, where he had no chance of converting me to cowardice as well, *then* we could speak again. Not before. "Just try to be quick, please," I said quietly. Then, with effort, "It isn't that I hate you. It isn't that I blame you for being afraid. It's just time for you to move out."

"You're an odd duck, Adrien," he said with resignation. He was holding a handful of clothes; he dropped them into a bag, still staring at me. "All right. I'll be quick."

I went into the atelier, and this time he didn't stop me. I locked the door behind me. If he found that suspicious, he didn't do anything about it. After so long, I knew exactly where the syringes would be, and I went digging through the cabinets without any particular hurry. I had all night.

I discovered them within a minute. How smart I had been, I reflected, to never throw them away. What foresight. I took one from the case, put it on a table next to the bottles of nepenthe and sanative alcohol, and went to go find some lucifers. Once I'd begun, the physical routine of injection overtook me. Sit down. Strike the lucifer. Run the needle through the flame. Wipe it with the alcohol. Into the bottle. Nepenthe smells like ozone and honey. I stared into the bottle, watching the light bend one way and another through the glass. Pretty, I thought. How pretty.

I wanted it. I wanted it. No repetition can convey how I wanted it.

Draw the plunger. A smaller dose than before, to account for starved tolerance. Into the vein, a sweet, pinching ache. No need for a tourniquet. And—

Ten years.

I'd wondered for so long when I'd finally break; it felt blissful to no longer have to wonder. I like to be good at things, and I've always been good at dosing myself safely. Not too much. Not too fast. Not too often. It was nice to feel competent at something again.

Forgive me if I decline to go into clinical detail about the ataraxiate effects, and the paradisiac effects, and their interplay, and how good it felt, and just how dearly I hated myself when I realized what I was doing. It can all be inferred.

My vision smudged. I took off my glasses and put my head down on the table. None of my doubts could overshadow the fundamental narcotic comfort; soon, the ataraxiate won. I finally slept.

Chapter 19

I took one bottle of nepenthe and half of the fresh set of needles to work with me the next day. Best to keep some in the office. Thankfully, the hangover from nepenthe is minimal, and the few hours or so before I injected again passed as pleasantly as they could. I wouldn't overuse it, I told myself. Not really. Just enough to get through the next few days. Even at the height of my use, I'd always controlled how much I took. I wasn't going to fall much farther, I insisted to myself.

For the first time in a while, I had interest in the classes I taught. The nerve-wracking grief of seeing so many empty seats dulled to a tolerable ache. I continued to warn the classes I hadn't gotten to yesterday, and I found that my voice stayed steady when I did. Above all, the daimon was quiet. I was more than an akratic again; I had emotions that weren't subject to its grasp. Sometimes nepenthe can worsen an episode or induce its inverse, but apparently, my risk had gone unchallenged. I was all right—I staggered a little, I slurred a little, my head spun, but I felt fine.

The threadbare relief lasted until I had to talk to Gennady properly again, rather than merely seeing him outside the lecture hall. We needed to ask Velleia for protection, and we might as well go to ask for it together. I took him aside in one of the hallways after classes were done—I had time; I wasn't going to see Malise. She could always tell when I'd been weak, and there was no need to disappoint her.

"So," I said to Gennady, with a brief look around at the empty hallway.

"You're looking chipper," he said suspiciously.

I might have been feeling better, but I didn't think *chipper* was accurate. "I slept well."

He shrugged. "Good for you, I guess."

"It's time to beg," I said. "We'll go to Velleia and beg. I don't think it'll work, but we can certainly try."

"Huh." He furrowed his brow. "You seem pretty okay with that."

I gave him a stillborn smile. "I've developed a new outlook."

He looked at me askance, but he didn't press it. "Actually," he said, "we already got summoned. She dropped me the word this morning—and we're not going to that administrative building, either."

I steeled myself. "Then where *are* we going?"

"She wants us to go and testify in front of a bunch of important Vigil people," he said. "We have to go to the Basileum district."

The Basileum district at the center of the city houses the Basilike Cyrene, the palace where the empresses live. The Basilissae. The twin thrones, all-seeing, sit in the Basilike Cyrene. There's no more intimidating place. We might not have been going to the Basilike itself, but even the proximity was worrying. "All right," I said. It might as well happen. "*When* are we going?"

He grinned nervously. "Tonight. Six."

"You'd think we would have been given more notice," I said. At least since I wasn't seeing Malise, there was no problem with the scheduling.

"I really thought you'd make a bigger deal about it," he said. "Where's the complaining?"

"There *was* complaining," I said. "Just now. *You'd think we would have been given more notice.* That's complaining."

"Not like *you* do it," he muttered. "What, did you finally give up?"

"Gennady," I said pleasantly. "Leave it alone."

It never occurred to me that he might be worried until I saw the look he gave me—spooked, sullen discomfort. "Whatever."

I tried my best to look unnarcotized. "There's nothing wrong. I'll see you at six tonight, yes? Just tell me the exact address."

He crossed his arms. "636 Via Saveni. It's the house of some Clementia exemplar."

The exemplars of the Curiae are only a step below Prefects. Our air was getting more and more rarefied.

"Lovely," I said. "Which exemplar?"

He thought hard for a moment. "Ocrisia . . . Ocrisia Moreau."

I didn't know the name, which was promising. If she wasn't notorious enough to be recognized, hopefully that meant she lacked Velleia's famous temper.

"I'll be there," I said, my mind wandering. Had the medical student from the night before realized yet that she'd been lied to? Had the unaccountable inventory been noticed? If I was caught, what would happen to me? Did I care?

I didn't care, no. Not really. My breaking point had snuck up on me. It had come in the night; it had come on a whisper. Now that it was here, I felt better than I had in weeks.

"Professor," Gennady said.

"Hm."

He leaned toward me. "Are you okay? You look kind of . . ."

I focused my gaze and waited for him to decide what word he wanted.

"You just look . . ."

He wasn't going to finish his sentence. "Thank you," I said absently, looking away again. I don't know why. To reward him for his concern, maybe, or maybe it was just the first thing my mind provided.

Lady whined.

"Goodbye," I said, and turned to leave. Gennady didn't stop me.

∼

Casmir was finally out. I went home to an empty house to get ready to testify in front of the Clementia. For good measure, I double-checked the kitchen knife's place in my bag and dosed myself again—barely anything, a tiny shot, but enough to wipe away the last traces of anxiety and anger. I needed an empty heart. Again, I told myself that it was just for now, that once everything was over, I'd put away the needles again, and the temporary detour would be over.

In retrospect, impairing myself before I went to talk with some of the most important curial officials was a bad idea. But my judgment was, as ever, suspect.

When Gennady and I met shortly afterward to take a caleche to Via Saveni together, I was more glassy-eyed than before, and his suspicions hadn't disappeared in the meantime. Still, he left the subject alone for the moment. He only said, "You ready?"

"As ready as I'm ever likely to be," I said, without resentment.

We flagged down our caleche.

∼

Gennady spent the entire ride staring at me. Lady joined him from the floor of the vehicle. I pretended not to notice and tried not to list too much to one side; I was well versed in how to compensate for the more obvious outward effects of nepenthe.

The wealth of the Basileum district was immediately, breathtakingly obvious from the moment we passed into it. White stone and dark wood ruled the space; intricate stone tracery graced nearly every building. Deme Palenne is comfortable enough, but I was far from prepared for the district's opulence. I wished I'd pressed my clothes.

When we entered under heavy guard, the exemplar's house felt more like the scene of an interrogation than any sort of meeting between equals. Only fitting, I thought. That was about what I'd expected. We weren't valued allies; we were sacrifices that had merited talking to just by virtue of our sheer, dumb luck in not having been killed yet.

The house was lavish and spacious, with gilded family portraits on the walls and the coat of arms plastered over every surface. A group of about fifteen Clementia waited for us: a few captains, several soldiers of higher rank, two Clementia exemplars, and Prefect Tessaly Velleia herself. In the corner, a handful of mekhania eyes whirled; some witchfinder lieutenant generals were lurking apart from the main group. They crowded the room; the air was close. There were no run-of-the-mill soldiers present, no general troops—this was not a rally.

When we entered, the room stilled. Every pair of eyes turned on us, and for a moment, I entertained the vision of every rache in the room rushing to tear us apart.

Velleia broke the brief silence and nodded us toward two empty chairs, set up in front of a long table. With that, the rest of the Clementia took their seats there, gazes still burning holes in us. Gennady looked at me briefly, looking for cues, and I smiled and sat down without a single word. He followed suit.

"Welcome," Velleia said. I didn't feel the need to thank her. Any pleasantries from her were hollow. "Shall we debrief?"

"Before that," I said, without thinking. Nepenthe has always worsened my loose tongue. "We have a request of our own."

The silence was disbelieving, deafening. Beside me, Gennady squirmed, looking at me with bewilderment.

"Oh?" Velleia said.

I shrugged. "Protection. We've been found out, I'm afraid. The traitor magicians know that Gennady and I are with you. Our lives are in danger. Would you be willing to do something to preserve your assets, as it were?"

One of the exemplars—Ocrisia Moreau, certainly, since the other was a man—spoke up. "What do you suggest?" Her voice was no less steely than Velleia's, if higher, but it didn't carry nearly as much weight.

You're the ones who did this to us. You figure it out. I restrained myself. "A protective guard, perhaps, or a warning to those who might harm us. I don't know. Anything."

"You are not in a position to make demands," Velleia said, more interested than outraged. "It would be best for you to remember that."

"It couldn't hurt to try," I said. "We don't have much to lose." The needles were talking over any shreds of better judgment I had left.

"Professor," Gennady said. Incredible, that he was now the one urging restraint.

"That will be decided after you finish giving us our information," Velleia said. "No sooner."

I crossed my legs, looking out into the crowd. There was a perverse pleasure to be found in frustrating the Clementia. "There isn't much to give, I'm afraid. We have more evidence, more eyewitness accounts, but we have no solutions."

"Again," she said, "that will be determined soon."

"Then shall we begin the briefing?" I said.

Gennady made a small, unhappy sound, clearly expecting some retaliation, but none came. Velleia and the other Clementia merely exchanged exasperated glances and settled farther into their chairs at the grand table.

"We shall," Velleia said, at length. "Speak."

Before I could, Gennady launched himself into the fray. "They figured out how to make the experiment work," he said. "They gave someone magic, or they made one of the magicians more powerful, or something—we don't know which."

"Yes," Velleia agreed. "One of the soldiers was made into a magician. There may be more, by now."

"Then we don't have anything for you," Gennady said, with near desperation. "We don't know anything else. We did what you said, but we couldn't . . ."

Ocrisia Moreau leaned forward. "You attended these meetings twice, correct?"

He nodded. Lady paced the floor in front of him, her tail lashing.

"That seems like more than enough time to formulate some idea of how to address the situation."

Thankfully, Velleia broke in before Gennady could respond. "No matter. Let's start by laying out the facts."

"Which are?" Moreau asked.

"The Vigil is turning," Velleia said grimly. "I'm sure you've all seen it. More and more of us have fallen for Mulcaster's lies. Those of us in this room and our closest allies can be trusted, but everyone else is an unknown."

A ripple of nods traveled the room.

"The opposition grows stronger," she continued. "Their ties with the traitor Pharmakeia magicians are holding. They have a few Chirurgeonate healers on their side as well, monitoring the second batch of unconscious test subjects. We can't extract the patients without incurring some sort of severe retaliation."

"So they're being left to their eventual murders," I said.

"Yes," she said, with neither rancor nor regret. "There are more important pieces in play."

"But some of them are Vigil," Gennady said, fidgeting hard. I could see him fighting not to pull his hair, not to fall apart in front of his superiors and let his mask slip.

"That's regrettable," the second exemplar said, speaking up for the first time. "No one's denying that. But our priorities are elsewhere."

"They're my friends," Gennady muttered.

"What was that?" Velleia said sharply.

I shook my head at him, but he lifted his chin and repeated himself. "They're my friends. Some of those people are my friends, and they deserve—"

"They deserve nothing," Velleia said. Amphion padded forward to sniff at Lady, dwarfing her unimaginably. "They aligned themselves with Mulcaster, and they'll get what they volunteered for."

Gennady had gone ashen. I put a hand out to touch his shoulder, and he whipped around to glare at me. I let him go. Our tenuous arrangement— keeping each other even—was starting to crumble. "Fine," he said.

"No," Velleia said softly. "You say *yes, Prefect*."

I closed my eyes; I already knew what was coming. Gennady was easy to push too far, and no matter his loyalty to his Curia, this was the moment he would break.

Beside me, I could hear him fidgeting faster. I knew, without looking, that he was checking the hilt of his saber, that Lady was turning in helpless circles.

"Say it," Velleia ordered.

"You're just like him," Gennady said, eventually. I looked up again to see the watching Clementia lean forward, an audience of predators sensing blood in the water. "You don't care about the Vigil either."

In an instant, Amphion had Lady between his teeth. The serrated maw enclosed her neck entirely. She was too small to stand a chance. He hadn't bitten down, not yet, but she let out a tortured whimper nevertheless.

Gennady stopped breathing.

"Am I?" Velleia said. "Am I indeed? What a curious judgment."

"Prefect," Gennady whispered, his eyes fixed on Lady. There was nothing else in the world for him but her fear. If Amphion bit down, Gennady would die with her.

I have no idea what the rache bond is like, what it must be like to feel another creature's pain and love entirely. Another mind fully entwined with your own. I don't know, and I'll never know. When I saw the look in Gennady's eyes, though, I wasn't sure that the risks were worth it. "Please," he said.

I decided that I was tired of it. The nepenthe was very warm in my veins. Unbidden, a crackle of lightning framed me, and every gaze in the room snapped toward me.

"I think we should all reconsider," I said. "Let's all reconsider our options and calm down."

"You're not a part of this, magician," one of the Vigil captains said to me. His comrades growled in agreement, their raches watching Lady and Amphion hungrily. "You don't want to be."

"Lieutenant Richter has been doing his best," I said impatiently. Who were any of these people to inconvenience us? "We've *both* done our best with what's been given to us, and he can hardly be blamed for some distress over the situation."

"He disrespects his Prefect," Velleia said, her face unreadable.

I nodded toward Gennady, to where he sat pulling his hair, cringing, half-reaching out toward Lady but unable to act. "He's a product of the Vigil, Prefect Velleia. He's the Curia's son. It seems impractical to hold him responsible for that."

"You're nothing to us," Velleia said.

Amphion's jaws tightened. Lady screamed.

"If I take both of your heads right here," Velleia said, "the loss won't mean a thing to our cause."

"There's no real reason to kill us," I said. "A fit of pique is hardly worth it." I paused. "And I assure you, there's no guarantee that you'd finish the execution unscathed." I meant the threat, for once. I was willing to give Tessaly Velleia a few scars to remember us by. If we were destined to die now, I wasn't leaving without marking her as she so richly deserved. Whether or not that would make me a witch was the last thing on my mind.

"Prefect," a captain said, a man who hadn't spoken yet. "This is below you."

"Just say you disagree, Idrisi," Velleia snapped. "There's no need to be a sycophant."

I couldn't help myself. "Oh? You seem to want Lieutenant Richter to be your sycophant. Is it only the higher ranks who are exempt?"

"Professor," Gennady said, his grip on the hilt of his saber tight enough to rattle it.

"It would be petty to kill us," I said. "Gennady deserves better. Gennady has served you. He's—"

"*Enough*," Velleia hissed. Amphion released Lady; she fell to the floor, trembling, as the larger rache went back to settle at Velleia's feet again. "If only to make you stop talking."

I thought it might be pushing it to smile. With effort, I kept my expression blank. "Excellent."

Moreau sighed heavily. "I think we should dismiss them. They're useless at best."

After a moment of dangerous contemplation, Velleia jerked her head toward the door, barely restraining herself. "Out of my sight," she said to Gennady and me. "Go, and count yourselves lucky."

We made our escape. Gennady and Lady scrambled out, and I followed at my own pace, not feeling the need to hurry.

Then, once we rounded the corner into an empty street, Gennady burst into tears. Lady keeled over and curled up; he knelt beside her and scooped her into his arms.

At last, something got through the narcotic haze. I flinched. Paralyzed for the moment, I only watched.

After a while, he glanced up. "Go ahead," he said thickly.

"What?"

"Go ahead and call me stupid. Say it was my fault. Say I messed up. It's true."

I sat down beside him and chose my words with utmost care. "I know you tried your best."

The surprise on his face lasted only a moment. "It's the same every time," he said dully. "It's always going to be the same." He gave me a rictus grin, and I fought the urge to recoil.

"Saints. I'm sorry," I murmured. I wasn't sure what for, exactly. I hadn't made him what he was. I hadn't been the one to press the sword into his hands as a child; I wasn't Hiram Corvier. Still, I *was* sorry, more deeply than I could say.

"I'm bad," he said. The perfect sunniness with which he said it, even clogged by tears, drew me to him. Awkwardly, I patted him on the shoulder.

"We should go," I said. "We should get away from here. Come on."

"Where?" he breathed.

"I don't know. Do you live nearby? Should I walk you? Should we—?"

He was parting the fur on Lady's neck, checking her skin. His fingers came away smudged with the faintest hint of red.

Just like that, he was whining like an animal, and Lady was crying like a woman.

"I can't help it," he gasped. "Professor Desfourneaux. I just can't help it."

The evening chill was setting in, and he was shivering terribly. I draped my coat over his shoulders. "That's enough, my dear."

I didn't try to get him to stand up anymore. I didn't say anything else. Whatever he was feeling, it was for him and Lady alone. We sat there until the nepenthe was filtering out of me and the streets were black. The smell of the night air drifted in.

Eventually, Gennady could stand again, and I was starting to waver.

"Deme Nymphes," he said quietly.

I blinked at him.

"I live in Deme Nymphes."

He was still shivering. "Should I walk you?" I asked again. It was close enough to offer.

He meant to say yes, I could tell. That was the entire reason he'd offered the information. But at the crucial moment, he turned away. "No," he snapped, straightening up. "I'm fine. I don't need it."

It seemed cruel to point out that he hadn't quite stopped crying yet. I wasn't going to force him to accept the offer. And, selfishly, I was looking forward to crawling into bed myself, the sooner the better. My fingers were a little numb.

He took my coat off and handed it back to me. "Why the hell did you put this on me?"

"You looked cold," I said, infinitely exhausted, feeling stupid for the gesture. The nepenthe had left me cold as well, and I put the coat back on with sheepish gratitude.

"I'm not your kid," he said, as Lady struggled to her feet as well. "You don't have to take care of me." He watched me suspiciously from the corner of his eye, swiping at his face.

"God forbid," I murmured, and turned away. "Be well, Gennady. I suppose I'll see you tomorrow."

Before I could start walking, he spoke again. "Hey."

"Yes?"

"I figured out what's wrong with you."

Reluctantly, I turned back to face him. "In what way?" By that point, he could be referring to anything.

"You're high," he said. "I knew a lady once who liked to take rosethorn. That's what you remind me of."

I waited to see if I would feel any shame and discovered that it was far too late for that. "Not anymore," I said reasonably. "I'm sober now. With luck, that'll change soon. Goodnight."

His face was perfectly shadowed. "Junkie," he said, just to have something to say.

I waved and started on my way home.

The walk was long and heavy. Once I was through the door, everything seemed far too quiet. I was missing Casmir's presence, his movement, his noise. I spent a long time staring at a fresh needle in my bedroom, wishing he were there to stop me. If I could abstain this one time, I thought, that would be enough to prove that I was still in control, that the detour was as temporary as I'd always intended it to be.

Junkie, I heard Gennady say, and opened a bottle. Ozone and honey. He could call me whatever he liked. He could think whatever he liked. If I was going to fail quite so spectacularly, I might as well revel in it.

In the end, I compromised. Before I took any more nepenthe, I made myself some tea. I ate something, however reluctantly. I gathered a few books to set on the bed and neatened up the atelier. I'd get around to fixing my ambric lights soon, I thought. Tomorrow, maybe. Soon. The meaningless distractions went a long way toward giving me the illusion of choice; surely if I was able to pause and take my time, it didn't matter if I eventually injected after all. If it wasn't done in a moment of desperation, surely it didn't count.

It counted. I sterilized. I threw away the used needle and read myself to sleep.

Chapter 20

Gennady ignored me the next morning, and I left him to it. If that was what he needed to salvage his pride, who was I to get in the way? My first classes passed in an unremarkable daze, and I went back to my office to think without a single word to another soul.

Malise was waiting for me, seated in the free chair in front of my desk. My instinctive pleasure at seeing her was immediately drowned out by the reality of the situation—of course she was here because I'd been skipping appointments with her, avoiding any time with her at all, and she was suspicious, and she was about to be mortally disappointed in me.

"Hello," she said with saccharine brightness. "It's been longer than usual, Adrien."

I dropped into my own chair and leaned back away from her, as if the distance would help. "Ah," I said, and waited.

She clasped her hands tightly together, watching me. "So you've decided to go off your treatment."

"Not forever," I said. "Just for a while."

"And why is that? What possible logic could there be behind that decision?"

I said something very indistinct.

"Speak up," she said softly.

"I didn't want to waste your time," I repeated. "All right? I didn't want to waste your time."

She glared at me, tiny and terrifying. "Why would it be wasted?"

"Oh," I said, fighting a breathless laugh. "I stole some bottles of nepenthe the other day, and I've been half-senseless ever since." A spark of lightning crawled from my fingertips and died midair. "So I thought it would be best to keep to myself until I've sorted it out."

She wasn't the least bit surprised. She already knew, I had to assume. That didn't stop the tears. I sat there, numb, as she cried into her hands.

I wanted to focus on her, to take in her pain as it deserved. I couldn't. My mind drifted until she shook me out of my daze with a particularly loud sob.

"Ten years," she said.

The weight of a decade crushed me down; I wavered. "I know."

"What changed? What happened?"

"Casmir," I said distantly. "He said something to me."

She turned away, sick with disappointment. "Casmir," she said. She sniffled, scrubbing her eyes to recover herself in admirable time. "Casmir, Casmir, Casmir. Always Casmir."

"One day that'll change," I said. For the first time, it felt true. Something would have to give. His spell would have to break soon. "Not today, but one day."

"Come to the Chirurgeonate," she said. She was begging. "Come get treatment. Come to a solarium and clean yourself up again. Please."

I had no real reason to refuse except for pride and an appetite for self-destruction. I knew that. It didn't change anything. "After everything is done," I said. "After this is all over." The other possibility, that I would die before things improved, wasn't worth mentioning.

She twisted her hands together, cheeks and eyes red. "Selfish."

I put my head down on the desk. At least she wasn't begging any longer; anger was better than pain. "I know," I said. "I know."

"Sit up," she said. "Look at me."

I did.

"You will quit again," she said sharply. "You'll quit, and you'll get better. You'll go back to treatment. It will be all right."

All I could muster was a shrug. "I'm tired, Malise."

She took a deep, shuddering breath, fighting off tears again. "Let me treat you now. Before you go deeper."

"No—"

"*Why*?" she spat. "You think you deserve to be sick? You think you deserve to suffer? Or do you think the nepenthe is all you need? Is that it?"

For the first time in a while, I had a truly clear thought: she would be far better off without my company. "Go away," I said tonelessly. "I think you should leave."

"I know what you're doing," she said, nearly snarling. "I know you. You're not getting rid of me."

"Go," I said.

She crossed her arms. "Are you going to drag me out?"

I recoiled. "Of course not," I said.

She gave me a grim smile. "Then I'm afraid we're at an impasse."

"So you intend to force me to accept a medical procedure I don't consent to," I said delicately, just to be difficult. "Very ethical, Tyrrhena."

She began to cry again.

I got up and left my desk. She scrambled up as well to stand in front of me; I wondered if I could gently move her aside and found that I couldn't fathom it. "Excuse me," I said. "I'm leaving if you won't."

Without warning, she crumpled into my arms. Normally, the force of her personality more than compensated for her height. Not then. She looked tiny.

Leave now and she'll never want to speak to you again, the daimon said. *Leave now and she'll be safe from you.*

But I was too weak to cut the final threads. I wrapped her up and rocked her. "I'm sorry, my dear."

Her tears were turning to frost on her cheeks; her magic was flaring. "I'm not your dear right now," she said, dragging a sleeve across her face. "Right now, I'm your doctor."

We'd used that form of address for years. It had begun as a joke and grown into an expression of something entirely honest, and to have her reject it stung as much as anything else. "I'm sorry, doctor."

That was no better. She hid her eyes.

"I'm sorry."

She shook me slightly. "I don't want you to be sorry. I want you to get better."

I had nothing to say. Nothing sufficed.

"You need a keeper other than Casmir," she said. "It can't be him anymore. Does he even know?"

I looked away.

"Then he hasn't done his job. Find another keeper."

I couldn't think of a single candidate—and a stranger was out of the question. I'd never been kept well by a stranger.

She set her jaw. "I'll do it."

"No," I said. The end of the word was swallowed in a little gasp. "Absolutely not."

"I could—"

"I will not do that to you," I said, very precisely. "I'll find someone else. I promise." I took her by the shoulders, finally feeling more or less sober. "It isn't that I don't trust you."

"Then what is it?"

"I need you as a friend. You're my friend."

"Casmir is your friend," she said, a jab at him through me.

"Not like you."

She sagged with exhaustion. "Let me treat you."

I gave up. My already-thin defenses against her tears had collapsed. "Fine. All right."

The brave smile she gave me cut deeper than any glare. "Sit," she murmured, and guided me back to my desk.

The problem with skipping treatments, other than the obvious backsliding, is that resuming treatment hurts worse and worse with each missed day. There's more of a barrier. There's more of a burn. I sat, braced myself, and waited for her to cast.

She smoothed my hair back, aware of why I was already wincing. "I'll be careful," she said; her blue light filled the room with a soothing chill.

I often like to imagine that the pain of treatment stems from the daimon digging its teeth and claws into my mind, holding on for dear life before it's banished back to the deeper reaches. I had let it fill me up, let the nepenthe make me think I was keeping it down on my own. When Malise cast, I felt it tearing me on its way out. The tissue of my mind gave way. A quiet whimper forced its way from my throat.

She finished up as soon as she safely could and gave my hand a squeeze. "All right?"

"All right," I said, but my voice grated. A wrenching headache settled in. I felt no happier, but something had quieted inside, by a bare degree.

"That should help," she said softly, almost hopefully. The alternative was too frightening to consider for either of us. The day healing treatments stopped working on me was the day I euthanized myself.

I crushed a small, ugly grain of resentment. "Thank you."

"I don't suppose I can convince you to throw out the nepenthe," she said.

I wouldn't lie to her, but I couldn't look her in the eyes, either. "No."

"Soon," she said. "Tomorrow, or the day after that, or the day after that. You'll be sober soon."

Are you a seer now? I didn't ask, although my lesser nature urged me to. I only shrugged.

"I remember how bad it was before," she said. "How you were. What it took to get you there, the first time. If you could deal with that, you can deal with this."

But for once, the danger I faced was real. It wasn't in my head; it wasn't something that could be exorcised by the return of my wits. It was here, and it was present, and it was crushing.

"Malise," I said.

She nodded.

"Are you safe? Is the Chirurgeonate in danger the way the Pharmakeia is? Are your colleagues going to be hunting you down?"

She had to consider it for far, far longer than I liked. "No," she said, moving back from me. "I don't think so."

"You would tell me if you *were* in danger?"

"I would tell you," she said. "I would hesitate, at first, out of fear of making you worse. But I would tell you, in the end."

I realized with muted dismay that I would die for her, and hoped sincerely that it wouldn't come to that. She wouldn't approve.

"That's what I care about," I said. "In the end. I care if you're safe. Please tell me if I can help you stay so."

She finished the last of her sniffles and shook herself. "I will. My dear," she added.

I forced myself to smile. It came with less difficulty than usual. "Thank you."

"I want to fix this," she said. "I want to make you come with me to the Chirurgeonate and keep you under observation."

"But you know you can't do that," I said patiently. "I don't consent."

"If you overdose," she said. The undisguised terror in her eyes made a monster of me. Who needs a daimon when you have yourself?

"I won't," I said. "I never have." That was true, at least, one of the few reassuring things I could say to her about my use.

She lifted her chin. "If you do, I shall never forgive you."

"I'd hate to disappoint you further," I said, with faintest trace of nauseous humor.

"Then let's both be careful," she said, dropping her gaze.

I nodded more decisively than I felt.

"I should leave after all," she said. "If I can't do any more, I should . . ."

I wanted to tell her that of course she could stay as long as she could, that of course I valued her company, that I wanted her around. But the truth was that I was tired, and no matter how I loved her, I could only take so much.

My hesitation was all the answer she needed. "Smarten up," she said, gave my hand a bracing squeeze, and left me alone in my office.

Nepenthe would have done a great deal to ease my building migraine. I abstained, just this once, in Malise's honor.

∼

I conducted my next class through the winces and hisses of the migraine, the bright stab of the lights. I ended class a few minutes early when I lost the will to talk and avoided Gennady's gaze as he watched like always, more curious and intent than ever before.

When the students were filtering out, Gennady took his leave as well. I wondered what he did on his breaks—did he go for meals? Did he spend time with friends? What did his life look like? But of course I couldn't ask.

Just as the lecture hall was clear, Casmir walked in, holding a paper bag.

I stared, apprehension gnawing.

He shook the bag sheepishly, looking somewhere above my left shoulder. "I brought you lunch."

When I didn't respond, he continued. "You were right. We can't join them."

The relief staggered me; I took a moment to gather myself. "Thank you." It came out pathetically breathy, and I was glad he wasn't looking at me. "You're not angry that I asked you to move out?"

"It was time," he said.

He came closer, and I hoped to God the nepenthe was far enough out of my system that he wouldn't be able to see it. He'd always had an uncanny sense for when I wasn't altogether myself.

"Here." He held the bag out to me. I took it; I smelled Eloran food, light and spicy.

My earlier resignation that Casmir would have to find out that I'd slipped sooner or later dissolved. All of a sudden, *he could not know.* He could not know. I turned away from him and started to rifle through my things, preparing to leave the classroom.

"Oh," he said. "Are you busy?"

"A little," I muttered, shading my face against the light to ease my migraine as much as to get away from his view. "We can talk later, all right?" I projected some warmth into my voice. "Thank you for the food, Casmir. It's very kind."

I thought I saw him go still, but I wasn't sure. It could have been a hesitation. It could have been my imagination. Either way, the moment passed quickly.

"Tomorrow? Should we talk tomorrow?"

I could be sober long enough to meet him tomorrow, yes. I nodded. "About the same time?"

He rewarded me with a wan smile. Again, I thought I saw something unreadable in it, but only for an instant. "Sounds perfect."

I started to walk past him, but I slowed. I needed to tell him that I wanted another keeper. I needed to tell him quite a few things.

He raised his eyebrows at me.

"Be well," I said hastily, bowed a stiff goodbye, and left in a hurry.

On my way, I threw out the food, making sure to be consumed with guilt over it. It wasn't that I didn't appreciate the gesture. Nepenthe and food just don't mix well.

Addicts are predictable. I went straight to my office to prepare one of the needles I'd kept in my desk drawer without a second thought. I apologized to Malise in the back of my mind, but that was as far as any hesitation went.

And I was sterilizing the needle when Casmir opened the door.

Naturally.

I did not panic. There was only a dull ringing in my ears. "You must learn to knock," I muttered, tapping the needle against the nepenthe bottle to rid it of a stray drop.

He came to me and took the syringe from my hand. I didn't resist, for fear of puncture—and to feel his touch, brief though it was.

"This again," he said, with the weight of a mountain.

"This again."

"Why?"

I allowed myself an irritated look. "If you'd like the pharmacopeiac explanation—"

He cut me off. "You really can't be pleasant for two consecutive seconds, can you?"

So we were both falling back into our worst habits. Wrath, for him, and my own were obvious. Chastised, I looked away. "I've always been careful. It's a temporary detour."

Slowly, deliberately, he took my chin in his hand and looked at my pupils before letting me go with a disgusted sound. "You've only just sobered up, hmm? Time for the next shot?"

"I'm sorry."

"Don't give me that," he said, gray exhaustion ringing his eyes. "I should have known."

"You certainly picked up on it quickly enough," I said. A cracked laugh shook me. I couldn't even be bothered to scold myself for my obviousness. Casmir hadn't seen me on nepenthe before now—yet even though this was uncharted territory, it felt familiar. I was forever disappointing him.

"Of course I picked up on it," he snapped. "I'm your keeper."

"Not for long," I said, bright and brittle. If things were going to come crashing down, I was going to do my best to enjoy the sparks. A collapse isn't complete until you embrace the spirit. The daimon cheered me on. "I need to find someone else."

He was still as a statue. I took the opportunity to retrieve the needle from his motionless hand and set it back on the desk.

"Good," he said.

It was my turn to freeze. I'd expected the disgust. I'd expected anger. Not whatever this was.

"Good." He stepped back from me. I stood up clumsily and moved toward him, gripped by a sudden panic.

"Casmir?"

"I won't watch you do this," he said. "You and I are done."

Finally. Finally, I'd saved him from my company. After so many years, I hadn't thought he'd call my bluff. I'd let myself think that his patience was eternal. I watched him shudder with rage and realized that I had a choice to make.

I could embrace it and happily show him out of my presence, or I could cry. I could do him one last indignity. I could provide one last akratic show.

"Thank God," he said, and took the decision away from me.

The tears came unevenly, unreliably, like Gennady's, like Malise's. I took a second stumbling step toward him, supplicant. Casmir shook his head, daring me to make another move.

"I can't help it," I said. "I can't help it."

"That's *enough*," he said, very dangerously.

Not even nepenthe could dull that.

"I'm sorry."

"You're always sorry," he said. With that, he turned to leave.

"It's the same every time," I gasped, and clung to him as though I were drowning. "Casmir, every time—it's exactly the same, and I never learn, and it's going to happen over and over again, and it's always going to be the same—"

He hissed and pushed me away. "Get off." The stone floor shook, his magic surging with his fury.

I let him go. "Please," I began.

He struck me.

I reeled and bit off a cry of pain and surprise; my glasses shattered on the floor.

We lived in that instant for a small eternity. Slowly, he put a hand to his mouth, his eyes wide with horror. "Saints," he said. "I'm sorry. I am so sorry."

"You hit me," I said stupidly, falling to my knees to find my glasses. I cut my finger on a broken lens and nearly dropped them again as I stood.

He shook his head, and I sat back down at my desk, cringing from him.

"I didn't mean to," he said. I saw him realize that he'd reached his own binary decision. Walk it all back, or commit?

He chose to commit. The horror on his face gradually resolved itself into determination. "Do what you want," he said shakily, swallowing hard. "It's not my responsibility anymore. You're an adult, Adrien. Make your choices."

He fled out the door. Right into Gennady.

Chapter 21

Casmir bounced off Gennady and jumped back into the room with a startled swear.

Gennady pushed him forward a step or so, making room for Lady to prowl inside. I sat frozen, still holding my broken glasses.

"What the fuck is going on?" Gennady surveyed the room. He settled on me and narrowed his eyes, taking in the unflattering scene as Lady began to whine.

Casmir moved away from him toward me, and I flinched before I could think, putting a hand up to shield my face. I didn't think he'd hit me again. My body wasn't so sure. An akratic is vulnerable to ill use by their keeper; I was lucky enough to have never been kept by anyone monstrous, but there had been unkindness.

"Keeper," I said, in a voice that was not my own. "Please."

Casmir stared at me, mouth half-open.

And then I was myself again, my skin crawling with disgust for whoever had just spoken.

The suspended moment broke; Gennady lunged forward with a snarl and shoved Casmir back. "Get away." He drew his conclusions in a flash, baring his teeth. "You hit him."

Although Casmir stuttered and winced, he didn't lie. "Yes, but—I didn't mean to."

Gennady readied his saber; immediately, Casmir made a horrible little noise of terror.

I stood up and made my painstaking way over to grab Gennady's sleeve. "Don't," I said tiredly. I didn't love Casmir anymore, but that didn't mean I wanted to see his blood pooling on the floor. I didn't want to smell the copper. "Please."

Gennady gave me a glare. I could tell it was nasty, even without my glasses. "Why not?"

I straightened up with some difficulty and looked him in the eye. "Honestly," I said, with a sternness I didn't feel. "Just leave your weapon alone. You're not killing anyone in the middle of the Pharmakeia."

He let go of the blade. "You've been crying. I can see it," he said, and began to pace, nervous energy radiating off him. He pulled his hair; Lady came over to circle my legs, so I stood very still for fear of offending her.

"It's fine," I said. "Gennady. It's all right."

"He broke your glasses," he said, and nodded to the smudge of red on the shattered lens. "You're bleeding."

"I'm not *bleeding*. I just cut my finger a little."

Lady lunged at Casmir. My heart seized—he suppressed a strangled yell and jumped back, but she pulled away at the last second before any damage could be done.

"Stars," Casmir said faintly.

"Time for you to leave," Gennady hissed, and dragged Casmir by the arm outside. After a moment of stunned silence, Casmir hurried down the hallway. I wondered distantly if any of my office neighbors had heard anything of our fight, and found that I didn't care.

I sat back down and reflected on the facts. Casmir had hurt me. Casmir had left me. Casmir was gone.

Gennady slammed the door shut with a resounding thud. "Professor," he said, coming to stand in front of me. He reached out, and I devoted all of my effort to not flinching again. Briefly, awkwardly, he patted my shoulder. The reversal of our roles was not lost on me.

"Why are you here?" I asked, looking away. I was ill-equipped for the humiliation.

"I had some news about what's going on," he said. A deep discomfort warped his tone.

I made a sound to encourage him.

"Mariya sent me a note. She says they're using their procedure on more and more people, and it's working, of course, and—"

He broke off.

"And."

"One of them's from my unit," he said. "Apparently. Finally. Masha heard about it from the witchfinders who were talking about it. They're sort of keeping tabs."

A petty flicker of frustration boiled over, and I crossed my arms. "Why don't they do anything about it?"

He shrugged. "They're waiting for the say-so from the higher-ups. They're not ready yet."

I was in no position to accuse anyone else of cowardice. I only shook my head.

"Also," he said. "I came because I just wanted to say thank you." He checked the hilt of his saber. "Thanks, and I'm sorry. I'm sorry I was mean before."

"Oh," I said. I had nothing better to say; all was empty. I reached for the abandoned syringe and bottle. "It's all right."

He watched me prepare the dose again with his alien eyes. Curious, cold. My hands shook, just a little.

"Right in front of me, huh? Right here."

I remembered his earlier barb. *Junkie.* "It's been a very difficult afternoon," I said. My voice was small and faint in my throat; it hurt on the way out. I recapped the nepenthe bottle.

Gennady picked his teeth. "Whatever." So it made no difference to him. With that helpful, bracing contribution, he moved on to the next item. "I can kill him if you want," he said. "Later. Your boyfriend."

I stared, holding the needle still in the air. "My God, no." More urgently, I said, "Do not do that. It's imperative that you don't."

He shrugged.

At a great delay, I added, "He isn't my *boyfriend*. He's nothing anymore." With that, I poised the syringe.

Patiently, he reached out and took it away. It made a difference to him after all.

I could have cried again. It seemed particularly unfair that I wasn't allowed to enjoy the consequences of my relapse on my own terms. "Give that back," I said, fighting my old stutter.

He blinked slowly, then took the bottle as well and dropped it into his pocket. "I feel like I'm not supposed to," he said with great deliberation. "I feel like that would be the wrong thing to do."

When he phrased it like that, there was no possible way I could argue any further. He was fixing himself. It would have been the act of a monster to get in the way of that. I sat back and cursed the stars.

He set the full needle back into the case I'd left lying on the desk and took that too. "Really," I said. "That doesn't belong to you." The fact that the nepenthe technically didn't belong to me either registered only after I'd spoken.

A cheerful nod dismissed my complaint. Gennady perched himself on the desk, looking at me sidelong. "I don't know what to say about this. I don't think I know anything about it."

I folded my arms to keep myself warm. "We're not talking about it."

He huffed, keenly dissatisfied. "Really?"

"Really."

The air went still. The thing that lived inside him was rising to the surface again, peeling away the superficial layers of skin and fabrication. "Do you trust me?" he said.

"God help me," I said, defeated. "I suppose so."

"Then you're supposed to talk to me about it."

My educator's responsibility to him dragged a sentence from me. "I went for almost ten years without this."

He submerged himself again into his daylight persona. "Okay," he said.

The track marks on my right arm caught my eye, blurry as they were currently. I should have felt ashamed. All it did was make the desire sharper, more precious. "And now here I am."

"Too bad."

I had to laugh. "Isn't it?"

"That guy's your keeper," he said thoughtfully. "That's what it's called, right?"

I folded up my glasses and replaced them where I'd left them on the desk. I had a spare pair at home, at least. "Not anymore."

"Good riddance."

The urge to argue came and went.

He hopped up again, gave Lady a scratch behind the ears, and offered me a hand. "Come on. Let's take a walk."

I stared at him before taking his hand and hauling myself up.

∼

Gennady led me out the door and through the Pharmakeia's halls in companionable silence. I found myself grateful for the opportunity to be quiet, for once; I barely paid attention to where we were going, or who we passed. "I need to go home and get my spare glasses," I said eventually. "You really don't need to walk me there."

He squinted. "I'll walk for a while and see if I get bored on the way."

I didn't complain.

Just before we cleared the gates, however, he slowed to a halt. Another uniformed figure and his rache were coming down the way toward us. "Hey," Gennady said hesitantly. I looked up and squinted at the Vigil officer in front of us, trying to resolve his face enough to determine if I recognized him.

Before I could make much progress, Gennady said, "Alim?"

"Genya," the officer said, stopping near us. "How've you been? Haven't seen much of you around."

"It's been busy," Gennady said. "What with all the stuff going on."

Alim tilted his head, hawkish. "What, Mulcaster and Velleia?"

Gennady shrugged. "Something like that. Who're you with?"

It was an unspeakably charged question, but Alim didn't hesitate for an instant. "Oh, Velleia. I don't have time for whatever Mulcaster's trying to do."

I felt Gennady relax at my side. My guard stayed up.

"Great," Gennady said brightly. "At least there's you, then. Not everyone else is as smart."

"So I hear," Alim said. At his side, his rache strolled over to groom the fur on Lady's face. "They've done it, right? They figured out how to make the experiment work."

Gennady nodded. "Mariya told me one of the successes is from our old unit, actually. She sent me a note."

Alim paused for a lengthy moment, as if trying to remember Mariya. "Oh. She still works for the witchfinders?"

"She does," Gennady proudly. Mariya might not be Vigil, but Clementia work was Clementia work.

The back of my neck prickled. Alim looked at me, trying to figure out what I could possibly be doing with Gennady. "That's good. Does she know who got turned?"

"Maybe," Gennady said. "I don't know. I think she would have said, if she did, but I don't know for sure." He frowned, faintly distracted, juggling probabilities. "She *could.*"

Alim tilted his head, a repetition of an earlier gesture, no less hawkish than before. He, too, showed the same strange remoteness as the other soldiers from Gennady's unit. "What are you going to do when you figure out who it is?"

Gennady looked him over. "I guess I'll have to kill them, eventually." He didn't sound like he enjoyed the thought. "Why? You have a problem with that?"

"You know I don't," Alim said mildly. "I'll help you do it myself if you want."

"Maybe I'll take you up on the offer," Gennady said. A flicker of unhappiness crossed his face. "Maybe. Maybe I'll just get Velleia to do it. I bet she would."

Alim stilled. "Velleia. You'll rat them out to Velleia?"

Immediately, Gennady bridled. "It's not ratting if they deserve it."

I began to feel somewhat useless at Gennady's side; I cleared my throat. The three of us stood in a deep, opaque silence.

"Well," Alim said eventually, and smiled. It wasn't a warm smile. "I won't keep you."

"See you around," Gennady said, startled, and awkwardly bowed goodbye. We continued on our way through Deme Palenne.

The instant we were out of sight and earshot, I said, "It's him. He's the success. He was turned."

Gennady stopped walking and spun to face me. I edged a step away. "What?" he said.

"Did you see his face? Did you hear how he was speaking?"

"No. Not him."

"I know it," I said. "Maybe I can't prove it, but I know it. Believe me, Gennady."

He stood with his mouth working, silent.

"I'm sorry," I said. I'd grown used to distrusting my suspicions, to examining them through the lens of akratic paranoia. Not so, this time. This was sound.

He tugged his hair. "Then what am I supposed to do about it?"

"You could ask Mariya first," I said, not without some reluctance. Suggesting any sort of contact between them seemed unwise, but she was the best hope for a confirmation, barring actual observation of Alim. It was a good place to start.

"I'll get around to it," he said. "Tomorrow, maybe. Come on. We have to get your glasses."

An undefinable trepidation settled deep in my stomach. "I wouldn't leave it until tomorrow. Best to know for sure before you risk running into him again."

He sighed heavily and pulled me farther down the street by my sleeve. "Later today, then. Fine. Come *on.*"

I let my mind drift until we came upon my house. "You really don't need to follow me around," I said thoughtlessly, before I could consider how that might sound to him.

He didn't take offense. "Well, you're coming with me to see Mariya next. So I do."

"That's news to me," I said, fishing out my keys. Their shine in the sun disoriented me for a moment.

"You have a problem with it?"

"No," I said, a flagrant lie. I hadn't been dosing myself for long enough yet that severe withdrawal would be an issue yet, but I was getting there. I wanted to be left alone to my next shot, my scheduled self-destruction, although it didn't seem prudent to tell him so. Either way, he wasn't going to be leaving me.

He stood at the threshold once the door was open. "You want me to wait outside?"

It was a marvel that he was even asking. I didn't have the heart to tell him to stay out. "You can come in if you like."

Lady ambled in first, and he followed her.

I was aware, suddenly, of what a perfect mess the place was. A sea of books covered the floor, covered every other surface; a hundred pens and pencils lay scattered across the house where I'd put them down and refused to pick them up. I was thankful Gennady couldn't see into my bedroom.

"Wow," he said.

"Feel free to sit if you can find a chair," I said, and went into my room to dig up my spare pair of glasses. The world came back into focus, finally. It occurred to me to find a plaster for my sliced finger, but in the end, I didn't have the motivation. It had stopped bleeding, regardless.

I stood above the bottle of nepenthe and the prepared fresh needle on my nightstand for a long, hungry moment. I needed it, I thought, to stand going to the Watchtower to meet with Mariya. I needed it to stand the memory of Casmir's disgust. I needed it to stand anything.

I decided that Gennady would probably make me regret it dearly if I came out of my bedroom high and walked back into the living room.

He was idly paging through a book without reading so much as a word, possibly looking for illustrations. When he saw me, he tossed it away onto a random pile. "What do you need all these for, anyway?"

"To read," I said.

He rolled his eyes, got up, and came over to inspect me. "You've got sort of a mark."

"It wasn't very hard," I said, embarrassed. "He didn't hit me very hard." It seemed insensitive to complain of petty violence to a soldier who had certainly done and taken much worse.

He was unconvinced. "Bet you went over like a leaf in the wind, though."

The scorn was far more comforting than any sort of reassurance could have been. I smiled. "Nearly."

He nodded toward the door. "Let's go, then. You said we should see Mariya sooner than later."

I *had* said that, I reflected with dismay. I'd set myself up for more responsibility, more time out of the house, more of Gennady's company, well-meant though it might be at the moment. I wanted to ask if we couldn't stop for a cup of tea, at least, but I thought my will might fail me if I stalled too much. "All right."

We left the house to find a thoroughfare. Via Archole was busy that evening, and I found it comforting—at least in the middle of everything that was happening, the city was still going about its business. Astrum's citizens still had their own lives; they still worked and danced and fought with each other as usual. My own collapse was insignificant in the grand scheme of things.

"She'll still be angry at me," Gennady said as we stood at the side of the street.

"She may always be angry with you."

I paid another caleche fare alone; Gennady didn't offer to make up any part of it. Whatever his worldview was like, it didn't include money. I realized with a start that I would need to make sure Casmir didn't have access to mine anymore.

The thud of the caleche horse's pace rattled my aching bones. I huddled against the side of the compartment and waited.

∼

This time, when we approached the Watchtower, we weren't let inside with the same rapidity as before. My standing as a magician with the Pharmakeia was now, understandably, considerably more suspect. Even Gennady's rache and uniform weren't enough to get us through without examination. We were stopped at the gates.

The examiners were two young men this time, a pair likely fresh out of their cadet's training with the corps. One of them, dark-skinned and painfully thin, grabbed me by the arm. I flinched hard.

"Easy," Gennady said, a growl underlining his words.

"Identify yourselves," the first witchfinder's partner said, lowering heavy brows.

"Adrien Desfourneaux," I said.

Gennady pried the witchfinder's hand off me. "Gennady Richter. What's your problem?"

For a single, exhausted instant, I thought there might be a fight, but the second witchfinder murmured something to his partner, and the two of them backed away.

"I'm sorry for his rudeness," I said, to meet them halfway.

Gennady growled, but he didn't ruin the apology.

"We're going to search you now," the second witchfinder said. "Understood?"

I suppressed a despairing laugh at the thought that they considered me any kind of danger and submitted to a thorough, businesslike frisking while the other witchfinder did the same to Gennady. Lady hissed softly, as if considering action, but the moment passed unshattered.

"What are you here for?" the second witchfinder asked, after they were done. He'd relaxed marginally, but that margin was thin. "You looking for your friend, Vigil?"

Gennady paused. "What friend?"

The second witchfinder jerked a thumb toward the Watchtower's gates. "The other officer who came through here just a minute ago."

The average Vigil soldier would have little reason to visit the Watchtower.

"What did he look like?" Gennady said. Very, very slowly.

They both squinted, trying to remember. "Sort of tall," the first witchfinder said. "Pale. Big gray rache."

Alim. Of course, inevitably, Alim.

The lightning bolt finally struck; I remembered the tilt of Alim's head as he'd spoken to Gennady. I remembered his words.

She still works for the witchfinders? That's good.

"Oh," said Gennady, as if he'd been punched in the gut.

"Did he ask to be shown to the mekhania office?" I said. It was not truly a question.

"Sure," the first witchfinder said. "Why?"

Lady shrieked. We ran.

Chapter 22

We had no idea just how long ago Alim had passed through, and there was no time at all to stop and ask the witchfinders. Mariya could already be dead— and if she wasn't already, Alim was bound to be in the process of trying his best to change that.

I should have known, I thought distantly, as we ran through the gates. The witchfinders cried out in surprise and indignation and took off after us, shouting orders: *Wait, stop, explain.*

"He's going to kill my sister," Gennady yelled back at them, and careened toward the mekhania office without another instant of delay.

Despite our lead on them, the witchfinders caught up to me quickly. They were trained to chase down victims, and I was not. One seized me by the back of the collar, and I choked a little as he jerked me to a stop.

"*Listen*," I snarled, once I had my voice back. My breath burned in my chest. "You can do whatever you like to me after we deal with this. Execute me on the spot, if you like. For now, if you'd like to prevent a murder, follow Lieutenant Richter."

For an agonizing moment, they conferred in furious whispers, their mekhania eyes grating loudly in confusion and concern—and then they let me go and ran after Gennady, each with daggers drawn. They didn't stop to alert any of their fellows; there were few in sight, in any case.

The mekhania office seemed much farther away than I remembered. It felt like an eternity before the group of us burst through the doors to get into the mekhanic's workshop. Gennady was inside first, saber held ready, with Lady howling at his heels.

Gennady and the witchfinders stepped over the dead bodies. Several office staff, older witchfinders who'd been run through by a Vigil saber. They bore deep bite marks on their throats; the room was red, a red I could smell.

I'd never seen a fresh murder before. I got one good look at their faces before my nausea forced my gaze to the ceiling. The blood was tacky on my shoes as I edged past them, begging myself not to look again, trying not to fall too far behind the others. I was going to remember those faces, I realized, for the rest of my life.

When we got into the workshop, Mariya wasn't lying dead. We'd come just in time. She was backed into a corner; Alim stood before her with his saber poised to run her through—there was more blood on the floor from a slash in her arm, where he'd missed just an instant before. His gray rache was snapping and slavering, worked into a frenzy. Mekhania pieces littered the floor, knocked from shelves and tables during the struggle.

I saw a certain serenity in Alim's face, reminiscent of Gennady's own coldness during his lapses. We'd surprised him, but he wasn't moved in the slightest. "Hello, Genya," he said. "I guess it's too late to keep you from finding out who was turned."

Gennady made a wordless sound of grief and fury.

"Too bad," Alim said, and moved to plunge his blade into Mariya's stomach.

Lady was half a second quicker. Her teeth sank into Alim's arm, tearing him away from Mariya. His saber still grazed her, drawing a thin line of red across her cheek, but she was alive.

With that, Gennady closed the gap between him and his former comrade.

Alim threw Lady away from him, and his own rache coiled, ready to spring. The two witchfinders jumped into the fray, their eyes whirling as they prepared cantrips.

They fought. Just as I'd never seen a fresh murder, I'd never seen a real fight before. Not between soldiers who had been trained from childhood to be ready to kill. The clash of blades was too fast to follow, and the baying of fighting raches was like nothing I'd ever heard before. I could have tried to send a lightning bolt or two their way, but I had a better chance of hitting an ally than otherwise.

I was beginning to wonder if Alim would use his recent augmentation to any real effect when he raised a hand and conjured a gout of green flame to send toward Gennady. Real magic, true magic. He was a wonder of innovation now.

With my question answered and nothing else useful to do, I ran to Mariya, grabbed her, and pulled her from the workshop. Once we cleared the threshold and she saw the bodies on the floor, she began to hyperventilate. We went outside, neither of us looking down.

For the first time, she looked her age—young, and scared, and bleeding. I took off my coat to wrap her arm.

"Gennady led him here," she choked. "Idiot. Idiot. He did this."

I had no helpful reply. "It'll be fine now," I said.

She took a breath to say something cutting, wavered, and threw her arms around me. I stood still while she panted, wondering exactly what it was about me that appealed to Richter children.

"He cut me," she said. I made a move to hug her back, and instantly, she jumped away, scrubbing her face furiously. I should have known better.

If I were less of a coward, I would have gone inside to see if there was anything further I could do. Instead, I was content to tell myself that I was protecting Mariya outside, and that I would only be in the way.

Mariya opened her mouth to speak again. At the same moment, the side of the mekhania office exploded in a burst of green flame. Gennady and Alim came tumbling out with their raches entangled behind them. The raches howled; the officers were silent. The two witchfinders lay in the rubble—I thought they were still breathing, but I couldn't be sure until one rose to begin patting the flames off his partner's clothes.

By then, witchfinders had begun to stream out of the nearby buildings, finally alerted to the violence.

I didn't see the killing blow. All I knew was that one moment Alim was wrestling with Gennady on the cobblestones, both of them smearing blood underneath them, and the next moment Gennady had stuck Alim through the throat with his saber.

The gurgling sounds of Alim's last few breaths were cut short when Gennady retrieved his weapon and sheathed it again in his chest. A few gouts of green flame shot from his twitching hands, and then that was it. Between Lady's teeth, his rache fell motionless.

As a growing crowd of witchfinders came to gather around us, Gennady dragged himself to his feet. Within an instant, he was inspecting Mariya, checking her for wounds, talking at her in quick, rough Aicorine.

"I'm fine," Mariya whispered in the same tongue. For once, she declined to follow it up with an insult. She didn't cling to him, didn't thank him, but she let him near her without complaint.

A woman wearing a lieutenant general's star strode toward us, pushing her way through the gathering crowd, and went to inspect the two witchfinders laying in the dust. They were both bleeding, but neither mortally, as far as I could tell. "Briande," the woman said. "Finlay. Care to explain?"

Finlay gasped for breath. "That dead officer tried to kill one of the mekhanics." He gestured up at Gennady and me before standing and helping his partner do the same. "These two came to stop him."

The lieutenant general narrowed her eyes. "And the explosion?" She turned to me. "You're dressed like a Pharmakeia magician. Was that you?"

I shook my head quickly, looking around for support. I had to remember my promise to the witchfinders that they could execute me on the spot later. Yet another stupid thing I'd said under pressure. "No, no. He was one of Mulcaster's people—he was given magic. He used it to do that."

The two battered witchfinders chorused their agreement. I allowed myself to relax, barely.

"One of Mulcaster's people," the lieutenant general repeated. "This is the one who was augmented?"

If the witchfinders had only deigned to do something about all of this earlier, they might not have an explosion on their hands, I thought. "So you're aware, but you did nothing," I said.

"I'm not the Witchfinder General," she said bitterly. "I don't make those calls. I wish I did." She turned to address the crowd of witchfinders. "Go about your business," she called. "Nothing to see here. It'll be taken care of. We'll call the cleaners for the dead soon."

After the scene was cleared, she turned to Gennady and bowed. "Vainna Ullford. Thanks for saving our mekhanic."

Gennady didn't bow back; he only stared, panting and bleeding from a multitude of claw marks and slashes, singed all over, feral-eyed. Lady paced around Mariya, dripping blood from her own wounds.

If Ullford was insulted by the lack of response, she didn't show it. "We'll need you to help put together an official report," she said to us and to our two witchfinder allies.

Part of me had assumed that the Curia Clementia was so accustomed to violence that such an incident would pass mostly unnoticed. I was wrong, apparently—even violence couldn't cure bureaucracy.

"Surely that can wait until tomorrow," I said. "They're both injured. They'll need time. There's no more immediate danger—can it *wait*?"

She glared at me, but she didn't argue the point. "Report tomorrow, then. All of you, at nine in the morning. We need to get this sorted out."

"May I assume Mariya has the rest of the workday off?" I couldn't help the small dose of sarcasm that bled into my voice, but apart from a narrowing of her eyes, she didn't call me on it.

"If you're going to take her to a healer, the Watchtower can only thank you," she said.

I moved to take Gennady and Mariya away, and she put out a hand momentary to stop me.

"Yes?"

"We'll come to find you," she said. "If you don't show up to make your report. We need it made. I just want to make that clear." It was less a threat than an extension of courtesy, from her tone. I still shuddered before leaving.

We fled the Watchtower for the Chirurgeonate. Our frightened caleche driver said not a word about the blood, and all of us were silent as well. Lady shivered and growled on the floor of the vehicle. Ostensibly, I could have healed the Richters' wounds myself, but none of them were mortal, and I hadn't been able to heal since the solarium. The Chirurgeonate would have to do.

The rushing in my ears didn't subside until we were halfway there.

∼

We arrived at the Chirurgeonate's campus awkward and unsure of ourselves. It didn't matter how familiar I'd once been with it—I'd never brought someone in for treatment following a gruesome killing. We were shown to a room inside the nearest hospital building immediately; Gennady's uniform went a long way toward assuring instant care.

Gennady and Mariya sat down on the cot inside the room. I stayed standing. The Chirurgeonate staff would have assigned us a doctor more or less at random, but I asked if Malise Tyrrhena happened to be available, and if she might consider treating the Richters, provided she had the time. The uncertain attendant in blue set off to find out, and within twenty minutes or so, Malise was scrambling into the room.

When she saw that I was unharmed, she relaxed, but it was slight. She turned her attention to the Richters. "What on earth happened?"

I paused to condense my explanation into as compact a bite as it would go. "One of Gennady's friends tried to kill his sister. We stopped him. Gennady killed him. He and his sister were injured."

She flinched at the mention of killing before facing Gennady with her spine straight and her gaze steady. He was the worse injured; despite her misgivings, she had little choice but to walk toward him and put out a hand.

"I'm going to heal you now," she said tightly.

"Mariya first," Gennady said.

She shook her head. "You're worse off. Listen to me."

He nodded, though not without a sullen hesitation. "Okay, miss." Apparently, his respect for healers held true even when the rest of his self-control had been eroded. Lady folded herself to the ground beside him.

There was a brilliant cloud of light in the air as Malise's magic flooded the room, bright enough that I had to shade my eyes. Slowly but surely, the gashes and burns showing through Gennady's clothes began to close and mend, scabs appearing.

Not even a healer such as she could entirely erase the traces of that violence, but she came as close as anyone could. The wounds were reduced to red scabs, and Gennady breathed easier.

"Your rache next," Malise said grimly. Clearly, the thought of touching a rache set her on edge. I wanted to tell her that Lady wasn't so bad, really, that she was as small and sweet-tempered as the creatures went, but Gennady was protesting before I could open my mouth.

"No," he said, teeth suddenly bared. "You're not touching her."

Malise closed her hands into fists and then slowly released them. "You don't want her healed? You want her to be in pain?"

"I just don't want you touching her. It's not personal. It's just—" He looked at me. "*You* can do it, right?"

Silently, ashamed, I shook my head. I wanted to. I could have, if I'd forced myself. But the barrier was far too great to overcome on command.

"We've gotten along just fine without healers before," Gennady said. "We'll do it again. I'll take care of her. You can't touch her."

Malise bit her lip hard, maybe forcing back some unkind words. "It's my understanding that raches are as smart as their people," she said.

Gennady blinked. "Sure. So what?"

"So why don't you ask her what she prefers?"

There was a deathly silence while he decided whether or not to be offended. Eventually, he said, "Lady, do you want to get healed?"

She lay down and rested her head on her paws, looking up at him calmly. We all stood, unsure of what that meant, until Gennady cursed and turned away. "Fine," he said thickly. "Go ahead. But you be careful. All right?"

Yet again, I was confronted by the fact that I had no idea what the rache bond was like. I was never going to understand that aspect of Gennady's existence. It would always remain a mystery to me, and there was no way to change that. All I knew was that it must be nerve-wracking to have a virtual stranger make prolonged magical contact with one's rache, with the being who comprised the other half of one's self. I put my hand on Gennady's shoulder, very carefully.

When Lady's healing was done, Mariya spoke up. She was still shaky, not quite over her shock. I doubted she would be any time soon. "Doesn't anyone care about me?" she said. "Don't I get healed?"

Malise had more tenderness for a child, no matter if that child was disagreeable. "Of course we care," she said quietly, and moved to stand in front of Mariya. "You agree to it?"

"Just fix me already," Mariya whispered. "It hurts."

It was nice to know that her eerie similarity to Gennady didn't go soul-deep. There was still a vulnerable child somewhere in there. I tried to imagine that there might be hope for her yet.

Again, the wash of lovely blue light. Again, the wounds closed slowly, painstakingly.

Gennady reached out to pull Mariya toward him, and she jerked away. "You have no right."

It hurt more than I expected it would to see him rejected again. She blamed him for his indiscretion, clearly, for its role in sending Alim after her. That was sensible, in many ways. I just wasn't sure he could handle it. "Sorry," he mumbled.

The urge for more nepenthe grew and grew, more insistent by the minute. I felt it tugging inside my veins.

"A moment outside," Malise said to me. Gratefully, I stepped out of the room with her.

"Why on earth were you with them when this happened?"

"Bad timing," I said. "It was just . . . an awful coincidence."

"You have a little bruise," she said with brewing suspicion. "On your face. Did the soldier—?"

Abruptly, my memories of Casmir came flooding back. They felt faraway now, but the ache remained. "No," I said quickly. "No, no. He didn't."

"Then who?"

The desire to protect Casmir wasn't there. If I was dealing with the consequences of my actions, he could too. "Casmir," I said, quietly.

Malise went rigid, her jaw set with fury. "Why?"

I tried to think. Of everything I'd done, what had been the thing to set him off? "He was angry with me for the nepenthe. He said we were done, and I asked him to stay, and . . ."

"I'll kill him myself," she said, and hugged me. The venom in her voice was pure, but her embrace was gentle.

Despite myself, I laughed. "I'd rather you not. I still need to untangle him from my finances."

She stood away again. "Do you think you're really done, after everything?" The question sounded hopeful, which I forgave her for.

A crush of pain threatened, then passed. "Probably," I said, trying to make my smile brave rather than merely sickly.

She didn't pursue that; as always, she knew where to press. "You told him you need another keeper?"

An unwelcome echo sounded in my mind: *Keeper, please.* "I told him."

She sighed deeply. "The nepenthe. You seem sober now."

"To my very great dismay," I said, "I am."

I didn't stick my comedic delivery, and she didn't laugh. "Are you going to let me keep you here overnight, maybe? Help you stay that way a little longer?"

I wanted to make her proud, to agree and let her take care of things. In the end, though, sedation won, as I was beginning to suspect it always would. "Another day, maybe," I said.

"You frustrate me," she said calmly.

"I know that," I said, and extended her the courtesy of not sounding contrite. If I wasn't prepared to do anything about the nepenthe, contrition seemed a poor offering. "I intend to stop someday."

She motioned for me to lean down. I obliged, and she kissed me on the cheek. I felt blessed, as though a saint herself had descended from the stars to give me her consideration. "You're looking thinner," she said. "Eat something, if you're not going to clean up."

I nodded. No matter how many times she proved that I didn't deserve her, I never numbed to the ache. "I can promise that."

We went back inside to see to the rest of the Richters' treatment. They complained and fought the whole way through, but it was oddly comforting. No matter the travails, they remained essentially themselves, and that was worth something.

～

The next day, Gennady, Mariya, and I met at the Watchtower to give our accounts for the satisfaction of the witchfinders. The process went smoothly enough, although we were all of us tired and out of sorts. We submitted to interrogation; we filled out forms. The witchfinders demanded a meticulous recounting—difficult to deliver, given the adrenaline of the experience.

We wracked our brains for salient details to offer up, and by the end, we left feeling assured that the witchfinders didn't hold Gennady accountable for Alim's killing. It had been taken care of as Clementia business, where killing was routine. The witchfinders were, after all, on Velleia's side.

Relieved, I dosed myself with restraint that night. Not too much. Just enough to restore me to my baseline, to send me to sleep dreamlessly. I regret it, in hindsight. If I'd kept my wits, I might have anticipated sooner that matters were about to come to a head.

Chapter 23

For a self-supposed genius, I'd made some truly awful decisions. Filing our report with the Watchtower, primarily. This was made apparent to me the next morning when a complement of Vigil soldiers and traitor magicians dragged me into a lecture hall with some of my other colleagues. They told us with gleaming smiles and sabers that the time for reckoning had arrived, and I resolved to die in as inconvenient of a way as I could manage.

That wasn't necessary quite yet. Myself and the other cornered magicians were corralled into the hall, whispering fearfully amongst each other; shortly, Kirchoff stepped forward to pull me aside individually.

"Well, here we are," he said. "You finally slipped. The pieces are falling into place."

"Just tell me what it was," I said.

Kirchoff smiled, oily and content. "Your pet Vigil's little stunt at the Watchtower. Did you really think it would go unnoticed? Especially after you *filed a report about it*. Did you think we wouldn't have spies within the witchfinders?"

I hadn't, in fact; too overwhelmed to remain suspicious, I'd believed the public image of incorruptibility the witchfinders cultivate. I felt singularly stupid. Poor judgment.

Kirchoff clasped his hands behind his back. "It came at such an opportune moment, too. Just in time for us to have cemented trust with Mulcaster. The plan is complete now; no one can back out. You being exposed won't have any bearing on us anymore."

"Congratulations," I said distantly. "You must feel so proud." I had to wonder if I would have a chance to beg protection from Velleia again, or if we were all up against the wall now.

"I do, actually. It's time to face your consequences, Desfourneaux."

Consequences, consequences.

He stepped away from me to address the wider group. The other Pharmakeia faculty stood rigid and ashen, shying from the Vigil officers' sabers and raches. I counted Gailhardt, Pavarotti, and Xu among them. They all looked like they were asking much the same question as I was: was it time to die?

"Attention," Kirchoff said. "You all know why you're here, I trust. You've been dissenting from the cause. It's time to pay for that."

All of us on the same side raised our magic all at once, ready to defend ourselves as well as a roomful of academic magicians was capable of. The air surged.

Kirchoff sneered. "Oh, put your hands down. This won't be a slaughter just yet. You're being offered a second chance." He gestured grandly, magnanimously. "Realign your priorities, and you'll live when everything comes due."

Pennyblood villain, I thought.

"Monsters," Gailhardt called, and then shrieked as a rache snapped at her ankles. A ripple went through the crowd; everyone near her flinched as well.

"May I assume that this doesn't apply to me?" I asked, loudly and clearly. Heads turned. My colleagues rustled in surprise. I didn't feel the confidence, but it was no time to show weakness. "I can't imagine you're keen to leave me alive."

Kirchoff shook his head. "Of course you'll get your second chance too," he said. "We're reasonable. We're generous."

I had to wonder if he was only saving me for some more spectacular fate. "You must know we're far beyond that," I said.

He smiled. "I have an offer for you that should give you pause."

I knew, down to my bones, that there was no offer that could sway me, until he said, "Would you like to be cured?"

It felt like a hot needle. "Pardon," I said.

"We're working miracles here," he said. "The things we've achieved have been beyond what anyone thought possible. Imagine what we could do with augmented mind magic—a cure for your little condition might not be too far behind. Wouldn't you like that?"

I went dizzy.

"Wouldn't you like to be healed?"

Oh, to be healed.

"You're a force to be respected, Desfourneaux," he said. "Imagine what you'd be with the augment. Imagine what you could do, if only you put aside your pride for a moment and considered the gift you're being offered here."

"No," I said.

He lifted a hand in consternation. "So you'd rather die?"

"I want to be healed," I said faintly.

He nodded. "Good. Then—"

It hurt to force my next words out; every lesser instinct was screaming for me to consider this just a few moments longer. There was a world where I said yes, where Kirchoff was telling the truth. I could see that world clearly. I could almost reach it, if I tried, and it looked beautiful. It looked like home.

"But not by you."

If Malise could not cure me, no one could. I would not chase shadows for Kirchoff and his empty promises.

With that, with the spell of his offer broken, the world faded back into view. I realized that some of the other magicians on our side were looking at me with surprise and something like admiration, turned toward me as though I could offer any sort of hope. I smiled at the small crowd, feeling absolutely nothing.

"Unfortunate," Kirchoff said flatly, and he was done with me. "Very well. All those who would like one more chance, stand here." He pointed toward one side of the room. "All those who'd like to die for their convictions, to the other side."

Everyone shuffled toward where he'd pointed, heads low. There was no debate. I didn't expect there to be; there was nothing to blame them for. I stayed put, however.

One of the Vigil shifted a hand toward her saber, but Kirchoff stopped her. "Leave him. I'm saving him for Tenniel."

I felt the beginning of something. Some manner of spiral. Some type of collapse. Another one to add to the pile, and nothing more. Nothing more. I put my hands in my pockets. "How many of these little meetings are you holding across the Pharmakeia, Marsilio?" I asked.

"Enough to start the ball rolling," he said. "The academy will be ours soon."

I was finished listening. I started for the door to the lecture hall. "If you don't need me for anything else," I said.

"Be here later," he said. "The Pharmakeia will be convening for its final decision at five tomorrow, in the hall of St. Cynanne."

"Fine." I turned.

"One more thing, actually," he said.

I stopped.

"Your pet officer." He smiled. "He's in custody now."

A crackle of lightning ringed me, sending the enemies a few steps back. Kirchoff moved back too, but his smile rekindled quickly. "There aren't many yet, but do you know that the successfully augmented soldiers turn out very obedient to their enchanters? *Unbelievably* obedient. He's being turned as we speak.

"You did that to him," Kirchoff said. "Enjoy the knowledge, Desfourneaux."

"Where is he?" I asked. The rest of our company had vanished from my mind. It was only the two of us in the room, as far as I was concerned.

He folded his hands. "Now, now. It wouldn't be much fun if I told you."

Quietly, without a fuss, I snapped.

I left the room without looking behind me, and I wasn't stopped. The rest of my fellows would need to deal with the situation as best they could on their own.

No classes were being taught at the Pharmakeia that day. I gathered my things and left to go break myself.

～

Over time, I've learned what sorts of things can induce mania. A lack of sleep. Caffeine, alcohol, nepenthe. Stress. Irregular treatment. Fighting with a friend. Loud noises, even. I had most of those covered already. All I needed to do was hit the others.

I was out of options. With the daimon's colder side dragging me down, I was useless. I needed its help. I needed it to take control, and maybe *it* would be able to think of *something*. I could think of where Gennady might be; I could think of how to get him back. I could think of how to save the Pharmakeia. That, or I'd get myself killed, and either way, the situation would be improved. Hopefully, Malise's last treatment had reset me strongly enough to allow for a second mental break.

So I went to the nearest market to buy some whiskey and coffee. Things were looking up.

When I got home with my shopping, I put a pot of coffee on. I'd mix it with the whiskey, I decided, for efficiency's sake. I took a double dose of nepenthe, ozone and honey and the pinch of the needle and the ataraxiate and the paradisiac and the pure synthetic bliss, and I stumbled to the kitchen to wait for the water to boil.

I drank. I played piano.

Loud, discordant noise has always helped to edge me closer to any sort of akratic disturbance. I hadn't played piano in years; now that I finally had a good reason to try again, I fell back into yet another old habit with surprising ease. I played nothing in particular as dust flew off the keys, no identifiable piece, just fragments my mind spat out, played with as little grace as I could manage. Without a thought for my neighbors, I played until the sun began to go down, opening my mind up to the tender, raw friction of pure noise, wired and increasingly drunk.

It's hard to stay awake after too much nepenthe, never mind with the addition of alcohol. The caffeine could only do so much. I forced myself not to sleep. Not an instant, not for the entire night. I made myself remember making Malise cry. I told myself I'd enjoyed it. I replayed my argument with Casmir. I replayed *every* argument with Casmir.

What exactly had he said? What was his exact inflection? How much would it hurt to see him again, knowing that we were done? *Keeper, please.* I fantasized about him fucking me to keep myself awake, too flooded with chemicals to feel any real desire. I waited for the sun to come up, and I prayed to my daimon like it was a heathen god.

Come to me. Come to me. Come to me. Come to me.

I was blind to the passage of time. Hours passed in instants. When the mania broke over me, around three in the afternoon the next day, I could have died for joy. It wasn't in full swing yet; it would take longer for that. I didn't care. I had what I needed. I went to the hall of St. Cynanne at five o'clock feeling better than I ever had in my life.

Mania was enough to blunt the physical complaints resulting from my excesses. They were a faraway matter, something for another person to deal with at another time. Maybe my head hurt. Maybe my mouth was dry. Maybe I felt, overall, like I was in the aftermath of being struck by lightning. None of that mattered.

The hall was a huge amphitheater with excellent acoustics, not unlike a larger version of the hall of St. Osiander, except that it had a raised stage. I filed in among a long stream of other Pharmakeia faculty, feeling some-what at home. There were no students; only the professors were being judged. Through my haze, I thanked the stars for that.

Everyone murmured and whispered to each other, awkwardly filling the seats. The air rang with paranoia and terror; at least half of those present were convinced that we had all been brought here to die. The other half reserved their judgment, undecided—from them, I heard mostly words of compromise. Whatever deal was about to be offered, they told each other, it would be best to take it. Whatever they'd been told yesterday in their own little meetings with the traitor magicians, they'd been swayed.

I recognized plenty of faces; I saw Casmir. I was proud of him, in a sickly sort of way—he'd never joined the traitors if he was here. He'd found some courage after all. He half-raised a hand when he saw me, but I turned away. I worried that I might see Malise, that the Chirurgeonate might be making its own decision as well, but as far as I could tell, there were no healers in the crowd. The Archmagister was nowhere to be seen. She was either dead, in hiding, or a traitor. I wasn't sure which one I preferred.

Kirchoff and Tenniel were up on the stage, along with a respectable complement of other magicians. They watched us all fill the seats distant smugness, lording over the space. Kirchoff caught my eye, and I smiled brightly up at him. He'd pay soon, the daimon told me.

Once everyone was settled in their seats and the thin sounds of frantic conversation had died down, Kirchoff took center stage. "You're all here because you're in need of a second chance," he said. "This is that chance."

He waited to allow us all time to squirm, soaking it in. Next to me, a pair of magicians from the Light Studies department vowed to do whatever Kirchoff required, if only it meant they'd live. In my right mind, I couldn't have blamed them. Manic, it made me angry enough that a few sparks of lightning dripped from my hands, and they looked over at me with bewilderment.

"It's time for the remnants of the old Pharmakeia to make up their mind," Kirchoff said. "Prefect Mulcaster, as the new Pharmakeia's patron, is willing to extend to you all a deal."

The new Pharmakeia. I shivered with outrage, my skin prickling.

"Join us, prove your loyalty, and you may eventually be given the chance to receive the augment. Power untold. Reject this offer, and you'll be dead within the week. A purge is coming. You can be a part of the academy going forward, or the academy can go on without you."

He got off the stage; the other magicians with him trailed obediently after.

Immediately, everyone was on their feet, seeking out the peers they knew best to discuss.

Around me, my colleagues milled and muttered, working themselves into a dusty frenzy. The cardinal question was passed around the room a hundred times: Should we accept the deal? Should we sell our souls? *Could* we? If we fought, what were the chances we could prevail?

I wasn't worried; their deliberations were a charming amusement. Things were going to go my way. Didn't they always?

It's difficult for me to navigate the world in that state. It's a process of estimation: How quickly am I speaking? How much am I smiling? Do I make sense? A bright haze covers everything in sight. And at the other edge of the blade, the hatred, waiting to strike.

I had been holding it together so admirably, I thought. A laudable performance, a skillful facade. No more. My daimon yawned and opened its eyes. My headache vanished.

It's a wonderful feeling when the daimon cooperates with me. The sharpest joy in the cosmos, and a rage fit to kill.

Unbidden, I heard Gennady's voice, dripping with gleeful contempt: *You are so dramatic.*

I smiled, purely entertained by myself, and went up to stand at the lectern onstage. "Pay attention," I said to everyone, very loudly, cutting through their murmuring. Their heads turned. I knew the look on all their faces, collectively: *What does the daimoniac want?*

The lights began to flicker.

In the crowd, Casmir mouthed, *Don't.* I waved at him.

"I am going to have a breakdown now," I announced, "and you are all cordially invited."

Kirchoff pushed through the crowd to me, as I knew he would, taking the stage as well to stare me down. He didn't get too close.

You, I thought pleasantly. *You brought me here.*

He glanced up at the lights above. "Control yourself," he said severely. "Those fixtures are difficult to replace. They're very expensive. If you damage them—"

I turned to him, and the room tumbled into darkness with the sound of a dozen filaments bursting. The crowd gasped.

"What?" I asked, as the lightning came to my hands. I smoothed it into a crown and put it on: if I was going to make a spectacle of myself, I was going to do it with style. "What will you do?"

The only light in the room came from me, just as it should always be. I spread my arms grandly for a moment, for the aesthetic benefit, dizzy with my various highs.

Kirchoff's eyes widened, shining in the lightning's glow.

I leaned toward him a bare inch. "Let me ask—have you had your power augmented? You haven't, have you? You're afraid of what it'll be like. For all your speeches, you're afraid it'll go wrong."

"Don't," he began, and fell silent when I came to stand close to him. Below us, our other colleagues chittered, voicing nervous objections.

"Do you know what that means?" I said. "It means that however I decide to hurt you right now, you can't stop me." I felt a definite warmth toward him, all of a sudden. He was certainly trying his best. "Marsilio, dear, you requested my presence, and now you have it."

"You would not make yourself a witch," he said, shying from me. "You would not kill—"

The daimon turned. I slipped over the other edge of the knife. The world inverted. Hate. "Shut up," I hissed.

He recoiled; I despised him all the more for it.

I called another surge, felt the lightning bolt rest in my hand and purr. Lazily, it stretched, until I held a staff with a sleeping serpent coiled along its length. The healer's sign, twisting and flickering.

"Tell me what I wouldn't do," I said. "Traitor. Coward."

He was silent.

I smiled again, placated, blissful once more. "Quite. I'll do whatever I like."

Casmir said my name from the crowd, urgent. The knife spun perilously. How I had loved him once. How I wanted to ensure, once and for all, that he'd never speak to me again.

I ignored him. "Luckily for you," I said patiently to Kirchoff, "I am no killer. Barring that, however, one way or another, you are all going to do exactly what I want."

The lightning flashed; the power felt good. I wondered what it would be like to make Kirchoff feel just a little static—if he would like to be put on trial. If I would enjoy being his judge. I would not, I decided, but he saw me wondering. He hurried back from me, down the steps, and hid himself in the crowd. For all his menace, for all his poison, once I'd finally shown myself, he was no contest.

I knew that I would hate myself later, that I would wish I had been struck dead in that instant. It was a problem for another day.

Grinning freely, I spun to address the crowd: a sea of faces, indistinct, all turned toward me. "Ladies and gentlemen," I said, enjoying the echo of my voice against marble. "Thank you for your attention. The discussion is over now. No deal. The Pharmakeia will not bow to Prefect Mulcaster. I will not allow it."

Gailhardt raised her voice from the back. "There needs to be a vote, Desfourneaux. I agree with you, but—"

I closed my eyes briefly and resigned myself to the real possibility that I would be charged with and convicted of witchcraft at the end of all this. I knew that Casmir was in the crowd, hating me.

I poured the lightning out and out, until it flooded me, gracing the stage, crawling scars marring the wood. A field of stars, I imagined myself, blue and white. The world was terribly bright.

I didn't let it strike. I wouldn't. *They* didn't know that.

"All in favor," I said. My voice was the daimon's.

To a one, they raised their hands.

In my right mind, I could never have committed the others to the cause that way. I could never have decided that their lives were in my hands. I certainly could never have threatened them into potentially dying to fight Mulcaster. This may sound, to you, like a moment of triumph. It was not. It was a moment of monstrosity.

But I was serene in my selfishness. We would fight, and there was no possibility but victory.

"You have your answer," I called to Kirchoff, finding him in the crowd. He and his cadre stood together, ashen and uncertain. "Would the handful of you, augmented or not, like to try your luck against half the Pharmakeia's force?"

Left with no choice, my allies gathered their magics. The air sang; the ground shook. In all the city, I was sure, there must be no greater show of power. Academics or not, at the end of the day, magic is magic.

Kirchoff's unease had turned to fear. Of course he hadn't accounted for the logistics of an actual fight. Of course he'd been so sure of our cowardice that he'd come prepared only for domination.

"Feel free to surrender," I said, and aimed my lightning bolt at him. "Or feel free to struggle. Either way, Mulcaster is going to be terribly disappointed in you."

He was mute. I dropped down from the stage; the crowd parted around me as I walked to him.

"Marsilio," I said softly, nearly tickling his chin with the bolt. "Talk to me, Marsilio. Tell me how you're feeling about all this."

He swallowed. "Daimoniac."

"Yes," I hissed. "Answer."

"Cease-fire," he said.

"Louder, for the audience."

"Cease-fire."

Some of the deadly, thrumming tension in the room dissipated—

But the traitor magicians had their own ideas. A few summoned their power and turned on the nearest foes, and like that, the room descended into the starfield I'd imagined before. Dozens of magics tangled into each other. The light and sound were unbearable, nearly physical.

It was of absolutely no concern. With that, I left the room, heedless of the petty violence around me, and went to go find Gennady.

Chapter 24

The Penumbra, of course. Gennady was in the Penumbra. I knew it. I would have thought of it much sooner, if I hadn't been numbed and weighed down. As soon as the daimon had turned, I realized that it was a perfectly logical place to keep a dissenting enemy of the new Clementia.

Wait, you say. Wasn't that dangerous? Wasn't I aware that I would only be throwing myself into the jaws of whatever was waiting? Didn't I understand that the Penumbra was too dangerous to approach, given Mulcaster's coup?

Of course not. Nothing can go wrong in certain states of mania. Everything is bound to work out. Barring the terrible anger, barring the times when every thought is nothing but a particle in a dreadful buzzing sea, everything is beautiful. I was assured a perfect victory by nature of my mere existence.

The moment I set foot near the Penumbra, I could tell that it had been given over to Mulcaster. Velleia's faction of Vigil had lost control over the city's prisons; every officer who staffed the prison grounds had the same look in their eyes, the same guarded, mistrustful hunger I saw in Mulcaster's people. A desire for more, at whatever cost. The only faces I recognized were faces from the warehouse meetings.

I waited to be apprehended the instant I was recognized, but apparently, I wasn't important enough to Mulcaster for him to let the average Vigil soldier know that I was to be watched for. It was gratifying to know that even now, the communication between the new Pharmakeia and the new Vigil was threadbare at best. That, or the average Vigil soldier couldn't tell magicians apart. Either was eminently possible. Perhaps my confidence was the key; I walked through the Penumbra's gates and into the main prison without a single pause, assured of my good fortune.

There was a separate office cut off from the rest of the sprawling prison where affairs of organization could be dealt with, and I walked happily into it to present myself. The Penumbra's overarching theme of grim grayness and solid, joyless stone held true in the front area, but I wasn't bothered by the architecture. The Clementia's subpar aesthetic sensibilities were none of my concern. Mostly, I was relieved to get away from the light; the sun hurt my eyes.

"Excuse me," I said to one of the Vigil officers staffing the front.

He looked up at me with undisguised hostility. "What?"

"I'm looking for someone you probably have locked up in here," I said, smiling just because I felt like it. "Gennady Richter. He's Vigil, actually. His rache is a little thing named Lady. He would have been taken in just yesterday. I don't suppose you could help me find him?"

"Not my job," the officer said. His rache showed me its teeth.

"A general direction would be lovely. Any idea?"

He crossed his arms and leaned back in his chair, glowering at me from behind the screen of metal bars at the counter that separated him from me. "I don't know."

"I'm going to wander the prison until I find him, then," I said. "Is that quite all right with you? It's that, or I stand here and bother you until the sun goes down."

I watched him decide that he wasn't paid enough to obstruct me. He nodded me toward the entrance to the prison proper and went back to staring into the middle distance.

The Penumbra is enormous, a deme unto itself. To scour every inch of it would have taken me a very, very long time. Time I didn't have. Fortunately, I was manic, and so I undertook the expedition with perfect optimism.

I'd never been inside the Penumbra before. I'd never seen the rows and blocks of cells, packed with the poor and unfortunate, a monument to human suffering. I wasn't sure which was worse—the prisoners who looked up at me and entreated me with their eyes to somehow help them, or those who ignored me as if nothing from the world of sunlight could possibly touch them. It made me waver, I'll admit, but the uncertainty was short-lived. I continued on.

There were wards, of course. Both magical and antimagical, they stifled my lightning as I walked, slowing my blood. I ignored them.

Curial citizens, people with connections to one of the three Curiae of the government, are given their own cells in specific parts of the prison. I learned this through one-sidedly amicable conversation with the Vigil guards I encountered as I strolled through the Penumbra. As Vigil, Gennady was a curial citizen; it was possible that even now, Mulcaster's faction would respect that delineation and put him in a curial cell.

I asked to be directed toward where those might be, and my request was granted. The new Vigil seemed to assume that I had some sort of nefarious intent toward Gennady, and they were more than happy to assist me with it.

The Penumbra's population of feral cats scuffled with the guards' raches, creating a background din; a few times, one of them ran past me, chasing something or fleeing somewhere. The atmosphere would have been oppressive on any other day, but I was unbothered.

When I saw a cell that was guarded by two more Vigil than usual, I knew with absolute confidence that I'd found Gennady. It had taken me perhaps thirty minutes, no more, a testament to how graciously the universe was bending my way.

I walked up. Gennady was there, slumped on the floor of the cell with Lady laid across his lap. He didn't raise his head when I approached. How lucky he was, I thought, that I was here. The attending Vigil raised their eyebrows at me.

"My name is Adrien Desfourneaux," I said, confident that if they recognized me, I'd be able to defend myself handily. "I'm here to talk to Lieutenant Richter."

They stood in silent confusion.

I pointed down the corridor. "Go on," I said. "Go away. I'll need privacy."

The absolute authority with which I said it worked wonders. I was, after all, the most important person in the prison. Why wouldn't I speak with authority? Vigil are trained to respect power; they're accustomed to accepting orders. Those orders would normally never come from a magician, but their alliance with the traitor Pharmakeia magicians had apparently softened that line. They turned and set off down the corridor.

I knelt on the floor before the bars in front of Gennady, unmindful of the dirt on the floor. "Gennady."

Slowly, his gaze rose to meet mine. His hair was sticking up every which way; his eyes were dull. His uniform was terribly rumpled. He was a mess, and the look on his face was one of consummate hopelessness. Lady was scarcely any better, lying there limp and slit-eyed.

"Professor," Gennady said, with thick confusion.

"Hello," I said brightly. I still had the sense not to speak too loudly, at least. "Are you feeling all right?"

Even in such a state, he was able to give me an evil glare. "Fuck you."

I put a hand through the bars for Lady to lick; she shuffled a little closer to the bars. I was filled with a sudden, unaccountable tenderness for them both, as though Gennady were a favorite pupil of mine. In a way, he was.

"They took my sword," he added in the same aggrieved tone. "They broke it. They broke my saber."

What symbolism that might hold for a soldier was a mystery to me, but it was likely nothing good. "Have you been turned yet?"

"Of course not," he said. "Idiot. But they keep trying."

The curiousness of that statement struck me enough to cut into my brilliant haze. "They keep trying?"

"The magician comes every so often to mess with my head. Cast on me. But it doesn't work. So she comes again and again."

"Which magician is this?"

"Your pal," he said. "The lady."

"Tenniel?"

"Whatever."

It would have to be Tenniel. She hadn't been at the Pharmakeia.

I had to marvel; Gennady was hardheaded enough that even Tenniel couldn't successfully enchant him. Of all the soldiers and converted magicians, as far as I knew, only he had been both willing and able to resist.

"Sit straight, my dear," I said. "Come on. Tell me about it." He wasn't going to be able to inform me of any technical aspects of the process, but a few details couldn't hurt.

But he shook his head. "I can't. It just hurts. She puts her hands on my head and it hurts." His voice broke.

It was enough to turn me toward unchecked fury.

At least he was unaffected still, I thought, and then he coughed, and a mote of plasma drifted out.

I saw it in him, then. A spreading, spidering curse, making its way through his veins and the pathways of his mind. It was taking him. Even his stubbornness could not deny enchantment. Not forever.

Impossibly, my fury grew.

It was a shame that Malise wasn't there, I thought, that she couldn't try to heal him. He was in an early enough stage that she might well succeed. Then, by degrees, I realized that I had been a healer too, and I might do it instead. A rush of nausea shredded my manic confidence in an instant. I hadn't healed for so many years. I couldn't. I couldn't. My poisoned touch wouldn't allow it.

But there was no one else. Either I could cleanse his mind, or I could leave him to his transformation. Only one was any sort of option.

"Help me," he said.

I rested my head against the bars, taken by a sudden fit of shivering. It could have been my bone-deep terror, or it could have been the caffeine. Does it matter which? Quickly, I jerked up again, keen not to be seen in a moment of weakness by the Vigil nearby.

"Help me," he repeated, more insistently, almost with irritation. "Aren't you going to help me?"

It didn't matter if the other Vigil soldiers were watching us from afar. If I worked some sort of magic on him, they'd only think I was furthering Tenniel's vision for her. I'd need to work quickly, in case their suspicions were rising, but I *could* fix Gennady. If only I could work up the courage to cast, he could be saved.

"Come closer," I said to Gennady, gasping a little. "Up to the bars. I can heal you."

I prayed that I was telling the truth, that I could hold up to that promise.

He crawled a bit closer and put his face up to the metal, looking at me with cool animal interest. "You'll be careful," he said, less a question than a statement.

"I'll be careful." If I hadn't been manic, I might have paused to consider that a delicate magical working would be best undertaken sober.

I reached my hands between the bars to rest against his temples, brushing aside his tangled hair. He closed his eyes, a reflexive gesture against fear. A crackle of lightning flashed around him, never touching.

Tenniel's instructions from the warehouse echoed in my head—*Tear it.* That wouldn't do. Driving out a physical contagion with healing magic is about the proper application of heat, in large part. Driving out a curse would be something different. I closed my eyes as well and sent my magic out into him; my instinct was to stay on the surface, not to invade, but I could feel Tenniel deeper. I could feel her hooks and barbs far below.

Slowly, with as much care as I could summon, I began to gather up the tiny pieces of her power remaining inside him, wrapped around his thoughts— binding his soul, digging away at the barrier between his life's power and his self. She was eroding him.

I swept away the acid she'd left behind; I thought of myself as a needle and thread. Use the needle to cut Tenniel away, draw the thread through the holes. Pull it tight, gather the excess. As I went, I took utmost care not to leave a speck of my power behind. I couldn't risk imposing anything of myself on him. Not if I wanted to live with myself.

When I was done, he slumped, and I feared the worst. Within a moment, though, he'd steadied himself. I couldn't see any difference, but I felt something, a bit more solidity to him, a mental barrier somewhat repaired.

I made a small, wounded sound, relieved beyond words, beyond sensation. The akratic confidence came trickling back in—of *course* I'd succeeded. Why had I ever doubted that I would? I was powerful; I was talented. There had never been any other possibility.

Before I had much time to enjoy that thought, Gennady looked up at me. No—not at me. Behind me. There were footsteps, I realized abruptly.

"Desfourneaux," Tenniel said, of course.

～

I staggered to my feet to face her. The Vigil from before were behind her, wearing the sullen expressions of people who knew that they'd been tricked.

"Winifred," I said pleasantly, lightheaded from standing. "I'm so happy to see you."

"You're not as smart as you think you are," she said.

I was feeling too accomplished to be offended. "I—"

"You're supposed to be at the Pharmakeia," she said, with keen suspicion.

"Well." I smiled winningly. "Ask Kirchoff about that later. Assuming he's still alive. Things didn't go quite according to plan."

Her eyes narrowed. She raised a hand. "Whatever you've done . . ."

"I have to wonder what you'll tell Mulcaster."

"Take him," she said. The Vigil set upon me.

One of them grabbed me by the arm; the vicious pressure against a recent injection site was painful, and I yelped. The raches circled me, hissing and rumbling deep in their chests, ready for blood. I stood still, barely breathing. It was, I admit, enough to faze me. Around us, the other prisoners who could see muttered in concern.

Tenniel took a key from one of the officers and unlocked Gennady's cell. "Up," she said.

He dragged himself up.

"Out."

He and Lady shuffled out of the cell. Tenniel gave Lady a kick on the way, and Gennady spasmed silently with sympathetic agony. The look on his face was unlike anything I'd ever seen before—a serene, primordial hatred. A killing look.

I moved forward, but the soldier holding me drew me back.

"Time to go," Tenniel said. "We're cleaning things up. It was good of you to present yourself for capture so easily, Desfourneaux."

I neatened my clothes, irritated with the Vigil officer for ruffling me. "You're welcome. Where are we going?"

"Just outside," she said, reveling in crypticity. I hated for her for it. "With all the others."

"And who are all the others, exactly?"

She thinned her lips and didn't answer. The second Vigil guard took Gennady by the collar, choking him a little. For a moment, I thought he'd bite, but he only swayed.

I could have defended us easily. Easily, if only I'd been willing to kill. If I had tried, I might have been able to break through the wards. In that moment, I was powerful enough for it. But I had no idea how to use lightning to incapacitate; I had no experience with attacking people. If I was going to use it, I would risk destroying whomever I struck.

It was more a question of squeamishness than ethics. Manic or not, I couldn't do it. So I obeyed carefully when Tenniel said, "Come on, now," and the Vigil began to march Gennady and me out of the Penumbra.

We passed several other captured Vigil officers being taken from the prison as well by their former comrades, their raches snarling as they filed out alongside us. By the time our procession was nearing the entrance, we were walking alongside dozens of other apprehended unfortunates.

I winced as we came out into the lowering sun, my various chemical influences all protesting the light at once. Behind me, Gennady swore weakly under his breath, a continuous stream of invective. We converged with the stream of other allies being corralled into the bleak stretch of packed dirt that served as the prison's expansive front yard.

I was the only captured magician; the few other Pharmakeia staff were all with Tenniel. All around, disobedient Vigil were forced to kneel in the dirt, surrounded by their victorious fellows.

Gennady stayed standing. The officer holding me let go and joined efforts with the other to kick him down to his knees. Lady snapped, but a rumbling growl from another rache quelled her. I stayed where I was.

In the distance, I saw Mulcaster stroll in from the front, accompanied by a grim handful of other high-ranking Vigil. Corvier was among them; my stomach turned. In the dirt, Gennady made a small, low sound.

The splitting of the Vigil was complete. It was absolute. Through Kirchoff's poor management, the Pharmakeia had been spared the final blow, but Mulcaster had made no such mistakes.

By the time Mulcaster was near enough to survey the scene in full, a deathly hush had fallen over the gathering. Every pair of eyes was on him. His faction was looking upon their god, and ours was looking upon their death.

I waited for a long victory speech that did not come. "Soldiers," Mulcaster called to the kneeling Vigil. "We've broken your sabers. It's over. I have one last order for you: find your unitmates. Your *first* unit." He spoke to them in the tones of a disappointed father.

There was no disobedience. There was no hesitation. Even now, a Prefect's authority was absolute. The kneeling soldiers staggered to their feet, pointedly unaided by Mulcaster's Vigil, and began to mill as one. The crowd mixed and converged as they singled out those from their unit to huddle together with, their raches piling near each other in solidarity. Gennady didn't move; his family came to him. I stood just outside the ring, with Tenniel breathing down my neck.

I had to wonder how many of the standing Vigil were unitmates with the kneeling. Did it hurt them to see this?

Once the gathering was divided properly, silence fell again. The mystery of what was about to happen seized me; I watched the scene with pinpoint obsession.

No matter how long I'd considered, I never could have imagined what Mulcaster had in mind.

"You will fight amongst yourselves," he said. "Fight to the death. Those who survive, one per unit, will be rewarded with the gift of augmentation."

The daimon, no longer enjoying itself, stretched inside me. Thin strands of lightning began to rise, lashing the air. The Vigil around me stepped away; Tenniel said, "Easy."

The Vigil all looked at each other. Nearby, Gennady pulled Lady to him, holding her close.

Mulcaster made a gesture, a lazy lift of one hand. "Trial by combat. Get to it."

They had no weapons. He intended them to tear each other apart with their raches. No one moved. No one breathed.

"If you don't fight," Mulcaster said, with infinite patience, "then *none* of you will have been proven worthy of the augment, and none will survive."

Nothing, still. The Penumbra had dropped out of time. We'd discovered a whole new world, a parallel earth where silence reigned.

For a moment, I dared to hope. I dared to hope that Vigil loyalty would prevail, that if not a single soldier broke, Mulcaster's people would understand the enormity of their crime. Maybe if the silence lasted, there would be no blood.

But of all the units, Gennady's was the first to fracture. A young woman with a massive brown rache split into a sob, turned to Gennady, and fell upon him with teeth and nails. Her rache snapped its jaws around his ankle, and he screamed, and the sound rang out across the waiting graveyard. Just like that, the dirt of the Penumbra began to churn red.

I wanted badly to cover my eyes; I wanted to look away. Mania could not blunt the horror. But I knew I owed it to Gennady to watch. I owed it to him to bear witness to the fall.

It was never in question that Gennady would be the victor over his kin. That knowledge did nothing to blunt the keen agony of watching him tangle in the dust. Lady had never looked smaller or sweeter than she did then, working the other Vigil into fine red shreds. Before I knew it, Tenniel had stepped away from me too, because all around me there was lightning.

One by one, Gennady tore the others down. They all knew that he was the most dangerous; they all came for him before so much as looking at any of the others. He fought ten at once, and then nine, and then eight. Seven. Six. Five. Four. Three. Two.

One. The young woman who had first attacked him. She'd survived until the end. I thought—I hoped—that Gennady might hesitate, might plead with her. I should have known better. He strangled her in front of me, methodically. She made tiny sounds, her last words trapped in her throat. She thrashed. She died.

"Watch," I heard Tenniel say from a very great distance. I watched.

There was nothing I could do. Even if I finally killed, I couldn't stop the violence. I looked out over the broad expanse of dirt in the setting sun and decided that the heathen concept of a hell must look a great deal like this. A rache can tear the throat of a human being in a few seconds with little effort. Occasionally, a captured soldier would fling themselves at one of Mulcaster's. That death was always instant.

Amidst the howls and the screams, whenever the din lulled, I could hear the true character of the slaughter: the sobs of the victors. Gennady knelt with Lady, ringed by kin, and stared up at me, almost inquisitive. It was the look of an innocent: *Are you proud?* I'll forever regret that I looked away.

Slowly, by degrees, the new reality crystallized. The dust settled again. The last bodies fell; the last writhings of downed soldiers faded into the air. Most of the units had their single survivor. A few of them had none at all—the final combatants had bled out shortly after their victories.

I turned my attention to the standing Vigil, trying to read their faces. Were they horrified? Were they pleased? The gathering was split, I found. Some of them watched with quiet smiles, and others fought dangerous tears, forcing them back as the liability they were. The illusion of a monolith was broken.

Corvier made his way over to survey the remnants of his children. "Traitor," he said when he saw Gennady alive, exquisitely casual. He spat in the red dirt.

Gennady reached one hand out toward him, dragging the other hand across his face and smearing a long red streak across his cheek. Lady whined. "Ain't no fucking traitor," he growled, the diction of the baseborn demes beginning to crawl through his voice.

Corvier pretended not to understand, raising his eyebrows; his sable rache snorted. "Remember your elocution, now."

Gennady exterminated the baseborn drawl and repeated himself. "I said I am no fucking traitor, Captain."

Corvier looked away from him without another moment of consideration, examining me behind my screen of lightning. "Tenniel," he said.

She nodded.

"Take care of this one."

Then I was on my knees, and I was choking, and the lightning had died. The air had gone from my lungs; I couldn't draw a single breath.

Every kind of magic has its particular horrors. Tenniel's talent was among the worst, I decided, as I began to starve for oxygen. Dust devils swirled around us, taunting me.

Of course Tenniel had been augmented; she was braver than Kirchoff. Her magic was now beyond anything I could reach. She was above the laws of nature. She was my better in every way, and she had only allowed me my freedom so long because it amused her to see me try.

Gennady stumbled to his feet and dashed toward Tenniel, but Corvier brought his saber up and forced him back. He came forward again. Corvier struck him brutally on the head with the hilt of the blade, and he fell. He didn't get up.

A dizzying rush of stars flooded my vision, dying away into brilliant blackness. I felt a few last sparks of lightning at my fingertips, valiant gasps, but I knew I'd be unconscious before long. The buzzing in my ears grew to a tremendous pitch.

In the far distance, I heard a woman's voice. Not Tenniel's; abruptly, Tenniel had stopped choking me. I could breathe again—the relief of it combined with the drugs, and I teetered on the edge of consciousness. Eventually, shapes began to resolve in front of me. I could see, little by little.

What I saw when I raised my head was Prefect Tessaly Velleia, and behind her, the ragged skeleton of an army.

Chapter 25

Corvier cursed viciously and stepped backward. A dangerous rumble echoed through the gathered traitor Vigil as the occasional sobs from the decimated units quieted.

"Everett Mulcaster," Velleia called, in her strong, low voice, the voice of an oncoming apocalypse. "I convict you of treason, by the authority of Basilea Illyria."

The Basilea who headed the Curia Clementia, one of the two empresses. I had to wonder where she had been throughout all of this—had she been unaware until now, somehow? Had she been watching and waiting to see who would prevail? Either way, it didn't matter; in the final hour, she had chosen Velleia. A wave passed through the gathered Vigil—the traitors wavered, and the defeated dared to hope.

Amphion tipped back his head and howled, a sound of raw, unmitigated violence. One by one, every other rache joined in, both the new Vigil and the old, baying together as one in response to a Prefect's call.

The howl of a rache evokes something primal in anyone who hears it. For the Vigil, it signals that there's prey to be had. For the rest of us, it reminds us of the days before civilization.

Only Mulcaster's mottled, half-tailed rache was silent. The two of them stood unmoving, unimpressed, almost bored by Velleia's challenge—or so it might seem to the unobservant. Mulcaster's expression was calm, but in his eyes there was a subtle fire.

When the deadly racket had died down, he walked slowly to Velleia, one hand on his executioner's sword. For the most part, those swords were intended to be symbolic, ceremonial. I had a sense that both Prefects would be willing to repurpose them.

Velleia ignored Mulcaster studiously. "The Basilea has given her orders," she called to the Vigil. "She's been presented with all the evidence she needs. She's issued her legal decree. Anyone who wishes to stand in the way of that stands against the city of Astrum itself."

Mulcaster turned to his troops as well. "Illyria is beholden to the Curia. The Curia is not beholden to her. We'll take our victory here, and then we'll see what she says."

"Sacrilege," Velleia said. The Basilissae are, in the civic liturgy, goddesses. A gasp swept the Penumbra's yard.

Velleia stood with a grim smile, as though by uttering the word, she'd decided the matter. She should have known that Vigil who were willing to sacrifice their comrades would never be swayed by such infinitesimal matters as sacrilege.

"Ready," Mulcaster said. His voice rang out across the dirt, and the traitor Vigil raised their sabers. The hatred on his face was a force unto itself. I recalled the rumor that Amphion had taken the other half of his rache's tail.

"You're outnumbered." Velleia drew her executioner's sword.

"Not for long," Mulcaster snarled. He turned on his heel and approached Tenniel, absolutely heedless of me as I knelt before her. She straightened up, ashen despite herself.

Mulcaster's rache—Leo, I remembered; what a darling name—came to inspect me as Mulcaster and Tenniel spoke. He was nearly as tall as I was, on my knees. The edges of my vision blackened again.

"You," Mulcaster said. "Where are the other magicians?"

"On their way," Tenniel said. "They were given notice to be here as soon as possible. There was some sort of trouble with Kirchoff, but they should be here."

And he was drawing a breath to interrogate her about the specifics of *soon* when the first magicians arrived. Magicians have a weakness for aesthetics, and the drama of timing is included in that category. Mulcaster's magicians had come in style. As they approached Velleia's army, I could feel their power, a pressure in the air. I could hear it buzzing in their veins. The Penumbra was packed.

Tenniel left me kneeling to join her fellows, content that I was no longer capable of being a threat. She seemed eager to get away from the Vigil, I realized, and they were glad to be rid of her as well. With that realization came the shaky, threadbare beginnings of a plan.

Gennady was just beginning to come to; I stood, not without difficulty, and went to shake him by the arm, pulling him to sit.

"Professor," he said.

I tried to stand him up, but he crumpled again. "Come on," I said. "Come with me."

With my shoulder under his arm, I helped him walk to the center of the yard, heedless of the gathering crowd of magicians and the arguing Prefects. No one stopped us. We were watched by some, with hope or hostility, but everyone had bigger concerns. Once we were at the center, I helped Gennady sit again.

"What the hell are you doing?" he slurred.

"I want to make sure everyone can hear me," I said.

He only shook his head, not willing to bother with questions. Blood shone through his hair where Corvier had struck him.

Mulcaster's magicians had fully filtered into the Penumbra's yard. Some of Velleia's soldiers made the beginnings of moves to attack them, but a raised hand from her kept them under control. I expected her to touch off a wholesale slaughter, but evidently, she was more interested in minimizing the damage than Mulcaster was. The Penumbra was a lodestone, I thought dizzily, pulling every vicious and unfortunate soul toward it bit by bit.

Some of the traitor magicians looked at me curiously as they took their places next to the soldiers. Kirchoff and his cadre weren't among them, of course. At least we'd taken that small sliver of their force away.

But this was not going to go the way of the hall of St. Cynanne.

It was time to try something. I turned to the magician nearest to me, a few paces away, and said, "Really?"

She narrowed her eyes at me, taking me in. I knew I looked awful; a distant pang of vanity made me wince.

"I mean, *really*?" I repeated, as Mulcaster and Velleia talked with each other up front, the hatred radiating from them like a spotlight. Others around us had turned their attention to me.

"Really what?"

"Allying with the Vigil," I said.

She shrugged. "A necessary evil."

"You know they hate us."

"It's only temporary."

I mimicked the shrug she'd given me. "Good luck betraying them before they can betray you."

"Aren't you Adrien Desfourneaux?"

I had to smile. "That's me."

"You've already lost," she said. "Time to stop talking."

Unfortunately for her, it is rarely time for me to stop talking. "You're telling me you don't remember how the Vigil used to treat us, before all this?"

"Of course I remember," she said softly, as a few of the other traitor magicians who had settled near us cocked their heads.

Gennady was staring at me. "Always threatening," I said. "Always with their sabers in hand. How many times have you seen them terrify one of your students?"

She set her jaw. "Plenty. That's not what this is about."

"Tell me," I said. "You don't expect me to believe that the alliance has been *easy.*"

"Of course not."

"How many times have *you* been threatened? Hmm? In the last week, say."

Her expression told me that the answer was, as I'd predicted, not *zero.*

A different nearby magician broke in. "They've all been brutes about it."

"The alliance was supposed to last until you perfected the process, wasn't it?" I said. "That happened a long time ago. Why are you still beholden to them?"

"Kirchoff said," he began.

I swept my hand in a cutting motion. "Forget about Kirchoff. He made his mistakes. He's . . . out of the picture." I didn't think he was dead, but *they* didn't have to know that. "Why are you still fighting the Vigil's battles for them?"

We were attracting the attention of a small crowd.

The first woman crossed her arms. "It's just for a little while longer."

"Oh," I said. "So you're willing to risk death for them."

She blanched.

"Because that's what you're here for," I said. "They're using you as fodder. If you fight here, now, Velleia's forces are going to rip you to pieces."

She looked uneasily at Velleia's ragged army.

"That's right. Is that how you want to end up? Killed by the Vigil after all— just how they threatened so many times?"

Hesitantly, she shook her head, and the growing group of other magicians around us that were listening shook their heads too.

Gennady spoke up. He'd caught the eye of a nearby survivor of the old Vigil, a teary-eyed young man with a broad slash across his face and a bloodied rache. "Listen to them," he said to his comrade, breathlessly. "Cowards."

"Hey," the first magician said. None of Mulcaster's magicians had been around to see me dragging Gennady to the center of the yard; she didn't know we were connected in any way.

"You are," Gennady said. "You're cowards. I can tell." He paused. "But then, all you Pharmakeia people are."

I was betting that the majority of Mulcaster's magicians would have no inclination to distinguish between the old Vigil and the new, bloodied or not. To them, a soldier was a soldier. Gennady's insults might as well be coming from Mulcaster himself.

"Better a coward than a vicious animal," I said to Gennady. I smiled at him; he smiled back.

"Better a vicious animal than a magician," he said.

One of Mulcaster's Vigil nearby broke in. "Shut up over here."

The woman I'd been talking to bridled. "You can't tell us to shut up."

The officer's rache showed its teeth, and she shied. A discontented murmur spread throughout the small crowd around us.

"Pathetic," Gennady said to Mulcaster's officer. "Right? Aren't they?"

The officer opened his mouth, possibly to tell Gennady to shut up as well, but before he could, I turned to Gennady again. "Quiet down." I made my tone as sharp as I could—quarrelsome, waspish, everything I did best.

That got the officer to turn on me instead. "Not another word out of you."

I glanced at the other magicians surrounding us. "Can you believe this? They never stop ordering us around."

My status as an enemy was quickly being forgotten. I saw them nodding. Evidently, deep-rooted prejudice was stronger than new-forged alliances. Magicians were magicians, and Vigil were Vigil. A sad lesson for humanity, a grim indication overall, but a godsend for me and my half-formed plan.

Slowly, the discussion spiraled out of control. First another single voice chimed in, and then two from the opposing side, and then a dozen more people were talking all at once.

Mulcaster and Velleia, meanwhile, put aside their standoff for long enough to walk over and investigate the commotion.

"Explain," Velleia said, standing a thousand feet tall.

Mulcaster was silent, surveying the scene with deadly consternation.

The quarreling crowd had stilled. Dust hung in the air.

I looked at Gennady and beckoned. He gave me a wide grin and launched himself at me, knocking me to the ground with a flying tackle.

It was all the powder keg needed. The magicians around us cried out in outrage and raised their magic, and the Vigil drew their sabers.

The lodestone of the Penumbra pulled everyone in close, and the violence spread like a virus as Mulcaster's soldiers and magicians sprang upon each other. Velleia's people obligingly joined in. A vast wave of magic and sound poured from across the prison yard, and for the second time that day, I found myself in battle.

The tide was coming, but I had the grace of a few moments before it broke. If Gennady and I dashed, I thought, we might be able to escape the Penumbra.

My akratic confidence was well and truly gone; I was no longer thinking in terms of guaranteed victories. It was time to *leave*, no matter how selfish that might be.

Gennady rolled off me; I struggled to my feet and gave him a hand up, amidst all the chaos. "Come on," I cried, over the din.

Mulcaster and Velleia had their executioner's swords out. As their forces dissolved around them, every possible crossfire running hot, they dueled. They moved like gods of death, like evil poetry. I saw Mulcaster cut Velleia open along the side; I saw her nearly take his head off.

If I watched any longer, I knew, I'd be entranced. I looked away and dragged Gennady toward the exit from the prison yard.

But he stopped. I felt his weight drag against me as he stood still, and I looked back at him.

He mouthed, silent over the noise, *Watch out.*

I turned to look behind me.

Corvier. I'd forgotten Captain Hiram Corvier. He stood, face twisted in unholy rage, hating his son. He'd followed us to the center.

The world quieted, just for us.

Corvier raised his saber to the setting sun. He stepped forward.

"Captain," Gennady said, and then he said, "please," and then he said nothing at all. Corvier drove that saber straight through him.

Corvier's rache lunged for Lady as she screamed and screamed.

I confess it. I lost control.

My daimon and my lightning were tired of me, I think, tired of my squeamishness and cowardice. They twisted into a whole new monster. That monster wore my face. I raised a hand.

For a brilliant, shining moment, the entirety of the Penumbra's yard was thrown into stark relief from the crash of lightning I brought into Corvier's chest. I could feel my magic driving through him like an arrow, like my needles, like his saber through Gennady's chest.

He was wreathed in blue. Healer's blue, I thought, and laughed.

Wait, I heard myself think, in the smallest little voice, standing outside the self I'd given up to the daimon and the lightning, tugging at the monster's sleeves. *Wait.* Corvier wasn't dead yet. I could feel his life through the perfect, divine connection that ran through us both, along the lightning. I could pull away and save him. I could break the bolt.

It wouldn't do, I thought, simply. It wouldn't do to kill in front of Gennady.

The cardinal problem was that I'd never used lightning on another living creature before, and I had no idea how to stop naturally. There was no way I could ease my magic gently away.

So I shattered it instead.

It was brutal; it was instant. The recoil began. *Oh*, I thought, as I started to burn. *This is what it feels like.* From my core, the lightning forged a path.

Corvier and his rache fell rigid on the ground. Lady went to Gennady, curling up against the pouring wound. I saw it all from another world, another plane, as my magic carved me. There was no real smoke, no real fire. The retribution was silent. I don't think I screamed, or if I did, I never heard.

I looked at my outstretched hand, a stranger in my own body. Slowly, a pattern crawled down it, red and raw: the branching, fractal patterns of a lightning strike, etching their way across my skin.

I felt quintessentially alive, and I was seized with the suspicion that the gift was temporary. I stumbled to Gennady and knelt.

The healing came without trouble, without the slightest instant of hesitation. It came as naturally to me as anything ever had, as if there had never been a Philidor solarium. If I were a god, I suspect, I could not have felt half as powerful.

I wondered if this was what the augment felt like. Whatever barrier the augmentation process was meant to tear inside a human being, I'd almost certainly torn it for myself. I could only hope that I'd done it properly.

I barely had time to see Gennady's wound close before the broken lightning fled from me. It left me enervated and gasping, huddled on the ground near Gennady; his blood stained my clothes. I leaned him painstakingly against me. The patterned scars carving themselves into me continued, up my arms and down my chest and back, and I shook.

The pain was—

Significant. Martyrlike, I thought, from far away.

Gennady was breathing, but he'd lost consciousness. I may have healed him, but there was no erasing that kind of shock. He'd be asleep for some time yet. I could see Corvier breathing too, but that concerned me significantly less.

I thought I'd try to stand. I thought I'd try to help Velleia's people fight. I thought I'd say something to Gennady, or try to use my magic again. I thought I'd do *something*. But in the end, I was too exhausted to do anything besides sit with Gennady and try not to feel the fundamental, uncompromising pain of the scars still slowly inscribing themselves into my skin.

The display of my lightning had cleared a space around us; none of the combatants engaged in their petty, feral struggles nearby dared to step inside the blackened circle of earth I'd left around Gennady, Corvier, and me. We sat undisturbed as the battle around us raged, and then began to turn, and then began to wind down as more and more bodies fell.

The sun had nearly gone. I closed my eyes against the sight and let myself drift off to the smell of war and ozone.

Chapter 26

I woke up still sitting with Gennady, as he tapped the left lens of my glasses like a child with a fishbowl. They'd stayed on, miraculously. From the look of things, it was the middle of the night.

"Wake up," he said rustily. I thought I heard more irritation than concern. "Wake up. Desfourneaux." Lady barked.

I batted Gennady's hand away. "For God's sake," I murmured, and then doubled over into a cry of pain as my skin lit on fire when I moved. The new scars were screaming.

I could feel my magic rushing loose and jagged beneath the surface. Whatever I'd damaged when I had broken the lightning, it was still torn. I could still feel the power flickering in sharp surges inside me.

There would be time to address that later. My augment, such as it was, could wait. I looked up at Gennady.

"Whoa." He put a hand on my back, and that hurt too; I leaned away. "Stop that."

He dropped his hand. "Sorry."

The events of the last hours came trickling back to me, and I hissed lowly. "How are you? Your chest?"

He felt the hole in his uniform gingerly. "It's fine. There's sort of a mark still, I think, but it's fine." He paused. "How'd that happen?"

I laughed, half relief and half disbelief. "How on earth do you think?"

"Yeah," he said, chagrined. "All right. Thanks."

"You're quite welcome."

I squinted around us, trying to make out the surroundings. It occurred to me that we were sitting there in a charnel house. There were bodies all around—not nearly enough bodies to account for all of the combatants of the evening before, but enough to turn my stomach. "Oh."

Corvier was not present as a corpse, at least. Maybe I'd avoided making myself a murderer.

Gennady sighed. "It's rough. I think we're the only ones here. Whenever everyone else left, they left us alone."

I couldn't blame them, given the obvious, manifest danger of my lightning—and perhaps they'd thought us both already dead—but it was still an affront. Being left alone in the bloody dirt in the aftermath of the battle, after having played no small part in swaying the affair toward Velleia's advantage, stung. "Bastards," I said.

"Oh." Gennady stood unsteadily. Lady picked herself off the ground. "Language."

The thought struck me like a second rush of lightning: *Malise*. Malise would think I was dead.

I scrambled up after Gennady, swaying, and spun until I located what I thought was the way out of the Penumbra's yard. "We have to go to the Chirurgeonate."

"Are you that bad off?"

"I don't know," I said. Everything hurt. Everything burned. I didn't think I was in immediate danger, but I was feeling unsafe in my skin, and getting medical attention might be wise. More important was reassuring Malise. "We still need to go. I need to find my friend."

"Which one?"

"The healer." I began to pick my way through the bodies on the ground, willing myself not to think about what exactly they were whenever my foot caught on one of them and I stumbled in the dark. Gennady steadied me as we went, and I steadied him, and I reflected with some surprise that it had only taken us dual near-death experiences to become something like friends.

"God, I'm tired." He yawned widely and nudged the arm of a corpse out of the way for me. I resisted the urge to shut my eyes entirely and just let him guide me.

Neither of us had any money on us. We were obliged to walk the entire way to Deme Palenne, and by the end, with my legs and chest aching from exertion, I thought I might die after all. Gennady fared only slightly better. We stumbled onto the Chirurgeonate's campus faint and still spectacularly covered in dried gore; Lady's pelt was thick with it too.

The Chirurgeonate was alive that night. The halls were full of patients. I saw plenty of magicians from both sides being tended to, and masses of Vigil soldiers. There were no faction distinctions within the Chirurgeonate's walls. Now that the battles were over, it was a time for healing—if Velleia and Mulcaster were still alive and still intending to continue their feud, it would have to wait until the healers had given their say-so.

I tried to leave Gennady and Lady in the capable hands of a passing doctor, but they refused to go.

"I'm sticking with you," Gennady said, hovering near.

I was too bewildered and grateful to protest. "Malise Tyrrhena," I said to the doctor, instead. "Please—where is she?"

Miraculously, he actually knew. "Seeing to room seventy in the Caserio building. Be careful, though. She's in a state."

With Gennady at my heels, I rushed to Caserio. Room seventy wasn't close, and it felt like miles.

When I opened the door, she was there—she was sitting at the bedsides of a handful of unconscious traitor magicians, and she was crying as I'd never seen her cry before.

"Malise," I said.

She shrieked and threw herself at me.

I almost buckled under the weight of her hug; she saw me unbalance and pulled back momentarily before reeling me in again with abandon.

"My God," she said. "My God, my God, my God."

"It's all right," I said, with my best attempt at helpfulness. Gennady hung back; I gave him a dazed smile before turning my attention fully to Malise.

She sat me down on a chair and framed my face with her hands. "You're alive."

"I'm as surprised as you are."

With a blink, she spotted the skin of my wrist and took my hand, examining it, pulling my sleeve up. "What are these marks?"

"Lightning," I murmured, and with the realization that I was safe came an unconquerable lethargy.

"What?"

"I broke it," I said.

She shook her head. "You broke your lightning?"

I nodded dreamily.

"You can explain later." She knelt to get a better look at me, and because her legs were giving out beneath her. She fought to choose her words: "I'm glad you're here."

"I'm glad too, my dear."

Finally, she glanced at Gennady. "You both made it out."

"Together," he said, in an attitude of defiance, expecting to be scolded. If I hadn't been watching closely, I wouldn't have noticed that his mouth trembled. It remained to be seen just how badly Corvier's last act at the Penumbra had broken him, but the signs were already there.

To show him that he was wanted, I said, "Together. Gennady made quite a comrade."

Malise got up to give him a brief, sharp bow. "Thank you," she said passionately. "Thank you very much." She looked to Lady. "And you."

Gennady was silent; Lady wagged her tail.

She turned back to me. My vision blurred. The alcohol and caffeine and nepenthe had left me, and whatever else the lightning had done to me, it had taken most of my mania away with it. The daimon was silent. "Would you mind," I said. "Would you mind finding me a bed?"

That was it for my wits. I barely remember her guiding me to the nearest free bed; I barely remember when Gennady decided that I was safe enough and took his leave to seek treatment for Lady and himself. Flashes managed to ingrain themselves in my recollection—halls filled to capacity, harried doctors carrying supplies, and once, the fleeting silhouette of a woman who might have been Tessaly Velleia. Other than that, the night passed in shadow.

～

Malise must have healed me in my sleep; I woke up feeling, if not quite *better*, more human. She wasn't at my bedside, which I couldn't have dreamed of begrudging her. She was still a doctor, and the Chirurgeonate was still overrun. Gennady and Lady, however, were there—and Mariya, and Casmir, and they were all engaged in a staring contest with each other when I came to.

I sat bolt upright, regretted it, and gingerly eased back again until I was no longer seeing stars and the lightning scars had quieted.

"Adrien," Casmir said. His voice cracked a little, and I chided myself for the guilty pleasure that brought me. I might not want him the same way anymore, but old habits die hard.

"Good morning," I said.

"It's midafternoon," Gennady said helpfully. Lady yawned.

"Thank you. Good afternoon."

Casmir's mouth worked soundlessly for a few moments before he found what he was looking for. "I thought for certain you were dead."

"As if their little squabble could kill me," I said. There was a great deal of self-mockery in it.

He passed a hand over his eyes. "That stunt you pulled at the Pharmakeia..."

I braced. "Am I going to be tried for it?"

"The Archmagister and Velleia are going to talk to you," he said. "Or so everyone's saying. They'll interview you and Lieutenant Richter at the same time."

"So the Archmagister wasn't in on it."

He shook his head. "No. God knows what she was doing with her time during the whole debacle, but she wasn't with Mulcaster."

If she was going to talk with me, I was going to have a talk with her, I decided.

"Mulcaster?"

"Dead."

Gennady snickered, an odd, empty sound. Mariya echoed him, a perfect mimic. I made no effort to quell them.

"Kirchoff? Tenniel? The others?"

"Due to be tried after they recover," Casmir said.

I had to marvel. "They both survived?"

He shuddered. "Barely."

A wash of relief took me for a moment. Now I could hate them properly, revel in their downfall without any pesky pangs of guilt to get in the way.

Apart from the little detail of my potential witchhood, quite possibly legitimately earned, everything had turned out as well as could possibly be expected.

I took a moment to breathe and tried sitting up again. The second attempt went much better; I swung my legs over the side of the bed to face Casmir and the Richters.

"I hope you've been getting along," I said. "No quarreling over me?"

Casmir thinned his lips while Gennady and Mariya smiled their identical smiles.

"Ah." I looked to Mariya. "It was nice of you to come," I said cautiously.

She shrugged. "I figured I might as well. Whatever."

Apparently, once I'd earned one Richter's loyalty, the deal extended to both. Again, all it had taken to strengthen the bond between them had been shared near-death experiences.

"I'll talk to you shortly," I said to Gennady. "For now, may we have the room?"

He took Lady and Mariya and shuffled out of the room, still walking stiffly. The healers had done their work on him too, but some wounds leave their marks regardless. I checked my arms and found that my own marks were just as vivid as before.

"You never did join Mulcaster," I said to Casmir, once we were alone.

He looked away. "I never did."

"You weren't hurt, were you?" I asked. "In the hall of St. Cynanne. There was fighting; was it bad? I left before . . ."

"No, I was fine," he said. "I was lucky. Though I think a couple professors died there. The Pharmakeia has some positions to fill."

The loss could have been much worse, but a wave of nausea kept me quiet anyway.

Casmir shuffled his chair closer to the bed. "Listen," he said.

I listened.

"Friends?" he asked, putting out a hand to me. He was more sincere than I'd ever seen him, wide-eyed and open.

I didn't take his hand. "You hit me," I said.

He flinched. "I'm sorry."

I nodded. "You resigned as my keeper before you hit me; you said we were done. If you hadn't said that first, I'd tell you to leave now."

That seemed to reassure Casmir, and I needed to temper his relief. "It was a very thin margin," I said gently. "The grace of a few seconds."

"I wasn't cut out for the job," he murmured, fidgeting, shaken. "I should have realized it earlier."

"So should I," I said, after consideration. "But God knows I've been difficult too. I made my choices."

"I'm willing to try again," he said. "We owe each other that."

"We might."

With a feeble sort of humor, he said, "You know, Malise doesn't approve. She would only let me in here as long as that soldier was in the room at the same time. She said I had to leave once I talked to you."

I knew what he hoped I would say; he hoped I'd offer to overrule her for him. Refreshingly, I found that I had the strength to deny him. Still, I had to ponder how to phrase my reply; I could either be charitable or precise, but not both.

Casmir blinked at me. I remembered what my infatuation had cost and decided that precision was key. "Even when I was in love with you," I said, "I still would have chosen Malise."

He took that with a nod. I added, "Things won't be the same, Casmir."

With a wince of recognition, he stood, getting ready to flee. I let him. "I understand," he said. "Goodbye for now, all right?"

His contrition was obvious; I summoned a wan smile. "All right."

Before he got out the door, he stopped.

"What?" I said.

"The nepenthe."

Abruptly, the urge for it was there again, sharp and sweet, as my body remembered what it was missing. Malise's healing had blunted withdrawal, but there was only so much she could do.

I prepared myself to snarl. "What about it?"

He looked away. "I just want to know if you'll get treated for that."

I knew my answer without thinking about it. "I'll go to a solarium soon," I said. "Once I'm well enough to handle it."

I would never be *well*. We both knew that. Equally, he knew what I meant.

He relaxed with bone-deep relief; I remembered why it was that I'd kept him by my side for so long. That was over, but I understood. "I'm glad, Adrien."

Then he was gone.

Before I had time to process it, Gennady came back into the room. Mariya had left, at least. It was just the two of us.

"So," he said. "A solarium."

I put up my hands and stood, staggering only briefly. "*Manners.* Don't eavesdrop. That's another conduct lesson for you."

"I'll learn it later." He took a chair again and stared at me. "That'll be good for you," he said. "A solarium."

"I haven't been in years." An age-old shame set upon me, sitting deep in my chest, and I looked away.

He was silent. Silent, silent, for a long, long time.

"I was thinking," he said.

"Oh, no."

"Shut up. I was thinking."

I softened my tone. "Thinking of what?"

"I want to keep knowing you," he said. "You've been good to me. You teach me stuff."

"My star pupil," I said. I didn't need to force my smile.

Again, a long silence. Lady paced in nervous circles.

"Gennady."

He said, "You should know something first."

"Do tell."

"My brother Vanya. I told you about him. I killed him with a knife."

I wanted so badly to ask more, but there was no way to change the past. I only nodded. Not an agreement, but an acknowledgment. "All right."

"You don't hate me."

"I don't."

"Then I'll be your keeper."

I did not move.

Anxiously, he began to pace, pulling his hair. "You need a new one, right? And it's not like you need someone *nice.*"

I had never hated being an akratic more than in that moment. The intimate ache of my new scars multiplied by thousands.

He spun to face me. "You just need someone who'll watch you. Tell someone else if you need help. I can do that. I can figure out when you need it." He took a deep breath. "I'm not so bad that I can't do *that.*"

"Why—"

"And you can keep me."

I put my head in my hands.

Worse than the horror of the offer was the horror of realizing that I couldn't dismiss the idea immediately. A little responsibility might teach him something. He was right—I didn't need nice. I didn't need normal. I needed stable, and I could keep him stable, just as he kept me. He wasn't an akratic, not quite, but he was *something.* He needed someone too.

From its place safely below the surface now, the daimon said, *Don't. Not him.* So just like that, I rushed to my decision.

"We'll try it," I said, my throat tight with humiliation—and with gratitude. "While I'm in the solarium. While there are backup measures in place. We can try it for a while." He wouldn't have much keeping to do, but it would ease him in.

He grinned fiercely; Lady purred, strongly enough that her whole body shook. "Nice. That's nice."

I might have accepted, but I couldn't bear to speak of it any longer. "Thank you," I said. "That won't be for some time, however. Let's move on."

"On to what?"

"Are you all right?"

It was his turn to freeze. "What do you mean, *all right*?"

"Well," I said, and began to enumerate the items on the list with my fingers. "Firstly, you were forced to slaughter your unit. Secondly, your captain tried to kill you, and he nearly succeeded. Thirdly, you saw me strike him with lightning right in front of you. Fourth—"

He sat down. "I get it."

"So? How are you, Gennady?"

Lady put her head down on the floor, gazing up at me. "I don't know," Gennady said. "I never know. It's always a mystery to me."

"You have time to recover now," I said. "From everything that was done to you." *By the Vigil at large*, I thought, but it was prudent to keep that sentiment to myself for the moment.

He crossed his arms. "I guess."

For his sake, knowing he'd reached his limit, I changed the subject. "Is Corvier alive?"

He smiled. "Yeah. He's going to the Penumbra after the healers fix him up. They might cut his head off or something after he gets tried, but for now, he's alive. I can tell him what I think of him now."

I inspected my new scars and wondered, for the briefest of instants, if the life of Hiram Corvier was worth marking myself eternally for.

But Gennady's relief wiped the question from my mind. "Do you know what you're going to be doing next?" I asked him.

"I asked to stay stationed at the Pharmakeia," he said. "I thought maybe you could sort of keep teaching me stuff."

I made sure not to hesitate an instant. "Of course. I'd prefer that."

"Great," he said, and stood up, uncomfortable with the effort of holding a sincere conversation for more than five seconds. "I've got to leave now."

"Wait a moment."

He waited.

"Be ready to be summoned by Velleia and the Archmagister," I said. "They want to talk to us about the whole affair." It seemed like an understated way to say *They'll be deciding my fate.*

"Yeah, I know. They're not going to convict you of anything," he said impatiently. "What would they get you for? Fixing stuff? Trying to help?"

"Witchcraft. I used my magic to harm someone. I threatened people with it. Strictly speaking, I did the same thing as the Pharmakeia traitors; it's only fair I be tried as well." I twisted my hands together. I'd deserved my first witchcraft trial for Philidor, and I deserved this one as well. I might not deserve a conviction, but the question was valid. Whatever that said about me, it wasn't good.

"I'll kill them if they try to convict you," Gennady said, as if that solved everything. Lady was growling.

I fixed him with a severe eye. "Don't."

He shut his mouth, clearly taken with the desire to argue.

"Don't."

"We'll see."

That was as good as I was going to get. Wordlessly, he turned toward the door again.

"Be well," I said, and with echoing footsteps, he and Lady were gone.

~

The only thing left was my trial, and it came with astonishing rapidity. The next day, in fact, before I'd had any time at all to prepare.

Even injured, Tessaly Velleia was a force to be reckoned with. She wore bandages around what wounds she'd sustained from Mulcaster that couldn't be erased by healing, and there was a dull, angry pain behind her eyes, but she sat straight; her eyes pierced just as deeply as ever. Amphion lay on the ground near her chair, licking the remnants of his own injuries.

Gennady and I stood before Velleia and Archmagister Vionnet LeFlore in a large, otherwise empty classroom at the Pharmakeia; we'd been summoned there with only a few hours' notice for the trial, such as it was. No attorneys, no witchfinders, no witnesses, no documents. At least they had deigned to try us in a familiar location.

"So," the Archmagister said after we'd made our preliminary conversation. She was a tall woman with iron-gray hair and an iron disposition; between her and Velleia, I felt a pale shadow. "Desfourneaux. You used your magic to threaten Marsilio Kirchoff in front of dozens of people, and you critically injured a member of the Vigil."

"Yes," I said.

"Do you regret it?"

"No," I said.

Gennady elbowed me hard; I hissed and clutched my side.

LeFlore smiled. It was a nice smile, considering the situation. She'd always had a reputation as a reasonable administrator. "No? That's very bold of you."

I had to step carefully. "I wish I had been able to achieve the same ends without using my magic," I said. "What I did will haunt me for some time. I'd also do it all over again, if presented with the opportunity. It was the right thing."

"You're marked forever for your transgression," she said. "I hear you sustained scars from your attack on Hiram Corvier. Some might call that a sign from the stars."

"I lived," I said, unable to resist. "Some might call that a sign too, if they happened to be superstitious."

LeFlore raised her eyebrows.

"Stars and saints," Velleia said. "You really don't know when to shut up."

"He's right," Gennady said, speaking for the first time since we'd entered the classroom. "He did good. What else was he supposed to do?"

"Some have advised me that your condition ought to be taken into account," LeFlore said, ignoring him.

To steady myself, I closed my eyes for a moment before looking up. "My condition."

She tilted her head, examining me, trying to figure me out. "It's evident that you were in quite a state."

"Yes, yes. Everyone knows I'm an akratic," I said. "That shouldn't have a bearing on your judgment."

"Even if it works out in your favor?"

"I'm competent to stand trial," I said. Whatever the consequences, I would not compromise on that. I might not have been in my right mind when I'd threatened Kirchoff, but I was willing to stand by my actions.

"You seem difficult," LeFlore said.

The looming specter of exhaustion sapped me. "So I'm often told."

"You're in good company, I hear." She nodded to Gennady. "Lieutenant Richter isn't under any formal charges, but I've been told plenty about him."

I let Gennady speak for himself.

"I'm fine how I am," he said. "I did fine out there, and so did he. Let us go."

Velleia cleared her throat. "You performed acceptably," she said with supreme reluctance. "Given very few resources."

"*You* gave us very few resources," I said. "We nearly died for you time and time again." I turned to LeFlore. "The Pharmakeia didn't receive much of a guiding hand from you, either."

"*We're* not on trial," Velleia said, her hand straying to the hilt of her executioner's sword. Amphion raised his head to look at me.

"It was strategically necessary," LeFlore murmured, showing some regret for the first time. "I didn't have the power to stop everything on my own."

I relented, finally. "I plead not guilty." Best to advance matters.

"See? Not guilty," Gennady said proudly, as though I'd already resolved the issue.

I will credit Velleia and LeFlore with this: they didn't keep us in suspense.

Velleia let her sword go. "Acquitted."

LeFlore nodded.

My breath left me in a sharp gasp of relief. The lightning scars tightened and then released, making me shiver; I leaned forward in my chair.

"That was nice and quick," Gennady said.

"I try to be reasonable," LeFlore said. She offered me another reserved smile as I sat up straight again.

Velleia tapped her nails irritably on the table they were sitting at. "You were useful."

My mouth was dry. I had only one question; it had been obsessing me since the moment I walked in. "Will I be reinstated at the Pharmakeia?" *Please.*

"You were never removed," LeFlore said gently. "Whenever you're ready, you're welcome to return. The academy is still rebuilding, but whenever classes resume, you'll have your hall ready."

I choked on my answer.

She graciously stepped in. "You might find that your colleagues will receive you more easily than us."

"Pardon?"

She rested her chin on her hand, watching me curiously. "I asked about you, to better educate myself for this decision. I've heard what people truly have to say about you."

Kirchoff's voice wormed its way into my head. *Daimoniac.*

I lifted my chin. "And what do they say?"

"Ask them yourself. You could be surprised." She pointed toward the door. "Now. I have a great deal of other work."

Gennady bowed clumsily to Velleia, and I bowed to LeFlore. Not daring to risk another moment in their company, we fled out into the Pharmakeia's halls, into my beautiful home—my home again, *still* my home.

I passed familiar faces on the way, and some of them smiled.

Epilogue

After the trial, I wobbled back to the Chirurgeonate to go find Malise and see if I couldn't help her with some of her patients. My first instinct was to go find nepenthe; a distraction was necessary.

The halls of the Chirurgeonate weren't quite as hectic as they'd been before, but traces of panic still remained. Small smudges of blood missed by the cleaners, overcrowded rooms. Regardless, the sunlight streaming through the glass of the buildings soothed me; finally, I'd emerged into the day.

I found Malise attending to the leftover comatose patients. I brightened to see them still alive; at least Mulcaster's people hadn't found the time or reason to murder the second wave of them as well.

She was sitting at a bedside with her hands on an unconscious Pharmakeia student's head, channeling thick bursts of healing magic into the girl. I stood aside, quietly, until she was done.

When she looked away from her patient and saw me, she broke into a broad smile. "It looks like the trial went well."

"As well as could be expected. Velleia is still terrifying, but I've escaped witchhood for a little longer."

"We would have all rioted if you hadn't," she said. "Oh, it would have been a disaster."

Awkward gratitude made me laugh. The thought of the other Pharmakeia magicians I'd used so poorly banding together for my sake produced a tender ache.

Malise dusted her hands together. "Are you sure you should still be out and about?"

"I'm really not badly hurt. It's just the markings." There was also whatever I'd done to my magic, however I'd shaken it loose with my self-induced augment—but I didn't think there was anything the Chirurgeonate could do for that.

She made a small face. "I'd offer you something for the pain, but . . ."

"Unwise," I said. "Yes."

"I'm surprised you're not complaining more about the scars. I'd have thought you'd be howling in outrage about them."

I traced a forking branch on my wrist, wincing as it sent traces of fire up my skin. "Why? For vanity?"

She raised her eyebrows primly. "Well. Yes."

Feeling silly, I said, "I think they might look nice, once they stop hurting. They'll match my . . ."

I waved a hand vaguely.

"Your *look*," she said with a theatrical sigh.

I covered my eyes, fighting a grin. "Am I really that vain?"

She beckoned me for a hug before turning her attention to the patient in the next bed, situating herself to heal him as well. "You are."

Then the patient she'd been healing before stirred slightly; I froze. "Did she move?"

Malise nodded. "Some of them are getting better. We're learning how to treat the coma. We might not be able to save all of them, but most seem to be recoverable."

The curse was breaking.

I took a deep breath. "Is there any chance—?"

She was silent.

"The Philidor solarium patients," I said, trying not to whisper, but my voice failed me nevertheless. "Have you tried the same method on them?"

Again, she nodded, and she said nothing else, which told me all I needed to know.

I bit my tongue hard until I knew I wasn't going to succumb to dramatics. "I see."

She looked away and focused on her healing. "I'm sorry, Adrien."

It had been a ludicrous thought. There was nothing I could do to fix the solarium. There never would be; I'd known that before.

"Come eat with me after I'm finished here," she said. "We don't have to go far."

I shrugged.

She pursed her lips disapprovingly. "Let me rephrase: you *will* eat."

That was difficult to argue with. "All right. After you're done."

Once our silence was more companionable than gloomy again, after Philidor's shadow had passed, I took a deep breath. "Speaking of solariums."

"Yes," she said. "Westbrook again?" Westbrook solarium had become my first choice over the years.

"I'm sure they'll be ever so glad to see me."

She didn't take the sarcasm. "I'm happy for you," she said. "You'll be better soon."

I'd heard the words too many times. Better soon. Better soon. "I'm tired of my life being about *better soon*," I said.

She finished up her healing and turned to me, smiling. "It's about other things, too."

I found, to my delight, that I agreed.

So I'd avoided martyrdom. I was alive, unclaimed by the stars.

There are other nations where the people pay tribute to saints, but it's only here that a saint and a martyr are always one and the same. It's in the name of the place—Martyr's Reach. A messy end is the nonnegotiable criterion for sainthood. That must say something about us, I think. A question for another day. I was content to let the mystery lie, for once, to revel in my newfound distance from self-canonization.

Aching and craving and exhausted beyond measure, I went to have a meal with my best friend. I knew that soon I would teach again, and I knew the Pharmakeia would mend. It was all, as ever, a matter of time.

There you are. There's my historical account of the events of 3016. Forgive me my narrative foibles; I gave it as well as I could.

Acknowledgments

Thanks to my family for their love and support.
Thanks to my tabletop friends, the funniest people I know.
Thanks to the educators who encouraged my writing and thinking.
Thanks to everyone at Red Hen.

Biographical Note

Madeleine Nakamura is a writer, editor, and lifelong fantasy devotee. She began writing her first novel the day she realized a computer science degree wasn't happening. She graduated from Mills College in Oakland with a degree in creative writing. She is based in Los Angeles, California.